SOMEBODY LIKE YOU

BONUS: ALL OF ME

HEATHERLY BELL

SOMEBODY LIKE YOU

CHAPTER 1

With any luck, Brooke Miller would not receive a marriage proposal tonight.

On a warm August evening, the wine flowed at the Serrano winery in Starlight Hill. George, the owner and her boss, wouldn't give Brooke much of a hint as to the occasion. Only said that tonight's announcement would be momentous, unprecedented, and a surprise to everyone in the community.

It just had better not be a proposal.

Having an affair with her boss was hands down, the singularly most stupid thing Brooke had ever done. When after a few months she'd realized that, as so many times in the past, the fizzled had fizzed and the pop had— well— popped, she'd avoided George. And it hadn't been easy.

How, exactly, did one break up with one's boss? Her first guess? Strategically.

One option would be to tender her resignation. Not going to happen. Brooke loved her job as general manager, and she was damned good at it. One stupid mistake shouldn't ruin her career trajectory.

She could just be honest and tell him the truth. And she would, eventually, but not now that he was considering her for a promotion to Vice President of Sales. In that position, she'd get an expense account and travel several times a year to Europe. More to the point, she was the most qualified person for the position and everyone realized it. George counted on her, relied on her, and trusted her. He'd assured her time and again that the position would be hers.

So for weeks, she'd had a cold that wouldn't go away. George had kept his distance. He seemed to understand when every time he approached any closer than three feet she held her arm out. "Still not feeling well." She did have the monthly excuse, but that only worked one week out of the month. Two if she stretched it. George was not the brightest light when it came to women.

Frankly, she was running out of excuses.

Yet despite all the hints she'd dropped: "I think it's great when a couple can remain friends after the romance is over. Sometimes two people don't click, and is it really anybody's fault?" George didn't seem to catch the hint. At all.

Instead, he'd taken to asking her about engagement rings: size, color, shape. She had no opinion.

Then he'd asked about honeymoon destinations. Which would she prefer? Paris? Italy? Spain?

She swallowed, and had no opinion.

Maybe, Brooke hoped, he would announce her promotion tonight. Even if, among all the marriage talk, there'd been no mention of her promotion. Brooke straightened the silver setting for the umpteenth time. She'd chosen a perfect shade of Burgundy for the tablecloth and napkins. The centerpieces were crystal vases filled with old wine corkscrews.

"Brooke, everything looks so awesome," Chelsea Ricci, their summer intern, said. "You have perfect taste."

"Thank you." Brooke stopped near the chocolate fountain. A nice touch and not the norm for Serrano parties, but she wanted tonight to be special. Just in case it was indeed the announcement of her promotion.

"Someday I hope I can be half as creative," Chelsea said.

"Of course you will be." Brooke said, picking up a name tag from a table. Tiny corkscrews with name cards. Everyone thought she was a genius, but part of her secret was Pinterest.

George had invited every vintner in town tonight. Even some from neighboring Napa. She recognized all the established names among Napa Valley vintners: Guglielmo, Dardanelli, Rapazzini. Some she'd worked with in the past, some she'd like to work with in the future. But obviously, going to another company after first being VP of Sales might be a better transition to make.

A couple of hours later, the party was in full swing and still no one had any idea of the occasion. They'd stop by and ask her occasionally, expecting her to know.

"Oh, you know George. He likes to surprise us every now and then," she'd answer, and then go find something to do.

Brooke steered clear of George as he walked around the tables, in his usual composed state, as though a tornado wouldn't faze him. Never smiling, head held high. He dripped with Alpha male confidence, which at first she'd found alluring and then after a while a tad disgusting. But since that was pretty much the pattern in her love life, it didn't exactly surprise her that she'd grown tired of him.

"I'm sure you all wonder why I gathered you all here tonight for this lovely occasion," George finally announced in his booming baritone voice. "I hope you all understand. When a man is in love...let's just say it's been difficult to keep this under wraps."

Brooke's hand rose to her neck. Oh no. Not here. Not

happening. How could she say no and save this night? She tried to mentally telegraph to George that he should not do this. Not now, so publicly.

Seemed that maybe this would happen. Happen right now. Her palms were sweaty. She couldn't marry him. She couldn't marry anyone. Marriage was for other women. Women that were not Brooke.

"Even the woman of my dreams doesn't know this moment is about to happen, as I've had to keep it quiet. You all know how I love a good surprise." It seemed a little strange when George moved in her opposite direction. He dropped to one knee in front of Chelsea. "My darling Chelsea, I know I don't deserve you but would you make me the happiest man on earth and marry me?"

It seemed that the room was a bit hazy, and Brooke was looking through a telescope lens. She couldn't for the life of her take in a deep breath, though she required oxygen at the moment. Stat! What had just happened? Chelsea? Twenty-two year old virgin and thirty-five year old playboy? It was a joke, that's what it was. A bad movie of the week. Sometimes George liked a good practical joke, although for the life of her she couldn't remember one.

Chelsea turned beet red as everyone stood up to applaud. "Oh, Georgie," Chelsea exclaimed. "Is this really happening?"

Georgie? Well, this was a surprise, and an explanation for why he'd asked so many questions about rings and honey-moons. Probably only trying to get a woman's opinion on the subject. And even if they'd never officially called it quits, maybe this was for the best. Brooke finally exhaled.

George was on his knees now, holding a diamond ring looked to be worth two years of Brooke's salary. "From the moment I saw you, I knew you were the one for me. I wanted to surprise you. Surprised?"

"Say yes, you'll marry him!" Someone in the crowd shouted.

"Yes! Yes! Of course I'll marry you," Chelsea said, and George slipped the ring on her finger.

The couple kissed and George turned to the crowd. "While we have your undivided attention, I'd like to announce our new VP of Sales."

Brooke smiled as she caught George's eyes, and moved towards him. Yes, this was her time. Her moment in the sun. Better than she could have hoped. She'd have the job, and no George to damper the celebration, or the tiny question in her mind that he may have given her the job for reasons other than her abilities.

"My lovely fiancé will take over those duties, as soon as we return from our honeymoon in Italy. After all, this is first and foremost a family business." He threw a significant look in Brooke's direction.

The words kicked Brooke in the gut.

"A la familia!" A gentleman from the Ricci table raised a glass of their best Pinot Grigio private label. Their latest prize winner, velvety with a hint of oak and fruit. Brooke had personally chosen it for the occasion tonight.

For several long moments, she couldn't move. She might have celebrated the fact that George had moved on, except for the fact that he'd taken her promotion with him. He'd dangled the promotion in front of her when he considered her to be his private play thing. When he realized that was over, he'd taken his toy with him.

Suddenly she needed a shower in the worst kind of way. George managed to make her feel cheap and incompetent all at once.

The newly engaged couple made their way around the room accepting congratulations, oblivious to the volcanic eruption that was building inside Brooke's stomach. She would need to give her best wishes to George privately, where she might have a chance at destroying the family jewels.

Chelsea approached. "Thank you for throwing my engagement party. No one could have done any better. I'm so surprised. Did you have any idea? How could you keep this a secret?"

"I had no idea. Didn't even know the two of you were dating."

Chelsea blushed pink. "Georgie wanted to keep it a secret. I didn't want to, but he said it wouldn't look good because of my internship."

"And he's right." Wouldn't look good, either, that a man-whore was marrying Tinker Bell. Brooke trembled with anger. Either that, or she had a fever.

"Can you believe this ring?" Chelsea held it out for Brooke, nearly blinding her.

"I really can't. Congratulations. Not just on the wedding, but the job. That's great," Brooke spit out.

"Wow, yeah. I had no idea about that but when George mentioned it to me a couple of weeks ago it sounded so cool. I mean, I get to go on trips to Europe and all. I don't know what I'll wear! I need to go shopping!" She squealed and bounced.

"I better go see if the kitchen needs anything."

Seemed like there should be blood and guts on the mason tile floor, and not little drips of chocolate from the fountain. George had given her promotion, the one he'd promised her, the one she deserved, to the girl he was currently sleeping with. And he hadn't bothered to tell her, or even give her a warning.

No sooner had she entered through the doors to the large utility kitchen than Eric had followed her inside. "Bastard."

"That job was mine, Eric. I deserve it."

"Do you want me to cut his nuts off? Because I will."

"Don't be ridiculous," Brooke said. " I'll do that."

"That's my girl," Eric said and left the room with a tray of wine goblets, but not before Brooke snatched two from the tray.

Definitely a two fisted night of drinking lay ahead of her. She would enjoy this damn wine, an amusing bouquet of earthy opulence, if it killed her. What an idiot she'd been. For the first time in her life, she'd made the mistake of sleeping with the boss. And it had cost her a promotion, not to mention a sense of self-respect.

She might have made the Dean's list at Chicago State, but she still hadn't cracked the mystery of boys. Or men that behaved like boys.

Well, hell, this was a party. Brooke joined in, and danced with several of the men who asked. Even George's youngest brother, Tony, who lowered his hand to her ass in a characteristic show of machismo.

Brooke resisted the urge to slap the face so like George's, and instead held up a finger and shook her head. "No, Tony. If you want to keep that hand you better put it back where it belongs."

He did, snaking it around her waist. "Man, Brooke. You are smokin' hot. It almost might be worth it to lose a limb."

"I don't think so. You're too young for me. What are you, twelve?"

He scowled. "I'm twenty-one, dude."

After a few more glasses of wine, Brooke started to feel a whole lot better about the situation. The Vice President of Sales would be a token position if he'd given it to Chelsea. He needed someone young and pliable, someone without ideas of her own. Meanwhile, Brooke had an opinion or two, and they didn't always agree with George's vision.

Like the name of their latest wine, for instance. George

wanted to call it Georgissimo, which made a lot of sense for a narcissist. Brooke had been steadily and aggressively promoting many other, far less ridiculous names. Tonight she had a few new ideas.

She swayed a little to the right, set her empty wine glass down on the tray that passed by, and made her way to the stage where the live band played. Time to offer heartfelt congratulations to the happy couple.

Eric reached for her elbow. "What are you doing? I don't like that look in your eye. You've had too much to drink. Let's think this through all the way."

"I'm fine," Brooke said, shaking him off and climbing up the steps to the stage to take the microphone from the lead singer. "Good evening, ladies and gentlemen. Not you, George. I don't mean you."

The crowd roared with laughter. *Oh right, they think I'm kidding.* "I'm Brooke Miller, and I work here. Most of you know me. I'm the general manager."

"Woot! Woot!" Tony shouted from the floor. Seemed he'd had one too many, because children didn't know how to handle their wine.

"I wanted to offer my sincere congratulations to the bride and groom to be."

Everyone cheered. Chelsea waved from the chocolate fountain. So far, this was easy. "Next month we'll be unveiling our new wine collection, and naturally George wants to name it after himself."

Ripples of laughter ensued, and George had on his I'm-the-King-of-this-Castle smile. Time to wipe that smug look right off his face. "I disagreed, and I had a whole list of other names. But that's not important right now. I agree this wine should be named after George. This is a momentous occasion."

The crowd cheered. George walked over by the chocolate

fountain to join Chelsea, and put his arm around her. "So the question is: should we name this wine Lying Sack of Shit, or Two Timing Bastard? Any thoughts? Comments? Suggestions?"

An audible gasp arose from the formerly engaged crowd, and every smile slipped off their collective faces. Tough crowd. Eating out of her hands one moment, glaring at her the next.

George's face had turned all interesting shades of red. The man could be scary looking when he wanted to be. But Chelsea. Damn. Brooke felt a pinch of regret deep in her belly. Chelsea didn't deserve this treatment any more than Brooke did. George was setting Chelsea up to fail, so that perhaps he could write off their honeymoon as a business trip. He of all people realized how unqualified Chelsea was to be his VP.

Eric walked up to the stage and took the microphone out of her hand. "Time to go now."

"Wow. I wasn't really finished, but okay." Brooke walked off the stage, the unnatural quiet of the room enveloping the night. The lead singer stared at her blankly, but before Brooke could tell him to play The Bitch is Back, a piercing squeal from the back of the hall drew everyone's attention.

It appeared Chelsea had slipped in some of the chocolate drippings on the floor. As Chelsea rose up she lost her balance, and fell into the fountain, toppling it to the floor. Oozy melted chocolate goodness now covered the tile. She slid into the chocolate, and one big piece attached itself to her Jimmy Choo heel. When she tried to get up, she slid again. Many of the patrons raced over to help, but George beat them to it. He bent down to pick her up, lost his footing and slid right into the chocolate mess. Both of them now appeared to be bathing in the stuff, chocolate smears in their hair, on their neck, on their faces. Clothes too, of course.

"This is a thousand-dollar suit," George could be heard bellowing. "Brooke! Who ordered a damn chocolate fountain anyway?"

"There's something you hate to see," Brooke muttered. "All that chocolate, gone to waste."

Eric slapped his forehead. "Oh man. It's been good working with you, Brooke."

Right. One more thing she had to say. She ran up to the stage again and grabbed the mic. "Before I call it a night, Georgie? I quit!"

With that she held the mic out to her side, raised it shoulder level, dropped it to the ground like she'd seen so many rappers do, and marched off the stage.

And she didn't trip once.

* * *

BILLY TURLOCK PICKED up the Chronicle at the 7-11, along with a gallon of milk.

Pitcher or Wine maker?

Although the two wouldn't appear to have a thing in common, Billy Turlock has been spotted in his hometown of Starlight Hill in Napa Valley. The word is he's scouting a location to start a vineyard. The pitcher retired from the Oakland Sliders after a year of injuries and surgeries on his nearly shredded shoulder. But the fact is even though he's not even thirty, the former darling of baseball had outlived his usefulness on the mound. So if wine making is in his future, we hope he can press grapes better than he can pitch a no-hitter. The last time he pitched a no-hitter…

Cockroaches. Vile filth. Billy set down the newspaper and grabbed a pack of beef jerky instead.

"No paper?" The checker said, ringing up the milk without even looking at him.

"I'll find something else to line my bird cage," Billy grunted.

That's when the man looked up. "Holy shit, Billy Turlock. In my store. Crap, hold up dude. Would you take a picture with me? Hey, Dad. Get out here, would you? Look at this."

Damn, that was nice. He should stop reading the sports section, like his older brother Wallace suggested. People were so much better. Before long some of the customers had congregated to ask for autographs and a photo or two. Or three. Of course Billy posed for pictures but he insisted on paying for the purchases, even if the owner wanted to give them to him on the house. He might not have a million dollar contract to look forward to this year, or any other year again for that matter, but he wasn't exactly in the poor house.

He wouldn't be playing baseball anymore, but he'd find something to do with the rest of his life. He was almost sure of it.

Of course, this wine making situation was a bit tenuous at best. But who was Billy to deny his grandfather's dream? Hadn't Pop been at every game since little league? It was certainly time to come back to his hometown and reward their support by sinking some money into the economy. Why not a vineyard?

Some of the customers followed him outside. "Is it true you're moving back?"

"I am back, and it's good to be home again." Billy threw the gallon of milk in the passenger seat of his convertible.

"You opening a sports bar?" One of the men asked.

"Not exactly, but you're in the ball park." Billy said, opening the door. Everyone got a kick out of that double entendre. "A vineyard."

"Another vineyard?" Billy heard someone say. "Like we need more of those."

"How's that like a sports bar?" Someone else muttered.

Billy didn't know the answer to that question, so he didn't even try. He hopped in his car and ripped open the bag of jerky. Eventually everyone wandered back in the store or went about their business, waving goodbye.

Vineyards.

He didn't know the first thing about them, other than the fact that he'd grown up in Starlight Hill. But Pop said a private label vineyard was the way to go. A family business. Even if Billy's mother's side of the family was proudly of Scottish descent, filled with men that had likely never even come close to the grape, Pop said he knew what he was doing. Billy believed him, even if he realized he'd probably be seeing a lot more articles like the one in the paper today. Retired pitchers were supposed to open sports bars and fade quietly into the background. Certainly not try to resuscitate an old vineyard.

His cellphone rang, and he could see by the caller ID it was Gigi, his publicist. Checking up on him again since it'd been all of thirty minutes since they'd last spoken. "What now?"

"Just checking up on my favorite ball player."

"Right. Well, it's been thirty minutes and no, I haven't fathered an illegitimate child yet. The minute I do, you'll be the first to know." Billy punched her in on the speaker phone, and drove out of the parking lot.

"Don't make fun of me because I try to protect you from those women."

Gigi referred to *those women* as baseball's version of gold diggers, and by now Billy could recognize them as well. He didn't need Gigi's assistance, not that she would believe him. "I'm in my home town. Give my home girls a little credit."

"Fine, but don't come crying to me if an old classmate comes to you with an eleven-year-old, claiming she gave birth to your love child," Gigi said without taking a breath. "I'm kidding. Do come to me when that happens."

"It's not going to happen." His teenage prowess had been greatly exaggerated, and he'd never been the man-whore the media liked to portray. If he had been, he wouldn't have had time to play baseball. "You should stop worrying. I'm with family now, and they look out for me as well."

"Believe me that single fact is why I haven't come down to scope out the place ahead of time. Besides, I'm still fielding some of these endorsement offers. How do you feel about kitty litter?"

"No." Was there anything more to say?

"I'm fielding offers, but nothing is quite right yet. I'll keep looking. What's wrong with you, anyway? You sound pissy."

Billy crossed over Merlot Bridge, and felt a grin coming on despite his mood. The prettiest girl he'd ever known had bungee jumped off this bridge back in high school. Memories. "I just took a look at the Chronicle. Mistake."

"What did it say? I'll demand a retraction."

"Never mind." They were right, much as it hurt. He'd been on a losing streak ever since the last surgery. He only wished he'd quit while he was ahead. But quitting the game had turned out to be harder than he'd imagined. He wasn't sure who he was without a mitt in his hand, but he was about to find out.

"Whatever they wrote, don't listen to them. You have a bright future ahead of you."

"Yeah." Except that future wouldn't involve baseball. No more surgeries. Time to retire, the doctor had pronounced. No more options.

"And you be careful with this vineyard venture. I've heard the business can be cut-throat."

"Unlike baseball?" Billy laughed.

"Laugh all you want, but those vineyard owners are probably going to scoff at a retired ballplayer acting like he can be any kind of real competition to them. You're not even part Italian."

"Let them scoff. Don't worry about me." He was worried enough for all of them. The last thing he wanted right now was a failed business. He couldn't afford another embarrassment, another failure.

As for competition, maybe it was time the old vineyard growers of Napa got some friendly competition.

A little something he did know about.

Not everyone regarded him as a useless retired pitcher with a shredded shoulder. None of the people he'd run into so far were questioning whether he'd ever been worth all the millions he'd earned out over his career. They were loyal baseball fans, like no other.

Damn, it was good to be home.

CHAPTER 2

It wasn't the first time Brooke had been sky-diving, and it certainly wouldn't be the last. But today was especially fitting as diving out of plane at several hundred feet would be better than committing murder.

The murder of George Serrano would have made front page news. They would have found her standing over his body with the bloody knife in her hands. "He made me do it." She would say to the cops.

Poor Ivey, her best friend, would be shocked. Mom would be ashamed. "I didn't raise her that way. I taught her to love the environment. Heck, to worship it. This isn't what I had in mind."

Not that Brooke cared what Mom (who should be re-named Mother Earth) thought. But there was the whole prison thing. She could plead temporary insanity, but face it she'd get a good ten years even for a slime ball like George. And she'd never looked good in orange.

So skydiving it would be. Today she and her fellow skydivers were flying over Napa where it seemed like every weekend there were hot air balloons covering the landscape of the skyline. Less often, a Cessna loaded with daredevils.

"Oh crap, I can't believe we're doing this." Frat Boy #1 said to his pal.

"I'm betting you won't at the last minute, Einstein." Frat Boy #2 said.

They were practically indistinguishable to her— same vacant party look in their eyes, same Converse shoes. She'd bet a year of the salary she no longer had that they were the Stanford elite. Money to burn.

"What about you, babe? How many jumps under your belt? Cause you look like a pro." Frat Boy #1 asked Brooke.

"Don't call me babe, asswipe." Twenty-four jumps to be exact and Joe the pilot knew it. But he was busy doing his job.

"Oooooh, you stepped in it." Frat Boy #2 said.

"How much longer, Joe?" Anytime now would be good. Today she would jump harder than she'd ever jumped before. She would jump so hard today the middle of the earth would hear it when she landed.

"I was just about to tell y'all to line up," Joe said from the cockpit.

Now why couldn't she fall for a guy like Joe? Beautiful blue eyes, sexy southern drawl. Retired Air Force, even. Served God and country. Willing to serve her, more than once if she recalled.

But since graduating from college, she'd had a definite type. George had been her type. Short-cropped hair, clean cut type, not a stitch of facial hair. Italian silk suited CEO.

Maybe it was high time to re-think her type.

"Brooke, we'll have the rookies go first, and we'll bring up the rear. What do you say?" Joe winked.

Damn he was good looking. "Sure."

Frat Boy #2 stood up first. "Let's do this thing, dude."

She had to sit through all the last minute instructions as Joe's co-pilot went through them one by one. She'd heard it all more than a dozen times.

Let's go, let's go. Time to get this show on the road. Frat Boy#2 and his tandem partner hurled out of the plane, but not before the stupid kid shouted, "Ha-ooh!"

Joe rolled his eyes. "Next."

"That would be you." Brooke slapped Frat Boy #1's back. His tandem partner hooked them together.

"Dude, I don't know about this. That's a freakin' long way down." He stared at the ground beneath him as if he'd only now noticed it was there.

"What's your name?" Brooke asked from behind him.

"Er, Terry. Why?"

"I've jumped about twenty-four times, Terry. And I'm still here to tell it. So go ahead and find your balls in there, and do this thing."

Terry didn't move. Joe talked to him, and so did the tandem partner. About how it would be okay to change his mind at this point. No harm, no foul. Nothing to be ashamed of. The usual.

"Don't listen to them, Terry. If you don't do this thing alone you're going to feel like crap. Your buddy did it and he won't let you live it down." Brooke patted his back.

"Dude, good point. Ah, hell." Still, he didn't move.

"We're going to need you to move if you're not jumping," Joe said. "We're losing our window."

In other words, she was losing her window. And she would jump today, one way or another. No one would take that from her, certainly not a spoiled rich kid.

"I just wish—" Terry began.

He didn't finish the sentence because Brooke gave him a good shove. He pushed into his tandem partner who must have assumed that meant a go, and out they both went.

"That someone would push you out?" She called out after him.

"Dudeeeeeee!" he yelled as he plunged into the air.

"Shit, Brooke." Joe said. He was nothing if not a stickler about rules. And it wasn't cool to push someone out, even with a partner.

"Sorry," Brooke said as she jumped.

Finally, the air rushed past her and she could fly. She stuck her arms out and welcomed the air rushing through so that she could at once be a part of the sky and a part of nothing at all. Falling.

The thrill of the ground rushing up to greet her. Rising up closer and closer, but unable to touch her from this high up. Seconds passed, always feeling much more like years. Falling like this, sometimes, was better than sex. Better because she didn't have to give up a part of herself. She only gave up her well-formed illusion that she was in control.

She liked control, liked her lists, and liked knowing where she was headed. Being a daredevil wasn't as crazy as some people thought. Every one of her risks were well thought out and planned ahead. And they forced her, for a few seconds, to let go.

To forget that, sometimes, she was scared. Not of the jumping, but of being alone for the rest of her life. Never finding that one person that felt like the missing piece of the puzzle. She told herself that it was because nothing was missing— she was full and complete on her own and if she never met the right man that would be okay too.

Yeah, and pigs fly.

She hadn't cried, and still hadn't called Ivey. Ivey would bring ice cream and commiserate but what would be the point? It wouldn't change anything. Only a time machine could do that. She'd get in one, too, if someone would hurry up and invent it.

Yes, she could have settled for George at one time. But an old friend had once told her she shouldn't settle for anything less than everything she wanted.

Joe, who had jumped right after her, was frantically signaling something to her, trying to get her attention.

Oh dammit, she hadn't pulled her cord yet. With seconds to spare, Brooke reached for it, and heard the familiar heartening flapping sound of the parachute slowing her roll. Whew. Joe would be pissed now, since he would be convinced she'd done it on purpose. She happened to hold the record for the closest amount of time to releasing, and Joe hated it. But this time, it hadn't been intentional. Not that he'd believe her or anything.

So she was a little bit distracted, and who could blame her? She'd just thrown her entire career away. Most of the other vineyard owners had been at the party, and had witnessed firsthand her less than professional behavior.

She'd acted impulsively for possibly the second time in her life, and it might have worked about as well as the first time.

The worst part of the jump was meeting the ground. It always insisted on being part of the deal. She landed with too much velocity as usual, and spread her legs out to slow down. One of her ankles twisted, causing a roar of pain.

Great, not another visit to the ER. She probably didn't have insurance any more. No way could she afford the Cobra payment. Anyway, she'd had enough twisted ankles in her lifetime to know how to treat one at home.

Frat Boy #2 had met up with Terry and in the distance she could see the two of them jumping in the air, high-fiving it, celebrating. Buddies.

And right then, Brooke wanted her best friend.

* * *

BROOKE'S ANKLE was pink and sore, but definitely not broken.

"Oh Brooke, what a jerk." Ivey Garner pressed the ice pack on Brooke's sore ankle.

Like a true blue friend, Ivey had run right over when Brooke had called.

"That's actually the nice word for him." They were at Brooke's postage stamp sized apartment, a place with a corresponding sized rent payment. A place she should have long ago outgrown.

"I never did like him."

"Neither did I after the first few exciting months. I was an idiot to go out with my boss. But I never thought he'd give the job I deserved to someone as green as Chelsea."

Another thing. George wasn't stupid enough to let her bring down his business, which must have meant that the Vice President job was nothing more than a figurehead position. And yet he'd dangled it in front of Brooke, and made her believe she could have that promotion. Made her believe she might finally be able to move out of this little place.

"Have you cried yet?"

Cried over that man? Not even if he deserved it, which of course he didn't. "I don't cry. But I might, if I can't find another job soon."

"Do you have any other options?"

"I'm going to put some feelers out. There should be something out there. Even though a lot of my prospective employers were at the event. They probably think I'm a little wacky now."

Brooke turned and reached inside her freezer for another ice pack. The kitchen was so small she didn't even have to get up to do it.

"You've forgotten that many of them don't even like George. For all you know they'd be willing to give you a medal. But why not take some time and think about what you want to do as your next step?"

She could do that, but Brooke knew what she wanted her next step to be. The problem was she wasn't entirely sure she had the stomach for it. She'd taken physical risks before, and plenty of them, but financial risks were different. She could risk death, but she sure as hell didn't want to be poor.

Still, she couldn't stop thinking about the Mirassu vineyard. For so long she'd had a crazy dream of owning a piece of land in the valley. For years she'd worked to make others a success, but maybe now it was finally her time.

"The old Mirassu winery got repossessed by the bank about a year ago. Maybe I might be able to get a good deal on it because it needs work." She stretched out her ankle so Ivey could put another ice pack on it.

"Sad what happened there." Ivey shook her head.

More like tragic the way family could turn on each other. The official word was that it had been a 'family dispute', another euphemism for a contentious divorce. Suing each other had taken so much of their money that they'd lost the one thing they'd been fighting over. Brooke knew a little about contentious divorces and how they could ruin people. All right, she could write a book with the knowledge she had.

"I say go for it. Sounds like perfect timing to me. Reach for your dreams. Why not?" Ivey asked.

Because the land might as well be gold bullion. "I don't want to be poor, for one."

"It might be a risky venture, but at least you know what you're doing."

"I've got some savings, but not enough. I'd need a loan." She couldn't ask Mom, who lived on an organic farm after the divorce. Brooke's father had left Mom almost penniless. Brooke still wasn't speaking to the man.

"Then get a loan. You're part of the community here, and I'm sure the bank would work with you."

Brooke felt the first twinge of hope. "You think so? I'll call the bank tomorrow."

Maybe she could make an offer on the vineyard. It wouldn't be much, but maybe with the lack of buyers in this recession they'd jump at the chance. Brooke had the experience and the know-how to turn things around. That alone should put her in the contending, even if she wasn't financially viable.

"This is exciting," Ivey said. "It's like when I first got the midwife job at the hospital. You deserve to have your dreams come true, too."

For Brooke, what she might deserve and what she got were rarely one and the same. But today was a day for dreaming. "When I buy the vineyard, I'll live right on the property as I get it ready to reopen. I've always wanted to live on a vineyard, and the Mirassu vineyard has that beautiful balcony that overlooks the land."

"That's the spirit. I like the way you said when and not if."

First she had to think the plan through all the way. Make a few pros and cons lists, then organize them point by point. She had to be smart about this. Draw up a business plan and get a few investors lined up in case she needed them. She'd start tomorrow.

"New beginnings all around."

* * *

On a cool early September morning, Billy stood at the curb with his grandfather and surveyed the dilapidated Mirassu winery. From the outside, the rambling stone mansion looked like an Italian villa manor from days of old. A manor with weeds overgrown from the house to the tree line. The place also needed a new paint job, and who knew what else?

He'd been assured the grapes, however, had been salvaged. The bank understood their value.

But with these looks, no wonder the bank was desperate. He was beginning to think the bank should pay him to take it off their hands. The place had fixer-upper all over it.

"I see that look on your face," Jean Jackson, Your Local Realtor with a Smile, said. "The same disgusted look on your face when Jeter hit it out of the park in the seventh inning. And like I told my husband, who said you should have thrown him your curve ball, it wasn't your fault."

Everybody was a sports critic. "Yeah."

Jean waved a hand in the direction of the vineyard. "Don't let the price scare you away. It's worth every penny. The Mirassu winery was one of the oldest in the history of the town. And if you want to start a winery, it's better to buy one that's established. You do know it takes two to four years for a grape crop to grow in if you start one from scratch. You won't have that problem here. The only work is cosmetic. Best of all, the bank will entertain an all cash offer for a considerable mark-down. They want it off their hands. Like yesterday. You can definitely make lemonade with these lemons. Or should I say grapes? Ah ha, ha, ha. You know what I'm saying?"

Jean led the way, through the waist high weeds to the ornate front door. "Wait till you see this place. This is the main manor house."

It reminded him of an old Spanish villa, stucco and red tile roof. Ivy vines climbed up the side of one wall. Like the stone headstone at the entrance, some of the outer walls were lined with large stones.

Jean continued chatting up the place as he brought up the rear. She opened up the front doors and led them through a small hallway into the larger room. Lots of work needed in here, Billy noticed. There was an odd peculiar smell he'd rather not try and identify.

A broken window meant that critters might have made their way inside. Another wonderful thought.

"That window broke not long ago. Probably some vandals. Anyway, a small fix." Jean said, as she kept walking towards the back.

The wine bar was near the back, just before the spacious stone balcony. Billy walked over to the balcony to what could possibly be his new backyard. Ah, yes. Here was the rub. All that land. It had a way of enticing a man, drawing him in. Rows upon and rows of vines heavy with grapes.

Pop, who had been mostly quiet until then, finally spoke. "This is something."

"There's twenty acres of prime California real estate." Jean looked down at her clipboard. "The new gold."

"It looks like more than that."

"The land, the grapes, the manor house – did you know it comes with a living space in the back as well? That needs a little bit of work too. And then there's a smaller cottage style house in back. In the old days, the head farm hand often lived there. Now it's just more storage space."

Billy put his arm around Pop's shoulder. "So Pops, what do you say?"

They'd been looking at places for the past two weeks, and while there were others that needed far less work they were all much larger enterprises. All finely tuned machines that were only waiting for someone else to take over at the helm. Someone with more money than time.

But Billy would let Pop be the final word on this deal. He knew grapes, he knew land, and even if he wouldn't be running the place for the family this was his dream. Just like baseball had been Billy's. The way Billy viewed it, he was the bank. He had enough to buy this place for cash, even if he wasn't at all sure it was worth it.

"It's like I've always told you, Billy, baseball is life," Pop began and Billy settled in to hear another baseball analogy. "Run at full speed. Maybe you're sure that the ground ball you hit to the short stop is going to be an out. But what do we do, anyway?"

"Run," Billy said, because he knew this story.

"That's right. Run anyway. Run hard. Showing that you run 100% of the time says a lot about your playing style. And your character."

"Interesting," Jean said. "So what does that mean exactly?"

Hell if I know, Billy wanted to say. Only Pops had any idea of what he meant half the time. "Pops? What do we mean by that?"

"We're going to run with it, of course!" Pop wagged his finger at Billy.

Yeah, he should have known. They were going to do this mess. Not for the first time, he felt grateful to have a contractor in the family. Wallace would help, and that could be his contribution to the 'family business'.

He turned to Jean. "It means we're in the wine making business. Let's talk numbers."

* * *

A WEEK later Billy had closed on an all cash deal with the bank, sanctioned and approved by his accountant. According to everyone, he'd made a killing on this deal. The bank was desperate, and he had the cash. Cash was king, they'd said. And he'd forked enough of it over.

Today he'd brought his brothers Wallace and Scott to introduce them to the new family business. He also then planned on putting them to work, because face it, with his brother Wallace in the contracting business, Billy would call in all the favors his big brother owed him for the past two decades.

Pop was the owner of a vineyard, and he'd need help. First, the fix-it phase. "Let's start at the edge and whack our way to the house. How about that?"

Scott looked doubtful. "I should have brought my machete."

No. Billy didn't need Scott the Army sniper to bring along any kind of weapon. "I should have brought my bat."

"Billy, get serious. You can't take these weeds," Wallace laughed.

"Not unless maybe it's the seventh inning and all the bases are full up." Scott passed him on the way to the house, trudging waist high through weeds. "Tell me you looked inside."

"We did. It's not as bad as it looks like from out here," Billy said. "Most of the work is cosmetic. I think."

"Great, because I was afraid I'd have to kill you." Wallace said, and was the first inside once Billy opened the door.

"I'm told there's good craftsmanship in here." Billy followed him inside.

"I can work with this," Wallace said, nodding.

His brothers followed Billy into the large utility kitchen. "Mostly cleaning needed in here."

"We'll get mom to do that. She wants to help out." Wallace said, running his hand along the polished wood counter tops. "We could replace these with granite."

"It's all about the grapes though. Isn't it?" Scott said, even though Billy would bet a seat on the first row of the next World Series that Scott didn't know the first thing about wine. Neither did Billy, for that matter. All the Turlock men were more beer drinkers. And, of course, Scotch for special occasions.

"That's what Pop says." Billy jammed his hands in his pockets.

"You let him talk you into this, didn't you?" Wallace threw him a look.

Unfortunately his older brother could read him too well.

"Oh man, Billy," Scott threw up his hands. "Hang on to your money, old man. You can't play ball any more. What are you going to do?"

"This," he glanced around the kitchen. "The new family business."

"But what do we know about wine?" Wallace asked.

"Pop knows about it, and he's going to lead this venture. C'mon, it's going to be fun." This damned adventure would be fun for the whole family if it killed him. He knew he needed a break from surgeries and physical therapy. The past year had been one big exercise in futility. They all needed some fun. It couldn't just be him. Could it?

"Billy, you're a sucker." Scott said. "Can I have some money for lotto tickets? You gotta play to win."

"No," Billy said. "If I'm a sucker for my family, so be it. Pop won't let me down. He never has before."

"How are we going to run a vineyard when none of us have ever done it before? Shouldn't we like, call somebody?" Wallace asked.

"Who do you suggest? 1-800-Start-a-Vineyard? Or maybe I should ask my competition if they'd be so kind as to help a nice guy out," Billy said.

"You know what? Don't discount that idea right off," Scott said. "People love you here. You were a superstar and now you're home again. The people of this town would do anything for you, and you know it."

From outside, Billy heard the roar of a motorcycle. With those pipes, it had to be Harley. He turned to the wide paned window facing the front, and sure enough someone had pulled up at the bottom of the long circular driveway on a Sportster. "It looks like we've already got the welcoming committee here."

Wallace was at his elbow. "Nice bike. Don't you have one of those?"

"Mine's a Road King." Billy still had his eyes on the bike when the rider took his helmet off and long blond hair spilled out of it. That's when he noticed the rest of her— including an ass that should be declared the 8th great wonder of the world.

Scott clapped Billy's good shoulder. "This is like a porno I saw once. Somebody pinch me. Am I dreaming?"

"Holy shit," Wallace said. "Look at her. Would you?"

"I am," Billy said. Unfortunately he was mesmerized. But she was probably some baseball groupie that had heard he was in town. He had to get this woman off his property. Now.

"What are you going to do?" Scott asked.

"I'm going to take care of this. She's trespassing." He slammed the front door, and made his way across the wide expanse of weeds. "Can I help you?"

The woman looked up at him, and her smile froze in place. Billy's heart began to sprint as he stared at the woman. It couldn't be. No way.

Brooke Miller.

CHAPTER 3

*B*illy Turlock. Here? Now? Why?

It made no sense at all. Not that Brooke kept up with the sports page, but wasn't superstar Sliders pitcher hometown hero Billy supposed to be busy fielding the million dollar offers? Somewhere up in Marin County where the streets might as well be paved in platinum? Had he retired, and gone into the real estate business? Why hadn't anyone told her?

"What are you doing here?" Brooke squeaked out. Damn Billy. He'd always made her so nervous with his easy smile, which didn't always make it up all the way up to the green eyes. Those eyes were now supposed to be the smiling, uber confident eyes of a multi-millionaire. *Get with it, Billy, and get the right eyes already.*

It was those eyes, frankly, that had haunted her dreams from their days together at Starlight Hill High School. Where he'd been the jock and she'd been— definitely not a jock.

"I was going to ask you the same thing." He cracked a smile.

"I'm here to make an offer on this vineyard."

That seemed to bother Billy, somehow. He looked at the ground and rubbed the back of his neck. "That's not going to be possible."

"Wow, well, you need to learn a little something about sales. That's not a good attitude to take with a repossessed property in need of some TLC."

"Huh?" Billy asked.

Now that was more like it, and what she expected from a jock. Huh? What did you say? Where's the ball? She smiled, feeling the confidence kick in. These were no longer the hormone driven days of adolescence, even if Billy did bring some of the memories back to the surface by just— standing there.

She set her helmet on the seat of her Harley, and walked towards the house. "It's your lucky day. I've been running the Serrano winery for the past three years. Before that, the Guglielmo winery. And before that, I was taught about everything from the grape to the bottle by my mentor, Anthony DeLuca. What this means to you is that I know the value of land. And I know my grapes, too."

"You do?" He gave her one his drop-dead smiles.

Good thing it had no effect on her, and that he seemed to be following right along. "So don't try to stiff me. I know exactly what this land is worth, but you might have to budge a little on the price. This place needs work."

"Oh, boy." Billy ran a hand down his face.

Good. He seemed to catch her drift quickly. Then again, Billy had been one of the few athletes at Starlight Hill High, home of the Panthers, to make the honor roll. She had him where she wanted him. "I should take a look at the vines, to be fair in my offer."

"But —" Billy began.

Uh-uh buddy, no buts. "I'm sorry. Where are my

manners? It's good to see you again, buddy." She held out her hand.

"You too, Brooke," Billy said, holding her hand and locking eyes with her for a beat too long for her comfort level.

Well, that wouldn't work on her. She was a savvy business woman and not interested in long haired jocks with facial hair— Billy still wore his dark brown hair long, and now he had a mustache and beard. Sure, he had a hot body, all big brawny arms, long legs and flat stomach. But he was definitely not her type.

"Hmmm," she said, pulling her hand away because he still hadn't let go of it.

"Really good to see you." He looked like he meant it too, taking a little tour of her face and having the decency to remember where her eyes were located. "It's been way too long. How've you been?"

"Well, you know I went to Chicago State."

"Yeah, I do." His smiled waned a bit.

"And I came back home right after college." She walked toward the vineyard, and out of the corner of her eye saw a couple of figures pressed up against the wide paned window of the house. "Who's that? You have other buyers here?"

No sooner had she looked in their direction than the two men turned away from the window like they'd been caught in the middle of some kind of lewd and lascivious act.

Billy scowled in their direction. "You remember Wallace and Scott?"

"You brought your brothers with you? The real estate business isn't like baseball. You don't need to bring along your entourage everywhere you go." She proceeded to march past him on her way to the vineyard.

"Brooke, wait a minute," he reached for her elbow as she passed him. Her stupid elbow seemed to remember his touch, as the tingle spread right down into her southern hemisphere. "You don't understand."

Oh, but she did. She understood men like Billy Turlock far too well. Men who had everything handed over to them either because of their good looks, connections, or talent. Billy had all three. Not to mention a fast ball that was legend around here. His face plastered all over town. His retired jersey number at the high school, and trophies that probably still lined the athletic department. Girls had always fawned all over him, and that had probably not changed much.

Once, she'd thought they were friends. But she'd turned out to be wrong about that.

The last she'd read about him in one of the gossip rags was a year ago when he'd been dating some gorgeous and towering blonde actress. "All right, I'll play. What is it I don't understand?"

He looked at the ground for a second, then his eyes met hers. "I'm not the real estate agent. I own this vineyard."

The words hit her hard. "I don't believe you."

"Well, believe it. I'm the proud owner of a fixer upper." He didn't look particularly joyous about it, somehow.

No, this couldn't be happening. She'd talked to the bank manager about a loan. She'd crunched the numbers, done her due diligence. Made two or three lists of pros and cons. It looked promising. "But I was going to buy this place. I even talked to the bank manager."

"Yeah. I got that idea. And I'm sorry."

"What do you want with a vineyard? Have you lost your mind? What happened to baseball, and your contract with the Sliders?"

He rocked back on his heels. "I'm betting you don't read the sports section."

"Good guess, genius. Did you get caught somewhere with your pants hanging down? Did they suspend you?" Maybe it was unfair to lump Billy into that category but it was all she knew about these athletes that believed they were God's gift to the world at large, and the female population in particular.

Billy scowled. "I'm retired. My shoulder gave out on me."

A strange thing happened then— Brooke thought she caught something in his eyes that looked strangely— humbled. "Oh."

"Back in Starlight Hill now, with the rest of the family." He waved in the direction of the picture window where Wallace and Scott had gathered again. Presumably to watch the show, and the fireworks when she found out the news.

She wouldn't give them the satisfaction. "So you're back in town, but why buy a vineyard? Why not open up a sports bar?"

"It's for my grandfather. It's always been his dream to own a vineyard. A family business. So I bought it for him."

"You bought your grandfather a vineyard?" Brooke managed to say. So typical of athletes, throwing their wealth around.

"Yep."

"Next time buy him a card. It gets the point across with a lot less fanfare. But maybe you like the fanfare. This place is going to be a lot of work. Good luck to you." She turned to walk back towards her Harley. Another opportunity snatched out from under her, but no point in crying about it. Crying was for girls.

"Wait," Billy said from behind her.

This was where she was supposed to stop and turn around because when men like Billy Turlock said sexy single words like 'wait' and 'stay' women were to melt in their tracks. Then turn around and ask what Master wanted. So of course Brooke kept walking. She strapped on her helmet only to find him at her elbow.

Now he admired her baby, or in other words, tried to get on her good side. "Nice bike."

"Thanks," she said, mounting it. And then because she did feel pretty mean at the moment, she made a show of squirming and wriggling into the seat, bucking and gyrating a little bit. She licked her lips (which she hoped he could see through the helmet) and gazed in his eyes.

He didn't say a word, and this time he wasn't smiling.

Brooke started her bike and roared off, leaving Billy 'I'm-the-sexiest-man-alive-and-you-know-it' Turlock in the dust.

* * *

BILLY COULDN'T MOVE for several minutes. He could only stare into the distance trying to collect his thoughts. Actually, to have a thought of any kind would be nice. Any thought that didn't involve mounting Brooke like she'd mounted that bike, where he'd show her how he could relieve the itch she seemed to have.

Brooke, the prettiest girl he'd ever seen, and the only girl in the class of 2004 at Starlight Hill High who didn't think he walked on water. Unless one counted her best friend Ivey, who only had eyes for the point guard on the basketball team. Jeff something. More memories.

Too bad she hated him because it sounded like she knew the business, and he could use a staff right about now.

He walked back inside, and Wallace whistled. "Seriously better than TV."

"That girl couldn't be any hotter if she was on fire," Scott whistled.

"You didn't recognize her?" Billy asked his brothers. He hadn't either for a second. Back in high school Brooke had unnaturally black dyed hair – black nail polish, black eyeliner. Even then she'd been breathtaking.

"I'd remember her," Scott said.

"That was Brooke Miller, our old high school classmate." Billy glanced back out the window.

"No way, dude. Brooke had black hair. And a big attitude," Wallace said.

"Still has the attitude, minus the black hair."

"Sure looks better on her than black. I remember when some of the kids were into that look," Scott said.

He did too. Kids he hadn't hung out with much, since they didn't tend to come to the games. Didn't think much of the athletic department, basically his life at the time.

But he'd hung out with Brooke once, a long time ago.

"What did she want? Welcome you back to town?" Wallace asked.

"Not quite."

"Don't tell me she asked you out. Damn that is so unfair, bro. Why didn't I take up baseball?" Scott hit the wall.

"You're not even close."

"Are you going to tell us?" Wallace pressed.

"She was here to buy the place. Thought it was still available." Billy raked a hand through his hair. Of course she'd find out that he'd paid cash for it, and make up her mind about him once and for all. Stick him in the category with other athletes who took what they wanted, no questions asked. Without giving him another chance.

Scott whistled again, this time imitating the sound of a bomb on its way down.

"Don't give me that woe-is-me look, bro. You can't have everyone loving you every minute of the day. So she's pissed that you bought the place she wanted. Too bad. She'll get over it." Wallace said, always the voice of reason.

"It's not that. She happens to have experience running vineyards. Lots of it," Billy said.

"She could help us out," Scott said, the light bulb finally going on.

"No, she won't. She's pissed."

"Did you ask her?" Wallace pressed.

"I know that look when I see it," Billy said. "It was a screw you and the horse you rode in on." Not that he didn't deserve it sometimes, but not today. How was it his fault that Pop wanted to own a vineyard? He was only being a dutiful grandson.

"You know what? If you were smart, you could turn around and sell it back to her for a neat profit. And poof! You're out of the vineyard business with a profit to boot." Wallace said.

Yeah, it had occurred to him for a nanosecond. But there was Pop to think about. "What do you think Pop would say to that?"

"He probably wouldn't like it?" Scott said from the stone fireplace.

Yeah, there was that. Not to mention the fact that the whole idea of a vineyard had taken on a fresh new appeal. He wondered how often he'd run into Brooke.

"Well, why don't you offer her a job?" Wallace asked. "I mean, you never know until you ask. Right?"

Right. Something to think about. Did he want to work with Brooke, who had once called him out on his bullshit? Who even back when they were kids had a way of seeing right through him?

Maybe not.

* * *

If Brooke were the crying type, this would be a good time to let loose with a big wail. No job. No vineyard. Nothing she could afford, anyway. Mr. Hometown Hero had swooped in and bought it out from under her. How had it happened so fast? It took at least thirty days for escrow to close on a property.

Brooke pulled off the highway after she'd put a few miles of distance between her and the vineyard, wrenched her helmet off, dug for her cellphone, and dialed the bank manager.

Once she was finally connected to Ted Elliott, all he wanted to do was ask about Friday night. Yes, she'd said she would go out with him because he'd been asking for months. Dinner wouldn't kill her.

She veered right to the point. "What happened to my vineyard, Ted?"

"Oh, um, that. I meant to call you."

"Start talking, Teddy-boy. I'm standing on the side of Chardonnay Avenue and there's no time like the present." A car whizzed by so close that her body was pushed a bit by the force of the wind.

"So you've been there?"

"I had to take a look at the grapes, didn't I?"

He coughed. "I was going to tell you Friday. It was out of my hands, Brooke."

"Don't give me that. How did this happen? It takes thirty days to close escrow, to get loan papers signed." Another car whizzed by, honked, and the driver shouted an expletive. Brooke rewarded him with her finger.

"There weren't any loan papers."

Brooke waited a beat. For there to be no loan, there had to be nothing but— cash. She might have known. Billy had plunked down cash, because he was Billy Turlock. "Crap."

"Once he put up the cash, there was no talking to my boss. This vineyard has been costing us. We've been paying for the upkeep so as not to lose the grapes. They're not a lot of buyers who can put down that kind money."

Probably not, but a retired baseball playboy immediately came to mind. "Why this vineyard? He can probably afford one of the nicer ones that are already up and running."

"You got me. Billy's actually a great guy, Brooke. He signed a ball for my nephew and didn't even charge me for the autograph, and he posed for photos with everyone in the bank. Everybody loves Billy."

She was familiar with that irritating fact. "You don't have to tell me that. I went to high school with him."

"Wow, yeah, so you know. It's hard not to like him, but I did try if that makes you feel any better." Ted coughed again. "So, about Friday night?"

"Screw you, Ted." She pressed 'end' on her cellphone, never feeling quite as significant about that gesture. Tucked it back in her jacket, and mounted her baby again, this time like a cowboy about to tame a bull.

Owning a Harley helped calm her tendency to speed, a fact she hated initially, but one which was relieved by the cruiser's known cool factor. Should have cut down on her speeding tickets and it did. Most of the time. But not today, as Chief of Police Burt pulled her over, clocked at her ten miles over the limit and issued his citation along with a finger wag or two.

"I can't afford this, Burt!" She waved the ticket at him.

"Then don't speed anymore. Have nice day!" He smiled and got back in his cruiser.

Great. So this is what she got for due diligence, for taking her time and not rushing into such a huge decision with her future. Someone else had beat her to the vineyard. Brooke made it back into the heart of town and headed to Mama's Diner near the hospital, since Ivey and her husband Jeff had breakfast there every morning.

Brooke tore off her helmet, and threw open the door to

the diner. She spied Ivey in a booth with Jeff. As usual, all over each other.

"Men suck!" Brooke shouted right after the bell over the door tingled announcing her entrance.

"Order up!" Si said from behind the kitchen partition, and banged his head. "Ah, hell."

"Tell me something I don't know," Em, his wife and co-owner, said from the register. Brooke marched over to Ivey's booth and sat across from the two love birds.

"Thanks for that," Jeff said from the other side of the booth where he sat entwined with Ivey.

Brooke wondered how they could eat that way. "You're welcome."

Em was at their booth, pad in hand. "What'll you have, hon?"

"One hometown hero over-easy. Fry him till he screams!"

"How about coffee instead?" Nothing fazed Em anymore it would appear.

"Yeah, that's fine, too," Brooke said.

"What happened?" Ivey finally asked when she'd managed to tear her attention away from Jeff for a second.

"I went to look at the old Mirassu vineyard on Humming-bird Lane. Guess who I ran into? None other than our old high school chum, Billy Turlock. I didn't even know the man was back in town."

"Don't you read the sports section?" Jeff asked.

"Is he kidding?" Brooke asked Ivey. You never knew with Jeff.

"Not everyone reads the sports section, babe," Ivey cupped Jeff's chin. "Or knows what's going on in the wide world of sports."

"You do," Jeff said, gazing at Ivey like she was the last piece of chicken at a picnic and he hadn't eaten in a decade.

"Half the time I don't even know what you're talking

about." Ivey blushed, probably because she could tell what he was thinking. Everybody with a pulse could tell. "I do remember hearing that Billy retired."

"Super. But did you know the man fancies himself a vintner now? He bought the old Mirassu winery. Right out from under me, the bastard!" Brooke said. "I was going to buy that place."

"The nerve," Jeff said.

"I'm sorry," Ivey said. "What are you going to do now?"

"I've no idea. I can't afford anything else. Vineyards don't come up for sale every day. This was a special deal. A once in a lifetime opportunity." Brooke rested her forehead on the table. This was a crappy day. If only she had a rewind button.

"Heads up," Em said as she filled Brooke's mug with coffee. "And don't worry about what some people are saying. We all know you're perfectly sane."

"Why? What are people saying?" Last year it was the blue and pink ribbons for Ivey and Jeff. What would they do next?

"Nothing much," Em continued as the patted Brooke's back. "Just that you might have had a nervous breakdown. But look at you. You're fine. My sister Jackie had a nervous breakdown and she didn't brush her hair for weeks. Your hair looks great."

"A nervous breakdown?" Brooke squeaked out. Her lack of sanity had been greatly exaggerated. As usual. Just because she liked to jump out of planes and had once bungee jumped off the Merlot Bridge. "Well this is all I need."

"Don't worry," Jeff said. "Some of us never thought you had such a firm grasp on reality to begin with."

Ivey might have kicked him under the table, because he scowled.

"What am I going to do?" She turned to Ivey. "Who's going to hire me if they think I'm nuts?"

"Maybe you should offer your services to Billy," Ivey suggested.

Jeff's pager beeped. "Gotta go."

Brooke counted exactly six "bye, babe" with their corresponding kisses, because she had promised herself to scream if they reached number seven. By the grace of all that is holy they didn't.

Finally, Dr. Jeff Garner was off to the hospital where he could stop bothering his wife and go do something useful like save someone's life.

"As I was saying, why not offer to run the place for him?" Ivey said, taking a nibble off Jeff's left over bacon.

"You want me to help him? Why would I do that?"

"Because you need a job? And he owns a vineyard. Plus, he wasn't there that night."

"It's also his fault I can't have my own vineyard. This was my one chance to start one. The biggest dream I've ever had, and the timing was perfect. And then Billy showed up with his smile, his hot body, and all his money."

Ivey's eyebrow lifted. "Hot body?"

"Don't look so surprised. People started to fall all over themselves to give him what he wants. In other words, it's high school all over again."

CHAPTER 4

New day, new problem. Now Pop couldn't find the prize winning grape tending tip from his oldest friend, the late Giusseppe DeNiro, not any relation to the actor.

They didn't need the prize winning grape tip now. They had rows of grapes which had to be harvested.

Wallace and his crew had been at work on the manor house for three weeks now, with Scott and Billy's help. The place was beginning to shape up into a place he'd actually like to live in, and he'd given that some consideration. The country air would be good for him. So would the solitude.

"It was in this box," Pops said as he sorted through the items in an old shoebox. Probably not where Billy would have put something special.

Billy turned another one upside down, finding pictures and useless old bank receipts with faded ink. "Could it be in any other box?"

The Turlock family had congregated at the sprawling mansion he'd bought for Mom with his first multi-million dollar contract. On the outskirts of Starlight Hill on county land, it was the one place that had served as a refuge during the past few years and all the shoulder surgeries, each one more painful than the last.

Sure, he had his own apartment in the city but even if he'd plenty of offers for after-care treatment, no one took care of him like Eileen Turlock. Right now he thought he could smell the pot roast stew wafting in from the kitchen.

It was time to discuss their next steps with Pop. He'd already been over a mock up plan with his accountant and projections for salaries. "Hey, Pops. We're going to need to hire a staff."

"Sure, but we won't want anyone knowing our secret. He almost took this one to the grave with him. He was one greedy son of a bitch, and my best friend."

Billy didn't want to bother with the juxtaposition of those two statements. "I ran into someone who has a lot of experience. She used to work for the Serrano winery."

Pops ears perked up at that. "The Serrano winery? They've won the Blue label the past two years."

"That's a good thing, right?"

"A very good thing. But you haven't thought this one all the way through, son. She could be a spy." Pop pointed to his head, narrowed his eyes.

Yeah. One too many James Bond movies. "A spy?"

"He sent her over, maybe to find out just how much we know."

"Kinda doubt she's a spy," Billy said, shaking his head.

"You never know."

"What I do know is that we need to harvest those grapes soon. Otherwise we'll lose our window." Okay, so he'd actually done some reading since running into Brooke. He was now the proud owner of acres of vines, and he hadn't a clue. Calling Brooke and offering her a job, even if she'd been less than happy to see him, had become a real possibility. It was at least worth a shot.

Pop continued to dig through boxes.

At the risk of yet another baseball analogy, Billy offered up the truth in a way Pop would understand it. "It's game time. We're up to bat."

"Don't worry, son. We'll hit this one out of the park."

Considering his batting average, Billy didn't want to think that way. Sounded like a long shot at best. He wanted, needed, this venture to be a resounding success, and didn't want to see any newspaper articles quoting their doubts that he could make this work.

"I'm going to give her a call and see what this woman has to say. I'll have her checked out, if it makes you feel any better."

He heard Mom call out dinner time, and offered a hand to Pop. "You can go back to this treasure hunt later. Time to eat."

Pop put the box down. "I'm a little tired. Think I'll take a nap first."

"Before dinner?" It didn't sound right. Was Pop getting weak on him?

"Not hungry. And tell Eileen not to save me any leftovers either."

Great. Even worse. He'd have to talk to Mom, and make sure Pop had been to the doctor recently for a full check-up. For now, he would let Pop think about other things besides grapes and vineyards. Truthfully, Bill could use a change of subject too.

* * *

"WHAT THE HELL IS IT?" Billy stared at Mom's dinner. This was not pot roast.

"Tofu roast," Mom declared. "We're all eating healthy around here. Good for Pop, good for me, and good for my children."

No wonder Pop had begged off dinner. "Mom, tofu and roast don't belong in the same sentence together."

"Word," Scott said with a fist bump. "You've missed out on all the fun around here. Mom's on a health kick."

"And I've lost twenty pounds and lowered my cholesterol and my blood pressure," Mom said pointing her fork at him. "So no more complaining. Eat your greens if you don't like my tofu."

The greens looked like someone had taken a pile of grass, wet it, and put it on a plate. In the old days, Mom had cooked. Somewhere, somehow something had gone terribly wrong. He put a spoonful of wet grass on his plate and passed the plate to Wallace.

Wallace held out his hand. "Thanks, I already ate. I eat an early dinner early these days."

Billy immediately made plans to join him from this day forward. For now, he changed the subject. "I'm meeting with some of the farm hands tomorrow. The bank manager said they'd be more than happy to stay on with us."

"I'll be out there tomorrow, with my crew." Wallace said. "We need to finish up the living quarters."

"Should you spend all that money on that now? Who's going to live there?" Mom asked.

"Maybe me," Billy answered.

"Don't be silly. You don't have to stay out there all alone. There's plenty of room for you here, in my house." Mom objected.

"I'm twenty-eight years old and I've been living on my own since I was eighteen. I love you, Ma, but I can't live with you." Especially not now, when he couldn't even look forward to a good home cooked meal.

Anyway, he did want the quiet of the vineyard at night. Maybe there he could think. Make plans. Plans that didn't involve baseball. He still couldn't wrap his mind around that one. How was he supposed to get through the rest of his life without the passion that had driven him since he was seven years old?

"Fine. Have I told you how grateful I am lately, that you're making Pop's dream come true?" Mom asked.

"At least three times a day. But honestly, I wasn't sure what I'd do or where I'd be headed until Pop suggested the idea." Where did a washed up ball player go when he hadn't even had the foresight to get a college degree? When he'd gone straight to the minor leagues to the majors without a second thought? Where the wind blew, apparently.

"I've got to say I'm proud of my Scottsmen, doing something out of the ordinary. Why can't the Scottish be successful in the wine making business?" Mom asked.

"I like a good Scotch, myself." Wallace said with a deep sigh.

As it happened, so did Billy. But he'd learn to love wine if it killed him. "Maybe I should give Brooke a call."

"Please, bro. Do that and I won't ever ask you for anything else again," Scott said, then swallowed a bite of tofu with a pained expression. This was saying something, since Scott mostly inhaled food.

"You mean Brooke Miller?" Mom asked as she tried to place some more roast on Scott's plate. "She's such a pretty girl. I see her every now and then at the farmer's market with her mother. She always remembers to say hello."

"She's in the running to be your next daughter-in-law if I have anything to say about it," Scott said, pulling his plate out of Mom's reach.

Yeah. Right over Billy's cold and dead body. "The point is she can help us."

"She can help me," Scott said. "Without a doubt."

Billy ignored the hot spike of anger that hit his stomach. It couldn't be the food since he'd barely touched it. No, it was Brooke, all right— even if she wasn't his and never had been.

"Hiring her, after you bought the place out from under her. It's not going to be easy." Wallace said.

Not easy at all, but then again had anything worthwhile ever been?

* * *

"HEY BILLY, is it true you're planning a comeback?" A reporter called out.

Okay, that one made him laugh. He'd barely retired.

"How's the shoulder?" Another reporter shouted.

Great as long as I don't throw a ball. No more surgeries. Did you hear?

"Slow news day, guys?" Billy asked, as he climbed into his convertible. He'd been going between the vineyard and his mother's house for the past four weeks mostly avoiding them, but today they'd found him at his mother's house. An easy thing to do if someone was looking for a Turlock in Starlight Hill. They were standing at the edge of the steep driveway.

All the better that he didn't plan on staying with Mom much longer. She didn't tolerate reporters, even if the woman was practically a saint. But from the first time one of them had called Billy a "has been" she'd painted all of them with one broad brush. Speak ill of my child and you will die a slow death, Mom said. In other words, she was a typical baseball mom. Hopefully these guys would follow him and leave Mom's Tulip garden alone, or the whole town might come to regret it.

Billy sighed and backed out of the long driveway. Pretty

typical to be asked about a comeback when he'd only retired a month ago. Baseball loved an underdog story, but as much as he might wish for it, it wouldn't happen for him.

He'd had his run, maybe not the way he'd planned but he'd been luckier than most. And even if he'd miss it every day for as long as he breathed, it was over for him. No turning back.

What might happen today, though, would be a meeting with one Brooke Miller. It wasn't difficult to locate anyone in Starlight Hill, particularly not with his long reach. Within hours of asking his investigator to check into it, he had Brooke's personal email, cell phone, home address and places she loved to frequent.

Not that he would stalk her. He only wanted to ask her politely if she'd care to take on the position of general manager at the vineyard. She'd probably refuse, but then he'd have done his best. And he'd get another glimpse of her too.

He'd been a bit shell shocked to see her pull up on that Harley, and since then she'd headlined a few fantasies of his own. Brooke remained, and always would be, the one that got away.

Not that he would let her know that. He could only imagine how she'd greet the news that a washed up ball player had the hots for her. And even though Brooke was an old classmate and friend, Gigi had schooled him about women. Even if he was out of the game, that lingering baseball pheromone remained. There were some women who couldn't help themselves. Ball players were their prize. Even if he knew Brooke was nothing like that, he should proceed with caution or Gigi might show up. She always did when she smelled women, bless her evil heart.

Billy thought he'd lost the reporters, all four of them, when he pulled in front of the old diner named Mama's. This was where he'd been told he would either find Brooke, or her best friend Ivey.

All right, so he'd give this a try. If Brooke wasn't here, he'd try somewhere else. In the meantime, it couldn't hurt to hang out with some locals and take some photos. It was necessary and expected, and he'd never be too good for it.

He opened the glass paned door and the overhead chimes sounded. A waitress had her back to him and called out, "It's self-seating. I'll be right with you."

He took off his shades and when the waitress turned he saw Brooke Miller for the second time in ten years. The black apron skirt didn't manage to take away any of her appeal, though he could much better see her in a French maid costume. *Okay, Billy, enough already. Front and center.*

But Brooke, a waitress?

"I suppose you want a big enough table for you and your entourage?" She glared behind him.

Sure enough, the reporters had caught up to him. "They're not with me."

In the next few minutes he'd been greeted by everyone in the establishment with a hug and a request for an autograph. Again, he posed for a few pictures. One of them with Si, the chef, and yes he'd agreed that Si could hang the photo in the diner and say Billy Turlock had eaten here. Signed a little boy's arm after his mother nodded in approval, and gave a few pointers to a kid trying out for the Varsity team next season.

Brooke ignored him, pouring coffees and wiping down tables. When he took his seat at a booth, she slapped down a menu without meeting his eyes.

All four reporters had settled into a booth nearby. She threw down menus for each of them. "Everyone here is going to have to order something."

"You heard the lady," Billy said.

"What'll you have, Hotshot?" Brooke turned to ask him.

He had half a mind to ask for the waitress, well done, but no. If they were going to do this, it had to be professional. Brooke would never go for it any other way.

So he ordered from the menu, which his old trainer (and now his mother) would call Heart Attack Alley. Everything sounded good, but he settled on the Santa Fe skillet with eggs over-easy.

A few minutes later, Brooke set his platter down and tried to walk away, but he grabbed her wrist. "Can we talk?"

"I'm working." She shook him off.

"Si," Billy called out to the chef, "Can your waitress take a break and talk to me?"

"Hells to the yes!" Si shouted, and banged his head on the partition. Had to hurt.

"What a shock. You get your way again." Brooke deadpanned.

"You're working here now?"

"It's temporary. I give Em a few days off a week so she can do her rescue dog training. And also because I can't buy the vineyard I'd planned to buy. Since someone else already did."

"Yeah." Billy said, but he hadn't missed the fact that the reporters were leaning a bit closer. Not exactly the privacy he'd hoped to have this conversation. "Didn't know you were looking for a job."

"I'm not." Brooke locked eyes with him. Had she already guessed he'd been about to try and hire her? It wouldn't surprise him. Seemed like Brooke had always been two steps ahead of him.

"Because if you are, I'm looking for a general manager."

"Is that right?"

"I think you know that I'm slightly out of my element here. I need someone who knows what they're doing. I could hire an outside firm, but I already know who I want." He tried his best to give her a significant, completely non-sexual look.

Which, let's face it, was not easy looking the way she did, face flushed, hair a bit plastered to the side of her face. Like she'd just had a good— work-out. Still the most beautiful woman he'd ever seen.

"And of course, everyone knows you get what you want." Brooke leaned towards him, giving him a generous view of her cleavage.

The reporters were practically salivating. Not to mention Billy. If he could bury his face in that fleshy rack, he'd die a happy man.

"Not true," he said, regaining consciousness. He swallowed some of his water, wishing he could splash it in his face. He needed to concentrate right now.

"Order up!" Si called out.

"Sorry, gotta go. But this was fun," Brooke said.

She flitted about the rest of the tables, where her attitude remained as bright and cheery as a monsoon. Waitress material she wasn't. A few times he noticed that customers wound up straightening out their orders after she'd left, unwilling, or perhaps afraid to set her straight.

He understood the feeling. If not for the fact that he'd faced a lot worse— such as rehab after the first shoulder surgery— he might have felt the same way. Brooke was like a tornado that fascinated as it drew people and objects in its direction with the assurance that if one got too close they faced certain death.

He still thought it might be a good way to go if he got to choose.

A couple of hours later most of the customers had left and even the reporters straggled out when Billy continued to silently read the sports section. Giving them nothing.

"You're still here?" Brooke asked, as if she hadn't been silently throwing him death stares the entire time.

"You need the table?" He scanned the empty room.

"No, smart ass. I don't." She headed toward him with the coffee carafe, but he finally had the mix of creamer and sugar where he wanted it to be. He covered the mug but too late. Brooke poured a splash of hot coffee right on his hand.

He drew his hand back as white blinding pain seared his skin, and Brooke's eyes turned to big amber saucers.

"Oh no, I'm so sorry. Let me get that for you." She ran out of the room and came back with a wet towel and some ice.

This was by far the best injury he'd ever endured. No stranger to blinding searing pain that cut like a razor blade, this didn't initially feel like much though he knew it might blister by tomorrow. But the kind of attention he was now receiving from a penitent Brooke was well worth it.

Brooke sat on the other side of the booth from him, wrapping his hand in a wet towel. "Si said the whole order is on the house."

He hadn't expected the funny pinch in his chest. "That's not necessary. It was an accident. Hey. I'm okay." He touched her wrist with his left hand.

She gazed at him as if she was actually seeing him for the first time, and the years melted away. Back to the time before he'd let her down. "Billy Turlock."

Man, the way she said his name. That alone could give him a hard-on, as if he were still a teenage boy. "Brooke Miller. I'm sorry."

Her eyes narrowed. "*You're sorry?* I believe I just tried to pour coffee on your hand. It doesn't even resemble a mug."

"I'm sorry I bought the vineyard you wanted. I didn't know."

"How could you know?"

So she was going to cut him some slack. At least she understood it wasn't personal. "Exactly."

"But I can't work for you, Billy." She stated this matter fact, like it was also nothing personal.

"And why not?"

"Here's the thing. I'm thinking my next steps through, taking my time. I'm not going to do anything impulsive. And besides," she gave a wave around the restaurant. "I already have a job."

Time for stating the truth. From his past experience with Brooke, he remembered she appreciated honesty. "Don't take this the wrong way, but you suck as a waitress."

For a moment he thought she'd slap him, but then she laughed. "You don't think it's cool to pour coffee on a customer's hand?"

"I have a feeling your talents lie elsewhere."

"You would be right." She rose. "But this is what I'm doing now, while I re-think my options."

No one had to tell him when he'd pushed too far. Brooke needed time to think about it. But first he'd give her something to consider. His offer.

He placed a bill on the table, and stood. "Fine. But if you change your mind, give me a call."

He scribbled his private cell phone number on the napkin. "I'm offering a generous salary, medical and dental. And a 401K. Nice to see you again. Have a good day, Si."

He waved, opened the door to the diner, and left Brooke staring at the napkin, her mouth gaping open.

* * *

"ACK. I HIT SEND," Brooke said from her kitchen table, where she sat with her laptop. She'd sent a simple one sentence email to Billy: we need to talk.

With an offer like the one he'd made, she'd be a fool not to want to at least open a dialogue with the man.

"You have to hit send. How else is he supposed to get your message?" Ivey said, popping the third chocolate cupcake from Genenieve's Sweet Southern Buns in her mouth.

"But I changed my mind. I can't work for Billy. I'm an idiot to think I can." She reached for another cupcake, before they were all gone.

"Well, you didn't say you accepted the offer. Wanting to talk shows you're open minded. That you're reasonable and will entertain the generous offer he made."

Generous indeed. Brooke still wondered if he'd added an extra zero by accident. In a way, part of why she wanted to talk.

"But he'll see it as a weakness. Like I'm giving in, but I'm not. The Mirassu vineyard was supposed to be mine. It would be mine had he not waltzed back into town."

"Maybe. But now you have a chance to show him, show the entire town what you can do. Turn the place around and back into the vineyard it used to be before all the trouble. And show George what he lost as well, by not giving you the position as VP."

Showing the community that she'd been the reason behind Serrano's success would be satisfying. George would be destroyed to find out she could be his greatest competition. Of course, if the vineyard would have been hers in name too, it would be much better. But being the general manager, and in control of it all. Resuscitating an old vineyard, saving it from ruin. A worthy challenge.

As long as Billy gave her control to make all the important decisions, and she wasn't at all sure about that. He didn't look like the kind of man who handed over control easily.

Brooke watched Ivey pop another cupcake in her mouth, and didn't even have to get up from the table to reach into the fridge for some more milk. "I don't get what you have against Billy. I mean, other than the fact he bought the vineyard."

"Isn't that enough?"

She didn't dislike Billy, not at all. Unfortunately Ted was right. It was hard not to like Billy Turlock. Particularly if you were a woman. Unless you were a woman who had something against hot bodies, sensual lips, a full head of dark hair begging to be tousled, and...what were they talking about?

"You have to know it wasn't personal. You both wanted the same thing." Ivey's eyes widened in that doe-eyed way of hers. "Hey, maybe it's a sign."

Brooke stuck out her tongue. "It's not a sign."

"Well, he bought the place only because he happened to get there first." Ivey added.

And wasn't it always the case with Billy Turlock? He had the athlete's air about him, testosterone pouring out all over Kingdom Come. Might as well have had Winner written on his forehead ever since high school, and the first time someone had clocked his fastball at ninety miles per hour. Even she remembered.

"He got there first with all the money." Overpaid jocks and all their wealth. Not her favorite subject.

"I don't think he's the over privileged athlete you think he is. And even better, he's not your type. So, good-looking though he is, you should be fine working together in a boss employee relationship."

That would be because Ivey hadn't seen the way Billy looked at her. Like he remembered her. "Wrong again. We kissed once, a long time ago. High school."

Ivey's jaw dropped. "And you didn't tell me? What's wrong with you? How could you hold out on me like that all these years?"

Because the whole thing was so embarrassing. "There's nothing to hold out on. It was stupid."

"Tell me every single tiny detail."

"What do you want me to say? He's a good kisser." She couldn't say any more because the rest was too humiliating. But it was a long time ago.

"That's it? You didn't—"

"No! I didn't sleep with him." She'd been a virgin, waiting for the right one. Someone who could love her, because she'd had a stupid silly dream. All of that lay in the past, where it belonged. She no longer believed in fantasies.

Brooke's phone rang, and the caller ID displayed Billy Turlock. "Oh, no. This is him. He's calling me. Do you think he already read the email?"

"Wow, he is fast."

"I can't talk to him right now. I'm re-thinking this whole thing." Brooke pushed the phone away. She'd let it go to voice mail. Right now his sexy baritone voice might send her over the edge and she'd say yes. One more night to sleep on it couldn't hurt.

"I'll get it." Ivey reached for the phone in one swoop. She was stealthy, and Brooke couldn't wrestle it back. "Brooke's phone. This is Ivey Garner speaking."

Brooke's stomach hurt, and not because she'd had six cupcakes. She shook her head and waved hands in Ivey's direction. Brooke wouldn't be getting on the phone. Ivey might answer Brooke's phone, but couldn't make her talk.

"She's not here right now, but I'll tell her you called. Is there a message? How are you, by the way?"

Sweet Ivey. She could talk the red off a stop sign. Interesting how she made conversation with someone she knew only in passing, but she managed to do it for a few minutes before she finally hung up.

"He even sounds sexy," Ivey said as she put the phone down.

Hence part of the problem. And he looked even better than he sounded which wasn't fair. "What did you say, Mrs. Garner? Who sounds sexy?"

Ivey blushed. "You heard me."

"What did Billy say?"

"He said he wanted to make arrangements for you to come out to the vineyard."

Of course. He'd want her opinion on the condition of the grapes. He'd want her opinion on everything if he wanted her as a general manager. "How did he sound?"

"He sounded like a guy."

"I mean did he sound pompous, like he's about to get what he wants? Again?"

"Not sure how you sound pompous, but I still have to say no. He sounded friendly, fun, you know, like a ball player. So are you going to take the job or not?"

It would be satisfying to help Billy's winery be real competition for Serrano's. "I'm thinking about it. Don't rush me. But you know, if I only bide my time and let him fail… then I could swoop in and save the day, and buy the vineyard after all." Maybe Billy would sell it back to her at a discount. Or maybe he'd even let her finance one of those seller notes she'd seen on late night informercials. Did people still do that?

"Or you might have to sit and watch the place be a resounding success with the help of some other general management firm."

"Ugh, yeah. So you see my problem. Damn him. Either way Billy has always been a thorn in my side."

CHAPTER 5

"*D*ude, have you heard from Brooke yet?"

Had to be the tenth time Scott has asked. It had been a week, and he'd heard no word from her after he'd followed up on her email to him. Seemed as though maybe she'd changed her mind again.

"No. I called, and it's up to her now." Billy massaged his right shoulder. It had been killing him today, and the carpentry work wasn't helping. Still, no way would he let an entire crew work on the place while he stood around and supervised.

He'd been staying on a cot here alone at nights, and it was everything he'd expected. The silence of the night, the cool evening breeze. Every part of this place agreed with him. It had been a great idea, even if Pop still couldn't find the prize-winning tip. No matter, Billy would make this new venture work.

With any luck, he'd have Brooke at his side too. And if he'd been overly generous in his offer, he could afford it and she'd be worth it. He'd asked around, and Brooke had built a solid reputation with the wine buyers he'd talked to. They spoke of her expertise and professionalism. Of course he hadn't talked to any of his competition yet, certainly not the Serrano winery. To hear most tell it, George Serrano was an asshole who treated his employees no better than a King would treat a pageboy. Made sense Brooke had moved on.

And yeah, he'd checked her out even more. Plenty of speeding tickets and one exhibition of speed which only peaked his curiosity. No marriages. No children. Still single, thank God. Not that he wouldn't keep it professional. They'd start off on the right note, and if something developed later, perhaps, along the way as they worked together and celebrated victories...well, he wouldn't kick her out of his bed. Let's put it that way.

Despite all that, if he didn't hear back from her in a matter of days he'd have to move on. There were several management companies chomping at the bit for the project. Any of them would do the job, but none of them were Brooke.

"Put that down," Wallace shouted over the sanding machine. "Do you want Ma to kick my ass? No more shoulder surgeries."

"I'm fine," Billy said, but he put the sheetrock down and walked outside to the balcony overlooking the fields.

He breathed in the sweet smell, and reminded himself he should be happy. Most people would die a thousand deaths to see the view in front of him. A view he would see every morning.

Instead all he could think about was another field— a baseball diamond, to be precise. If he closed his eyes he could smell the freshly cut grass, the chalk outlining the field, the leather of his worn mitt. But that was his past, and this vineyard was the future. And he had to admit, every time he thought of Brooke the future began to appear increasingly ... appealing.

"The guys are taking a break," Wallace said, walking up to Billy with a cold beer. "And of course Scott is taking one with them."

Billy took a swig. "Think we're putting a curse on this place by drinking beer in front of it?"

"Turn around and don't let them see if you're worried about it," Wallace said with an eye roll.

"Right." Billy chuckled. Wallace had a way of bringing things back to perspective.

"Did you give away your Series tickets yet?"

"How do you know I'm not going?" One of the most annoying facts about having brothers was the way they could read his mind.

Wallace waved his arm around the place. "This."

Billy shoved his free hand in his pocket. "It'll take up most of my time, until we get it off the ground."

"Doesn't mean you can't go to the series, but something tells me you're not."

Late September, and the Sliders were already out. His replacement, a trade from Milwaukee, had a fair season but not a series worthy-season. Billy could relate.

"What's the point?" He couldn't be on the mound or in the dugout, so he might as well not be there at all.

"Have you heard from Brooke yet?"

"Not yet." He'd had enough. An athlete didn't sulk. Not much anyway, and then it was time to move on.

"You know, just because you're not playing ball anymore doesn't mean you can't go to the games." Wallace changed the subject.

But other times, walking away from something or someone you loved deserved a clean break. "Right now, it does. Otherwise I'll just tease myself with what I can't have."

Wallace clapped his back. "I hear you. But no one's ever

going to stop associating you with baseball. Just so you know, bro."

And he wasn't altogether certain he wanted them to stop, either. There was the rub. "Who knows? Maybe someday they'll associate me with wine." He held up his beer bottle.

Wallace glanced from him to the bottle and back again. Then he reared back on his heels and let out the Turlock laugh. All right, it was funny. He'd need to start drinking wine. Pronto.

"We need to talk about something else," Wallace said.

Sounded strangely ominous. "You have my attention."

"It's Ma. She's signed up for some internet dating service." Wallace scowled.

"No."

"Yeah. She said she's sixty-three now and has a few good years left in her, and now she's lost twenty pounds and feels like Elizabeth Taylor."

"I knew it couldn't just be a health kick. She lost weight to get a man."

"I don't know. I can't even let my mind go there."

Billy nodded. "Understood."

"So you should talk to her."

"Me?"

"She listens to you. But I was thinking, maybe if we get her a bit more involved in this place. We could keep her mind off it."

That had been the plan, though he still wasn't sure what Mom could do. "What did you have in mind?"

"Hell if I know. Add some stuff to the menu? At least, that's what I suggested to her."

It was one of the many items he wanted to discuss with Brooke. He'd seen the former Mirassu small menu of appetizer food to compliment wines, and wondered if they could expand on that.

"I'll think about it. But no wet greens. Or tofu." This was a winery. There should be cheese, and crackers. Fruit, probably. Beyond that, he had no clue.

Wallace nodded. "I hear ya. And we're almost done here with your renovation. I'll be taking my crew after we're done here up to Sausalito for a job."

Right. Wallace never stayed in one place for long, going where the work took him.

"This place is amazing," Mom's voice could be heard carrying through the empty main house. "Come along, Pop. A little faster. Right up these steps. Here we go."

Billy walked back into the house. "Hey, Ma. What do you think?"

"It's like paradise. Like Italy or something. And to think it was all Pop's idea." She patted Pop's back.

"Well, Billy's realtor found the place," Pop said. "I think I better go take a look at those grapes, son. It's time to harvest."

Billy realized that, hence the pressure to get Brooke on board.

Right now he couldn't picture Pop walking the length of ten acres along the hilly land. "Did you find what you were looking for yet?"

"Nope, but I'm getting close. I can sense it."

"Boys, I brought you all a snack. Don't worry, there's enough for everybody." Mom headed to the kitchen with whatever kind of punishment she had for them today.

"Thanks, Ma, but if I want to finish this renovation on time I need to get back to work." Wallace said with a wince.

"Fine, but you'll regret it. They're whole wheat brownies made with carob. None of the horrible processed sugar that has single-handedly killed so many people."

"I wish it would kill me now," Pop said with a scowl.

"Let's take a look at the grapes," Billy said as he clapped a hand on Pop's back.

* * *

"ALL RIGHT, HERE WE GO." Brooke said out loud to no one.

She'd just passed the stoned entryway with the Vineyard placard and photo of a hummingbird, Mirassu's trademark. Putted up to the top of the circular driveway. Now all she had to do was get off her Harley, walk up to Billy and check out the grapes.

Any time now.

Crap. Brooke took off her helmet and rested her forehead on the handle bar. Why had Billy always had the ability to at once draw her in and also make her want to run in the other direction?

So what if she still remembered that kiss? The one in which he'd pretty much sucked the marrow right out of her. It was a long time ago and she was certain he didn't remember it. He'd had a lot of experience with women even back in high school, and she'd had zip with boys.

None of this mattered because he wasn't her type. Long haired baseball jock with a beard and mustache. Dressed in baseball caps and not GQ suits. Probably didn't even own a suit.

He wouldn't be expecting her, because she hadn't called ahead. If they were going to do this, she had to be certain Billy was serious. Wanted to make sure she wouldn't find a harem of baseball groupies at the place. Did he want to make wine or collect women? Today she would find out.

And okay, maybe she shouldn't get her news from Look Here! Magazine, but in the past the periodical had portrayed Billy Turlock as a love 'em and leave 'em playboy. And it's not like she had any other image with which to replace him, since she didn't know him anymore.

Billy could date whoever he wanted to, no skin off her nose, but he'd have to put this business first if they were going to beat George at his own game. She wanted that almost as much as she wanted her own piece of land. To see Mirassu rise up again, courtesy of one Brooke Miller. Let the townspeople talk about that.

Nervous breakdown her ass.

Revenge wrenched her off the bike. Marched her up to the entrance, where workers came out of the main house carrying sheetrock. There seemed to be workers everywhere. In the yard, on the roof. Definitely some improvements going on here. A good sign.

Scott Turlock waved to her. "Brooke! Over here."

She remembered Scott, the youngest Turlock brother, a soldier and Jeff's roommate for a time. He'd been welcomed home with a parade when he'd returned from a tour of duty a year ago. She'd been one of many in the crowd.

"I'm here to see Billy," Brooke said. "And the grapes." Just in case Scott didn't realize how serious she was about all this.

"Of course you are. Right this way." Scott hooked his finger and turned to lead the way.

Brooke had only been in the Mirassu winery once, a few years ago. She was gratified to still see the fine rosewood floors, Tuscan gold walls, and the balcony leading to a breathtaking view of the vineyards below.

Speaking of breathtaking, Scott pointed towards Billy before he turned and walked back outside. Billy, the picture of concentration, had a pencil over one ear and was measuring some sheetrock. His long shirt sleeves were rolled up to the elbows, displaying cords of muscles. A tool belt hung low on his blue jeans. For now, she would excuse the turned around baseball cap on his head.

This ex-ball player made one fine construction worker.

Brooke cleared her throat. "Ahem."

Billy turned, the concentration shifting into a smile which took over his entire face. "Hey."

Brooke swallowed. "I'm here to check out the grapes."

He set down his pencil and shrugged off his tool belt. "Does that mean you're considering my offer?"

"That's what it means." She'd be an idiot not to consider it, and she might be a lot of things but idiot was not one of them.

"That's great, Brooke. Just great."

"Well. Let's not get ahead of ourselves."

"Right. Come this way."

She followed him to the balcony trying to avert her eyes from his fine ass. How pathetic would it be if someone caught her staring at his ass?

"Quite a view, isn't it?" Billy asked.

Oh dang, busted. Wait. Was he now complimenting his own ass? Aha! He was every bit the conceited jock.

It took her a minute to realize Billy was talking about the vineyard, as he reached the balcony. "It's twenty acres."

"I know."

Twenty acres of prime California real estate. A large manor house with a banquet room, kitchen, large wine bar. Living quarters in the back. She wondered what it would be like to survey the land below and realize it was all yours. She could only guess: pretty freaking awesome.

She caught a sight below which startled her. "I don't know how to tell you this, but an old man is sitting there in a lawn chair. Right along the first row."

"Yep. That's Pops." He turned to her like that should explain everything.

"Who is Pops and why is he sitting among m—" Brooke corrected herself, because she was about to call them her grapes. "Your grapes?"

"You don't remember my grandfather? It's a long story, but he's a big part of this enterprise. It was his idea, actually. He's always wanted to own a vineyard. As a young man, he used to occasionally work the fields. He had a small vineyard in his backyard in Saratoga before he retired."

Brooke blinked. She happened to know the Bay Area was replete with do it yourself wine connoisseurs. "Oh, good. But this is a little different."

"That's why you're here." Billy smiled again, something she wished he wouldn't do quite so often, and something went limp inside Brooke.

"Right. Let's take a look at those grapes."

Together they made their way down the hilly rows and rows of vines, Billy always leading, and never failing to look behind him and offer her his hand. She didn't take his hand once, but it didn't seem to faze him.

The grapes on the Chardonnay row looked good. Great, even. Same with the Pinot and the Cabernet row, though they were as ready and ripe as they'd ever be. Billy explained the bank had seen their value, and made sure to take care with their upkeep. Smart, and something she'd have expected.

"Everything looks fine here," Brooke said as she turned to follow Billy back down a hill. She lost her footing and fell right into Billy's rock hard chest with a smack.

She noticed he didn't waste any time steadying her, putting large hands around her waist. "Okay?" he asked.

Okay was a relative term. She wasn't okay with the fact that his touch had sent a small shiver down her spine, and the way he gazed at her with hot eyes wasn't helping the situation, either. "I'm not usually such a klutz."

"Too bad. I'm thinking all I need is for you to say yes to being my general manager, and this becomes the best day I've had in months." The smile stayed in his eyes this time.

Just like that she was thrown back to a time years ago when he'd kissed the fear right out her.

"Look—" she began, and was startled by the sound of someone shouting Billy's name.

"Did you hear me, son?" It was Pop, the old man, calling out from his chair several yards away in the Chardonnay rows.

Great. Had he seen the two of them? Brooke pulled out of Billy's arms.

"Yeah, Pop? I'm right here." Billy marched in his direction. If he was disappointed at their interruption, he gave no indication.

Brooke breathed a sigh of relief as she followed him.

They found the old man staring at the grapes as though he could breathe in their goodness. She knew the feeling. "You know what I'm thinking?" he asked Billy.

"What's that?"

"I'm thinking this is a real good start." Pop said, winking from his chair.

"Yeah," Billy said, throwing her a panty-melting look. "I'd have to say the same."

"And who is this young beauty?" Pop asked, finally noticing her.

"I'm Brooke Miller, sir." She stuck out her hand.

"If we're lucky," Billy added, "she'll be our new general manager. Brooke knows the business, inside and out. And we used to go to school together."

"Is that right? Well, well, well." The old man said, and then shut his eyes like it was time for a nap.

Brooke worried a nail between her teeth. If this were a family affair, Grandpa here should mostly serve as a mascot. She hated to break it to him, but the grapes didn't need him to keep watch.

"It's time to go, Pop," an older woman said as she joined them. "Oh, hello. Who have we here?"

"Mom, this is Brooke Miller." Billy made the introductions. "We went to school together."

Eileen Turlock enveloped her in a sweet mother hug. "Nice to see you."

"Okay," Brooke said, a bit unnerved. She saw Eileen Turlock on occasion around town and at Mom's farm where Eileen bought organic tomatoes, but they'd never hugged before.

Eileen Turlock was still attractive for her age, tall with short straight dark hair and gentle green eyes. Billy took after her.

"We should talk menu sometime," she directed this comment to Brooke, "but for now Pop has to get home for his afternoon nap which it appears he's already started. C'mon, Pop, let's get you home."

Brooke followed them up the hill, Billy doing most of the business of getting his grandfather moving, even if Billy grimaced and rubbed his shoulder. Eileen waved goodbye at the top of the hill, slapping Billy's hand away from Pop.

When Billy walked back to her, he might have noticed the questioning look in Brooke's eyes. "My family is a little over protective about the shoulder. I'm not an invalid just because I can't pitch any more. So why don't we go back to the house and discuss my offer?"

Billy led the way and together they wound up back at the balcony, where rolling acres of ripe vines lay out before Brooke, like a magic carpet. A view she could grow accustomed to.

"What did she mean by talking menu?" Brooke wanted to know how much of a family affair this would be, and how much control would Brooke have as general manager. All of it, she hoped, if this were going to work at all. They both needed this venture to be a success, for different reasons.

He took off his cap and ran a hand through his hair. "I want to improve on the menu."

"Sounds great. I have lots of ideas for you, but what does your mother have to do with any of it?"

"Not much, but could you use her help?" Something unspoken remained in those green eyes, almost pleading, and Brooke's stomach did a weird somersault.

"This isn't going to work if I can't have control over every aspect. Do you want me to be the general manager or not?"

"I offered you the job, didn't I?"

"That's not an answer." Maybe it had been a mistake coming here, even if she did need the generous salary. She turned to go.

Billy reached for her wrist as she passed him. "Hey. What's going on here? Why are you being such a pain in the ass?"

Maybe it was time to put some more cards on the table. "All right, fine. Here's the thing. Let's just say George Serrano and I did not part on good terms."

Billy nodded, understanding passing in his green haze. "I had a feeling. Creative differences?"

Creative differences. Yes, it sounded so polite. "Exactly. I'll be honest with you. I want this place to rise up from the ashes and clobber Serrano's nose till it's bloody. And I'm going to need control to take this place in the direction it needs to go to be a success. I want that as much as you and your family do. Maybe more."

He laid a hand on the balcony's stone ledge. "I see. And you don't think I'm going to let you have control?"

"Are you?"

Billy's eyes shifted, and damned if he didn't look like he was reconsidering everything. A car door slammed in the distance. He took way too long to answer.

"That's what I thought."

He leveled her with a look of such intensity that she'd swear her ovaries quivered.

"You should know that I don't mind a woman being in the driver's seat."

And why did she now wonder if he meant the job? "Good." She swallowed.

"So yeah, I'll give you control."

Brooke took a big breath. "Then I accept your generous offer."

Billy grinned. "Should we drink on it? We definitely have quite a selection. You can pick."

"All right." Brooke followed Billy's back through the large utility kitchen.

Even more possibilities in here. It occurred to her that Eric might like to work here, and that made her wonder how many of George's employees she might be able to spirit over. All of them? But that would come later, in good time.

They continued past the kitchen, their footsteps echoing down the stone steps into the wine cellar. Following Billy, her breath hitched and her palms began to sweat when they were plunged into darkness. She stopped in her tracks. How could she explain this to him without sounding like a fool?

"Are you coming?" He asked from a few steps below her. "Give me your hand. I don't want you to fall."

Before she could speak, he'd taken hold of her hand. She was walking down the steps into the darkness holding Billy's strong capable hand. He held hers in a tight grip. Those hands were probably good at so many things…things she should definitely not be thinking about right now.

Billy flipped on the light switch. Brooke almost had a small orgasm, and shockingly, Billy had nothing to do with it. Rows and rows of wine. She picked up a dusty bottle of Cabernet Sauvignon 1998 and set it back down. They might save that for a special occasion.

"Do you know how lucky you are?" Brooke eyed Billy. Sometimes she wondered if he had any idea, or if he'd become so accustomed to luck that he expected to see it rise every morning with the sun.

"Tell me," Billy said.

"I had no idea this place was worth this much money." In this room alone, thousands upon thousands of dollars' worth of wine which had been kept under the right condition.

"I paid enough for it."

"I think you got your money's worth, if that helps." She picked out a Merlot and handed it to him. "I have one more condition for my employment."

Might as well move in for the kill. Billy wanted her expertise, which gave her a bargaining position. She had the salary and the benefits. But there was one more thing she wanted, and she might as well go for it.

His eyes widened. "Why am I not surprised?"

Go ahead and say it. "I'd like to live in the little house. It used to be where the head farm hand used to live, back in the day."

"You want to live there?" Billy's eyebrows lifted. "It gives new meaning to tiny."

As it happened, it looked to be about twice the size of her apartment. Which, of course, Billy hadn't seen. "Yeah. I don't need much room. I like to sink my teeth into my work, so to speak. I'm going to live and breathe this place."

"Yes, you are." He grinned.

"Is that a yes?"

"It needs to be emptied and cleaned out, but okay," Billy said. "We can make it a part of your salary."

Right. And how would that look? "Absolutely not. I'll pay rent, of course. Something fair."

"Whatever you say." He lifted a shoulder. "I can have my business manager draw up something."

Spoken from the mouth of a multi-millionaire who didn't need the money.

Brooke would live here. The land wasn't hers, no, but she would get to wake up here every morning and … pretend for a little while. And she would work for this winery like it was her own, because in some small way it would be.

"Now I have a question for you." Brooke turned to him, and looked him square in the eyes.

"Go ahead, Ms. General Manager. Ask away. You know you're going to anyway."

"Why me, Billy? Why not go with a general management firm? You said I'm a pain in the ass. And sometimes, you'd be right about that."

Billy didn't speak for a long moment. "You can be. But a long time ago I knew a girl, my friend, who was the only one who didn't fall for my bullshit. The only one who wouldn't let me off the hook and tell me it was okay to take the easy way out. Honestly? Except for my family, I'm surrounded by sycophants. But what I need is someone to tell me like it is."

"And you know I will." It was the perfect end to their meeting, and she didn't want to taint it with any more talking. Sooner or later he'd say or do something to piss her off. She held out her hand so they could shake on it.

Billy returned it with the usual man crushing experience, and she tried not to wince. "You can move in as soon as I hire someone to get it cleaned out. Probably next week. I'll let you know when my business manager draws up the contract. But there's something else you should know."

"Uh, no, Billy. Stop talking. Everything is perfect and I don't want to ruin it." She didn't want to give him a chance to change his mind now. She brushed by him and marched up the steps before he could shut off the light. At the top of the steps she turned and glanced down. "You taste that wine, and let me know what you think of it."

"But—"

She held up a hand. "Not now. Let's end this on a pleasant note. I'll talk to you soon."

"If you say so." He smiled, showing his rare dimple. It was hard to see along all that scruffiness on his cheeks, but she spied it.

"I do," Brooke said, because she would make this work. One way or another.

CHAPTER 6

A week later, Brooke woke on her first morning in the vineyard's cottage and stretched. The first thought that came to mind was that she could get used to this kind of quiet. So quiet she might have heard the flapping of a hummingbird's wings.

She'd made the right decision. Even if thinking it through had possibly cost her an opportunity to buy the vineyard, making Billy wait had meant she got to call the shots. Now she'd be living at a vineyard, as she'd always dreamed. Maybe not a land owner yet, but who knew? Maybe someday. She had to be patient. Even if she wasn't good with patience, she'd have to learn.

She threw off the covers, and put her bare feet on the cold hardwood floor. Thanks to Billy, the place had been cleaned and freshly painted. A very nice shade of copper brown, which added to the rustic sense of the place.

Nothing about it was new, and happened to be what she loved the most, in addition to the privacy. For the past few years she'd lived with units so close together that she and Mrs. Monroe had to coordinate shower times. And when

Officer O'Toole had the early morning shift the following morning, everyone pretty much had to stop talking at eight o'clock in the evening.

And of course, she'd never dream of stepping outside of her apartment in nothing but the panties and tank top she'd slept in.

But she was definitely considering it this morning as she waited for the coffee to brew. She reached for a mug from a moving box labeled Kitchen, unwrapped it, and rinsed it out. She poured coffee into the mug, pulled up the blinds and looked out the window into the bright seamless sunshine of the valley.

She had a great view of the vineyards here. Not quite like the view from the manor balcony, but spectacular regardless.

Yes, this could work. It would work. She and Billy would keep it professional. Even if they'd been less than that in her dreams last night.

She'd dreamt of that time, years ago, when he'd kissed her. When he'd then pulled away to stare at her, like he couldn't believe he'd just done that. She hadn't believed it, either. Billy and Brooke didn't hang out in the same crowd. They weren't dating material. But somehow, when they'd kissed it had been like connecting the dots.

It was a long time ago, and it hadn't worked out for many reasons. She'd forgiven him a long time ago for the way he'd let her down. Today, she was an adult who realized that Billy Turlock hadn't owed her a thing. Not ten years ago, and not now. But they could be friends again, and partners in this endeavor. Not that they were partners. She was his employee.

And her dreams of Billy? Well, they'd remain in her subconscious where they belonged.

Brooke grabbed her mug and tiptoed outside to the small porch, feeling decadent. The nippy early October air hardened her nipples, only adding to the thrill. She set her mug down on the rail, rose on her tip toes and stretched in the early morning air. She might start practicing yoga again, out here in the early morning hours. She squeezed her eyes shut, tossed her hair back, and tried not to giggle.

"It's official. I've died and gone to heaven."

Billy. What the hell? Brooke turned to find him leaning over the manor balcony, a mug in his hands. Grinning.

Brooke had too many expletives running through her mind at once, so that when something finally came out of her mouth it sounded like, "Gah!"

She ran back inside and slammed the door shut. She should have considered he might be an early riser. But why get here so early? All the construction had been done. He could at least have given her a warning that he'd be here.

Well, they were going to have words. No one saw her in her panties without paying for dinner first. She searched for her fuzzy bathrobe, slipped it on and marched back outside.

He was still standing where she'd left him. Still smiling, this time biting his lower lip like he wished he could stop. "Sorry."

"If you're going to be here this early, you need to give me some notice."

He raised his mug to her. "Brooke? I'm going to be here this early every day."

"Why would you do that?"

"I live here too. What did you think all that construction was about?"

She'd had no idea. The manor house had living quarters but no one had lived in them for decades. "You should have told me!"

"I tried to tell you, remember? You said we'd talk later. It wasn't a good time."

"You should have tried harder," Brooke said, pulling her

robe tighter. "I thought I was alone. I don't usually parade around outside in my underwear."

"That's a real shame. Don't worry, I didn't see much. I've grown used to averting my eyes."

"I don't have business meetings in my bathrobe but we need to talk." With that, she opened the door and slammed it again, probably waking the rest of the wild life.

Billy again burrowing himself under her skin. It could have been a simple misunderstanding, a joke they'd laugh about later. But somehow the look in Billy's eyes made her think twice. He wouldn't soon forget he'd caught her half naked. Her own damn fault.

The worst thing about it was that she wasn't even wearing her best panties. Her good fortune today was that she had worn her panties with the kites being flown by kittens. *Real sexy, Brooke.*

And then there was her rattiest bathrobe, the one within reach. The one she wore when she didn't care who saw her. But worse was the fact that she cared. About all of it. Maybe she should be worried about that.

Brooke hopped in the small shower, dressed in jeans and a t-shirt, and stuck her blow-dried hair in a ponytail. She didn't want to wait much longer to talk to Billy and straighten some things out.

There was a soft knock on her door, so he'd wizened up and come to her. Probably to apologize again. Good.

When Brooke opened the door, she was surprised to see a middle aged woman in a pin striped suit. She had straight salt and pepper shoulder length hair which flipped at the ends in a classic pageboy-style.

"Hi, Brooke. I'm Gigi Rosenberg, Billy's publicist." She held out her hand, and Brooke took it, moving to allow Gigi inside.

"You'll have to excuse the mess. I just moved in." Brooke waved in the direction of her boxes.

"I heard. And you didn't know that Billy would be living in the manor house when you asked to live here?" Her stiletto heels made a clackety sound against the hardwood floor.

"No idea." Brooke waited a beat. "Where's Billy?"

She didn't know this woman, and the tone in her voice sounded strangely accusatory. She might be imagining things, though. Billy could, and should be the one to explain to his publicist. This was her cottage now. Billy had said it could be. Brooke didn't care if Attila the Hun moved in next door. She wasn't budging.

"He's taking a quick shower, so I sneaked out here to talk to you, woman to woman."

Uh-oh. Seemed like maybe Gigi might be Billy's woman, and naturally she didn't appreciate the arrangement. But tough luck, she'd have to live with it. "Look, I don't have any designs on Billy if that's what you're worried about. I'm not here to steal your man."

Gigi's eyebrows rose to her forehead and she let out a little cackle. "Is that what you think? How old do you think I am, dear?"

Brooke hated this game. Mom and all her friends played it with her on different occasions. They claimed their healthy way of living stopped, and at times even reversed, the aging process.

Brooke erred on the side of caution. "I don't know, forty?"

"Fifty-eight!" Gigi announced with a hair flip. "This is what staying out of the sun for twenty years can do for a woman."

Damn, she did look good. "Wow. Well, that's a big age difference, but I'm not here to judge you."

Now Gigi looked at her with pity. As if: poor, simple

Brooke. "No, no, dear. Billy's like a son to me. And I look out for him. It happens to be my job too, but naturally I love Billy."

"Doesn't everybody?" Brooke sighed and moved a cardboard box labeled 'books' so she could sit on her crowded loveseat.

"Both his blessing, and his curse." Gigi nodded, arms folded across her chest.

Brooke for the life of her couldn't imagine why everyone in the whole world loving you could be viewed as a curse. "Uh huh."

"At least once a year Billy's had a woman claim they had a love child together. Lies, all of them." Gigi waved her arms around in the air. "But those DNA tests can be time consuming. If he'd slept with all the women the media claims, not only would he have a bad shoulder, but he'd have no knees left. All of it greatly exaggerated. Don't you read the sports section?"

Why did everyone ask her that? "No, but I'm going to start." It sounded saucier than some of her romance novels.

"Anyway, it's my job to keep the baseball groupies away. Women who would love nothing more than to sink their teeth into Turlock, Inc."

Brooke would have thought Gigi's job would be fielding endorsement offers and issuing press releases, but what did Brooke know? "I get it. So you think I'm here to get knocked up and stake my claim? Don't worry about me. I don't even like kids."

This was not going well. Brooke resisted the urge to pummel the publicist. Pummeled publicist. It even had alliteration.

"I didn't say that," Gigi said, waving a dismissive hand. "But appearances do matter. What if the media gets wind of this arrangement?"

"I don't care. Billy said I could live here, and I gave my thirty days' notice to my landlord. Too late."

"We can find a better arrangement for you."

"Not a chance. I want to talk to Billy." It had been a long time since she thought she'd find an ally in Billy Turlock, but today might be that day. She headed towards the front door, when she heard a much harder pounding on it.

Brooke opened the door to see a freshly showered Billy, hair still damp and pulled into a ponytail. He wore low slung faded jeans and an equally faded Giants jersey. He smelled like soap, looked devastatingly handsome, and was missing his ever-present grin. "I can't leave you alone for a minute. Can I?"

"We were just chatting." Gigi smiled, reminding Brooke a little bit of Cruella DeVille.

"Yeah," Billy said. "I can imagine the chatting."

"You told me I could live here," Brooke reminded him.

He stood in the frame of the door, filling it with his presence. "I did, and I haven't changed my mind about that. As long as you don't mind having me as your neighbor. I like it out here as much as you do. Are you cool with that?"

"I'm okay with it." Brooke waved him inside. Too late now, anyway. Billy did have a right to live in his own house. Even she had to concede that.

"Oh wonderful, I'm glad you two kids are happy with this risky and tawdry arrangement." Gigi threw up her hands.

"It's only tawdry because you're making it out to be! And besides, I never step out of the house half-naked. I only did that today because I thought I was alone." Brooke felt her cheeks burn as she locked eyes with Billy. Not only did he not break the gaze, but his eyes were smiling even if his lips were not. "Believe me, it won't happen again."

"Are you satisfied?" Billy turned to Gigi. "You don't have to protect me from Brooke. She's not even interested in me."

"Exactly." Brooke pointed her index finger at Gigi.

"Hmmmm," Gigi glanced from Brooke to Billy. "Just friends, huh? That's it?"

"Old friends," Billy said, hooking his finger towards the door. "Now can we leave Brooke alone? You and I have business to discuss."

Gigi moved towards the door. "I usually have a sixth sense about these things. I see I was wrong this time. My apologies."

"You and I have to talk business, too. The winery," Brooke said from the front door. "There's so much to do and plan before we open."

"Absolutely. It's at the top of my list. Come over in a couple of hours," Billy said, smiling and shutting the door.

At the top of the list? This winery should *be* the list, and if he required a reminder, Brooke would be more than happy to set him straight.

* * *

"YOU MUST BE out of your ever-lovin' mind if you think I believe this 'we're just friends' line."

Billy opened the front door and made room for Gigi and her attitude to walk inside. "Even if I wanted to marry her tomorrow, which I don't, it's not your business."

She stopped in her tracks, turned and pointed a finger in his direction. "Billy, don't even joke about that. Tell me you wouldn't marry her, or anyone, without a pre-nup. Tell me or I won't be able to sleep tonight."

Just like that they were back to a discussion they'd had once a year ever since she'd signed on as his publicist. He'd never come close enough to giving it much thought, but couldn't help but think that the words pre-nup weren't exactly the start of great foreplay. For now, he didn't see the need to think about it.

"You'll sleep fine."

"Not with that vixen next door. Good heavens I thought your eyes would have to be surgically placed back inside their sockets. Why do you think I suggested you take a shower?"

"So you'd have time to go hatch your evil plans?" To destroy any chance in hell he had with Brooke, who might never forgive either one of them.

"What part of protect do you not understand?"

"You don't need to protect me from Brooke." Though she might need to protect Brooke from him. He wasn't sure how long he could go without at least giving it a shot. For now, he'd have to. He could read it in Brooke's thinly veiled contempt. He wouldn't be seeing a glimpse of those panties again anytime soon.

"You say that about all gorgeous women, and you're always wrong."

"Look, Brooke was the one girl at Starlight High that wasn't part of my fan club."

"Oh no, it's worse than I thought. Every athlete has one. She's the one, right? The one that got away. Be smart, Billy. Let her stay away." She made a shoving motion in the air.

Scary how on target Gigi had come to his own somewhat convoluted feelings, even if she was a drama queen about the whole thing. "Let's stop talking about my non-existent love life, thanks to you, by the way. Let me see some of these endorsement deals."

For the next two hours they went over some possible income generating leads, but Billy wasn't interested in any of them. Not like he thought a washed up pitcher would get any significant opportunities, but he couldn't see attaching his name to the newest wood shining product or kitty litter.

More exciting to him were all the local schools who wanted him to bring a pitching clinic to them. Gigi said there was no money in that, not to mention the time and organization efforts it would take. Also, he wasn't supposed to be diluting his star power or some such nonsense.

Still, it would be something to be near the diamond again, even in some small way.

More embarrassing were the offers of renaming local parks after him, and the new wing at St. Vincent's Hospital. Of course, in lieu of a generous donation.

A couple of hours later, he'd bid Gigi goodbye. She'd be flying out to LA on her broomstick in the afternoon, and not a moment too soon.

Brooke was at his door within minutes. "Is Cruella DeVille gone?"

Such a good name for Gigi. He almost laughed but Brooke, dressed in a tight Hensley shirt that hugged her succulent breasts, didn't inspire laughter so much as pure unbridled lust.

"The coast is clear." He moved so she could come inside.

"We have so much to talk about." She held a laptop, a notebook, and a smart phone.

"Right. Let me start with an apology. Gigi means well."

"I don't like the way she sized me up. Walk out your house half naked and people start to make all kinds of assumptions."

It wouldn't help for her to keep bringing that up. He could still picture the hard nipples pressed up against the tight cotton t-shirt, the butterfly tattoo on her shoulder, belly button with something shiny in it, the curvy bare legs and that scrumptious ass that headlined many a fantasy.

He needed a drink. "Coffee?"

"Yes, please." Brooke didn't waste any time setting up her

laptop on the kitchen table, pulling out her notebook and pen. "Cream, no sugar."

He gathered the mugs and met her at the table. "I'm all yours."

Brooke leveled a gaze at him. "Don't say that in front of your publicist or she's bound to take it the wrong way."

He probably deserved that. "Don't worry about her, she's gone back to LA. Mostly we talk over the phone, but every once in a while they'll be a chill in the air. My skin will crawl, and I know Gigi must be thinking about me."

Brooke smiled, and holy shit, she should do that more often. Why had she stopped smiling like that, and what was the jerk's name? "First things first." Brooke tapped the pen on her notebook. "A name."

"For...?"

"The winery, of course. I mean, I figured you'd want to rename it the Billy Turlock Winery or something like that." She looked serious.

He couldn't help but laugh. "No. Doesn't have a nice ring to it. Too bad I'm not Italian. They have the best names for wineries. Turlock— now that sounds like a good bat, but not a great wine. What do you think?"

"Well, hear me out." She looked tentative, unsure for once. "I was going to suggest we keep the name. The Mirassu winery has a long history in Starlight Hill, and for years it was a good one. We could say it's under new ownership and management."

"Fine with me." Billy reached for another gulp of coffee. "I don't even think Pop would mind, but I'll run it by him."

"That was easy," Brooke said, making a note, even if she did sound surprised.

He leaned back in his chair, gratified he'd straightened her out on the assumption that he was another big headed narcissistic jock. Even if something told him he had a long way to go in convincing Brooke. "I aim to please. What's next?"

For the next few hours, Brooke talked about the harvest, crush, marketing, a new website, appointments with some of the restaurants in town with which she had connections, and hiring a staff.

"I'm sure I can get Eric to come over from the Serrano winery, and he's a good employee. You'll find it's hard to find good help. I believe in holding on to what you have when it's working."

"I'll trust you with those decisions."

"Great. I like that you're giving me all this control, but don't forget I'll need you to be around. To attend meetings and be the face of this business. I'm not naïve enough to believe that our success won't partially hinge on one popular baseball player."

"You'll have me whenever you need me." He meant that in more than one way, but it likely went right over Brooke's head.

"Thanks, Hotshot."

"You know, you're the only one who ever got away with calling me that. I've decided I'll let you keep doing it."

Brooke leveled an uncertain gaze in his direction. "O-kay."

He glanced at his watch. "We've talked business for over an hour. For two people who hadn't talked in ten years before a few weeks ago, we haven't talked anything personal yet."

"Billy, you saw me half naked and haven't even bought me dinner yet. How more personal do you want to get?"

Well, for one he'd actually like to get underneath those panties but that wasn't something he would share. Yet. "What happened to you after high school?"

"I went to Chicago State. You know that." She tossed that ponytail and stared at her smart phone.

"Yeah. I wanted details." A painful subject, but one they'd have to broach sooner or later if they were going to work together.

"There's nothing to say. I got my degree, and came back home. I don't like winters in Chicago." Brooke leveled him a look that told him he might be swimming near a rocky shore.

"If it will make you feel any better, you can say I told you so." If he'd been to college instead of going straight to the minor leagues, he'd at least be a washed up player with a college degree. Not only that, but who knew what would have happened with Brooke?

Most of his team mates had married their college sweethearts. Would Brooke have been the one?

"Why would I say that?" Brooke asked.

"I should have stayed in school. I know that now. You tried to tell me."

"You're kidding, right?" She put her phone down. "I was wrong, and you were right."

This he had not expected. Brooke, hater of all things athletic, now believed he'd made the right choice? "No, you've got that backwards."

"I don't think so. You've done pretty well for yourself. Wouldn't you say?" She waved around the room, no doubt meaning the winery.

"Brooke, what I made might have to last me for the rest of my life. And I'm not even thirty." Not to mention that he couldn't do the one thing that he still had passion to do, just because his body had given out on him. No one seemed to care about that.

"Let's not have this conversation." Brooke got up with her laptop.

He knew what this was all about. They'd had this argument a handful of times as kids. Even then, Brooke knew her own mind. And it was different than ninety-nine percent of the people he knew.

"Let's." He stood up. "I'm not the one who sets the salaries. None of the players do."

She looked at the ground as if praying for patience. "If we paid teachers what we pay athletes, maybe we'd have the best educational system in the world. But you know how I feel about this."

"I do. I just wish you'd stop blaming me for the way things were set up long before I even picked up a glove and a ball."

"You always said that, but you were a part of the system. You accepted the status quo. All of you do."

"I just wanted to play ball. You of all people know that."

For one second it looked like she would understand. But that kind of acceptance didn't happen in one conversation. Too many years stretched between them like a wound up coil ready to snap.

"Say what you want, but you'll never convince me that you're not the luckiest man I know."

"I wouldn't even try." He'd had a great career, been smart enough to stash away a small fortune, enjoyed a loving family's support, and now stood in front of Brooke Miller.

She cracked a smile. "I'm going to set up some meetings, and I'll get back to you. We have work to do." She moved towards the front door.

"You bet." Maybe if he played this inning right, he'd have a second chance with Brooke.

This time, he wouldn't drop the ball.

CHAPTER 7

For the first time in her life, Brooke might have too many lists. There was so much to do she didn't even know where to begin. She'd never been a part of a venture from its inception in this way. Not that they were starting from scratch. They had rows upon rows of grapes. They needed to be harvested. Like yesterday.

Harvest time usually began no later than late August, and they were now in early October.

Back at her kitchen table, she tore off another piece of paper and made a list of items to be done in order of chronological importance.

1. Harvest.
2. Check on the tanks.
3. Apologize to Billy for being a bitch.

Brooke tore off that piece of paper. No, she didn't need to apologize, but dammit if Billy didn't make her feel like she did. It was in those eyes— they said so much without words.

The eyes said that yeah, he knew he'd been lucky, but no,

he wasn't happy. In case anyone cared. And of course she shouldn't, but unfortunately she did. Because he was Billy, dammit.

He thought she'd been right, which was hysterical since she'd been thinking for the past ten years just how wrong she'd been.

He'd taken the offer into the minor leagues instead of the college scholarship at Chicago State against her advice, and though it hadn't guaranteed he'd make the major leagues, he'd done it anyway. Hard work and dedication to the thing that had always been, would always be, his first love.

And the rest was history. She'd gone to Chicago alone, and made friends, had a couple of boyfriends. Lost her virginity to one of them, even though it should have been Billy. Would have been, on that night when it became clear that they both wanted more. But she'd been too good for the jock. Wanted to save herself for the right man. It might have been Billy, and a hundred times she'd imagined that it had been. But no matter what, she couldn't change the past.

And that was the end of it.

Her cellphone rang and she glanced at the caller ID. Great. "Hey, Mom."

"Hi sweetie. I'm going to be at the Farmer's Market this Saturday."

"Why would this Saturday be any different than any other one? You're always there."

"It would be nice if you'd come by. I've made a new herbal shampoo with your favorite scent. Cranberry."

"I still have six bottles of shampoo I haven't used yet. I'm good."

"Oh. Okay, then. I'd still like to see you."

Brooke felt the guilt press down. She hadn't seen Mom in a while. "I've got a new job and its harvest time as you know. I'm going to be busy."

"Right. Harvest time. You usually disappear for weeks." Mom's voice got a bit tinnier. Possibly tinged with a whine.

"Yep. Everything okay, otherwise?"

Mom sighed. "Well, I might have to go on a statin because of my high cholesterol. Except that I refuse."

"Why?"

"Honey, don't you realize they make that medicine with a pregnant mare's urine?"

"Ew, mom. Please."

"Well, I'm only telling you the truth. I ask you, would you take a pill made with someone's urine?"

"Not if I had a choice."

"Exactly. So I'm going to take the herbs that Sally makes at our farm. She swears that her cholesterol went down forty points…"

Brooke let Mom's voice fade into the background while she doodled on her pad. It was better, really, to tune it all out because Mom only wanted to be heard. Brooke made sure to say "Uh-huh" every few minutes.

"And so that's why I think all doctors are quacks."

Brooke let out a breath. "All right. Well, then. Gotta go. Talk later, okay?"

After a few more false starts, she finally hung up. Maybe Brooke could and should pay more attention to Mom, but it would help if she would talk about something interesting for a change.

Sighing, Brooke wrote at the top of a new list:

1. Try to be a better daughter
2. Stop thinking about Billy
3. Write down something you have a prayer of getting done

* * *

A FEW DAYS LATER, every grape had been harvested. Even if Brooke had to call on every single one of her resources, she'd done it. Not one grape gone to waste.

Naturally, her resources notwithstanding, she'd had no shortage of volunteers. It was now official news in town that Billy Turlock was back in town and the new owner of Mirassu winery. Those records were public, after all. Consequently the local media made a habit of parking at the end of the long sloped driveway. Brooke had campaigned for that, since Billy often allowed them up into the tasting room parking lot.

But he'd listened when Brooke told him that they might chase away prospective customers. He hadn't listened when it came to the so-called friends and 'fans' who had assembled to help in the frantic push to harvest in time. She couldn't very well argue that point since she needed all the help she could amass. And frankly, with the before dawn hours the job entailed, it meant that the crowd of volunteers were hard-core fans.

She was grateful, even if it meant she'd had to rise before dawn too so she could issue careful instructions and make certain all the volunteers were doing it right. But now, every grape had been harvested. Time to crush.

"Next year, we'll have special wine crushing events – folks love that stuff. One place even sells t-shirts with the customer's wine stained footprints on it."

"Great idea," Billy said.

They were in the tank room, where they'd place some of their newly crushed grapes. "I'm going to check the tanks right now. Abe will help me with that."

"Something wrong?"

"Abe said he thought there was a leak in tank ten. I'll check it out."

"Let me know if you need me. I'm meeting with Coach Buchanan in the tasting room."

"Again?" Seemed like the coach at Starlight High was always hanging around, like a little puppy dog at Billy's elbow.

"If he wants my advice, he'll taste the wine." Billy grinned, making Brooke's knees a little weak.

Even if she should be a little upset with him, for parceling out his time the way he did. His family and the winery did come first, but he still found plenty of time to talk baseball with the locals. Now the baseball coaches from the entire Bay Area had zoned in on the fact that Billy was generous with his time.

Which meant Brooke was getting ready to stick a plug in that, whether he liked it or not.

No matter, today Pop was here and he'd turned out to be one of her greatest allies. Once you got past all the baseball analogies, which went right over her head. Maybe she could get him to talk to Billy.

She'd left Pop guarding the Pinot Grigio row in his favorite lawn chair. He'd take a nap or two there and when he woke he'd remind Brooke that he was very close to finding out the prize winning tip.

She wasn't holding her breath. "Abe, help me push this ladder to the tank so I can check it."

"No miss, I'll do that."

She waved him away. "Don't be silly. I know what I'm looking for. It will only take a minute."

Abe found the ladder and pushed it to the tank, and Brooke clattered up to the top. The tank room had an equal mix of modern tanks and the old wooden barrels, because tourists enjoyed the old ways. Today she would check out one of the modern tanks because the level was lower than it should be.

"Careful," Abe warned.

Funny how no man in the business, whether farm hand or owner, believed a woman could know what was wrong with a tank. Maybe she couldn't fix it, but she'd know if it required fixing. Besides, this was part of getting her hands dirty, and being in every part of the business.

"Abe, can you give me a hand?" one of the farm hands called out.

"In a minute," Abe answered, spotting Brooke.

"I'm fine. Go ahead." She was almost done here anyway.

Brooke stepped back down the ladder, but she probably shouldn't have worn her flip flops as the edge wanted to stick to every step. Cal-Osha would have her hide. A casualty of living on the premises. She'd begun to feel too safe, too much at home in the work place.

Brooke lost her balance halfway down the ladder, and no matter how hard she tried to recover, she was falling.

There was that damn ground again, rising up to meet her.

* * *

"I'M SEEING TOO many injuries at younger and younger ages," Coach Buchanan was saying. "I figured you would understand better than anyone. I have half a dozen players who remind me of you. They're that promising. But my pitcher has been injured twice this season."

"I hear you." Billy understood, but had no clue how to help. Injuries happened. The shoulder or elbow wore out sooner or later.

"We need to change the way they throw."

"That's tough."

"Don't I know it. But they're still young, and I figure if we're going to do this, now's the time."

"We had someone come out and try to teach us a new way

to throw, and it didn't go over well." After throwing one way for most of his life, he'd been worried about losing speed. Same with most of the other players.

"I wish I'd known about the better way to throw when you were in high school. Who knows? It might have saved the shoulder."

He wondered if he would have listened even then. "Do you think they're open to it?"

Coach sighed. "I doubt it, but I have to try. Did you know I'm retiring this year?"

"Congratulations." It seemed about time, since Coach had been a fixture at Starlight Hill even before Billy had attended.

"Well don't congratulate me yet. I've been tasked to find my replacement."

Billy didn't like the way Coach looked at him now, like maybe he thought he'd just found his replacement. "Any luck?"

"Not much. Do you think you might be interested?"

Nothing like coming straight to the point, but that was Coach. "Well—"

Billy was about to decline when Abe came rushing into the tasting room, white-faced. "It's Miss Brooke. She fell. Hurry."

Billy didn't hear anything else but the thudding of his heartbeat in his ear drums. He recognized that his heart rate had spiked, not an easy thing to do any more.

He ran after Abe, and found her lying at the bottom of Tank #10. Luke, one of the farm hands, held her hand. "She's so white. She always this white?"

Billy knelt beside her and grabbed her other hand. Her eyes were half-mast, but thank God she was conscious. "What happened?"

"No Mom, I don't want any more shampoo." Her hand reached out and swatted him away.

So the floor had beaten the sense out of her. "What are you talking about, Bungee?"

Her eyes fixed on him, and comprehension dawned in her eyes. "Hey, you haven't called me that since…"

"Right after you bungee jumped off the bridge?" He let out a breath and gathered Brooke in his arms. If she remembered his nickname for her, he wasn't too worried. "I'm taking you to the hospital."

"Good idea," Abe said. "Best to get checked out."

"Bad idea. Put me down. I haven't been to the ER in three months. I don't want to break this streak."

"You just broke it." Her hair smelled sweet, a little like cranberries, as Billy carried her to his convertible.

"Can I help?" Coach Buchanan had followed him to the car.

"I'll call you later. But would you get my grandfather home?" He climbed in the driver's side.

"If you insist on taking me, go get my purse. I have my member's discount card in it," Brooke said.

"I hope you're kidding, but it doesn't matter. I'll take care of it." Within seconds he'd pulled out of the lot.

"That stupid ground," Brooke kept muttering to herself on the drive.

Unfortunately she kept dozing, and he saw no other way of keeping her awake than periodically pinching her left arm. This did work and accomplish its purpose, even if it earned him Defcon 4 glares peppered with some cuss words.

Luckily the hospital was only a two mile drive into the heart of town, and Billy pulled in near the ER entrance. He carried a groggy Brooke in through the revolving doors and set her down in front of the reception desk. Brooke still seemed unsteady on her feet, so he held her up by keeping one arm wrapped around her.

A pretty redhead named Donna was the triage nurse, and

she recognized Brooke. "Oh, Brooke. What now? Another concussion?"

"She fell, and seemed disoriented." Billy explained, looking down at Brooke. He'd forgotten how petite she was standing next to him.

"Don't let them stiff you." Brooke turned her head up to him. "I come here a lot."

The nurse had Brooke sign a form and then wrapped a name band around her wrist. "Follow me," she said and he walked through the double doors with Brooke.

It would take someone large and burly to keep him away. No one tried, even the security guard who stared like he was trying to place Billy.

Donna settled Brooke on a cot and then glanced at him. "Usually no one back here but family, but I think we can make an exception for you."

"What a surprise," Brooke said, eyes barely open.

"She keeps dozing off. I've been pinching her to keep her awake," Billy said.

"Don't worry," Brooke said to Donna. "I will pinch him back. I just need to regain my strength."

He watched Donna set a blood pressure cuff on Brooke and he assumed, take her vital signs.

"I'll get the doctor." Donna smiled and touched his shoulder right before she pulled the curtains shut.

"Billy, I think she's sweet on you," Brooke said once Donna left the room. "Isn't everybody?"

He sighed. No, not everybody. There was one hard headed woman who had put up walls too high to climb. "Whatever you say."

"Now he tells me. Don't try to get on my good side."

"Do you think you have one?" Although as far as he was concerned, every side was a good one. Left side, right side, front side, and his favorite: the back side. The problem was her heart. Closed up tight.

Maybe even because of him.

The doctor arrived, and other than a brief nod to Billy, the man's focus was entirely on his patient. The consummate professional, thank goodness.

Billy waited for the tests he knew would be coming. As a kid he'd once been knocked out by a fast ball so he recognized the procedure. He also realized someone would need to stay with Brooke tonight to make certain she'd wake every few hours. And that someone would be him, no matter what she had to say about it.

"Mild concussion. Again," Dr. Lewis said a few interminable hours and several tests later. "So you know the drill. Someone to wake you every few hours. Do you want me to call someone for you?"

"No," Billy said, standing. "I brought her and I'll take her home. We're neighbors. It makes sense."

"Don't let him. He only wants to have his way with me," Brooke said. "And all he's getting is one helluva pinch."

"How long will she talk crazy like this?" Billy asked the doctor.

"I don't know," he deadpanned, "Another forty years, maybe?"

"Look at that, the doctor made a funny. It happens once every ten years, and you were here to see it, Billy." Brooke sat up, appearing nearly recovered.

Billy knew better. The interminable night stretched out in front of him, and damned if he didn't anticipate every last second of it.

* * *

BILLY TURLOCK WAS a royal pain in the ass. Not just because he'd swooped in and picked her up in his arms like he was some kind of firefighter hero, but also because of the pinching. He'd brought her home, plopped her down on the couch and wouldn't leave. To add insult to injury, now he wouldn't let her sleep.

Sure, she understood she had to wake every few hours, but did he have to take such pleasure in it?

"Wake up, Bungee." He nudged her. "It's been long enough."

"Stop calling me that," Brooke swatted his hand away. "And stop waking me up. I was enjoying myself."

"You're telling me," Billy said with a grin. "What were we doing in your dream? You said my name a couple of times."

"What?" Brooke sat straight up, stone cold sober. "I did not. I'm not sleepy any more. How about some coffee?"

She couldn't figure out if he was teasing her, or if some of her subconscious mind was out of control. Had she been dreaming of him again? She got up and starting switching lights on.

It needed to be bright in here. "These stay on all the time."

"I thought it didn't matter since you were asleep."

"Well, it matters." She wasn't going to be telling any more of her secrets tonight.

After they'd argued for a few minutes over who would make the coffee she finally let him, then flicked on the TV to a re-run of Gilligan's Island. Billy sat next to her, uncomfortably and achingly close.

"I changed my mind," Brooke said after a few minutes, changing the channel. "I don't want to watch this stupid show. I always wanted to be like Ginger but instead I was Mary Ann."

"No way. You're a Ginger if I ever saw one." Billy set

down the coffee mugs, grabbed the remote and switched it back on.

"Stop teasing me. I don't have red hair and I'm not tall. That would be Donna the nurse. I'm sure you noticed her?"

"You're a short blonde Ginger," he said with a sexy grin. "A short, stacked, blonde Ginger."

"Give me that," she said wrestling the remote control back. "What we need is a scary movie to make you think twice about teasing me again. Something about those women who snap."

"I'm all right with that. If you get scared, I don't mind holding you until it passes. It would be a hardship, but I'm willing to do it. You fell on my property and it's my responsibility."

Brooke channel surfed for a few minutes but there wasn't anything as scary on TV as those words had hit Brooke. She settled on a program about the rain forest.

Was it the concussion, or was she starting to feel some deeper affection for Billy? For the man who was, let's face it, a jock *and* her boss. *No, Brooke, do not go there again.*

Especially not with him.

She must have drifted off a while later because the next time she woke sunlight filtered through the curtains, and her head was in Billy's lap. She raised her head to find him asleep as well, all the planes of that handsome face oddly relaxed. Usually he was so upbeat, friendly, energetic. Wound up tight as a guitar chord. She'd never seen him so— helpless. Vulnerable.

This would be the perfect time to pinch him. Instead she wanted to take a tour of his face, of his arms, his chest, and his abs. What he didn't know couldn't hurt him. Or her, for that matter.

He had bed hair, tousled and spilling over one eye. Unfairly long eyelashes. Damn him. She wasn't so set on her type that she didn't notice Billy put the H in hunk. Earlier he'd pushed up his long sleeves to his forearms, and she admired the cord of muscle strands in his arms. She took a closer look at the tattoo on his forearm. A nautical tattoo of an anchor, with the words *Hold Fast* across the top. He had one arm slung over her, and the other stretched out on the back of the couch. All her movement under his arm, and he hadn't moved a muscle. Poor guy was probably exhausted, keeping her awake. Of course he hadn't tried the fun way of keeping her awake.

Mostly because Billy Turlock was a gentleman.

She could straddle him right now, and wake him up a way she didn't think he would mind. Then together they could stay awake for hours. She'd thread her fingers through that long silky hair, and kiss along the beard stubble until she reached his mouth.

She wanted to connect the dots again. Even if this time it would have to be different. They were both ten years older, and he'd been around the block a few times since then. And she'd been, if not around, then at least nearby.

She moved on to his lap and straddled him, and he still didn't wake. Did the man sleep like the dead, or what? Brooke was about to touch a single lock of his hair when a tiny alarm sounded from the direction of his wrist.

An omen. A literal alarm, setting off the warning that should have been in her head had it not been hit so hard today. She scrambled off his lap as he shifted and opened one eye. Whew, that was close.

He fiddled with his wristwatch. "I set this to wake you up, but you beat me to it. How long have you been awake?"

"Oh, um, I just woke up too." Brooke ran her tongue over her teeth. Did she have morning breath? Did he? Should she find out?

Bad idea, Brooke.

Even if it was risky and dangerous, two of her favorite things in the world. It so happened she was too vulnerable right now. Probably starting to miss sex. Well, no probably about it.

"You can go now, Hotshot. Its morning and you've done your duty."

"Are you sure? Because I provide a shower service as well," he said with a mischievous grin.

And wouldn't that be fun. It took every muscle in her body to restrain herself from tackling him.

His cellphone rang before she could answer, and he glanced at it and scowled. "Gigi."

"Go ahead, take the call. But please don't tell her you spent the night with me, concussion or not. I don't want her flying out here again."

He cracked a smile. "You're probably right."

"Sure. I'll see you later." She walked with him to the front door, shut it behind him and leaned against it.

Time to meet a man. She had to start dating again. Since she literally lived at her job, it might be difficult but she'd have to find the time. If she was ever going to get her mind and heart off the bright and shiny distraction that was Billy Turlock, it would be necessary.

CHAPTER 8

Gigi had to be psychic. Otherwise, how could she have such evil timing?

He could see something shift in Brooke's amber eyes. Maybe she'd opened up to him a little bit. He didn't want to embarrass her, but at least in her dreams he was getting somewhere. Now to translate that into real life so he might enjoy it as well.

"Yeah?" he answered on the third ring.

"Oh easy there, slugger. Did I wake you?"

"I'm up. What is it?"

"It's official. They're going to rename the new hospital wing after you. And the donation isn't as bad as I'd anticipated. I recommend you do it."

"Fine," Billy said, scrubbing a hand across his beard. "Let's do it."

He'd only made it a few feet from Brooke's door, and it would take every vestige of will power not to turn around and go back to her.

Brooke. He wanted her so badly his teeth hurt. It wouldn't be the disaster Gigi predicted, either. But he had the distinct impression he would have to convince Brooke of that as well. As much as he thought he'd caught a hint of desire in her eyes this morning, he was still an athlete. On the field or off, that wouldn't change. Unfortunately he represented everything Brooke believed was wrong with the system. Even if he would have thought she'd be over it by now.

"…you haven't heard a word I've said have you?" Gigi was saying.

He pulled his attention back to Gigi. "Sorry. The, uh, vineyard is heavy on my mind."

"Uh-huh, sure. The vineyard. As I was saying, the hospital wing will be finished by April and we'll have a nice ceremony and you'll mention all the great work being done there. Yada yada yada."

He half-listened to the rest of the conversation, and had reached his door by the time he finished the call with Gigi. No going back now. Brooke would be taking that shower by herself, no doubt. What a waste.

Time to take his morning run now, come back, take a shower, and stop thinking about Brooke. Once upon a time she'd made it clear how she felt about him and all athletes in general. He wasn't about to defend his life to her. She'd been right, and that was the end of it.

How many times had he regretted it? How many nights in those early years had he thought about Brooke and wondered how she was, alone in a big city? Her eyes had lit up when she'd heard about his scholarship to Chicago State. And he'd taken the light right out of those eyes.

But regrets did nothing for a man. It was the reason he wouldn't be watching the world series this season. Correction: trying not to watch any of the world series. Best to move on from all the reminders of that time. He'd had his time in the spotlight, and now it was time to move on.

According to Gigi, coaching little league or even the high school or college teams would be a huge step down. Laughable, even.

He should have taken the free ride to Chicago. But all the should haves in the world wouldn't change the fact that he and Brooke had gone in two different directions many years ago. Just because he viewed the fact that they'd wound up in the same place again as some kind of second chance didn't mean she felt the same at all.

An hour later, Mom called with her usual great timing, as he was dripping wet from his shower. "Yeah, Ma? Everything okay?"

"Yes, dear. It's just this world wide web. The Internet."

Oh hell. This had to be the online dating website. He'd neglected that altogether. "What do you need help with?"

"Well, I don't get it. I've been on The Internet for a few years now, with reading the gardening and food blogs. But these chat rooms are different. I asked Wallace about this and he specifically told me to call you. It's all these abbreviations. Have we lost the art of conversation to the point where it's too much of an effort to spell words out?"

"Yes," Billy answered.

"What a shame. Is there some kind of dictionary available to figure this out? What's DH, DD, and WTF?"

"Wait. Who said WTF?"

"It's this gentleman. We've been chatting online and the other day he wrote: WTF, are we going to meet or what? Does that mean well that's fantastic? Because Wallace said no, and that's when he told me to call you."

Billy groaned. "Ma, do me a favor and stop talking to that guy. Anyway, I was about to call you about the menu."

"Oh, the menu."

"Why don't you come by in a few days and you and I will talk with Brooke about your ideas?" Please God, let this work. He didn't want to have to tell Mom what WTF meant.

"That sounds wonderful. I'll get busy in the kitchen. I have so many ideas you're absolutely going to love. And so will that darling Brooke."

She might not be calling Brooke darling after they were done meeting about the menu. In fact, he was almost sure of it. "Yeah, it's great. She's going to love all the suggestions," Billy lied.

Sure, he'd have to play referee between the two women as he didn't think Brooke would appreciate losing any control. But she might just have to budge a bit.

He had to distract his mother from the World Wide Web.

* * *

A FEW DAYS LATER, Brooke was back to business. Still wondering about the leak in the tank, but she'd called someone to come take a look at it. One couldn't be too careful.

And she was still eternally grateful for Billy's alarm, or life might be wildly off course at the moment. Instead, progress on opening night moved along swiftly. Which is why she was now in the kitchen discussing the menu with Eileen, at Billy's request. A couple of things were becoming clear to Brooke. Firstly, Eileen Turlock might have too much time on her hands.

Secondly, Brooke didn't share Eileen's obsession with tofu.

"I know it's usually cheese and crackers, but this is my own personal healthy spin on that. After all, cheese will slowly kill your customers. So instead of cheese, a little slice of tofu. With a sprig of mint on top."

The crackers were fine. The sprig was a nice touch. The

tofu would be served over her cold and dead body. "But Eileen, people don't come to a winery for a health experience. They come to be a little decadent for a short time. To indulge."

"Ask yourself if that's a good idea. Do you want your customers to live long enough to come back again and again or do you want them to drop dead of cardiovascular disease?"

I don't want them to drop dead, but I'd like this tofu to drop dead. Instead Brooke said, "I'd rather they not drop dead."

"Let me tell you a little something about indulging. After my husband left I spent twenty years indulging. And poof, before I realized it I was 50 lbs. overweight. And now, look at me. Lost all that weight, and I'm ready to date again." She twirled around.

Ready to date again? Hmmmm. "You look great."

"Thank you. By the way, how's your head? I heard you took a bit of a fall."

"It was nothing."

Eileen continued to slice tofu. "And you'd be shocked how fast your taste buds die off. I can't even eat sugar anymore."

"No sugar?" Brooke felt a bit faint.

"Diabetes is a raging epidemic. I can come up with some sugar-free recipes, too."

"But I doubt we'll have many diabetics as customers."

"Don't you want diabetic customers?"

"But Eileen, there's sugar in wine too. It occurs naturally."

"I have some ideas for that, too."

Oh hell no. "I see," Brooke said, praying for patience. "Excuse me just a minute. I have to talk to Billy."

"He went for his afternoon jog."

She hadn't seen him since several mornings ago when she'd wanted to jump him. Thankfully that urge had passed. Maybe she'd been hit in the head a bit harder than she'd realized. Billy represented everything that was wrong with the world. Sure, it wasn't his fault that he'd been paid millions to have fun, and she couldn't begrudge him his success. If not for that, she wouldn't have this great job with its salary and benefits.

But athletes got paid way too much money for throwing a ball around.

Brooke took a little walk around the vines, trying to calm down. Eileen was driving her a little bit crazy with the tofu and the health kick. Pop usually appeared daily to sit for a while with the grapes, but him she could handle. She'd grown to expect his crazy baseball analogies, trying to link everything under the sun with the game. But he was harmless, especially after she'd convinced him that she was not a spy.

Scott she wasn't all that certain about. He seemed to enjoy the attention of several women whom he occasionally brought by the vineyard for a tour. At this point tours weren't open to the general public, but Brooke couldn't seem to get this fact through to Scott.

Wallace was almost never around, and he was the strong silent type. She appreciated that.

The vines were beginning their metamorphosis to fall's golden colors, despite the unseasonably warm October. Soon enough they would be dormant. Then they'd need to guard against any frost, such a rare thing in the valley that she hadn't thought about it in years. And of course, in the spring, she'd suggest some new cuttings. Maybe by then Pop would have found this tip she was beginning to think was a figment of his imagination.

She wondered if anyone had missed her leadership at Serrano by now. Soon enough she'd find out when she got the latest report from Eric. He'd kept in touch, and asked her to call when she landed somewhere.

Well, she'd landed all right. Right in a pile of manure, it would appear.

She couldn't do Mothers, evidenced by her own less than great relationship with Mom. She didn't do family, either. And now she was smack dab in the middle of Billy's family. When she didn't even put up with her own, why did she have to deal with his on a daily basis?

Billy had told her she could have control. She didn't know how to explain this basic fact to Eileen without sounding like a first class bitch.

Well, she was pacing the vineyard now. If Pop were here today, he'd tell her to take a load off. He'd sit there and gaze at the vines, just taking it all in. Why couldn't she do that? She didn't know how to relax, that was the problem. But how could she relax when she had to whip this place into shape by December fifth?

She heard him before she saw him, the thudding sound of footsteps gaining in proximity to her.

Billy was jogging through the vines towards her. One large heaping of male testosterone coming right up. With a double side order of lust.

Had anyone looked so good before, in the history of history? He wore jogging shorts with a green and white t-shirt. Not on him, where it belonged, but tucked into the waistband of his shorts. His chest was sweaty and glistened in the October sun. His pace slowed as he came closer and she heard the sound of his breathing— ragged, like he might sound after he'd just— *stop it, Brooke!*

"Boundaries!" Brooke shouted as he stopped in front of her.

"Come again?" Holy cow, that smile.

Yes, she'd love to but that wasn't going to be possible right now. She put her palms out, like that could stop him. "If we're going to work together, and live a stone's throw away from each other, we need to establish some boundaries."

He pulled the shirt from his waistband and used it to wipe away the sweat on his forehead. "I get it. So you'd rather not run into me when I'm all sweaty and half naked?"

"No, that's not what I meant."

"You do want to see me sweaty and half-naked?" He grinned. Evil, evil man.

"No! That wouldn't be appropriate."

"Says the woman who walked out her front door in her panties."

"I thought I was alone!" Would he ever let her live it down? Answer: probably not in this lifetime.

"You keep saying that." Billy just kept smiling. "I take it your meeting with my mother didn't go well?"

"It's still going. I needed to take five when she suggested she might have found a way to remove sugar from the grapes. I couldn't listen anymore."

Billy winced. "There's got to be a way to compromise. Can't you explain that you have a different vision?"

"I don't know how to do that and not sound like a bitch. You deal with her. I'll be in my cottage." Brooke turned around and marched up the hill to her cottage. Let Billy deal with Eileen. She had a winery to run, and more lists to make.

The door had been shut for all of two minutes when there was a knock. Billy.

"Did you talk to her already?"

"No. I want to talk to you first." He didn't look pleased, the grin wiped clear off his face.

Brooke moved aside, and he walked past her. Shirt back on, thank goodness. But he was still a little bit sweaty with that Alpha male aura emanating off him. Hair pulled back in a ponytail, which unfortunately served to highlight his face and not his long hair. This was a problem because he had a great face. Even with scruff all over the jawline.

"Why is it so bright in here?" He asked. "Do you have the lights on in the middle of the day?"

"So what? Sometimes I forget to shut them off." She flicked the kitchen light off. "I pay the PG&E. I keep the place neat and tidy. Are you going to complain?"

He glanced around the small living area. "The place is immaculate."

Thanks to her great housekeeping skills, thank you very much. She'd learned how to make much of small spaces. "What did you want to talk to me about?"

"My family."

"What about them?" She took a few steps away from him, and all those sexy male pheromones.

"Look, let's get this straight. I understand that my family can be loud and intrusive. But they mean well. You have to get along with them. If you're going to work here."

Crud. Billy was laying down the law, but a strange thing happened. Rather than piss her off it started to turn her on. His jaw was tight as though the words cut.

She jammed her hands on her hips. "*If* I'm going to work here?" No way could he take this away from her now. She'd quit before she'd let him fire her. "Billy, you told me I could have control!"

"You do have control. Just make her feel like she's got some, too. Even if she doesn't. Got it?"

"Do you want me to make this venture a success or not?"

"You know I do. But it's a family business first."

One in which a non-family member had the control, mostly because she was the only one who knew what she was doing. "Do you still want me here?"

"You know I do, and I think I've made that clear enough.

But this is a family business and everybody has a place in it. My family means everything to me."

Brooke's breath caught. "I thought baseball meant everything to you."

He sighed and ran a hand over his face. "You have a lot of stereotypes about jocks, and you need to get over them. Maybe you don't know me at all."

"All right, I'm sorry." This was new, backing down.

But the look on Billy's face was all badass and protective and she found herself wishing she was a part of his family. If she'd been part of his family, she'd bet that George would be regretting the way he'd passed her over for that promotion. Or rather the way he'd dangled it in front of her like some carrot, so she might consider marriage to a narcissist.

"Why can't you handle her? It's hard for me to believe that a hell raiser like you can't handle a middle aged woman."

"Oh please, all that hell raising is greatly exaggerated. Just because I drive a Harley and jumped off the Merlot Bridge on a dare."

"And skydive. Yeah. I know about that. You don't seem to be afraid of anything."

Oh but she was, only she wouldn't let him know about it. It was a small phobia, and she now had it under control. Mostly. "Fine. Here's the thing. I don't want Eileen to hate me if I'm too honest with her. I don't like family conflict, so I just stay out of it."

"Deal with her like you would with your own Mom."

"I can't even handle my own mother. Mostly I ignore her."

Billy continued to stare, like he was trying to decide if he could believe her. "Bummer."

Well. Why did he care? "Sorry, not everybody can have your perfect family."

"Perfect? We are talking about my mom, right? And Scott?

Let's not even start with Pop, who put a prize-winning tip in an old cereal box he now can't find." Billy cracked a smile.

That stupid grin made Brooke's special parts start to tingle. "Don't try to act like you don't realize your mom could easily win Mother of the Year."

"Once upon a time, sure. Okay. If I'm being honest here, I do have a hidden agenda. You deserve the truth."

They were still standing near her striped blue and white couch in the middle of the small room, and Brooke found that she backed up a few more steps. A man, being honest. Would wonders never cease? "I'm listening."

"Well, you can bring your eyebrows back down to your forehead. It's not that shocking. Not in today's day and age."

What kind of bombshell was he about to drop on her? Who was gay or needed a transgender operation? "It's okay." She tried to sound reassuring.

He shook his head slowly. "No, it isn't. My mother has been introduced to Internet dating."

"Is that all?" The whoosh of relief fell out of Brooke so audibly she was worried about what Billy might think. "You made it sound so serious."

"You might think it's not a big deal, but my brothers and I aren't happy about this. There are a lot of creeps out there. Unfortunately, I know some of them. And I sure in the hell don't want my mother dating them."

"Of course you don't. So you want to distract your mother with the winery? Is that it?"

"You're catching on. Wallace thought she could help with the menu. Except I'd hoped she'd leave her new health kick off the menu. She tried to serve me tofu roast for dinner."

Brooke winced. "Tofu and roast don't belong in the same ..."

"Sentence," Billy said with her.

For a moment Brooke only stared at the man. She wished

her boss didn't have to be so sexy, and also finish her sentences. "Thanks for telling me. Now I can think of ways she can help around here, without re-inventing the entire winery experience."

"I want her to feel needed. Relevant. That's all she probably needs, anyway."

"Sure. Of course."

"Pretty sure every mother needs that. Right?" He grinned.

"Right." She thought about Mom, and the farm. All that shampoo Mom made that she simply wanted Brooke to use and enjoy. So what if she already had enough to last her a lifetime?

Billy was a good son, and Brooke was such a bad daughter.

Brooke spent the rest of the afternoon with Eileen, listening to her suggestions and nodding. Writing notes as if she would actually consider serving lemon grass as an appetizer. Please.

The point was, she and Eileen were both women. And Brooke knew a little secret about women, since she happened to be one. No matter the age, they wanted to be cherished. And Eileen had probably not been cherished in a long, long while. Brooke knew the feeling.

She had a plan, but Billy didn't need to know the details. The last thing he'd want to hear about was the fact that his mother needed a love life. Brooke certainly hoped she'd still be making love in her fifties. Weren't those supposed to be the golden years? The problem was Eileen had gone about it the wrong way, probably because she didn't know how to meet a good man.

When Eileen had finished with her rhapsody on the health benefits of Kamboosha, a drink she thought should be added to the wine list, Brooke set the notebook down on the counter top. "Well. That's truly enlightening. Thanks for sharing. I have so much to think about."

Faking got a bit easier. Kind of like a first date with a man when Brooke would pick at her dinner, and talk about how there was really nothing like a home cooked meal.

"I'll start taste testing in my own kitchen and then when they're perfected, I'd be happy to bring them over for you to taste."

"Great. How long will that take you?" Brooke found the plastic wrap and began to help cover all the samples Eileen had brought.

"I don't have much else to do these days, so it shouldn't take long at all."

"Take your time. So... now that we're done here, Billy mentioned something about Internet dating?" Brooke coughed.

"Oh Lord, he told you that? I'm not going to anymore. It's hard to do with all the new words and abbreviations. I don't have time to learn all that. If I were going to learn another language, it would be Italian. Oh, how I'd love to go to Italy someday. You see, my ex-husband was German and he hated Italians. Did I tell you that? It's my side of the family that's Scottish, and we've always loved the Italians ..."

Brooke let Eileen ramble, while the idea cooked and formed. She'd fix Eileen up on a date. That's what Brooke would do to help. Help and distract, which was what Billy wanted anyway. He just didn't understand that the kind of distraction Eileen needed wouldn't come from tofu or plan-ning meals. It had to come from a man. Of course, not just any man.

No, she was with Billy on that one. She'd check the guy out first. After she found him, that is. Make sure he wasn't an ax murderer. And also that he didn't need Viagra, although what was the harm if he did? That pill had been invented for a reason, hadn't it?

Brooke steered the conversation back from Scotland and bagpipes and Eileen's sonofabitch ex-husband who wouldn't even pay for Billy's little league. "I'm sure I could fix you up with someone. You don't really need to go through the Internet to date. You're a beautiful woman."

Eileen Turlock blushed. "Thank you. But it's so hard to find men my age."

"Well, why does he have to be your age?" Brooke winked.

"You think I should go out with someone older?" Eileen seemed to consider it. "There are even less of them."

"How about someone younger?"

Now Eileen clasped a hand over her mouth, then slowly brought it down. "Younger? How young?"

"Have you ever heard the term cougar?"

CHAPTER 9

Once Brooke had explained that she didn't mean for Eileen to go out with anyone her sons' age, but someone in the forty-something club, she had actually considered the idea. Brooke promised she'd get back to Eileen, probably even before she was done with the taste testing. They parted, and Eileen had a little spring in her step that Brooke didn't think she'd imagined.

Now Brooke not only needed to start dating, but she would need to find a suitable companion for Eileen. Someone that Billy and his brothers wouldn't reject. It might take a while.

Night had fallen at the vineyard, one of her favorite times of the day. The evenings were getting colder now. Even if the days were warm and sunlit, nightfall had a way of reminding every northern Californian of the proper season. But even from inside, the wide paned window offered a breath taking view of the evening sky, hundreds of stars twinkling in the inky black sky.

She never knew, and tried hard not to think about what Billy did every night in the manor house. Sometimes he did get in late, occasionally with Scott or Wallace in tow, but usually alone. She realized this much because from time to time she spied on him. Hard not to do since their houses practically faced each other. Tonight, she saw the light on and realized her sexy neighbor slash friend slash boss was home.

What's more, he wasn't alone tonight. There seemed to be several people over, all of them as near as she could tell, men. She heard an occasional shout, and quickly determined they must be watching a sports game.

Brooke took a shower, dressed in her sweats, put her damp hair in a ponytail and popped her dinner in the microwave. Tonight she'd be paring her Lean Cuisine with a chilled bottle of Guglielmo Chardonnay. No matter how horrible the meal, it could be saved with a good vintage.

She'd just pried the cork off and poured it into a glass to smell its properties when someone knocked at her door. That wasn't Billy's knock. By now, she could tell. His was always rather forceful and strong. This was more like a tap at her door. A rap-a-tat-tat.

Brooke glanced out the wink window to see Ivey, holding a box from Mama's. "Were you going to tell me that you had a concussion?"

Brooke waved her friend in, and stared longingly at the box. "It was nothing. An entire week ago, and I'm fine. Are those Knock You Naked Brownies from Em?"

Ivey's favorite dish, and Brooke had become a convert the first time she tasted the yummy chocolate caramel concoction. Brooke brought out some paper plates. It wouldn't be the first time she'd eaten dessert first.

"It's been a while, but I've done concussion duty with you before. Why didn't you call me?" Ivey asked as she set the box down on the small kitchen counter.

"I didn't need to," Brooke said, reaching for a piece of

chocolate heaven. "Billy took me home and he stayed with me all night."

Ivey's blue eyes widened. "Billy stayed with you all night?"

"Take it easy. It's not what you think. Nothing happened." Like she would make that mistake again, so soon after. Usually it took her at least a few months to forget about a mistake so that she might actually repeat it again.

"That's too bad." Ivey frowned. "Although, this gives new meaning to the phrase 'I have a headache'. You really did. Didn't you? Have a headache?"

"I didn't have to refuse him. He was a perfect gentleman." Other than the suggestions he'd made about the shower the next morning. But he hadn't acted on any of it because he'd probably had second thoughts. So had she. They couldn't start fooling around and stay professional. She'd already been to that movie. Spoiler alert: don't sleep with your boss.

"I'm sorry to hear that." Ivey took a brownie out of the box.

"Even if I were ready for a relationship, which I'm not, I couldn't have one with Billy. We work together. Do I need to remind you of my last disaster?"

"Well, that was George. But lots of couples make it work. Jeff and I work together at the hospital."

"But he's not your boss. Stop comparing us. You and Jeff were high school sweethearts, written in the stars and all that crap."

"Don't get all romantic and gushy on me now." Ivey rolled her eyes.

Brooke thought about Billy during high school. Lean, athletic Billy dated a lot. Fallon had been his last girlfriend before he'd graduated and headed off to the minor leagues. Fallon the head cheerleader, because she'd been part of that world. Not Brooke.

"He's not my type. Jocks were never my type. Not in high school, and not now."

"Maybe it's time you reconsidered your type. This isn't high school anymore. You're both older now, and wiser."

"Exactly." Brooke leveled a significant look in Ivey's direction. "We have a good grasp of consequences."

"All right, so you're not going to have a love affair with your sexy, handsome, wealthy, gentleman boss."

"I am going to start dating again."

Ivey's eyes brightened, but before she could say another word Brooke held up a hand to stop her. "And I don't need you to fix me up."

"Suit yourself. I was going to suggest Noah, a male nurse I've worked with before. He's thirty-something, smart and cute."

"A male nurse?" Brooke didn't like the sound of that. Crap, listen to her judgmental self. What the hell had happened to her?

Ivey raised an eyebrow. "Men in the health profession have a good grasp of anatomy. Including a woman's anatomy. Hear me?"

"Hmmmm," Brooke said. "He does sound … intriguing."

"Hey, have you heard anything from Camp Serrano, or George? Anything at all? Does he know you're working for Billy?"

Brooke shrugged. If he did, and she could hope so, no doubt he'd be worried. Worried she'd make Mirassu his worst nightmare. His biggest competition. She found that she warmed at the idea.

"When's the big day for the grand opening?" Ivey asked.

"I still have to talk to Billy about that, but the way things are going I feel like we could be on track to have a celebration in December. The fifth is my target date, because maybe we could coincide with the town parade." It wasn't a typical grand opening date, and that's what she liked about it most. She wanted to open with a bang, do something new and unexpected.

Surprise everyone. This time in a good way.

* * *

BROOKE COULDN'T RECALL EVER BEING this nervous. In the next twenty minutes, she and Billy had one of several meetings set up with a couple of the more respectable restaurants in town. But Billy was late. She'd told him to let her know when he arrived and they'd leave together.

He'd told her he'd be here after his meeting with his old high school baseball coach, a man he'd been spending way too much time with. Just as she'd suspected, Billy's heart was still on the baseball diamond. Once a jock, always a jock. But now he was a vintner, or at least said he was. Pop was counting on him, and so was she. He needed to be the face of the new Mirassu line.

Brooke picked up her phone and texted Billy a pithy clipped message: *You're late.*

Within seconds she had her reply: *Two seconds.*

Brooke took one last glance in the mirror. Not much time to primp now.

Why did it feel like a date, when it was no such thing? That would come later tonight, when she'd agreed to give Ted another chance. It hadn't been his fault that Billy had swooped in with an all cash deal, and now she saw it more clearly with the benefit of time. So tonight she'd be having dinner with Ted at Chateau La Salle.

If any nasty rumors had spread regarding a mini breakdown she'd had at Serrano's, she'd put those to rest. The truth was that she had no idea what kind of reception waited for her. In a town like Starlight Hill, the gossip flowed as freely as the wine, and she was certain she'd been part of some of the mill since her rather unfortunate goodbye speech.

Billy knocked, and she opened the door to see his long hair falling around his neck line, dressed in slacks and a black blazer. Filling the doorway with his large frame and his equally big grin.

"Where were you?" Brooke grabbed her purse and shut the door behind her.

"I told you. I was with Coach and we—"

She interrupted him. "I thought you were a vintner now."

"You know I am. Anyway, he just needed some advice." They walked to the top of the driveway where they had small access parking for employees. Her Harley sat in the back, covered.

He opened the door to his convertible for her, making her feel for a second like they were on a real date.

"You know, people are going to try and take advantage of your experience and your knowledge." Brooke clipped on her seatbelt as he turned on the car.

Billy rolled down the driveway and glanced sideways at Brooke. "Don't look now, but you're starting to sound a little like Gigi."

"That's just plain mean. I'm only worried about the time you spend away from the vineyard. It might give people the wrong impression."

"Right," he said making a turn on to Hummingbird Lane. "And Gigi is worried I'll dilute my so-called star power by hanging with the local high school coach."

"See, those are two different things," Brooke said and ignored Billy's scowl. "Our first stop today is at Giancarlo's. They pride themselves on their extensive wine list, and we need for Mirassu to be on it."

"Got it."

"Okay, listen up. Giancarlo is a widower with four daughters. Sophia is the youngest and sometimes she waitresses for him." She went on reciting facts about Giancarlo's. Everything she knew personally, and then some. Was there anything more flattering than a celebrity who considered one to be important?

Sure, she would go ahead and use Billy's fame to their advantage. Not to do so would be stupid.

Giancarlo greeted them in the bar area of the restaurant. "If it isn't Billy Turlock. So pleased to meet you. Brooke, I haven't seen you for a while. How've you been?"

Introductions were made all around as Giancarlo led them to a table nearby. Giancarlo talked about the World Series, going on at the moment (news to Brooke).

"I've got old friends on the team, so of course I favor the Giants," Billy said, "But with a catcher like …"

Brooke tuned him out, focusing instead on Billy's quiet confidence. He should have been out of place, but he didn't give a hint of unease in those green eyes. Finally the conversation turned to her.

"So no longer with Serrano?" Giancarlo asked Brooke.

"We had a parting of the ways."

"His fiancée was in here not long ago, and she doesn't know a grape from a pea." Giancarlo scowled.

"Would that be Chelsea?" Poor girl would be so far out of her comfort zone she might as well be flying a spaceship to the moon.

"Yes, that's her. Anyway their wine pretty much sells itself. Can you arrange a wine tasting for us here? We haven't carried Mirassu wines in a while. Naturally, we'll order several cases."

Naturally.

"I just want to know what kind of pairings I can suggest." Giancarlo finished with a gentle smile.

She'd always been fond of him. A fairly young widower in his late forties, he'd been like a father to Brooke. He'd once strongly implied that he had connections to other wineries in the area, in case she ever wanted to move on from Serrano. She hadn't remembered that until now.

On the way to their last meeting, Billy turned to smile at Brooke. "So glad you're on my team, Brooke Miller."

"Ditto. You have a way of making everyone relax and remember that we're all Americans. And we all love baseball."

"Well, not everyone."

"I love baseball. That's my story and I'm sticking to it." This made Billy laugh, and Brooke caught her breath at the warm, rich sound.

On their way into Maurizzio's, which was kitty-corner to the bank, they ran into Ted.

"See you tonight," Ted said to Brooke after shaking hands with Billy and behaving as though he'd just run into his long lost brother from a different mother.

Billy gave Brooke a long look after Ted had walked away. "You have a date with Ted?"

"Yes," Brooke answered. "I have a date with your biggest fan. You should be happy."

He didn't look happy, but he didn't say another word on the subject. Billy held the door to the restaurant open for her, and she strutted inside. Or tried to strut, but wound up tripping on the rug in her high heels.

Billy caught her, and she narrowly avoided a face plant. "Walk much, Bungee?"

"Oh, shut up."

"Are you all right?" Stephan, Maurizzio's son, asked.

"Just a little trip," Brooke said, pushing away Billy's arm, still snaked around her waist.

"That's not what I meant. I heard you had a nervous breakdown. I didn't believe you'd actually show up for the meeting. Billy Turlock, how you doin', man? Big fan here. Would you mind signing a few balls? For my sons." Stephan said with a cough.

He didn't have any sons. Did he really expect that Brooke wouldn't let Billy know that? Stephan had taken over the restaurant's management because he hadn't much choice. Maurizzio had pulled him back from a career in his first love, gossip. Stephan ran a blog he called *My Two Cents, for What it's Worth.*

"Who said Brooke had a nervous breakdown?" Billy asked, still standing a bit too close to her.

Oh, please let's not go there. It mattered, incredibly, that Billy not know what a fool she'd made of herself. "That's not important."

"Not to worry," Stephan said, ushering them to a table, "I of all people know how rumors get spread around this little town. I can see she's fine. But it was George, the owner of Serrano. He and his fiancée were in here not long ago."

Red hot lava coursed through Brooke's arteries, but she took a deep breath and smiled. "Creative differences can lead to all manner of stories, and lies."

While Billy didn't look as happy as he'd been earlier chatting baseball with Giancarlo, his jawline tight, he did sign a few balls for Stephan's imaginary sons. Brooke would let it go. For now.

Stephan concluded the meeting by ordering several cases without asking for a private tasting. She wasn't about to suggest one. The less time she spent around "two cents" Stephan, the better for her reputation.

* * *

BROOKE HAD CHANGED out of her business pant suit and put on a pair of slender cut black jeans and matching sweater by the time Ted showed up promptly at seven o'clock for their date.

She was still thinking about how good Billy looked. Most men needed a clean shave to look that shiny. But not Billy. She still wanted to talk to him about his baseball commitments. As long as he kept denying that he was still interested in being involved in baseball in some way, shape or form, it wasn't going to help anyone. He needed to be honest with himself and Gigi. Too bad if she didn't like the idea.

Brooke was getting on board with the concept. Why couldn't he be both a vintner and a high school baseball coach? Or assistant coach, or whatever they called it? As long as he could balance the two, she didn't see a problem. The problem was in his near constant denial that he wanted anything to do with baseball.

He drove them to Radcliffe's on the outskirts of town, a nice change of pace. Ted suggested an entrée, but didn't order for her. So far, so good. He wanted her advice on a wine pairing. Smart man.

So far this was going beautifully, and Brooke had managed to push Billy out of her mind for hours. She hadn't once thought about how nice it felt to be around a man who opened doors for her (literally and figuratively), someone who seemed to be at ease with the world at large and his place in it. Someone who looked as good in slacks and a blazer as he did in gym shorts.

Someone who had stolen the vineyard out from under her.

Which reminded her, she owed Ted an apology. "I'm sorry I was so angry with you after losing the vineyard. It wasn't your fault."

"Perfectly understandable. It had to be disappointing, but hey, it's worked out rather well for you. Hasn't it?"

Right back to Billy again. "Yes, Billy's a great boss. He's generous, listens to my advice and lets me do my own thing."

It's just that it hadn't worked out quite the way she'd pictured it. She couldn't claim ownership. That dream was gone. But there was nothing to say that someday another opportunity might come up, and she'd be ready for it. First, she'd make Mirassu rise again. That would show George a thing or two. His enormous success had been at least partially due to her.

The waiter opened the wine, and let Ted smell the cork. Even if Brooke should have been the one to do so, given her expertise.

Ted took a sip and nodded. "I should have let you do this."

"It's all right. I don't mind a man taking the lead sometimes." But why did an image of Billy pop into her head unbidden?

At the end of the date, Ted took her home, and insisted on walking her to the cottage. Of course it wasn't possible to walk to her cottage without passing the manor house. As they approached the balcony, who should be outside in the late October air but Billy?

"What's Billy doing here?" Ted asked.

"He lives here. Didn't I mention that? In the back," Brooke said. She hadn't wanted to share that information yet, and honestly hadn't expected Billy to be hanging around when she got back from her date. Not like she'd seen him hanging around the balcony on any other night.

"Hey Billy," Ted called out. "How about them Giants?"

"Looking good," Billy said, raising a bottle of what looked like beer.

Beer? They were going to have words. "Would you like to come up?" She turned to Ted.

Ted's eyebrows joined his hairline. "Really?"

Why was that so shocking? Ted had been perfectly

pleasant and nice all evening. He'd held her hand, put his arm around her waist, and it was all fine. Quite nice. She wasn't going to sleep with him, but she wouldn't mind being kissed for the first time in weeks. She missed kissing. When it was done well, naturally, and she wouldn't mind testing Ted out. He might surprise her. Stranger things had happened.

Before she could answer Billy walked down the steps to join them, shaking Ted's hand and talking about scores and lingo she could barely comprehend. Ted was a goner when Billy asked for his advice regarding which team had the best chances of winning the World Series.

Brooke's eyes glazed over as she listened to the men talk. She tried not to be offended by the way Ted gazed at Billy with the eyes of a sports fan. Wasn't he *her* date? Didn't he want to come upstairs, or did the man have Attention Deficit Disorder? Didn't everybody these days? Was he so easily distracted, or was she just not sexy enough?

"I'm really tired," Brooke raised her arms and yawned softly. *Hint, hint. I'm going upstairs. Take it or leave it, Teddy.*

"Okay Brooke. Good-night. I had a really good time tonight. I'll call you." Ted smiled in her direction, and continued to chat with Billy.

Well, of all the nerve.

Brooke didn't return any of Ted's calls the following week, and he got the message. She hoped Billy and Ted would be very happy together. Brooke moved on.

It wasn't until two weeks later and two dates that were sidelined by Billy that Brooke wondered if Billy were trying to chase some of these men away. When Billy offered Sean Kowalski, one of the guys she'd met skydiving, his season tickets to the third game of the World Series the man became so discombobulated that he seemed to lose the power of speech. He waved in her direction as he left, holding tight to the tickets as if he'd just found the map to the Fountain of Youth.

"That's incredible." Brooke stared at Billy.

"Not really. I'm not going to the game, and they would have just gone to waste." Billy lifted a shoulder.

She faced him, squaring her shoulders. "That's not what I mean. Why have you been outside every time I've come back from one of my dates?"

"Sorry, I wasn't aware I had to hide inside. I'm always awake at this time."

"And you're not usually outside ready to make a new best friend."

"Don't make anything of it. I happen to be up, you happen to come home from your date. Coincidence."

"Right. I guess that's true. There must just be something wrong with me, then." Brooke took off in the direction of her cottage. She threw open the door, and prepared to spend an evening alone with Housewives of Beverly Hills. That show always made her feel good about herself, and tonight she needed a big shot of self-esteem.

She didn't like playing second fiddle to the enigmatic Billy Turlock. Women loved him, and men admired him. The women thing she couldn't do anything about, but she would have to find a man in this town who didn't like baseball. There had to be someone. Somewhere. She'd have to ask Ivey if Noah the male nurse liked sports.

Brooke had just served a heaping serving of Rocky Road ice cream into a bowl when she heard Billy's forceful knocking again.

She threw open the door, and there he stood in his entire super jock splendor. "What do you *want*?"

He braced himself inside the frame of the door. "Just wanted to say that for the record, if I were your date there isn't anything short of a category five hurricane that would keep me from joining you upstairs."

"Save it. I don't believe you. You're trying to sabotage my dates." She moved aside so he and his athletic ego would have enough room to come in.

He lumbered in and held out his palms. "Look, I happened to be up when you came home. Totally unplanned."

"Every time? So you aren't trying to scare all my dates off?"

He grinned. "Okay, that part is totally planned."

"Aha! I knew it. Why, Billy? Why would you do that to me?"

He reached her in two short strides, grabbing her arms and pulling her roughly to him. Brooke felt all the breath leave her in one single rush when he kissed her. He wasn't particularly gentle about the kiss, but the way he held her made her feel both precious and breakable. Her mouth opened under him and he took the invitation and explored. She'd remembered that Billy Turlock could kiss, but this was different. He kissed her now like he had every right to do so, with a kind of possession and authority that left her reeling. She felt the powerful tug of lust ping deep in her belly, just as it had years ago.

Billy pulled away, released her, and walked back to her door. "You're smart, Brooke. You figure it out."

Brooke didn't move for a minute. Billy Turlock had kissed the breath right out of her. That kiss—and he — was so much better than her teenage brain remembered, and that said something. How could he kiss her like that and just walk out? Brooke followed him out the door, climbed the short steps to his residence, and found herself knocking on his door for a change.

She'd only been here once before, trying to stay away

from the place where he laid his head at night. Where he showered. Where he couldn't, or didn't cook. Where he made love. She didn't want to know, didn't need the image burned in her corneas.

When he opened the door he didn't look at all surprised to see her. "What was that about?" Brooke demanded.

"You still need help figuring it out?" He pulled her inside. "Come here, I'll help you."

He pulled her roughly against him again, and her palms went up and against his hard muscled chest. She could stop him, she knew. By saying a single word. Only they didn't come easy staring into that green gaze. The eyes said too much, and she became overwhelmed by the emotions radiating down to the soles of her feet. She'd never known anyone to talk with his eyes before, but dang if it didn't seem they were having an entire conversation.

His thumb swept her jaw. "You're even more beautiful than I remembered."

This time she was the one who lifted her hands from his chest and wrapped them around his neck. He took that as the only invitation required for his sensual mouth to come crashing down on hers again.

His kiss was more of a sensual and decadent experience than a simple kiss. Billy Turlock made love with his mouth. With his talented tongue, hot, wet and probing.

She pulled away, breathless and incoherent with yearning. "Wait a minute."

Of course he listened. His arms fell away from her and he took a small step back. "Say it, Brooke."

She already missed him. "Maybe this isn't such a great idea?"

"It's a great idea. But you're right, it will change everything. I don't know about you, but I've been waiting for a long time for this kind of a shift."

"You're my boss." No point in telling him how badly her last relationship had turned out.

"Actually, you're Pop's employee. Not mine."

"What are you talking about? You hired me."

"Yes, but the way the corporation is set up I've made Pop the owner. It was his dream. I'm bank rolling it."

"So you're not my boss?"

"Not in the truest sense of the word. No. Why? Is that a problem?"

Brooke swallowed. "No, it's not a problem. But you and me? Gigi will hate it. She doesn't trust me."

"That's only a bonus, and not the main reason I want you."

"Don't joke about this."

"I know what I want. Maybe it's time for you to decide what you want. Because what I want is to change everything, and there's no going back."

"You make it sound so simple."

"It is."

"Is it? You and I are so different ..."

"When we were kids. Now we're adults. I don't think we have to stay inside our cliques anymore. Do we?"

"But— I like to think we're friends."

She didn't want to ever regret Billy like she did George. Didn't want to watch Billy throw her over for the young fertile ingénue, and really, what were the odds that a wealthy athlete would get tired of her? After he'd had his fill, of course. She'd probably win big in Vegas on those odds.

"I already have plenty of friends. I want more with you. And if you're dating, you need to at least give me a shot. Let me take you out."

So that's what this was all about. Simple envy for something he couldn't have? And dating Billy Turlock? The jock? The man who'd let her down once before? "That's impossible. Everyone is watching. It's like being under a microscope. They all know who you are, and they'd soon enough figure out who I am."

"So what? It's not like I'd want to keep our relationship secret, but there are ways for us to find our privacy. Believe me."

She'd bet he knew every one of those ways. Brooke backed up to the door and pressed her back against it. "I'm going to go now."

"Think about it." Billy again, talking with his bedroom eyes this time. Her imagination was going on a thrill seeking ride thinking about how else he used that tongue.

"I am." She felt her face grow hot. "I mean, I will," she said and turned to walk out the door.

She already knew very well what she wanted. She wanted to lie under him in his bed, to discover all his hidden talents. But there was a lurking danger to all of it with Billy. It already felt like he had a piece of her heart, and she hadn't seen him for nearly half of her life.

What would he do to the rest of her heart, given any more time?

* * *

THANK GOD FOR BASEBALL. For training and discipline, mind over matter. For ignoring the body when it was about to give out on you. For realizing your body was almost always more capable than what your mind believed.

If not for baseball, Brooke would be in his bed right now. Consequences be dammed. Because he could sense, given the way she'd kissed him, that she wanted him. And he wanted her so much that it had become a burning ache in his chest.

She kept holding back, and while there were reasons they shouldn't be together, he could hit every one of them right out of the park. This could work, and he wouldn't miss this second chance with her. Somehow when he wasn't looking, he'd fallen headfirst into a haze of lust and longing for Brooke Miller.

His covert plan had nearly not worked for him. He might have chased every lame suitor away, but he hadn't been prepared for the gentle beat against his heart when he'd caught the pained look in her eyes. He couldn't let her believe for one second it had anything to do with her. Those men didn't deserve her if they could be so easily swayed by Series tickets and the attention of a has-been like him.

No, she deserved better than that.

Even in high school, Brooke had deserved better. She never seemed to think so, though. With her jet black hair and black nail polish, she scared most of the kids at Starlight High. As far as he'd been able to tell, she'd had one friend. Ivey Lancaster. But that was also due to the fact that her parents fought over her constantly, and Brooke was forced to spend every summer out of state and living with her father's new family.

Each time she'd come back she seemed a little bit more pissed off with the entire world, but jocks in particular. And then there were all her causes. At the height of them a little something called world peace, ironic for a girl with a chip on her shoulder the size of Texas. Regardless, Brooke championed one cause after another. She stood outside the cafeteria and collected signatures for petitions. Save the Whales, Save the Arts, Save the Koalas, Better pay for Teachers (and for some reason no one considered her a kiss-ass because of it).

In their senior year, a favorite English teacher had died in a horrible car accident. That's when he'd discovered that Brooke didn't cry like most girls. Every girl had bawled uncontrollably, but Brooke had stared into space with a bitter, hard look in her eyes.

She'd scared him a little bit too.

Mostly because she went against every expectation he had about girls, and they were hard enough to understand without Brooke throwing everything off kilter.

In high school he'd been a serial dater. Never had that first love that burned so brightly it threatened to extinguish everything in its path. That wouldn't have been wise given his aspirations to the Hall of Fame. Wise or not, it hadn't happened. He dated one girl after another, which might have been how he'd gained his reputation. Because he didn't kiss and tell, and everyone just assumed. Naturally he'd let them, since he'd been a teenaged jock.

The whole image had suited him well, until Brooke. Now he was half convinced Brooke didn't want to be one more on the supposedly long list of Billy Turlock conquests.

Even if he'd known from that first kiss long ago that this was the fire that could burn too brightly. That had scared him too. But now —well, now he was ready for one hell of a sunburn.

He picked up his cell phone and dialed Brooke's number. She answered after the second ring, sounding breathy and like sex on a stick.

"Hey," he said. "Would you go out with me Friday night?"

There was a short pause. "Listen up. I'm going to tell you something you've probably never heard before: no." She hung up.

Ironically, Brooke had no idea how many times he'd heard the word 'no'.

No, another surgery won't help. No, your contract hasn't been renewed. No, no, no.

He could let that piss him off, and make him angry at her clichéd assumptions. But he was too busy to be angry.

He needed a Plan B.

Apologizing to Billy for being a bitch had wound up on Brooke's list again. Just because she didn't think it was a good idea to date him didn't mean she had to be mean about it. Yet a week later, she hadn't seen much of Billy, much less apologized to him. He'd taken off to LA for a few days to do a commercial for some promo shot with some of the other retired Sliders athletes. He'd been gone four days now, and yet he was supposed to be the face of this business.

He wasn't fooling her. Billy Turlock was not done with baseball, no matter what he said. Sure, he was currently retired but didn't all athletes do that to get attention? Retire once only to opt back in. That might be fine with her, because with him gone she'd do even better pretending the place was all hers.

Even with Billy gone, Pop and Eileen still dropped by every day for a few hours. Surprisingly, it wasn't as horrible as Brooke had thought it might be. Thankfully Pop was just as against the tofu menu appetizers, and he kept trying to talk some sense into his daughter. To Brooke, hope still sprang eternal. She might be able to eventually talk some sense into Eileen.

Meanwhile, Eileen had looked up the definition of cougar, and confided in Brooke that she thought she had the goods to be one. Unfortunately, the search for the perfect man for Eileen moved slowly. Forty-something-year-old eligible gentlemen didn't just grow on trees.

Eric had now officially come on board and Brooke made him head of Marketing. It was through Eric that Brooke had finally been updated on the inner happenings at Serrano Winery. Chelsea was a disaster as interim general manager, the VP of Sales position wasn't even mentioned any longer, and George wasn't happy. So unhappy he was already cheating on Chelsea, to hear Eric tell the story. Not that he wouldn't have done that eventually, happy or not.

Brooke sighed, stretched, and rose from her laptop. She'd been at it for four hours this morning, had a planning meeting with Eric, and then spent another four hours at the laptop this afternoon. She'd written another list of goals to accomplish before the Grand Opening, which they'd slated for December fifth, but she still had to discuss all of it with Billy.

Brooke's cell phone rang, and when the caller ID showed Billy's name, she didn't know why her chest expanded like that of a kid on Christmas morning. "Hey. Are you back yet?"

"Just got in about a half-hour ago. I need to shower and change, but meet me down by the Chardonnay row in about an hour. There's something I have to talk to you about, and it's important."

"O-kay," Brooke said. She didn't like the sound of his voice, short, clipped, and to the point. Was there something wrong on the Chardonnay row that she didn't know about? Maybe he only sounded short because of the plane ride. Or maybe Gigi had finally convinced him he should get rid of

Brooke now rather than later. Maybe he wanted the privacy of the Chardonnay row because he thought she'd have a temper tantrum.

For reasons she decided not to examine too closely, Brooke took a shower again, reapplied her make-up and fluffed her hair into submission. A nippy early November air had settled into Starlight Hill seemingly overnight, and it was serious sweater time. That didn't mean she couldn't find a nice one. Brooke dug through her closet and found her tight camel cashmere sweater and paired it with her sleekest pair of jeans. She then stuffed her pant legs into the long black leather boots that reached her knees. Ivey called them Ms. Dominatrix boots.

If Billy was going to fire her, at least he'd do it while she looked smoking hot. She gave one last assessment in her full length mirror. It would have to do.

But he wouldn't fire her. He couldn't. Her legs were shaking just a bit as she walked up the hill to the row. In the middle of the row, a sight surprised her. Someone had laid a blanket on the ground and a bottle of wine stood in the middle. There were two glasses of wine, and a picnic basket.

This was so unacceptable. People couldn't just come on to private property and have themselves a picnic. And now they were hiding, because they'd been caught.

Suddenly she heard Billy's voice behind her. "You're a little early."

She turned to see his perfect grin. He wore jeans and a leather jacket that did all kinds of badass things for him. It made him look equal parts bad boy and jock.

She was early, true, because she'd been so nervous. But something split down the middle inside of her, because Billy had put together this spread for her. Now he took her hand and led her to the blanket.

"You made a picnic." Stating the obvious always worked for her when she had no words.

"You've been working so hard. I wanted you to take a break." Billy went to work on the corkscrew.

This wasn't a date. He was simply taking care of a hard working employee. Brooke sat down on the blanket.

Billy handed Brooke the cork. Most people didn't know its importance. Even less of them had appreciated the fact that Brook knew what to look for in one. But Billy did. "This looks fine. Is it from the cellar?"

"Yep. It's a 2000 Mirassu Merlot." Billy poured, sniffed and handed the glass to Brooke. "It was a good year, right?"

The irony wasn't lost on Brooke. That was the year they'd both started at Starlight High. The year they'd met. "You should have saved this for a special occasion."

"You're more than deserving," Billy said, sitting across from her and raising his glass. "To the start of a great partnership."

Brooke clinked her wine glass with his. This was so much better than what she'd been worried about. "I'm glad you're back. We need to talk about the Grand Opening."

"Sure, but we should eat first." He reached inside the picnic basket. "In case you still don't eat meat, I bought some vegetarian sandwiches. There's fruit and cheese in here, too."

"I'm not a vegetarian anymore," Brooke admitted. That had been one of many causes in her pent-up angst youth. When every other week there was a new animal or a new country that required saving. Now she left all the earth saving to Mom. The earth was covered.

"You're not a lot of things anymore," Billy stared at her. "Not a brunette or a vegetarian."

"Not a virgin," she added, and immediately regretted it. Why she would bring that up right now only the much younger and sexually frustrated Brooke would know.

It didn't seem to faze Billy. "I didn't think so."

Subject change. Quick. "So how was LA?"

"Predictable." Billy popped a grape in his mouth. "Gigi says hello."

Brooke raised an eyebrow. "For real?"

He nodded and grinned. "That's not all she said, but that's the only part you want to hear about."

"That I believe." Brooke played with the frayed edges of the blanket, while she tried not to imagine how many other women had sat on it. It didn't matter because this wasn't a date.

"Tell me what you're thinking," Billy said because he did always have that annoying way of hearing her thoughts.

"No."

Billy laughed out loud. "You do enjoy saying that word to me, don't you?"

Brooke couldn't help but smile, maybe because of the wine, both a bit stout and smooth. "Actually, no."

"Nice. You're going to have a hard time convincing me of that."

Brooke laughed out loud. "Yes. You're probably right."

Somehow it would seem that she and Billy were holding hands now. It hardly seemed possible, but it was also the most natural thing in the world. Billy played with her hand, raising it up, bringing it back down again. Leave it to him to actively hold her hand. She wished he would sit still for a minute. But when he brought her hand to his lips and brushed a kiss on it, everything in the vineyard did seem to still for a moment. He could be serious too, when he wanted to be, and she'd almost forgotten that. He could be heart-attack serious.

And suddenly this felt a little bit like a date.

She wanted to kiss him more than she wanted another sunrise tomorrow morning. His kisses were like crack and she probably should have just said no the first time. Forgetting herself, Brooke straddled his lap and her legs came around his back.

She threaded her fingers through his thick hair. "Oh, Hotshot, why do you always do this to me?"

Then she kissed him softly, his only answer a ravaging kiss that seemed to reach inside her chest and take her heart for ransom. For the next few minutes every cell in Brooke's body was one long cord of need that only Billy could fill.

"Brooke," Billy rasped near her ear, and then trailed a line of kisses down her neck.

Brooke didn't want to think anymore, but only feel. That's what Billy did to her. He woke her up. She didn't know why, but he'd been the only one ever able to do it. From the first time he'd kissed her, and she'd understood why girls behaved like fools over him.

She thought she heard a sound coming from behind them and froze. Billy did too.

"Did you hear that?" Brooke scrambled off his lap, something she seemed to forever be doing these days.

Billy rose and walked to the end of the row, his head turning in each direction. "No one here. We're alone."

"I know I heard something." She wasn't paranoid. It was a distinctive clicking sound. But the reporters and photographers had finally made themselves scarce. Still, what if one of them had sneaked up here to spy on them?

Billy walked back towards her. "Where were we?"

"I think we were at the point where I regain my senses."

"I don't like the sound of that."

She almost laughed. "When Gigi thought I might be interested in you, she suggested I move. I like living here."

Billy reached for her arm and whirled her around. "You don't have to go anywhere."

"Maybe it's a good thing this happened. Gives us a chance

to put the brakes on. For some reason, when I'm around you I stop thinking."

"Ditto."

"Well, see, that's not good. One of us should be thinking."

He looked at the ground, and rubbed the back of his neck. "You're right."

"Damn you. Stop agreeing with me."

He seemed to be biting his lip, like he wanted to smile. "What do you want?"

"I like that we're friends. We never got to be that when we were younger. Now we can be, and I don't want to ruin that."

Brooke walked back up to her cottage, Billy following.

When she was just inches from her door, Billy twirled her around and she wound up back in his arms. "If you ever want to be more than friends, you know where I am."

She had her palms against his chest, but this time she wouldn't raise them to his neck. Billy scared her a little, and for a girl who liked a thrill, saying no to him was beginning to take on a Herculean effort beyond mere mortal capabilities.

She hadn't answered him for several seconds, only stood in his arms staring at his chest. He raised her chin and brushed his lips across hers. "Brooke?"

"I need some time to think." *Yes, you idiot. Let the hot man go so you can go inside and stare at the ceiling.*

Billy's arms slipped from around her waist, and he let her go. The man understood 'no' better than any man she'd ever met before. "Take all the time you need."

Just like that, he'd gone, taking all his seething male hotness with him. Brooke slipped inside the front door of her cottage, and took off her Ms. Dominatrix boots. They wouldn't see any action tonight. When she placed them beside her bed, the top half flopped over the bottom half and they looked as deflated as Brooke felt.

A few hours later, after yet another frozen dinner alone, she undressed and put on her flimsy satin pink baby doll nightie. The one Billy wouldn't be taking off her tonight. That one.

Why couldn't she just let go and make love to Billy? Why was she making it such a big deal? Was it because Billy had taken her back to the days when she was pickier, choosier, and when even he wouldn't have been able to storm the castle?

They could be discreet, and Billy wouldn't kiss and tell. That was obvious. But while she'd bounced back from George throwing her over, she didn't think she could when Billy got tired of her.

Brooke cuddled up on the couch with a book. She'd just gotten to the good part, where the hero finally confesses his love for the heroine, when all the lights went out. Every. Single. One.

No, not this. It hadn't happened in years. The power was out, and in the pitch black darkness Brooke couldn't take in a solid breath. She was prepared for this eventuality. With a phobia like this, the doctor had suggested it. That is, after he couldn't talk her into the full immersion therapy. No way would she spend fifteen minutes in a dark room voluntarily. Was the man crazy?

She crawled along the floor and felt her way to the kitchen drawer where she kept the flashlights. As luck would have it, tonight there was a sliver of a moon outside. It wasn't shining through the window closest to the kitchen, so she had to fumble her way.

I'm not going to die, this can't kill me. It's just the dark. The dark can't hurt me. The dark can't kill me.

Brooke repeated her mantra, but as usual it didn't help. She still couldn't draw in a real solid breath. *Please don't let me pass out here all alone.* She found the flashlight and pulled it out. Turned it on. Nothing. It had been so long since she'd used it the batteries had died. Should have checked the batteries. The moon would have to do. She started to crawl towards the door.

* * *

THE POWER WENT OUT in the middle of an ESPN's commentator's opinion on the new 49er line up. All things considered, very good timing since the man didn't know what he was talking about. This was turning out to be some day. He'd been shut down twice. Once by Brooke, and now by PG&E.

He dialed PG&E and listened to the recording that there had been an outage in the area and they were 'working on it'. Right. Using his cell phone for a light, he searched for his flashlight. He thought of Brooke, and aimed the flashlight in the direction of her cottage. He couldn't see a single light on in there. Had she already gone to sleep? Doubtful. Maybe Brooke needed a hand finding a flashlight or some candles. As he walked out his door, he told himself this was the only reason he was going back to the cottage to check up on her, and nothing more.

It didn't have anything to do with the fact that being with her was beginning to be a drive he couldn't ignore. Not that he wanted to. The kind of woman that cared about their friendship was exactly the kind of woman he needed in his life. Someone like Brooke. Well, not someone like her. It had to be her. She just didn't know it yet.

He'd been hit on no fewer than six times before getting a taxi cab home, and none of them had done a thing for him. Beautiful women who'd hardly registered a blip on his radar. Brooke was in his head 24/7. He didn't know how she'd done that when he'd only occasionally thought of her over the past ten years. Okay, about once a year. But seeing her again, right in front of him, had brought all those memories back to slam into him like a freight train on steroids.

He found Brooke lying on her back outside her front door, staring up at the dark night. Odd. When he approached with the flashlight, she turned her head in his direction.

"Thank God, your batteries work!" She said from the ground.

Billy shined the light directly on her. This was especially cruel, and he began to wonder if Brooke secretly hated him. She wore some kind of barely there lingerie that showed her milky white shoulders. The thing barely covered her thighs and her long curvy legs were bare, feet covered by fuzzy dog slippers.

"Any particular reason you're on the floor?" He squatted down next to her.

"I have the best view right here," she said with a completely straight face.

"The best view of —?"

"The moon, you ninny!"

He looked over his shoulder. "Ah, yeah. The moon. It's just a sliver tonight. But it can be enjoyed in a standing position as well."

"That's easy for you to say."

He offered her his hand, and she took it and rose. "Yeah."

"My flashlight's batteries were dead, so I came outside for the moonlight."

"What about your cell phone?" He held open the front door for her, shining the light into the dark room.

She slapped her forehead. "Great idea. Where is it? I'll need to hold it until the lights come back on. Help me find it."

They found it next to her purse on the table, and she used it to light her way to the couch. "I hope the charge holds.

How long will the lights be out? Do you have any idea? How long till morning? Do you know what time the sun rises? I'm not 100% sure since the time change."

She sounded like a wind-up doll someone had pulled repeatedly. All at once, he understood. "Brooke? Are you afraid of the dark?"

She looked like a sex siren advertising a new cell phone plan as she held it up in her hand like a display and kept glancing at it. "Define afraid. If by afraid you mean that I feel like I'm going to die when it's pitch dark, that I can't take in a solid breath of air, okay then, I guess I'm a little afraid of the dark."

A little? Sounded like a full blown phobia to him. Brooke Miller, finally afraid of something. He'd never imagined for a moment it would be the dark. He joined her on the couch. "Want me to stay with you? Until the lights come on."

"Sure, but only if you want to. That's a nice big flashlight." She said this with the same tone of reverence in her voice a teenaged boy might bestow on his first sweet ride.

He slung an arm around her shoulders and pulled her closer. She was trembling. "Would you like to hold my big flashlight?"

"Okay," she said and put her cell phone on the couch's arm rest. "This all probably seems silly to you."

"Nah. You're talking to a guy who used to shower three times for good luck on game day, and before my first batter up I made sure to look right, then left, then right again. And of course, make sure to have bananas for breakfast the morning of the game."

"Bananas?"

He nodded. "It would help if I could rub Scott's head twice for good luck, but he couldn't come to every game so that had to stop. And then of course I had to put on my socks before my boxers. The order was vital."

"Of course."

"Don't laugh. The night I did that particular ritual for the first time I pitched my first no-hitter. It all seemed to contribute to whether or not I had a good game. Don't ask me why. Baseball is full of superstition."

"You jocks are weird." Brooke snuggled into him, laying her head on his chest.

He caught the scent of her hair again. *Cranberry.* Good enough to eat. But he was getting ahead of himself. While she had practically crawled in his lap, he fingered the edge of her nightie. She hadn't worn this for him, because unless she was psychic she couldn't have predicted this particular outcome. "Were you expecting someone?"

Brooke raised her head and shone the light in his face, making him blink. "No!"

He moved her arm, and the flashlight, down. "Take it easy, Bungee. I wondered because of um, what you're wearing."

Brooke sighed and made a little sound in the back of her throat, as if she'd only now remembered what she was wearing. "I hope you don't think I'd kiss you the way I did this afternoon and then be— expecting someone else."

He might be pushing his luck, but still he asked. "Why, then?"

"You know, Hotshot, a girl buys nice lingerie and every once in a while she might decide to put it on even without a guy around. Just to feel pretty. Besides, it stays on longer that way."

"Good point." He'd wanted to take it off since he saw her lying on the ground in front of her door. Amusement mixed with full blown lust, another first.

Brooke had laid her head down on his chest again, which wasn't making any of this easy. "And, if I have to, I can always take care of myself."

He hoped she hadn't heard the sharp hiss of his breath,

but just picturing Brooke— taking care of herself— was not an image conducive to a steady heart rate. He swallowed.

"I love the way I've left you speechless."

"Face it, that's not hard for you to do." He forced himself to think about puppies and kittens. One thing he wouldn't do is press his advantage on a weak and vulnerable Brooke. She'd stopped trembling in his arms, at least. He glanced at his cell phone.

Brooke raised her head. "Who are you calling?"

"PG&E. I want to see how much longer before these lights are back on." Please people, make it soon. My physical and mental health might depend on it.

She laid her head back on his chest. One arm was clinging to his waist, the other still holding the damned flashlight. "You can go if you'd like. I don't mean to keep you here."

It had never occurred to him that she might think he had better things to do, or any place he'd rather be. He kissed the top of her head, as he listened to the recording of the outage update. "I'm not going anywhere."

"Thanks, Hotshot."

He hung up. Sounded like it might be a while. "How long have you been this afraid of the dark?"

She spoke as softly as he'd ever heard Brooke Miller speak. "I was a typical kid, afraid of the dark. Always had a night light. But it got bad in college the year our part of the city had a brown-out. I had a roommate that was never in our dorm. Of course the power went out when she was off with her boyfriend somewhere. I've never seen it so dark before, or since then. I stayed in my room alone and waited. I'd only been there for a few weeks so it's not like I had any friends to call. And the other people on my co-ed floor were having way too much fun out in the halls. I didn't feel like hooking up with someone whose face I couldn't even see, and that's what it sounded like they were doing out there. I locked the door and hid under the blanket. I've been terrified ever since."

Just the thought of Brooke alone in that room, far away from home, and he found that he held her tighter. Even pulled her into his lap a little bit. "I should have been there. I would have been if—"

"No, you would have been in the jock's dorm. They had the best one, across the campus from mine."

"Doesn't matter. I would have found a way." And he'd find a way this time if it killed him. It just very well might, but he wouldn't leave Brooke again.

"Right," she said, her breath falling on his ear. "But I don't think I would have made the Dean's List had you taken that scholarship."

"Yeah?"

"You would have been one huge distraction."

"I don't know about that, but I would have given it a hell of an effort."

"I'd like to see you give it an effort now." Brooke straddled him, and the flashlight dropped to her side.

Like a clock striking the hour, the lights suddenly went on again in the room. Brooke startled in his lap. Light radiated as though someone had turned the sun dial to high. He blinked to adjust his eyes. Every light in the room was on, but Billy couldn't take his eyes off the woman in front of him. Brooke blinked a few times, but didn't move from his lap. She gazed at him, her eyes soft and pliable with heat. Staring at his mouth.

He took the invitation, and this would be a whole lot better with the lights on.

CHAPTER 11

*M*ind numbing fear combined with body slamming lust turned out to be the biggest thrill Brooke had ever experienced.

Forget skydiving and bungee jumping. All she needed was Billy and the dark. No use in pretending she didn't want him. Didn't need him inside her like she needed her next breath. Billy lit her up from the inside out, right down to her bone marrow. She might have fantasized this moment dozens of times in the past, but it hadn't come close to the searing reality.

Then the lights slammed back on, and it seemed like the sun itself shined in her cottage. Spraying light all over what she was about to do. Because this couldn't happen, boss or not.

Not her and Billy.

Friends were one thing, but how could she yearn for someone who represented everything she hated?

But damn it, she had ten years ago and still did now. The lustful feelings had never gone away. And every time he had smiled at her, every time he signed her petition to save the whales, or whatever her cause du jour at the time just because she'd asked him to, he'd stolen another piece of her heart.

Now she had her heart back in one piece. He couldn't just waltz back into her life and start taking pieces of it again.

She scrambled off his lap before they'd both do something they would regret. This made twice now she'd nearly attacked the man. Or was that three times? Good, she'd already lost count.

He turned off the flashlight and stared at her, a puzzled expression on his face. Achingly vulnerable, heartbreakingly sexy. "What's wrong?"

"What's *wrong*? I came on to you."

"Uh, Brooke? I'm not exactly fighting you off."

"Of course not. You're a gentleman and you don't want to make me feel cheap." She glanced down at her nightie. Great. Giving him a free show. "Look at me!"

She ran to her bedroom for her robe and the ratty one was closer. So what. A deterrent would be handy right now.

Billy joined her, arms braced in the doorway of the bedroom. "Good idea. Your little couch is too small for me."

She tied the robe tight around her waist. "No! I didn't come in here for the bed."

"You think that stupid robe is going to stop me? It's made out of cotton."

How was she supposed to get out of her bedroom when he blocked the frame with his big hot body? She drew in a deep breath. "This isn't a good idea."

"Why not?"

Why not? As it so happened, she had a list somewhere. But for right now, she'd have to fly by the seat of her pants. For starters he now knew about her phobia.

She'd never been this naked in front of a man, without even taking all her clothes off.

He didn't wait for an answer as he stepped toward her and reached for her, his strong arms pulling her close. "You don't have an answer, do you?"

She put her hands up against his hard chest, feeling the strong beat of his heart beneath her fingertips. "I— I do have an answer—"

"Not one good enough for me." One sexy finger tucked a lock of hair behind her ear.

"You and I are from two different worlds."

"Doesn't feel like that."

He kissed her then, rough and a little bit wild and she closed her eyes pretending for a second she would let him into her heart again. Let him in so he could walk away without a word.

She pulled away after a few minutes. Those kisses of his were going to be the death of her. Her lips were nearly as bruised as her heart. "No. Stop."

He let her go, stepping away. "This isn't over."

"It has to be."

He walked through the doorway, turning once to give her a pointed look. "The only thing that has to be is you and me in your bed together. Or mine, if you'd prefer. To be honest, we don't even need a bed."

His words wrapped around her southern region and went straight to soles of her feet. She couldn't move.

Once he was gone she took a solid breath of air, now free of the absolute maleness of Billy Turlock. She couldn't understand how he managed to pull her in the way he did. Good looks were one thing, but he kissed with such authority and passion, being both rough and tender at the same time. He made her skin too tight.

The digital clock in the kitchen flashed the number twelve. She'd need to reset all the clocks because of the power outage. And buy new batteries and extra flashlights. She grabbed a piece of paper and started to make a list.

Yeah, she needed to get a handle on this phobia of the dark. A grown woman shouldn't still be unable to face such a ridiculous fear which had no real explanation. She was a daredevil, not afraid of anything.

Except Billy had reminded her there was one thing she feared more than the dark. Right now that fear had morphed into a six foot tall long haired baseball player.

Sleep. She needed to rest now, and forget the man who'd left a trail of heat in his wake.

Brooke folded up the blanket he'd pulled over her and threw it on the loveseat. They'd both been here not long ago in near total darkness and yet she'd felt safer than if every light in the house had been left on.

And wasn't that the scariest thing of all?

* * *

THE NEXT MORNING at Henry's Market, Brooke crossed batteries off her list. Two twelve packs of double As should last through a few power outages. She'd have to get the flashlights at the hardware store, since Henry's didn't carry those.

All morning long she'd fought to keep her thoughts of Billy in line. She would not daydream about him. She would not remember what it felt like to be in his arms, to feel the heated waves of intense desire nearly electrifying the room. She would stop thinking about the kissing.

Well, one challenge at a time.

Next on her list: milk, Munster cheese and fruit. She pushed her squeaky wheeled cart to the dairy section.

Ophelia Lyndstrom from the fabric store Sew and Tell nearly bumped into her shopping cart right next to the milk

156

aisle. "Brooke! Is everything really all right? You seem perfectly normal."

"Why wouldn't I be?" Probably just another rumor thread in town. Well, she'd squash it like a fly. She kept moving towards the milk aisle, Ophelia following.

"Keith told me you flipped out at Serrano's and had to be restrained."

Brooke stopped her cart and turned. "Restrained?"

"Yes, apparently some irate patron called George a horrible name and you hauled off and slugged him. I believe in company loyalty, but isn't that taking it a bit too far?"

For the love of Pete, the rumor was so far removed from the truth she wasn't sure how to respond. "I didn't hit anybody."

"Then why did Keith say that?" Ophelia really did appear confused.

"I'm sure he heard wrong. You know how rumors get around."

"You're right. Probably just an exaggeration, as usual. What did happen?"

"George and I had a parting of the ways. I don't work for him anymore." Brooke leaned in and reached for the fat milk this time. Screw the 2%. Sometimes you just needed fat. "Maybe I was a little loud when I handed over my resignation, but we're good. Everything's fine."

"I heard you're at the old Mirassu winery now."

Why bother talking when everyone already knew everything? "Yes, under new ownership. You'll be hearing more soon."

"You know I'll support whatever you do, honey. What about the photo? Was that you? Some say it's you but I'm not sure. It kind of looked like you, but I couldn't see your face." Ophelia blushed.

"What photo?" But even as she asked, Brooke feared she had the answer to the question.

"Billy Turlock kissing some woman in the Chardonnay row. I would have picked the Cabernet row myself, but there's no accounting for taste. White wine is good with fish, and that's about it. Don't you agree?"

"Yes, but where did you see this photo?"

"On Stephan's blog. Someone should really stop him. He has no shame, but what can you do? It's The Internet. God help us all." Ophelia threw a non-fat carton of milk in her cart.

Brooke whipped out her phone right in the milk aisle and found the blog.

Ophelia looked over Brooke's shoulder. "That's the one."

Front and center on Stephan's blog lay a photo of her and Billy emblazoned with the caption: *Love in the Afternoon?*

Retired ball player Billy Turlock wastes no time when it comes to the ladies. In this photo of him and a local woman it is clear if not love, there's at least lust in the air. I'm offering $50 to whoever comes up with the name of the woman Billy has in his lap. I do have my suspicions, but I need evidence...

The picture wasn't a good one, thank goodness. They'd captured Billy's back mostly, but it was clearly his long brown hair, and her fingers curling through it. Fortunately Billy's big body had mostly covered her, although her legs were seen to be coming around his back. Wearing her long black Ms. Dominatrix boots. The boots she'd had to order from a catalog, because of course there was no store in town that carried them.

"Come to think of it, those look like your boots," Ophelia said. "Aren't they?"

"Like I'm the only one who owns a pair of those boots?"

"I think you might be. Take a look at him, would you? If I

were only twenty years younger. What I wouldn't do. Ah, well."

Sweet the way he'd prepared that picnic, even if he'd made it an underhanded date. Because he wasn't used to not getting what he wanted.

"Yes, he is pretty good looking. Just not my type."

"Honey, this man is every woman's type." Ophelia breathed. "So you do work for him now, don't you?"

She'd just admitted as much. "Yeah."

"And you own a pair of those boots?" Ophelia's eyes narrowed.

Brooke didn't like this line of questioning. She put away the phone in her bag and headed to the fresh fruit section.

"Where are you going?" Ophelia called out.

"To finish my shopping. See you later."

Paul Smith stopped in the middle of bagging some apples to recite statistics for the Oakland Sliders, and swear himself a lifelong true-blue fan. Why he thought that mattered to her she had no idea. Brooke finished her shopping in record time, ignoring winks from some other customers.

She'd nearly made it to the checkout line before Fallon Andrews almost slammed into her cart.

"Ooops! Sorry about that."

But she didn't look the slightest bit sorry, smiling with that ex-cheerleader mean girl look she'd perfected at Starlight Hill High. "Out of my way. I'm in a hurry."

"We need to talk," Fallon said, "And I think you know why."

Brooke could hazard a guess. Fallon, being Billy's last girlfriend before graduation, had probably never given up on Billy. "I've got no idea. Why don't you spit it out?"

Fallon leaned in and spoke softly. "There are only two women in town with those boots, and I'm the other one."

Brooke froze. "Now how do you know I have a pair?"

"Please. Give me some credit." She tossed her wavy red hair. "Like those boots don't have your name written all over them. They're your style."

And not Fallon's, which would be short skirts and pom-poms. "Sorry, that's not good enough."

"I'm friends with the UPS guy. And when he delivered my boots he complimented me on my taste. Said only one other woman in town had— what did he call it— bitchin' good taste. And that was you."

"So what? Maybe that's me in the photo. Maybe I let someone else borrow my boots. Did you ever think of that?"

"It crossed my mind for a second. But then I thought, gee, doesn't Brooke now work at Mirassu's since she had her hissy fit at Serrano's? Oh sure, I heard about it."

"Well, I have a lot to do today, so if you'll get out of my way—" Brooke shoved against Fallon's cart.

But Fallon put up a decent resistance, which must have meant that she hadn't been only marrying three different men in the past ten years but apparently also spending some time at the gym. "And then I also remembered that no matter what you said, you had a thing for Billy even back in high school."

"I did not!"

"Save it. I think he broke up with me because of you."

"And I think it might be time for you to get back on those meds."

"Funny. Look, here's what I propose. You and I both know it's not me making out in the vineyard with him—"

"We weren't—"

"Shush. Do you want someone to overhear you confess? I think you should turn me in. Tell everyone I'm the mystery woman. Pass go, and collect your $50."

Brooke didn't see this coming. "Why would you want that?"

"Are you kidding me? Billy and I were supposed to be the golden couple, get married and leave town together. Instead he broke up with me."

"So even if it's not true, you want a return to your high school glory days?" Brooke didn't like the sound of it. Fallon wanting to capitalize on Billy's fame made her stomach feel tight and queasy. Gigi was right about some women. They were coming out from the town's soft under belly.

Brooke hated living in a world where Gigi was right.

"For some reason, it doesn't sound like you want anyone else to know it's you in that photo. I could help you out." She lifted a shoulder.

"You want to help me out? Get out of my way," Brooke gave one last swift kick to Fallon's cart. Those kick boxing DVDs were coming in handy.

"Think about it," Fallon called out as Brooke got in line and paid for her purchases.

Think about it. Sure. She'd think about how Fallon suddenly wanted to be friends, after mostly ignoring Brooke since Fallon had waltzed back into town after her third divorce. Not like they'd ever been besties. Fallon had been part of the preppy squad back in high school, right along with Billy.

She put her groceries in the saddle bags and hopped on her Harley. Fifty dollars were coming to whoever identified her in the photo. In this town, someone would do it for fifty cents. It was like igniting a flame of competition among the townspeople, all a bunch of nuts with way too much time on their hands.

At least Stephan's blog was followed by about twenty people. So it wouldn't go far, not that it mattered if it went any farther than Starlight Hill because people were going to try to make her miserable until she fessed up.

Well she wasn't going to do that. Brooke Miller was made

of stronger stuff. Their little afternoon indiscretion was the end of it, anyway. Running into Fallon had only reinforced the fact that she and Billy were too different. They were friends now, and her goal was for Mirassu to rise again and clobber Serrano.

She'd happily do that with a smile on her face, but she wasn't going to be one in a long line of Billy Turlock baseball groupies.

After she'd dropped off her groceries at home, she headed out for the baseball diamond at Starlight Hill High. That's where she knew he'd be, probably signing more autographs and acting like a demi-god. She'd have to take him away from his admirers, because there was a fifty dollar bounty on her head thanks to her unique taste in boots.

Brooke pulled up to the back of the school and the field. One thing you could say about Starlight Hill besides its perfect grape growing weather was its unflagging support for sports. She'd been on the wrong end of that loyalty more than once. The turf on this field had been replaced before it needed to be, all while the theatre still had the same cloth ripped seats since the 1960s. Brooke wasn't into theatre, but she had always supported the underdog, not that it had done much good.

The resounding crack of a bat sailed through the nippy November afternoon. Brooke turned and saw Billy up to bat.

"Better. Try again," she heard him yell.

Then he dropped the bat and walked out to the guy in the middle who'd been throwing the ball.

Giving up baseball? Who did he think he was fooling? And why did he have to look so good while not giving up baseball? He wore blue jeans, a jean jacket that had seen better days and a ball cap on backwards. And still he made her mouth water.

Brooke didn't know much about the game, but she

thought she could identify the pitcher. He was standing in the same spot Billy had during the one game she'd been to years ago. Then let's see, there were first base, second base, third base and fourth base. Or was it home run base?

She marched to the edge of the field and shouted Billy's name. Before long, she not only had Billy's attention but the attention of every jock on the field. They all turned to stare at her. It's as if they could tell just by her posture she didn't belong here.

But Billy smiled, and walked towards her. "Hey. What are you doing here?"

"I should ask you that question."

"Isn't it obvious?"

"It looks like you're playing baseball."

"Very observant of you." His hand scrubbed his beard, and he grinned even bigger if it were possible.

"But I thought you were done with baseball."

"I am." Still smiling.

"Doesn't look that way." She jutted her chin in the direction of the boys, who seemed to be throwing the ball around now.

"I'm done, but these boys aren't. They need some help." He turned in their direction, then back to Brooke.

"Why? He threw the ball and you hit it. Seems to be working just fine."

"Well, Brooke, he needs to throw the ball so I can't hit it."

"Why would he want to do that?"

"Because if he throws the ball over the plate fast enough, no one can hit it."

"But what's the point?"

"Getting me out. No one makes a run if the pitcher is doing his job."

"Are you kidding me? Are you telling me the whole point of this game is for nothing to happen?"

He sighed. "Do you want me to teach you baseball? Because I can do that later."

Brooke handed him her phone. "We have a little problem. It seems a picture of us wound up on a website and there's a bounty on my head."

Billy frowned as he looked at the blog she'd pulled up. "It's not a very good photo."

"No, but it seems fairly clear what these two people are doing. I told you this would happen."

"All right, but who cares? How many people are going to see this?" He handed her back the phone.

"It doesn't matter how many, if one of them is Gigi."

He shook his head. "This is a small blog run by someone with too much time on his hands. She won't see it. And it doesn't matter if she does."

"You kissed me and someone took a photo of it!"

"Actually, Bungee, you kissed me. Not that I was complaining."

Had she kissed him first? He'd certainly kissed back. "Either way. I'm not sure this is the kind of publicity we need. Do you want everyone in town to think you're a playboy?"

"I learned a long time ago I can't control what anyone thinks of me." Billy suddenly reached out to the side of her head and caught a ball midair with his bare hand.

Shouts and whoops of amazement came from the boys on the field.

Billy turned and threw the ball back. "Guys, let's keep it on the field."

"Doesn't that hurt?" She stared at his red hand. The ball sailing through the air was supposed to be stopped with a gloved hand. Even she realized as much.

"I'm fine. But your head wouldn't have been, and you've

already had one concussion on my watch." He grinned again, shaking his hand out.

Concussion. Yes, it could be the reason she kept staring in his eyes. She'd been hit in the head too hard. On the other hand, maybe she needed something or someone to knock some sense back into her.

"Thanks. I guess you saved me."

"You're welcome." He grinned, and reached out to tuck a hair behind her ear. "Now do you want to go and stop distracting every male here?"

She glanced in the direction of the kids, still throwing a ball around. "I'm not distracting them."

"You're distracting me. I'm not thinking about baseball right now."

"Are you thinking about wine? Because you should be."

"Not even close."

She realized she was asking for it, but couldn't seem to help herself. "Tell me what you're thinking about."

"I'm thinking about you and me. How good it's going to be when you finally stop thinking about the past. When you stop worrying about what other people think."

"But I'm not—"

He interrupted her. "I'll see you later for the tasting."

Then he turned and went back to the boys.

He had it all wrong. She didn't care what anyone thought, never had. Did he know her at all? Okay, she cared a little bit about what Gigi thought because she might have some influence on Billy. Had intimated that Brooke might want to find another place to live. But more and more, it became apparent that Billy was in Starlight Hill living his own life and accountable to no one, least of all Gigi.

Still, ten years ago he'd let her down. Then as now, he'd owed her nothing. And that's exactly what he'd delivered.

* * *

BILLY LOVED BASEBALL. He liked talking baseball. Loved playing baseball and always had, but now found he also liked watching the game when he had no skin in it.

But as much he'd enjoyed being on the diamond with the kids, concentration had been in short supply. Especially when Brooke had arrived, back to the place where they'd first met, framing the fact that maybe it had been for the best that they'd never taken their friendship to the next level. With her ability to distract him, he might have never made it out of the minor leagues.

Brooke was a mess of contradictions.

A vixen and the girl next door.

A daredevil and a scaredy-cat.

He couldn't figure her out, and knew better than to try. He'd meant what he said. She needed time to figure it out. And he'd be there when she did. It would be good. Hell, it would be fantastic. If only he could convince her of that fact.

The photo bothered Brooke, and Billy understood that. Having photos taken without permission could be a helpless feeling, and Brooke wasn't used to this kind of attention. If he'd learned anything from Gigi, it was how to control the media. Someone had once taken a photo of him scowling in the dugout after a bad inning. It got to the point where he didn't want to move a muscle, self-conscious that his every move was being photographed and displayed on HD television.

Contrary to many of his colleagues, he'd never grown comfortable in the limelight.

But this was Starlight Hill, and Stephan had a two-bit blog he played around with. He refused to worry about it.

And now, a few hours later at the tasting with Brooke, he had to admit, the romantic candlelit ambience at Giancarlo's was perfect for a first date. Or a second one, if he wanted to count the picnic. But he was pretty sure Brooke didn't count this as a date. It was, unfortunately, business.

He watched with an odd mixture of pride and lust as Brooke stood at the bar nearby and uncorked bottle after bottle, pouring for Giancarlo, and discussing the attributes of each one. Even making suggestions as food pairings.

"How about this girl, Billy?" Giancarlo said, pointing to Brooke. "Is she something? The woman knows her wine."

"She does." She also knew how to fill out a sweater. Also how to kiss a guy till she'd sucked the marrow right out of him. He felt certain there was so much more she could do, and do very well, if only she'd let him find out.

"Sit down, you two. You're my guests for dinner tonight. It's the least I can do." Giancarlo waved them to a table.

Billy pulled out the chair for Brooke, and she sat down. "I can get the chair for myself, you know."

"You're going to argue with the man who saved you from a second concussion today?"

She cracked a smile. "No. I guess I'm not."

"Good plan."

She leaned in and whispered across the table. "What are we doing about the blog?"

Again they were back to the blog. "Why do we have to do anything about it?"

"Should we just let them have their fun and guess who the mystery woman is?"

"I think everyone knows it's you, Brooke. What's more, they want it to be you." For good measure, he threw a look in Giancarlo's direction, who smiled in their direction.

"Not everyone."

"Who doesn't?"

"Gigi, for one. And your ex-girlfriend, Fallon."

He hadn't spoken to Fallon in years. "What does she have to do with this?"

"She accosted me in the market, and asked if I'd let people think it's her. She has a pair of boots just like mine."

Of all the news he'd heard since arriving back home, that singular piece was probably the most upsetting. He'd thought to be rid of Fallon years ago, and she hadn't even approached him since she'd been back. "Did she tell you that?"

He felt pinned under Brooke's stare, those hazel eyes shimmering in the candlelight. "She did. I'm guessing your ex is not over you. And even if she can't have you, maybe she can have everyone think she has you."

"Yeah." The burning sensation in his gut was not altogether unfamiliar. "Or maybe she can sell her story to the rags."

"Why would she do that?" Brooke reached for her wine glass and took a big swallow.

"Money." Maybe he'd have to call Gigi about this after all. Dammit.

He didn't want Gigi swooping in now. She'd find out about Brooke and try to make her sign a binding press agreement. He'd never been comfortable with having the women he dated sign on the dotted line and promise not to talk about their relationship after it ended. Why begin a relationship assuming it would end? Had he ever started a game assuming he would lose, he'd have had to kick his own ass on sheer stupidity alone.

But he wasn't just Billy Turlock any longer. He was Turlock, Inc. and he couldn't forget it. His family depended on him. But Brooke depended on him, too. He liked the idea. It didn't make him want to run in the other direction.

"She wouldn't dare," Brooke said.

Brooke was probably right. "If she hasn't tried to sell her

story of the ex-high school girlfriend by now, why would she?"

"Because she's on her third divorce?"

Three marriages? He hadn't exactly kept up with Fallon. "I'm not worried. You shouldn't be, either."

"Is this why Gigi is so protective? Did something happen with a woman in the past?"

Self-confession time. He had a stupid past with women. "A few something's, actually. About a year ago I dated an actress."

"I think I saw a photo of you together in one of those tabloids."

"No doubt. There were quite a few of them. Every time we'd go out paparazzi would appear out of nowhere. Gigi began to get suspicious and sure enough, we found out every time we had plans to go out Mandy would call them so she could be sure they'd be there."

"She'd call the photographers?"

"She'd give them the names and places we'd be. Little did I know she was trying to resuscitate a flagging career. Trying to stay relevant."

"You're kidding. So she was just using you?"

"Don't look so surprised. But it's one of the reasons Gigi is protective. The other one is more complicated. "

Brooke's eyes were fixated on his, as if begging him to say more, even as he wondered if the whole thing made him look like a first class idiot. "And?"

He guessed it was his cue to spill his guts. "And there was the time I was engaged."

Brooke blinked. "Oh. I didn't know you'd been engaged before."

"Not my proudest moment. I didn't know her very well, which of course was my own fault. She told me she was pregnant, and it seemed like the most natural thing in the world to ask her to marry me."

Brooke studied the tablecloth. "Did you love her?"

"No." He was no stranger to love, having plenty of it all his life. Love from his mother, grandfather, brothers, friends, faithful fans and colleagues. He'd always expected when he did fall in love it would be a little something like the deep love he had for his family, but it hadn't ever happened. Plenty of lust, epic fails on love.

"So you were going to marry someone you didn't love?"

"I was willing to try to make it work for the sake of the child, but she wasn't ever pregnant. Faked the whole thing. Fortunately, she walked away with a promise not to talk about it for a nice sum of money."

"Geez. I feel like I have to apologize for my kind."

"I wish it had been the only time someone tried the fake baby angle. Problem was I'd never slept with any of those other women. I'd like to think I'm good, but damn, I'm not that good."

Brooke smiled. "I seem to remember some pretty big jock scandals made Look Here! Magazine."

"Everything they've ever printed about me is a lie. Please don't tell me you read it."

"It depends on how long the line is at the supermarket."

"Good answer. I've been luckier than most, or maybe it is because I have Gigi. But I've never been accused of a crime." Even when allegations were proven to be false, for too many of his colleagues the stain remained. Mom and Pop wouldn't have been able to bear it.

"Suddenly Gigi is sounding rather compassionate. If it were me, those women wouldn't be getting settlements. They'd be getting sentences."

"No mercy?" He rather enjoyed the same fierceness she'd once displayed for the whales and any other endangered species fixed on him. Brooke the fighter turned him on. She always had, except for when she pissed him off.

The bus boy appeared for the third time to refill their water glasses. "Hey man, can I have an autograph?"

"Sure." Billy said, and took the man's pen.

"It's great you don't charge for them like everyone else does," the kid said.

Brooke raised a brow and stood up. "I need to talk to Giancarlo anyway."

He signed the autograph made out to Carlos and watched out of the corner of his eye as Brooke walked over to Giancarlo. Not like he should be jealous of a man who looked old enough to be Brooke's father. He needed to get a grip if that were the case.

He wasn't a jealous man, but right now he wished Giancarlo wasn't standing quite so close to Brooke. Their conversation peaked his interest when Giancarlo put a hand to his chest for a moment as if he'd just heard amazing news. Then he nodded, and wrote down something on a piece of paper.

Brooke rejoined him at the booth. "Ready?"

He stood, and waved to Giancarlo as he rested his hand on the small of Brooke's back. "What was that all about?"

Brooke looked up at him and seemed to hesitate. "I gave him my phone number. You know, so he could call me personally when he wants more wine cases."

"Right." Billy kept walking, bothered more by every step.

Part of his media training had involved spotting the tell, the language of liars. Over the years, he'd fine-tuned it. He didn't know why, and could only hazard a guess as to why Brooke Miller had just lied to him.

CHAPTER 12

Why hadn't Brooke thought of this before? Giancarlo would be the perfect date for Eileen. Even with all the distractions tonight, Brooke couldn't ignore the obvious.

Giancarlo was a family man, a kind man, a generous man, and a man who should be the spokesperson for handsome older men. Maybe she should have told Billy the entire truth. She hadn't just given him her personal cell phone number for business purposes, but so that she could arrange a meeting between him and Eileen. The rest would be up to them.

Of course, eventually she'd tell Billy, but the timing had to be right. First it was up to Eileen to share that information with her son. She couldn't wait to call Eileen and talk up Giancarlo. She'd been patient, and now Brooke had a winner behind door number one.

"What are you thinking about? Not still thinking about the blog?" Billy asked as he slid the key in the ignition.

Well, she hadn't been but now her attention was right back on that subject. So many hurdles to overcome. Life should be easier. "What will Gigi do when she finds out about it?"

"Who cares?"

"I do. She'll get to be right. She didn't believe it when we told her we weren't interested in each other."

"And now?"

She'd walked right into that one. Was he going to make her say it out loud? Make her say how she thought about making love to him every night and sometimes during the day? What it would feel like to be under, or on top of, Billy Turlock? Not that she was picky about the position.

But she didn't want to be another one in his long list of conquests. No, it didn't matter to her what anyone else thought any longer. It mattered what she thought. And she didn't want to be added to the list. Period.

"I think it's pretty obvious we're attracted to each other." She folded her arms across her chest and tried not to look at him as she said the words. Didn't want to see his smug little grin.

"I agree."

"But I'm not going to sleep with you, Billy. I don't want to be one of your many female conquests." There. She'd said it, and let the chips fly where they may.

The car veered off the highway so quickly she thought they'd had a flat tire. Billy turned to her. "Dammit, Brooke, is that what you think of me?"

Fantastic. Pissed off Billy was even sexier than always-smiling Billy. She knew this, and still she'd poked the bear. "C'mon, I—"

"I thought I told you not to believe what you read. I didn't date half of the women who claimed I did."

"But even if you dated half of them—"

"Look, I have a past. It's not nearly as illustrious as the rumors. But this is different, you and me."

"No, it's not. I'm just someone you want now because you never had me." Back in high school, there'd been that undercurrent between them. That nameless something that led to the first and only time they'd kissed in the school parking lot. If they'd been any older, and she'd been any more experienced, she was certain it would have led to the back seat. And she'd have been one of many.

"Are you telling me what I want?" He asked through gritted teeth.

She was pretty sure the answer should be no, so she went for the safety of a non-answer. "I'm not an idiot."

Billy didn't say another word as he veered back on the road. They drove in a tense silence all the way to the vineyard, and Brooke jumped out of the car before he could open the door for her. She nearly ran to her cottage and opened the door.

She didn't need this. Another pissed off man. Turned out she had a certain talent for it with Billy. Still, she hadn't seen him this angry in a while. Or ever.

And now she'd had an argument with her employer, or non-employer as he was calling himself these days. Regardless, he owned this place and she'd insulted him. Might as well have called him a man-whore playboy.

Crap.

She went to the fridge and poured herself a chilled glass of Mirassu Chardonnay, her guilty pleasure. Maybe she should apologize, but she'd wait until tomorrow when he'd cooled down. Then she'd calmly explain her position. What they both needed was a few hours to calm down, and see reason. This thing between them couldn't happen for a lot of reasons, the main one being that they were both too explosive, and this thing between them, whatever it was, far too out of control.

The sudden raucous banging on her front door startled

her enough to spill a little wine. "Brooke! Open the door! We need to talk."

Great. Talk now? She didn't want to get in a yelling match, but she opened the door and moved aside to let Alpha Boy in.

"Can we talk tomorrow when we're both calmer?" She was now apparently the voice of reason, a frightening fact.

"No. We're going to talk now." He reached for his wallet, pulled it out of his back pocket and handed her a weathered card.

She glanced down to see Billy Turlock's official membership card to the Save the Whales Foundation. A long expired membership. She held it up. "This is expired."

"Yeah, no kidding."

"Don't you ever clean your wallet out? Why would you carry an expired card around in it?"

"Brooke." He said her name on the edge of a breath, sounding a little exasperated.

She met his eyes, now so warm and with no hint of anger left in them. A sudden thought rose to the surface, but it couldn't be true. "Is this the same—?"

"The one you gave me when I made the donation."

"Ten years ago? And you still have it?" She remembered that day. One more cause, one additional signature. Most of the jocks and cheerleaders had passed by and ignored her table and banner at lunch time. But not Billy. He'd stopped and signed the petition. It had entitled him a year's free membership. She still remembered the smile on his face when she'd handed him the card.

"Why do you think I still have it?" He asked softly.

He was talking with his eyes again, this time telling her things she was afraid to believe. "I don't know."

"If you think about it, you know the answer."

Instead of believing what she wanted to believe, her mind

took her back to a bad memory. "You made me believe for once that maybe we could be friends, and left, like I was nothing. You never even said goodbye."

He reached and pulled her into his arms, that crushing, bone melting feeling coming back to her in waves. "I didn't say goodbye because I couldn't look in your eyes and tell you I wasn't going to take the scholarship to Chicago. I was a chicken shit kid, and I was running in the other direction of all the things you made me feel. It was easier to leave without saying goodbye to you. I'm sorry."

Her arms came up around his neck. "Why is it you always do this to me? I'm shaking. You're scaring me."

"You're not afraid of anything but the dark, and we can keep all the lights on if you'd like." He bent down to kiss the softness under her earlobe, and she shivered.

She was afraid of a lot more than the dark right now. Afraid she was going to lose even more than her heart to this man. Maybe even her soul.

"I want you so much, and I don't know how to stop wanting you." She'd tried and failed miserably every time.

On the outside, they didn't match. But their hearts, somehow, fit together.

"Stop trying." His mouth came down on hers and she welcomed him inside, opening up to him like a flower.

After all this time, they would finally be together. The teenage jock and the decidedly teenage un-jock. But she didn't want to think about that now. Best not to think at all. There was only Billy, and his beautiful eyes and smile. His warm skin and strong heartbeat thudding against the pads of her fingers as she touched him. Everywhere.

They were connecting the dots again. He was the map and she was the road. She hoped she would survive the ride.

* * *

THEY'D LEFT a trail of clothes from the kitchen to her bedroom, and Brooke discovered jocks didn't limit their stamina to the playing field. Even with all her disdain for organized sports, she couldn't deny this was a nice perk.

After all the years dreaming and fantasizing the reality managed to top her wildest fantasies. Billy could be rough and gentle, fast and slow— no wonder her head was spinning. She'd gripped his shoulders as every deep and powerful thrust seemed to drill deeper into her heart.

Lying next to him now Brooke slept fitfully, and not only because of Billy's naked proximity. But simply because everything had changed.

She glanced at Billy, still asleep, his long eyelashes and peaceful expression making him look achingly vulnerable. He lay on his side, one arm splayed over her. Billy Turlock, in her bed. Billy, the man she couldn't help but want even if her head knew better. She softly traced the edges of a large scar on his left shoulder, and wondered exactly how many surgeries had taken place in the name of baseball. She'd heard many people suffer for their art, but she hadn't realized that a jock could suffer for his sport. The scar made it clear some amount of suffering had occurred.

How is it that she hadn't noticed the man's level of hotness before last night? Well, okay, she had because she wasn't blind. She could appreciate a red sunset, but it didn't mean she wanted to make love to it.

Long-haired guys with scruffy beards? Definitely the way to go. She should have switched types a long time ago. Washboard abs? Check. Strong and defined biceps? Uh-huh, check. Well, no point in staring. She'd already taken a full accounting and any more ogling was plain indulgent. She should let the man sleep. She'd definitely worked him out.

Brooke managed to slip out from under his arm and out of bed, throw her good robe on this time and not the ratty one. She softly closed the door to her bedroom and padded into the kitchen to check the time. It was eight o'clock in the morning. She and Billy had made love on and off for hours. Like they were trying to make up for lost time.

The coffee had started to percolate when she heard the bedroom door open and turned to find Billy framed in the doorway to the bedroom. Wearing nothing but a smile.

"Come here." His morning voice sounded low and throaty, and the gaze in his eyes left no doubt as to what he wanted.

"I'm making coffee."

"That can wait. I can't."

From the looks of a particular part of his anatomy, that much was obvious. Resistance was futile. She took his outstretched hand and followed him back to bed where he disposed of her robe like a magician. She let him push her back on the bed and he rolled on top of her.

"Billy, you're in my bed." This moment seemed surreal, as though she were walking around in a living and breathing fantasy.

His long dark hair fell around his face as he looked down at her. "Brooke, you're in my arms."

She reached up and threaded her fingers into that silky long hair. Funny thing, the beard hadn't even itched her at all. It only seemed to heighten her sensations. "You better not think I'm easy."

"Ten years isn't easy." He kissed the hollow of her neck.

"Ten years and two months."

"I stand corrected."

"And yes, I will go out on a date with you."

Billy's face split with a grin. "Thanks, babe."

"No, thank *you*."

"Mmmmm. You taste so good," Billy said, his lips grazing her nipple.

"Like what?" Brooke moaned.

"Like a woman. My woman."

Brooke drew in a sharp breath. Not only because of the words that hit her heart with the subtlety of a sledgehammer, but also because of what Billy could do with his mouth.

She heard the knock before Billy seemed to, since he was otherwise occupied. "Did you hear that?"

More rapping at her front door.

Billy raised up on one elbow. "We should punish that person's lousy sense of timing by ignoring them."

"Billy? Brooke? Are you in there?" There was no mistaking the shrill voice of Gigi. "Billy! Did you forget our meeting?"

Brooke froze. "Shit. It's Cruella."

"Calm down," Billy said, palming her ass. "Don't go anywhere. I'll get rid of her."

"No you won't. You have a meeting." Brooke closed her legs, and everything inside of her rolled and dried up. She was pretty sure her ovaries had just shriveled up and died.

"And it isn't for another two hours." Billy got out of bed and started picking up his clothes. Unfortunately some of them were still in the kitchen where she'd ripped them off him.

Brooke laid her head in both hands. "This does not look good. What are you going to tell her?"

Billy smiled. "That it's none of her business?"

"Good plan. I'll stay in here," Brooke said, and pulled the covers over her head.

"Chicken." She heard Billy's soft laugh as he left the bedroom, and a few seconds later heard him at the front door opening it.

"Your timing is spot on, as usual," Billy said.

Brooke didn't hear Gigi say anything but, "For crying out loud, put your shirt on."

Then they were both gone.

Guess he was going to that meeting after all. Well, that was fine. She'd use this alone time to gather her thoughts, and maybe get her sanity back.

She flounced out of bed, naked again, because Billy had a way of doing that to her. The robe went back on and she went back to the kitchen and her coffee.

So he'd stormed the castle after all. All because he'd kept a membership card she'd given him ten years ago. He was good. No denying that. Unless it was all real, and the odds of that were probably not in her favor. How good was he at cleaning out his wallet? Maybe he'd had a good game the day he'd found the card again. Refused to get rid of it after that. Superstitions, nothing more.

Wait. How pathetic could one woman be? Why couldn't she believe he wanted her? That just maybe they'd had something special between them, that unidentifiable spark even ten years ago?

Brooke picked up her cell phone and dialed the one person who might understand. "Are you busy?"

Ivey sounded groggy. "Just getting up. I had a delivery yesterday."

"How did it go?"

"Poor Jessie was in labor for twenty-two hours. She actually begged me to go find a gun and shoot her."

Brooke gulped her coffee. "Great. And you still want to have a baby?"

"Are you kidding me? I can't wait. She had a beautiful baby boy. All's well that ends well."

"If you say so."

One more baby boy brought into the world. In those rash moments when the moon was full and Brooke allowed herself to even think about having a child someday, all she'd ever wanted was a baby girl. A tough little girl who would kick ass everywhere she went. A girl she could teach not to be afraid of anything, certainly not something as stupid as the dark.

"What's up? Everything okay with opening night?"

"Everything's on schedule for December 5th. A very Christmassy opening, white garlands of light hung in the trees. I'm even thinking about getting a horse and buggy for old fashioned rides. Not sure about that yet, but either way it's going to be great. And I slept with Billy."

"Wait. Did I hear you right? There at the end. It sounded like you said—"

"Yes! You heard right."

"Wow. Okay, just wow. You slept with your high school crush."

"No! He was never a crush. He was my enemy."

"Your frenemy, you mean." Ivey giggled.

"We were friendly, when he wasn't annoying the hell out of me. When he signed my petitions."

"Stop trying to distract me with petitions. Tell me what it was like and don't spare me any details. You owe me!"

But Brooke found that she couldn't kiss and tell. Not this time. She couldn't put her finger on it, but this was new. Different. Tender somehow. Strange because she didn't think guys could be tender. And he'd certainly been rough and strong too, when he needed to be. And stamina. Yeah, there was that.

"Well?" Ivey was on the other end of the line, waiting.

"What do you want from me? I'm not a poet."

"Oh, so it's like that? You can't even speak of it. Wow."

"No! It's not like that."

"All right, then, give me something here. I haven't seen Jeff in 24 hours. Remember, he started a new rotation? I'm the wife of a resident. Give me a break."

"I'll give you one word: stamina."

Ivey sighed. "Oh yeah, that. That's important."

Brooke laughed. "I should go."

"No, wait." Ivey said. "What you going to do about this? I mean, he's your boss."

Whether he'd officially signed ownership over to Pop didn't really matter in the end. Billy had been the one to hire her, like it or not. "I don't know."

Brooke said goodbye to Ivey and put her phone down. It promptly buzzed across the Formica counter top. A short text from Billy read only: *dinner tonight, 6 PM my place.*

Not a question. This time, his confidence didn't piss her off. He'd have to be crazy not to realize she wanted to see him again. And again. It took all of a second for Brooke to type in her reply: *sure.*

Brooke spent the rest of the morning working in the small office next to the tasting rooms. Her staff was finally coming together. George, Eric told her, had been apoplectic at Eric's resignation. She still had plenty of more resumes to go through, though, and maybe even more of George's employees to hire. Not to mention spreadsheets the accountant had sent and a forecast budget for spending. She'd start out with a small crew, which was fine since this was a small family operation.

She'd already hired Genevieve from Sweet Southern Buns to cater on opening night. Her beautifully decorated Bundt cakes were becoming a legend in town. They tasted like they'd been dipped in a mixture of milk and heaven. Sooner or later she'd tell Eileen that the menu was set, and by then she'd likely be too preoccupied with her new dating life to give it a second thought. That was the plan, anyway.

Not that her plans always worked out smoothly, with no kinks along the way. As in her original plan to keep it professional with Billy, which had died a thousand deaths last night. They were now so professional that she was acquainted with his scar, and the way every muscle in his body tensed when she licked his earlobe.

Very professional.

Twisting away from the front door, Brooke worked on her computer, firing off a few emails, personal and otherwise. Mom wanted to know about Thanksgiving, which was coming up. Brooke fired off a quick reply that sure, she'd be spending it with Mom at the farm.

She checked in on Stephan's blog. Quite a few comments, none of which she took seriously. Several women claimed to be the woman in the photo. One of them calling herself "HollerGurl" claimed that the boots belonged to none other than Billy's ex, Fallon. One commenter wanted to know why anyone should care, while another one insisted he had the scoop if Stephan cared to raise the price to $1,000.

For the love of Pete, they really needed to get a movie theater in town.

The social media campaign was gaining followers every day, and their mailing list had grown to two hundred subscribers. Before long it was lunch time and Brooke's stomach growled. Gratified, she realized she hadn't thought of Billy in about two hours. Brooke got up to stretch and turned to see Gigi standing just inside the door frame.

She startled and fell back in her chair. "Make a sound next time! You almost gave me a heart attack."

"Sorry about that. I thought you heard me come in." Gigi closed the door to the office.

Uh-oh. Why did she suddenly feel like a caged lion? "So. How are you?"

"Good, good. I would ask you that question, but I already know the answer."

"Now wait a minute—"

Gigi held up her hand. "Save it. I've already heard it all from Billy. You two are together now, and I'm to sit back and accept it. Even if you both denied it a few feet from here, not two months ago."

"But—"

Gigi sighed deeply. "Honestly, I get so tired being right all the time. Is it wrong to want to be surprised every now and then?"

That pissed Brooke off and she reached across her desk and pointed. "You aren't always right."

"Really." She folded her arms across her chest.

"I meant what I said then. I wasn't interested in Billy."

"But things have changed."

"Well, yes." She squirmed in her seat, not used to being interrogated about the men she dated. But this was Billy Turlock, and she tried with every ounce in her being to give Gigi the benefit of the doubt. She'd heard the stories. Understood protection mode all too well.

"Why now? Did you suddenly realize how much he's worth?"

It seemed as though the top of Brooke's head would fly open with steam, cartoon-like, and rip right through the ceiling. "What did you say to me?"

"I know you wanted this vineyard. I know you'd approached the bank about buying it. Maybe this place is what you really want. Is it true?"

"Why is it so unbelievable to you that someone would want Billy just for who he is? Have you ever taken a good look at him?"

"Because I know you, Brooke, and women like you. Beautiful women who take what they want, and always have a hidden agenda. Always. The guy is never enough. They want more. Stability. A future. Money. You're no different. There's a reason, I know it, and I'll get to the bottom of it before all is said and done."

"You're not just insulting me, you know. You're insulting Billy. Acting like he alone isn't enough."

"Of course he is. He's a family man, grounded and down to earth. He's perfect for the right woman, but I think you and I both know that's not you."

Brooke sucked in a hard breath as the words kicked her in the gut. She would have argued, except that Gigi was probably right. Brooke wasn't the marrying kind and she wasn't going to spit out a bunch of kids. If that's what Billy wanted, she wasn't it.

But she couldn't give Gigi the satisfaction of knowing she'd hit the Bull's Eye. This was all a passing fancy on his part, because in the end they weren't right for each other. Sooner or later, Billy would figure that out.

"Listen. Billy misses baseball, no matter what he says about being with family again and back in his hometown. The vineyard is never going to satisfy him, and neither is this little town. The best thing for him to do is audition for the sportscaster job at Fox Sports next week," Gigi said.

"Next week?" There was still so much to do before their Grand Opening. Besides, wasn't he getting enough baseball hanging out with the local team?

"I'm sure he'll take care of his obligations here, but after that he needs to re-think everything. I encouraged this little sideline diversion of his, but I knew he wasn't done with baseball and the next logical step is broadcasting. This is what his agent wants him to do, and I said I'd help."

She couldn't see Billy sitting behind a desk. Brooke's mouth grew dry. "Is that what he wants?"

Gig scowled. "He doesn't know what he wants, like most men. He needs to be told, and led in such a way as to think it was his idea in the first place. I have four sons. I know whereof I speak."

Really. And Brooke thought women like Gigi ate their

young. "Well, I think Billy knows what he wants, and he'll let you know once he figures it out."

"Okay, we'll play it your way. Maybe he'll stay in this little town and be miserable. Is that what you want for him? You don't even know what *you* want. First you're not interested in him, and now you are."

Enough already. Brooke stood up and came out from behind her desk. "You want to know why I changed my mind? Fine, I'll tell you even if it's none of your business. He had a membership card!"

The puzzled expression on Gigi's face would have been comical had Brooke not felt like a homicidal maniac. With one swift move, Brooke turned Gigi around in her tracks and shoved her out the door.

* * *

BROOKE WOULD DRESS in her sexiest undergarments just in case. The silky black thong and matching demi bra would be perfect for tonight. In case Billy was thinking along the same lines she was. They'd been unfairly interrupted this morning by a woman who wouldn't be getting a Christmas card from Brooke this year. Or any other year. Ever. The woman was so obviously trying to get between Brooke and Billy by intimidating her. Feeding her with vicious lies about sports casting jobs Billy wouldn't be interested in if hell froze over.

He was here to stay in Starlight Hill. Kisses like that couldn't lie.

Brooke found her come-and-get-it-big-boy bra in no time, but not only could she not find the matching thong, there was no clean underwear in the entire house. Her kingdom for a pair of panties! This is what happened when she worked too hard and neglected to do laundry. Well, no time to do it now. She'd just go commando.

She pulled on her low slung jeans, praying she wouldn't chafe in her special places.

A few minutes later she knocked on his back door, and when he opened it in jeans and a long sleeved Hensley that strained against his pecs, Brooke sucked in a breath. His hotness factor had grown by leaps and bounds since this morning.

He pulled her inside the door and straight into his arms. "Should we take up where we left off now, or are you hungry?"

Nice the way their thoughts ran so parallel to each other for a change. Then he kissed her, so deep and long and hard that she lost her footing when they came up for air. It also rendered her temporarily incapable of a reply.

"Let's eat." He smiled and nodded, as if kissing her the way he had was a daily occurrence.

Meanwhile she felt pinned to the spot, practically incoherent. "Um, yeah. It smells good in here."

"Steaks." He walked towards the kitchen and she followed him.

"Who taught you how to cook?" Hopefully Eileen had. Brooke didn't want to hear about an old girlfriend, and she realized too late she'd taken a risk asking. Maybe his ex-fiancé had taught him how to cook. If so, she didn't want to hear about it.

"I did one of those local news spots a few years ago which was a cooking demo. The cook went on to get her own show. Me? I just begged her to show me how to cook a good steak."

"Which I'll bet she was more than willing to do." Brooke took a seat at the small two person round table in the kitchen nook. Her lips still felt bruised from that kiss, and she ignored the pinch in her heart that made her miss him when he was only four feet away.

"Lucky for me, her fiancé was a fan." Billy smiled and flipped the steaks.

Brooke's heart flipped right along with them. It happened every time he smiled. What was wrong with her?

"But don't get too excited. It's the only thing I know how to cook. That, and scrambled eggs. I hope you can live on that."

"Fortunately, you have many other skills."

Oh wow, panty-melting look again, which was of course, unnecessary seeing as she wasn't wearing any.

She fidgeted in her seat, her special places indeed chaffing. "Gigi came by to see me earlier today, and it wasn't social hour. She hates me."

"Ignore her. What did she say now?"

Brooke left out the part about how she wasn't the right woman for Billy. Not for a grounded family man. "She told me you're going to audition for a sport casting job at Fox."

Brooke wasn't imagining the fact that Billy froze for a second as he pulled a plate from the cupboard. She thought she could see the muscles bunching in his back.

Brooke stood up, and regretted it. More chaffing. "It's true, isn't it?"

He turned to her. "I was going to tell you."

"So I was right all along. This vineyard isn't your dream. I just never thought it would be sitting behind a desk on TV." She couldn't help it, but the thought of him leaving now after being gone for so long tore off a little piece of her heart.

"It isn't my dream. Look, I owe it to my agent. She went out of her way to get me this audition." He shut off the stove.

"Is this what you want?" Her breaths were coming short and shallow. *Get a grip, Brooke.*

He's not yours, and he never was. Time to let him go. Again. They both traveled in different circles, and all that.

She'd known it all along, just allowed herself to believe for one moment it could be different now.

Billy crossed the distance between them in one short stride and pulled her close. "I miss baseball, it's true. But I'm not convinced sports casting is for me. I'm doing it to appease them both."

Her hands went up against his strong pecs. "Won't they make you cut your hair?"

"I thought you hated my long hair."

"It's growing on me."

Billy laughed. "It took ten years, but good to know. Look, if it comes to a job offer, I'm not going to make any decisions without talking to you first."

Her heart seemed to stutter. "You won't?"

"Yeah. This thing between us? I'm not playing. And you —" One hand skillfully slid up her back and caressed her, making her shiver down to her toenails. "Are what I want."

She wanted to say that he shouldn't make promises he couldn't keep. That he shouldn't come waltzing back into town and make her feel like a virgin again. Like someone no man had ever touched before, because that's what making love felt with him. New. Scary. Thrilling.

Those green eyes were talking to her again. Maybe she hadn't imagined the tenderness she'd seen in them. Or maybe she was imagining all of this— getting caught up in fantasies she'd had many years ago. But all she could do was thread her fingers through long dark hair and say only a little of what was in her heart. "Okay."

Billy kissed her again and again, slipping his hand down to the small of her back. She tensed a little as his finger slipped inside the back of her jeans, obviously searching for a string.

He stopped kissing her and smiled against her mouth. "Not wearing any underwear?"

"Um, no. It's laundry day."

He pulled back and held her gaze for a long moment. "Sexy."

"I didn't do it to be sexy. Honestly, these jeans are kind of uncomfortable with no panties on." She squirmed under his touch.

"Let's see what we can do about that." One hand on her stomach, he slowly backed her out of the kitchen and up to the family room couch.

She fell back on the couch willingly, but tensed as he unzipped her jeans and slowly slid them off. Stripped half naked, she felt as vulnerable as a baby lamb.

Both of his hands swept down her legs from the top of her thighs to her knees. "So soft. Is that better?"

"Not really," she said, reaching to pull off his shirt, and letting him know what she wanted. All of him. Her palms went up against his warm, hard chest, feeling the pulsing beat of his heart.

"You're right. You're way ahead of me." He smiled, stood up and didn't tear his gaze away from her as he slowly unbuttoned his jeans.

"Hurry." She couldn't stop staring, watching him undress for her, biting her bottom lip in anticipation.

"Please never wear underwear again."

"I can't promise that," she said. "Because of the chaffing."

By the time they got around to eating dinner, the steaks were cold.

CHAPTER 13

hoever said some things were worth waiting for (Pop, more than likely) wasn't exaggerating. Billy still couldn't stop thinking of Brooke— the way she tasted, the sweet way she said his name as she came. His own rolling climax always left him feeling an unexpected pinch in his heart. He had one word running through his mind and it hadn't been the one he'd expected. Not 'more', although that one was a no-brainer. The one word that hit him scared him as much as it surprised him. Mine.

One day in Los Angeles, and he already couldn't wait to get back to Starlight Hill, but now he sat across from Gigi in his least favorite LA Bistro, the one which made him feel like some kind of antique. This was a place to be seen, according to Gigi, but he didn't care to be seen. Was it too much to ask for a burger, hold the fame?

He'd already satisfied both Gigi and his agent with the audition. With no idea how he'd done, he decided to put the whole ordeal to the back of his mind. They couldn't pay him enough to sit behind a desk and critique other players. To talk about their injuries, and try to forget that not long ago that had been him on the field, trying to play through the pain. Getting criticized for every failure.

Speaking of injuries. "I've been working a little with the local high school team. There's a new way to throw that can prevent injury, especially the Tommy Johns elbow. The trick is getting the kids to throw the new way."

"High school coaching?" Gigi asked.

Billy grinned. "The Starlight Hill Panthers."

"And I'll bet you're their only claim to fame."

"Hey, they haven't done too badly without me. State Division two years in a row."

"Really. State division. Well, that's sweet." Gigi took a sip of her iced tea.

He didn't much appreciate her tone. "*Sweet?* It's where dreams start."

"Don't tell me you're considering coaching high school baseball. Billy, we can do much better than that. Just give this broadcasting thing a chance."

He stared at her. "I am. What do you think I'm doing here?"

"I know it's hard being on the other end of the game, and suddenly being the one to critique and comment from an armchair."

"Yeah." He was fairly certain she didn't know the half of it, but he let her continue.

"But what you have to add to the game is still important. No one knows the way another pitcher feels but one who has already been there. You know the stress, the pressure. Most of all, you know the game."

He did know the game, which is why he could do some good out on the field with those kids. Teaching them early on how to avoid career ending injuries. Gigi wouldn't understand.

"Are you about ready to go?"

"Let me just visit the Ladies' room," Gigi said as she got up.

Billy pulled out his cell phone and checked for messages from Brooke. Nothing except her last text this morning, a simple: *miss u.*

Brooke happened to be the single thing he missed most about Starlight Hill. He missed her smile, missed the way she hadn't worn panties, hell he even missed arguing with her which was plain weird. Sure, he'd known the sex would be great between them but even he'd had no idea how mind-blowing.

He quickly texted Brooke: *Steak tomorrow night, clothing optional* just as Gigi came back from the powder room with a tall brunette in tow.

He stood as Gigi made the introductions. "Billy Turlock, meet Jonie Taylor. You won't believe this, but she's one of your biggest fans."

"Nice to meet you." He was no idiot. If Jonie was a fan he was the Easter Bunny.

She fondled his hand and licked her lips, tossing her hair back. "I can't believe I'm meeting you. Have you thought about acting? You definitely have the looks for it."

He coughed. "Acting?" Although truthfully, it could be said he was doing a good job acting like he was interested in having this conversation.

"I'm an actress and I need someone to help me run lines."

"I'm sure Gigi knows someone who could help. Good luck with that." Billy took a seat and went back to his phone. Brooke hadn't texted him back which meant she was work-ing. He probably should let her do that.

Jonie took her cue and said goodbye, while Gigi sat back down. "That was impressive, and borderline rude."

He looked up from his phone. "Was that some kind of a

test? To see how vulnerable I am to a beautiful woman? Because it was a little too obvious."

Gigi pursed her lips. "It was a test, but not the way you thought. I didn't see you check her out once."

It took him half a second to realize she was right. He hadn't even checked out her ass as she walked away, and he was an ass man through and through.

He swallowed. What the hell was wrong with him? "And your point?"

"My point is that your General Manager has entered into dangerous territory. I know it's her on your mind. Isn't it?"

Billy put away his phone. He'd just texted Brooke to be sure to forget to wear panties again. "Yeah. So what?"

"Have you considered the fact that as your general manager, you've probably given her more leverage over you than any other woman? Ever?"

Here we go. Gigi was about to bring up a sexual discrimination lawsuit, an abuse of power allegation. "Say what you have to say. Go ahead, don't let me stop you."

"She's got you where she wants you. Boss/employee relationship. There's already that photo of the two of you on the blog. All she has to do is make an allegation of improper advances and suddenly you're making front page news."

He couldn't deny they'd been improper with each other, not that either one of them had any complaints. "You don't know her."

"Maybe you think you know her, Billy, but the need for money can and will change people. Once upon a time she might have been a friend, but now she's the woman who wanted the vineyard you bought."

He hadn't thought of it that way. Not Brooke. He'd been fooled before, but this was different. They had a connection, and he wasn't imagining it. This was his second chance, dammit, and he wouldn't blow it.

Then again, Brooke had wanted to buy the vineyard and he wouldn't soon forget how pissed off she'd been to lose it. But she'd also been the one to resist coming to work for him.

Until he'd sweetened the pot. There was an uncomfortable pinch in his gut. "I appreciate your concern, but you're wrong."

"I know about the photo of the two of you on that insipid blog. Did it ever occur to you that she might have been the one to hire a photographer?"

"Not for a minute." He'd seen how upset she'd been, worried Gigi would find out and make her life hell.

"She knows most of the people in town, and maybe she wanted them to know she was with you."

"What would that accomplish?"

"It's proof, in case she ever wants to sue you. She would wind up owning the vineyard if she plays her cards right."

"If she wanted proof, she could have a lot better than that lousy photo."

Gigi held a hand to her neck. "For the love of all that's holy, please don't tell me you're sending nude photos to each other. Sexting, or whatever you kids are calling it. Please tell me you're not doing that, or I won't be able to sleep tonight."

"Calm down. I went to fame school, didn't I?" No nude photos of him, even though he wouldn't mind receiving a few from Brooke.

"I don't get it. Why her?"

"Because it was my idea." Seemed like all his life he'd been chased by girls, and then women. Sad women who didn't seem to want to be anything but an attractive accessory to him.

But one girl had never chased him. He hadn't allowed himself to think what might happen if she didn't feel the same. No way were those amber eyes lying to him. She was all in.

Of course, she had wanted the vineyard before she'd ever wanted him.

* * *

BROOKE FELT good about progress towards opening date, and they were on target to open on time as long as nothing went wrong. Even better, Billy had been asked to open up the city's parade with the Boy Scouts, a nice segue to their Grand Opening. If all went as planned, maybe this year might be the one to erase the trajectory of all her past Holiday failures. She wasn't exactly Ms. Christmas.

And tonight, only one week from the upcoming dreaded start of The Holidays that began with stuffing the ass of a dead bird and eating until passing out, Eileen and Giancarlo would have their first date. Brooke was standing by, ready to hear a full report as soon as Eileen returned from her date.

She had a good feeling about this. Even if Giancarlo was at least a decade younger, Eileen was in great shape and looked much younger than her years. They'd probably go out a few times, keep each other company, and who knows what might develop? Maybe a nice romance for Eileen, and Billy would thank her once he found out. She happened to love the many ways he said thank you.

Brooke had poured herself a glass of Merlot and sat down on the couch to watch a marathon of *Sex Sent me to the ER* when there was a soft knock at her front door. She opened it to find a rather disheveled looking Eileen, her dress a little rumpled. Her hair stuck out a little bit in the back. Unnerving, as Eileen was one of the most put-together women Brooke had ever met.

"I thought you were going to call me." Brooke waved her inside.

Why did Eileen look so flushed and so— Oh. No.

"Whew. That was something." Eileen plopped down on Brooke's couch.

"I thought you two were going out to dinner." Where had things taken a wrong turn? Dinner. That was all she'd arranged for these two sex maniacs.

"Oh we did, dear. And afterwards to his place for a movie."

"His place?" Brooke tried to keep the rising panic out of her voice. And here she'd thought she could trust Giancarlo. He looked so harmless. What the hell did she know?

"Yes, it was a good movie. It was the one about a man who comes home from war and—"

Brooke sat next to Billy's mother on the couch. "Eileen! What happened? Are you okay?"

"Heavens, yes. Better than ever. Only I didn't know sex had changed so much." Eileen patted her hair, smoothing it down in the back.

"You had sex? With Giancarlo?" Billy would kill her for this. His sainted mother having sex with Giancarlo. On the first date! And all Brooke's damned fault. Because she didn't want to share the menu.

"Don't worry, we were safe. You know, I've read about this before but I never thought it would happen to me. It really is true that Italians make the best lovers. No wonder my ex-husband hated them."

Brooke swallowed the contents of her wine glass like a shot of Whiskey. "So you're okay with all this? He didn't hurt you did, he?"

"Hurt me? Oh my dear, no. In fact, it was all my idea. He thought we should wait. He's such a gentleman, really."

Such a gentleman. Brooke wished he were here right now so she could tell him how *much of a gentleman* she thought he was. She cleared her throat. "Did you by any chance mention to Billy that you were going on this date?"

"No, and I don't want him to know, either. A mother can't share these types of things with her sons. But that's what I have you for." She patted Brooke's knee.

Brooke got up to pour herself another glass of wine. "I don't feel comfortable keeping this from him."

"You want me to tell him I had my first real orgasm tonight? What are you thinking?"

Brooke went from filling up her glass halfway to filling it to the rim. She'd prefer a shot of anesthesia right now, but this would do. "I was thinking maybe you could just tell him you're dating Giancarlo."

"Sure. Well, there's nothing wrong with him knowing that. That is, if I decide to keep dating Giancarlo. Could I have some of that, please?" Eileen gestured to the wine.

"Wine? You're drinking wine now?"

"I was thinking about what you said. Being a bit decadent once in a while won't kill me. And my son and father do own a winery."

Great, she was being all kinds of good influence for Billy's mother. She poured far less than a half of a glass and handed it to Eileen. "What do you mean if you decide to keep dating him? I thought it went — well."

"It was fantastic, but if that's what I've been missing maybe I shouldn't just rush into settling for the first man that comes along."

"But I thought you said Giancarlo was a real gentleman."

Eileen took a sip of wine. "He was, but shouldn't I see what else is out there? What do you think?"

What she thought is that she didn't want to see Billy's mother meet some serial killer and wind up on Dateline. Eileen waited, as though she expected an answer from Brooke's vast wealth of experience. "I think you should date one man at a time, and see how it works out."

Eileen sighed. "I do wish I could talk to Henrietta about

all this. She's my oldest and dearest friend. What a bitch. If I told her what I did tonight, she'd blab it all over town. I *do not* want my sons to hear about this. A woman's got to draw the line somewhere, and I know you'll be discreet."

Discreet? Basically, Brooke would take this conversation with her to the grave. "You better believe it. No one will hear it from me."

"I've got loads to think about." Eileen set her wine glass down. "What about Thanksgiving? You are coming, right?"

While Brooke was grateful for the subject change, Eileen had segued right into another difficult subject. *The Holidays.* Yes, Billy had mentioned it to her, and of course she didn't want to say no to him. So she'd hemmed and hawed and kissed him until he forgot what he'd asked.

Brooke detested family holiday get-togethers, and then there was Mom. She'd be expecting Brooke to come to the farm since she'd done that every year for the past several. Since she didn't spend all that much time during the rest of the year with Mom, Brooke gave Mom *The Holidays.*

"Well, there's my mother. I told her I'd spend it with her. She expects me."

"Invite her, too. I have the room."

"Um— well." Billy's family might be large, but they'd started to grow on her. But adding Mom to the mix?

Why not just start a fire and let the whole place burn down to the ground?

What if she talked about her natural shampoo line throughout the entire dinner? What if she saw the mansion Eileen lived in and started talking carbon footprints? Ever since Mom had become Mother Earth she was annoyingly intolerant of people who would have resembled her younger self.

"When Billy first bought me that house, I thought I'd spend a lot more time entertaining. But then Pop started to need me more. Speaking of which," Eileen said as she rose, "I should go since Scott is hanging out with Pop. If I don't get home soon who knows what could happen? Last time I left him with Scott he took Pop target shooting."

At the front door, Eileen, who was a hugger, put her arms around Brooke and gave a little squeeze. "Thank you for this. I feel like I'm a new woman after tonight."

"You're welcome, but it's not my faul—, I mean it's not my doing."

"Nonsense, if not for you I'd have never considered dating someone younger. Someone like Giancarlo, who still has a bit of pep left in him, if you know what I mean," she elbowed Brooke. "I think I'm going to enjoy being a Cougar."

* * *

"You can do this." Brooke stared at her reflection in the bathroom mirror. No matter how many affirmations she recited to herself, her eyes were telling her she didn't buy it. The Holidays had arrived, and with them dread had settled into the pit of her stomach and made a picnic there. Mom would be coming and that was bad enough, but there was every possibility that Eileen had invited Giancarlo.

Brooke hadn't told Billy. There just hadn't been time between selecting tablecloth linens for the grand opening, taste testing the new November crop (Billy had a natural talent for detecting oak flavors), ordering glassware and carafes. And yes, the menu. A thousand tiny details had been discussed and agreed upon. And even if Billy did seem to sneak out every afternoon for what she suspected was a coaching session at the local high school, she had his attention the majority of the time. So did the vineyard.

Billy walked through her front door at precisely four thirty, just as Brooke had changed into a sweater dress. The man was so punctual it hurt. He no longer knocked on her door, and she no longer knocked on his.

"I'm not ready." She glanced at him, dressed casually in a button up shirt and a jacket that for Mom's sake Brooke hoped was faux-leather. No tie, because he hated those. Amazing how well he cleaned up even if he always looked his best in a baseball jersey, cap on backwards. Or wearing nothing at all.

"You look ready." He opened her refrigerator and helped himself to a glass of juice. Weird how familiar they were becoming with each other, when she hadn't been that way with anyone since— had she ever felt this relaxed, this connected to any guy?

"I have to wear something cute, but environmentally friendly. Also something that doesn't look like I paid more than ten dollars for it."

"I'm a guy, so I'm a bit clueless but how does an outfit look environmentally friendly?"

"It should be something that you can air-dry or hang on a line."

He cocked his head. "People still do that?"

"People like my mother." This dress wasn't going to work. In a minute she would reach for her blue jeans and to hell with everyone. Brooke pulled off her dress and ran into her bedroom. Of course Billy followed because he always did when he saw her removing clothes.

Somewhere in her closet she had a nice pair of slacks. Brooke moved clothes and the hangers made their slappy, snitty noises as they were shoved up against each other.

Billy came up behind her, drawing his arms around her waist and pulling her back into his chest. When he lowered his head she felt the gravelly feel of his beard, which always tickled.

"I didn't know your mother would make you feel like this."

Brooke sighed deeply. Men. "It's not so much her as it is The Holidays. But they are so closely intertwined I can't tell the difference anymore."

"What do you want to wear?" He practically whispered in her ear. It sounded so much like when he asked 'does that feel good, baby?' and 'do you like that?' that Brooke's spine tingled.

"I want to wear my boots, but those are leather which means a cow died for them, and also they cost me an insane amount of money."

"Is the price tag still on them?"

"Don't be silly."

"Wear them. And as much as I'd like to see you in nothing but your boots, let's wait until later for that. What will you wear with the boots?"

She turned around to meet his smile. He was right. She was going to wear what she wanted. Brooke settled on her little black dress with matching boots.

They picked up Mom at the farm, who was dressed normally in a red simple dress with her normally braided hair in a bun. She didn't make a single comment about Billy's convertible, probably because it was a hybrid.

Instead she made light conversation with Billy about baseball and the World Series. Brooke didn't even know Mom new anything about baseball, much less the actual name of the team that had won it. Naturally the conversation changed as they pulled up to Eileen's home. Home wasn't quite the word. Mansion on steroids more like it.

"For the Love of Pete, it must cost a small fortune to water this lawn and keep it this green." Mom stared, jaw gaping.

"Mom, please," Brooke hissed when Billy got out of the car to open the door for Mom.

"I'm only stating the obvious. We use some wonderful new irrigation methods at the farm. Maybe you'd be interested," Mom said to Billy when he opened the passenger door.

If he was surprised to discuss irrigation systems before Thanksgiving dinner, he gave no indication. "I'd love to hear it sometime."

Sure he would, because that's what they'd all like to do tonight. Talk irrigation systems. They had a great one at the vineyard, and neither one of them could talk about it for long without their eyes glazing over.

Eileen met them at the door, and the smells of turkey and stuffing wafted out to greet them. "Come in. Wallace is already here. We're just waiting for Scott. And don't worry, Billy, we have plenty of real turkey and mashed potatoes because I do realize some people have a death wish."

"Thanks, Ma. You know me. Life on the edge." Billy smiled and introduced Mom to Eileen.

Brooke followed her inside, feeling suddenly nervous. As though he might realize it, she felt Billy put his hand on the small of her back and guide her inside.

If ever there were a home that split the line between extravagant and homey, Eileen's home fit the bill.

Rich and expensive looking tapestries stood in stark contrast to family photos everywhere —from Billy pitching at a Sliders game to Scott in his Army fatigues. A photo of Wallace in front of a large cabin, dozens of photos of Pop with the boys. Very few of Eileen, but one photo of her sitting like the Queen Bee between her three boys. Billy looked to be about thirteen in that photo. That young face devilish and happy, the way she remembered him. He always seemed to be smiling.

Eileen led them into the large and open family room with

floor to ceiling windows, and Brooke's breath hitched when she saw Giancarlo alone in the corner.

"What's Giancarlo doing here?" Billy asked to know one in particular.

Eileen wrung her hands together. "Ah, well, I thought you might like to have someone in the business. Good conversation."

"Hey, thanks Mom. Great idea. Isn't it, Brooke?" Billy's arm lingered around her waist.

"Great." Brooke could use a few minutes alone with Giancarlo, but this was not the time or the place. Too late anyway, as Billy walked right over to Giancarlo and began to chat.

Eileen pulled Brooke to the side. "You have to help me get rid of him."

"Get rid of him? But why?" If anything, this was an issue for Brooke to worry about. Eileen had done nothing wrong, unless you counted poor impulse control but Brooke wasn't in any position to judge.

"The fool has come up with the most outlandish idea. He wants to marry me."

Brooke nearly choked on her own spit. "M-m-marry you?"

Eileen leaned in closer to whisper. "He said it's the honorable thing to do, and that he's afraid he's disrespected me."

Brooke covered her mouth to avoid cussing. This was turning out to be far worse than she could have anticipated. Ever the gentleman, Giarcarlo would now want to make an honest woman out of Eileen. If only someone would drag the gentle Italian into the twenty-first century.

"Okay. Here's what we're going to do. I believe we can count on him to be discreet, so no need to worry on that account. He'll keep his mouth shut. Let me talk to him."

"Thank you. I can't deal with a love sick gentleman caller, although it is kind of nice. But I have potatoes to whip and butter to melt. A turkey to baste. Marriage is not part of tonight's agenda." Eileen recited the items off while she threw occasional lustful glances in Giancarlo's direction.

Brooke took a deep breath and flew into crisis mode. She caught sight of Mom, seemingly under Pop's spell. Laughing, even. That seemed under control for now.

She moved to join Billy, still talking to Giancarlo, less that situation veer wildly off course. Surely Giancarlo would not think to confide in Eileen's son, or ask for her hand in marriage. No, that would be highly irregular.

Brooke sidled up next to Billy, and he threaded his fingers through hers without missing a beat. It didn't take two seconds to realize the men were talking grapes. Thank heavens for that. She gazed up at Billy, amazed at how much he'd learned in the past two months.

The past few late nights spread out in front of his fireplace tasting different vintages— encouraging him to develop a sophisticated palate— they were beginning to make a difference.

"Who's carving this year?" Wallace asked.

"I probably should," Giancarlo said and both Wallace and Billy looked at Giancarlo like he'd just said the world was flat.

Brooke swallowed.

Fortunately, the men ignored Giancarlo as if maybe he'd been overcome by a spell for a moment.

"Odd years it's Scott's turn, and even years you and I toss a coin," Billy said to Wallace.

"Guess it's coin tossing time," Wallace said, pulling a quarter out of his pocket. "Heads or tails?"

Brooke pulled Giancarlo aside while the coin tossing was going on. "How've you been?'

Giancarlo pulled out a perfectly folded handkerchief out of his pocket and wiped his brow. "I'm a little nervous."

Brooke played dumb. "Oh yeah? Why?"

Giancarlo leaned in. "Between you and me, I've proposed to Eileen."

"So soon?"

"When its right you know. I've waited a long time to find a woman good enough to replace my blessed late wife, but it's finally time."

"Did she say yes?" Brooke turned to see Billy had won the coin toss. Some amount of ribbing seemed to be going on between the brothers.

"Well, not exactly. She looked a little bit surprised and then she said she had to beat the potatoes."

Brooke cleared her throat. "I'm sure she didn't expect it. Maybe you should take it a little slower. You had one date."

"Three dates now, actually. But we're very compatible, believe me. And – what's done is done. It's my fault, really."

Brooke didn't want to go there, but maybe speaking in euphemisms might work. "Nothing is done. You don't have to buy the cow because you had some steak. Do you get me?"

He smiled and narrowed his eyes. "Why are you talking about cows?"

Brooke sighed. "I just think that Billy and his brothers might need a little time getting used to the idea. They don't even know you two are dating. Can you imagine how a marriage would go over with them? They're a protective bunch. Why not ease into it? Maybe first you could tell them you're dating. Wait a few months, and then tell them you're engaged."

The doorbell rang and out of the corner of her eye Brooke saw Billy open the door to Scott and his date. The brothers grabbed each other in a bear hug even if Brooke would swear they'd seen each other a few days ago at the vineyard when she caught Scott giving free tastings out of tank number ten and solved that particular mystery.

Another thing Brooke would have to talk to Billy about regarding his family. Scott couldn't keep bringing women around to sample the wine, family business or not.

Yeah, she'd told him that when she'd caught him red-handed, but he'd only smiled with that trademark Turlock grin. Told her he preferred beer, but when in Rome ... He didn't take her seriously, of course, and why would he? She wasn't the owner.

Tonight he was here with — no.

When Billy's big body was no longer blocking the way, Brooke noticed Fallon. Dressed casually in jeans tucked into the long Dominatrix boots that were like Brooke's.

And as much as Brooke would try to enjoy The Holidays this year, throwing her lover's gorgeous ex into the mix might be a little more than she could handle stone cold sober.

She tried to ignore the pang of hot red angry jealousy churning through her gut when Fallon and Billy hugged. Fallon lingering a little too long, and whispering something into Billy's ear.

"Wine?" Giancarlo handed her a glass which she couldn't accept fast enough.

Fruity and nutty. Way too sweet for a red wine so obviously a port of some kind. Mirassu didn't do port. "Who bottles it?"

"From my collection. Aged since 1960, a very good year for me. I brought it since tonight is such a special occasion. Thanksgiving, and the day I proposed to Eileen."

Brooke swallowed hard, and Giancarlo walked away, an idiotic smile on his face.

"Hey Brooke," Fallon said as she strutted over. "Like my boots? I know you do."

"Nice touch, wearing those tonight. Are you hoping someone here will notice and want to collect fifty dollars?"

Scott joined them, a beer in each hand, and handed one to Fallon. "You two getting reacquainted?"

Fallon smiled and Brooke tried to paste one on her frozen face.

"Brooke's the general manager at Billy and Pop's vineyard. She's the bomb," Scott said with a grin.

"Oh, so that's why you're here. I wondered," Fallon said.

Right. It couldn't be because she and Billy meant anything to each other. Fallon was going to go ahead and pretend she didn't realize it was Brooke in that photo with Billy kissing the breath out of him.

And why had Scott brought her here tonight anyway? Was he being passive-aggressive about the tank sampling? The Holidays were right in line with making Brooke feel small, insignificant and alone. And Mom hadn't even had anything to do with it. Yet.

She scanned the room for signs of Mom, but didn't see her. All she could see was Billy, coming toward her. Brooke's heart sped up a little bit, like it did when she'd had a shot of espresso. Was this what Ivey felt like when she saw Jeff?

The feeling was a bit like a shot of adrenaline coursing through her body. Like she'd just run long enough to get a runner's high.

Oh, she didn't like this feeling one bit. It could get addicting.

"Can I get you anything, babe?"

Brooke hadn't expected this at all. Hadn't expected him to be so— obvious.

Fallon squealed her surprise. She was one horrible actress. "Oh, so you two are— together? Wow. This is something. Do you remember how much you hated each other back in high school?"

Scott laughed. "My brother never hated anyone in his life. Well, except for reporters."

Fallon tossed her hair and one hand on her hip, turned to Brooke. "You hated Billy. And all jocks. Don't try to deny it now."

"I won't. But I've recently discovered that jocks have many ... redeeming qualities." She threw Billy a significant look. "Like stamina."

Scott laughed again.

Dang, she felt mean right now. She was definitely going to hell.

Billy grinned, kissed her neck and lingered. "I'm not done showing you all my redeeming qualities, either."

His fingers trailed down her arm and then curled around her hand, squeezing it tight. Brooke could have sworn she felt her womb contract.

"You two need to get a room," Scott said, taking a pull from his beer. "Huh, Fallon? What do you say?"

Fallon appeared speechless. Brooke had seen that particular look in someone's eyes before. Specifically her own. Raw and unbridled envy. Pure and simple.

"Everyone! Dinner is served," Eileen announced. "First, I have an announcement. Some unexpected but fantastic news."

For the first time, Brooke noticed Giancarlo standing next to Eileen, proud as a peacock. Oh. No.

"We're getting married!" She beamed at Giancarlo.

Billy stiffened beside her, and let go of her hand. Both he and Scott said at once, "What?"

"Are you out of your mind?" Pop shouted from the other side of the room. "You're too old to get married. And we have real problems now. Melinda helped me find the secret recipe, and that sonofabitch stiffed me again. From beyond the grave!"

Super. The Holidays would be awesome this year. They were already off to a great start.

CHAPTER 14

Billy couldn't have heard right. Mom getting married? To Giancarlo? Since when had they even been dating? Before he realized what he'd done, he'd dropped Brooke's hand and moved towards Mom and Giancarlo. An explanation would be nice. Mom could do what she wanted with her life, but why spring marriage on the family at Thanksgiving dinner?

"What do you mean you're getting married?" Wallace asked in his pissed off tone.

That's when Billy realized that both of his brothers flanked him on either side. Which couldn't be good for Giancarlo. He almost felt sorry for the man for a nanosecond.

"Look, just because I'm a woman of a certain age doesn't mean I can't be happy and in love again. It's my second chance, boys."

Giancarlo, who had to be a good decade younger that Mom, had a sappy look on his face. "Mine too."

"Well, hell. Congrats. Welcome to the family." Scott put down his beer bottle and embraced their mom. He shook Giancarlo's hand.

"Mom, just a few weeks ago you were asking me about online dating. You're moving a little too fast," Billy said.

Mom laughed. "I didn't need online dating. Thanks to Brooke, I've met the man of my dreams. I have to admit, I was a little shocked when he asked but somewhere between whipping the potatoes and stuffing the pie shell, I knew. I just knew."

Billy froze. What did Brooke have to do with this? He'd asked her to talk to his mom about the menu, not fix her up. "Brooke introduced you?"

"Wasn't she just here?" Mom asked, scanning the room.

Billy turned to where he'd just left Brooke. She'd moved and now stood behind the eight foot Ficus fern he'd given to Mom last Mother's Day.

"Here she is," Fallon said, pointing in the general direction of the potted plant.

Brooke emerged from behind the fern, scowling at Fallon. It couldn't feel great to have every eye in the room on you, yet Brooke handled it, which made his chest pinch oddly.

"It's true, I fixed them up. Dinner. I arranged for them to have dinner. I, for one, think they make a great couple."

There was a ringing silence in the room. Brooke stood alone, chin tilted up slightly, and again an odd feeling pinched his chest. He had the sudden incomprehensible urge to wrap his arms around her. He'd never been consciously aware of the desire to hug a woman before. A strange feeling. He'd wanted to touch Brooke a lot in the past few weeks, but not once had he thought about how much he wanted to hug her. Right now, she looked like she needed one.

Even if she'd lied to him. But if he was honest, he felt relief flood through him as he realized what she'd kept from him. It could have been worse.

Still, he didn't like it. Brooke should have cleared this with him first.

"I think that's such a loving thing to do." Brooke's mother stepped forward, and put her arm around her daughter.

"Yeah, it's great. Now does anyone at all care about my problem?" Pop asked. He still stood waving around an index card.

"Let's talk about that later," Billy said.

"I agree," Wallace piped up and turned to Giancarlo. "Seems like you two are rushing into things."

"Listen to my boys, talking to me about rushing into things," Eileen laughed. "Each one of you never listened to me when I told you to slow down with a decision. Because you always realized when a choice was right for you. Now please, give me the same respect."

"Sorry to say, gentlemen, but your mother has a point. This is her business. Her decision." Melinda said.

"Thank you, Melinda!" Mom said.

Had his mother taken leave of her senses? Getting married again, at her age? After Dad left, she'd never even dated anyone else. Now one date and she was engaged. How was he supposed to be okay with this? Or fine with the fact that Brooke had arranged it all? Without telling him?

"Maybe we should eat and talk about this later?" Brooke asked.

"Good idea, but there's not much to talk about. There's lots of planning, though. A wedding! At our age." Mom smiled next to Giancarlo, and strangely she looked excited and not at all in need of Prozac.

Billy shut his eyes and pinched the bridge of his nose. A wedding.

"Does anyone want to hear about my problem now?" Pop asked. "If you're done prying into your mother's personal life?"

"Yeah, Pop, what is it?" Billy asked.

"It's not instructions to grow the perfect vine. It's advice for a happy marriage. The stupid man thought he was a poet. He's likened a marriage to a healthy vine that produces good fruit. Respect each other, put each other first, and never go to bed angry, blah blah blah. Nothing we can use!" Pop said.

"Maybe we could," Giancarlo piped up, with a longing look towards Mom. Blech.

Melinda now stood next to Pop, rubbing his back. "There, there. It will all work out."

Before long, they were all seated around the table, watching Giancarlo carve the turkey. Strange to see his mother, a man by her side. Not that Giancarlo didn't seem like a perfectly harmless man, even if Billy hadn't had him checked out yet. He would have already accomplished that, had Brooke thought to share that bit of information with him.

She sat next to him, still not saying much. Despite his confusion, Billy grabbed her hand under the table and squeezed. She had plenty of time to explain all of this to him later, and explain she would.

Scott was another one who had some explaining to do. He was the brother who always brought home strays, but this was over the top. Billy didn't need one of his high school exes sitting next to him, where she'd made sure to find a place. She kept leaning a little closer than necessary to pass him a dish. Accidentally brushing her leg against his. Laughing a little too loudly at everything he said. That sense of desperation was no more attractive to him now than it had been in high school.

"Can we have the wedding at the vineyard?" Mom asked.

"Sure," Billy answered.

"That sounds *so* romantic," Fallon said from next to him, brushing up his leg again. "Don't you think?"

Billy didn't answer, since he wasn't the best person to decide on the romantic virtues of a wedding in a vineyard.

But if his mother wanted to get married there, she would. After he'd put Giancarlo through a proper background check.

"Are you thinking of a summer wedding? In June the vines are full and it's beautiful." Brooke spoke up.

"Summer? I wasn't thinking we'd wait that long," Mom said, batting her eyelashes at Giancarlo.

Billy froze. He was close enough to feel Brooke's thigh tense next to his. Turns out all along he'd inched his way closer to her, and away from Fallon.

"But Eileen, you need time to plan the wedding. We're going to have our grand opening in a few days. June would be great," Brooke said, and Billy thought he heard a little desperation in her voice.

There was every possibility that this turn of events had shocked her as much as it had everyone else.

"When you put it that way," Mom said. "Let's do it up right."

"Makes sense." Giancarlo nodded.

Billy relaxed, grabbed Brooke's hand and squeezed again. This time she squeezed back.

Fallon put her hand on his thigh and rubbed it. "It's so awesome that you can give your mother the wedding of her dreams."

Carefully, he dislodged Fallon's hand from his thigh. "Yeah. Awesome."

Later, after everyone had their fill of turkey and then some, and the guests began to trickle out, Billy waited until he saw Giancarlo leave. Satisfied that the love sick man wasn't going to be staying the night, he and Brooke left last, dropping off Melinda at the farm.

Finally, they had a moment alone in the car.

"I'm exhausted," Brooke said, throwing her head back on

the headrest of the passenger seat. "How will I get through Christmas?"

He reached for her, putting his hand on her knee. "I don't know what you're complaining about. Your mother was great."

"For once. But The Holidays seem to bring the craziness out of people. Billy, I didn't know your mother would want to get married to the man." She glanced at him, and though he only took his eyes off the road for a moment, he swore her eyes were watery.

Which couldn't be true. Brooke, to his knowledge, didn't cry.

He spoke softly. "Why didn't you tell me you'd fixed them up?"

"I meant to, but then I thought ..."

"That I wouldn't like it?"

"And I don't like this, either. I arranged dinner for the two, not a lifetime together."

"Kids these days." Billy laughed, and tried to make light of it.

It was easier to laugh than to take the love sick expression on Mom's face seriously. He wanted that for himself, but not so much for his mother. Selfish, okay, but damn.

"It's not funny. We have less than seven months. Maybe they'll change their minds. But what if they actually go through with this?"

"Then we'll have a wedding." They'd reached the manor house, and he shut off the car. "As long as the background check clears."

Brooke followed him up the steps to the main house. "Background check? I wouldn't have fixed your mother up with someone I didn't trust. Foolish romantic that he is, Giancarlo is a good man. He's a fixture in Starlight Hill. A widower ten years now, who raised four beautiful daughters."

"I'm sure you're right, but a background check wouldn't hurt." He opened the door and waited for Brooke to walk inside.

She didn't make a move to come in, and her eyes flashed with heat. "You don't trust me."

"What? Of course I do, Bungee." He reached for her, and pulled her inside.

"Face it. You don't trust me to find a proper man for your mother."

"Not true."

"Then you would forget the background check. You have to admit, this is better than online dating!"

"No argument there, but I asked you to get her input on the menu. Not fix her up."

"Well, it turns out she needed this more. Besides, she wanted tofu on the menu!"

So that's what this was all about. "Did you fix her up so you could have total control over the menu?"

She didn't meet his eyes. "Maybe."

"Brooke ..."

"She needed this. She'd become obsessed with tofu. Obsessed! I was doing her a favor. Can't you see how happy she is?"

"She wants to get married, and she just met the man!"

"What can I say? Apparently he works fast."

"All I can see is that you like control in every aspect of the business."

"I told you that when you hired me, and you still hired me!"

He couldn't argue with that. He had. And actually, he still didn't regret it. "All right. Look, from now on let's just be honest with each other. Tell me when my family is driving you crazy."

She looked him square in the eyes. "Billy, your family is driving me crazy."

"Thanks for all the honesty." He grabbed her wrist, and easily twirled her into his arms.

She put her hands against his chest and gave him a little shove. "And why were you holding hands with your ex tonight?"

Yeah, now they were getting somewhere. He'd have to guess Brooke had seen him slide Fallon's hand off his thigh, and made other assumptions.

"Ah. She put her hand on my thigh, and I took it off."

"Oh. Well, what was she doing there anyway? Am I supposed to believe it was an accident she wound up at Thanksgiving dinner?"

Thanks to Scott and Fallon, Billy found himself on the defensive, when he'd hoped for a passionate apology tonight. "Believe me, I'll have words with my brother. But I have to believe, knowing Scott, she asked if she could come. Sometimes that's all it takes with him. He's got a hero complex."

"She's interested in you, I hope you know." Brooke moved to the lighted balcony, where she stared into the dark night. There was a new moon but even so out here in the country the darkness was encapsulating. Complete. It had to be difficult for someone who feared the dark.

"But I'm not interested in her." He came up behind her, one of his favorite places to be. He slipped his arms around Brooke, pulling her into his chest.

She didn't resist, but leaned back into him. She was so small in his arms, it felt like he could pick her up and put her in his pocket.

"Billy, what are we doing?" She almost whispered.

If his head hadn't been bent down next to hers, he might not have heard her. He turned her around his arms.

"Whatever you want. Right here. Right now." His hand drifted up underneath her black dress and palmed her glorious ass.

Underneath his palm, Brooke shivered. Hopefully not just from the cold that had descended on the autumn night. "Here? Now? It's cold."

"I'll keep you warm. We're alone, no one around for miles, and the balcony is your favorite place. Admit it." He drew her tiny face to his lips and kissed her hard and deep. When they came up for air, her eyes had softened.

"But if we do this, I'll never think of the balcony the same way." Brooke smiled against his mouth.

"I'm good with that."

She pushed away from him and scooted herself into a sitting position on top of the stone ledge of the balcony. One finger beckoned him to her side.

He didn't know how Brooke managed to pull at two different organs at once, but she did. She'd been the only one who ever had. He felt the sharp thrust of pure lust as he got between her legs, and she pulled at his belt.

He took a condom from his pocket, and she slid it on with a smile. "Always ready."

When it came to Brooke, he'd be crazy not to be. He pushed up her dress to her waist and slid off his pants. Then he was inside of her, wet and slick, driving into her. When she cried out his name and he followed, nearly screaming too, he realized he'd been so distracted his thrusts had pushed her dangerously close to the ledge. He pulled her back.

"I got carried away," he said with a groan. "Sorry."

"Don't be. That was fun." She moaned softly, and for a

second he wondered if he had fallen in love with the female version of Evel Knievel.

The thought stopped him short. Holy shit. Since when was he in love with Brooke?

"What's wrong? You looked scared. I wasn't going to fall. And anyway, it's a short six foot drop. We'd only get a little bit banged up. Not like we would die."

He pulled up his pants, smoothed down her dress, picked her up in his arms, and carried her inside. "I'm not going to lose you over the balcony."

Later in bed, as Brooke lay on top of him, all her glorious wild hair splayed over his chest, she pushed up on her chin. "It goes both ways, you know."

"What does?"

"You're not being honest with me, and you know it."

He tugged on a strand of her hair. "I already told you, she put her hand on my thigh. I took it off."

"Not what I mean," she said, caressing the scar on his shoulder. "Does it hurt?"

"No." Sometimes, when he was with Brooke, he forgot he had a shoulder much less a bad one.

"Because when I saw you helping the guys play, I wondered if you should be doing that."

"The reason I had to quit is I can't throw the way I need to in major league baseball. Not on a consistent basis."

"So you could maybe coach?"

"Yeah. Actually, Coach is retiring and he'd like me to take his place."

"Really? Why don't you do it?"

He wouldn't expect Brooke to understand, but coaching a high school baseball team would be a step down. According to Gigi, and pretty much everyone. "Is this you, trying to get rid of me so you have the vineyard all to yourself?"

"No, this is me trying to get you to be honest with yourself. Maybe this vineyard isn't what you want. It's what Pop wanted, and you're doing it for him."

"So what's wrong with that?"

"Why not do what makes you happy?"

"I am happy. Especially when you stop talking and use your mouth for something else."

She laughed. "I'm serious."

He grinned. "So am I."

She grabbed his face and framed it between her hands. "Billy. All I'm saying is it doesn't have to be all or nothing. You could coach. Or maybe you should take the sports casting job, if it's what you want."

She wasn't fooling him. The sadness in her eyes was gratifying. "I'm not taking the job."

"If you want it, you should. I want you to be happy."

"What I want is to stay right here. With you." His hand slid down her silky smooth back and down to her perfectly shaped ass. A guy could get addicted to Brooke.

"Even in this boring little town?" She laid her head down on his chest, and he couldn't see her eyes.

"Who called my hometown boring?"

"Gigi said you'd never be happy here."

Every muscle in his body tensed. He was so damned tired of Gigi trying to protect him. Those careless words had obviously hurt Brooke.

He grabbed a handful of her hair in his hand. "She had no right to say that to you."

She lifted her head, her hair disheveled the way he loved it, a wild mane around her face. Her eyes were soft and liquid. "I kicked her out of my office."

"Good."

"But later I thought, maybe she's right. Maybe you can't be happy here. It's not fair that you spent most of your life working towards a goal, and then you have to leave it all behind."

"You know, we find ourselves in a precarious position right now. You, hater of jocks, encouraging the man you're sleeping with not to give up his sport. Ironic, isn't it?"

"Believe me the irony is not lost on me. But for once, I want to look in those green eyes and see a man who looks as satisfied with his life as by all accounts he should be."

He rolled on top of her. "I'm satisfied with my life. Do you want me to show you how much?"

Then he showed her without words. No more talking, but only touching and feeling. Learning and memorizing the landscape of her body.

Forgetting everything and everyone because she made it so easy.

* * *

FIVE DAYS from their Grand Opening on December 5th, and Brooke's lists were making her crazy. She had at least ten of them. Pretty soon she'd need a list of her lists.

A ten foot tree sat in the middle of the open floor, and some of her temporary staff were decorating it. Garland and white fairy lights were hung and wreaths every few feet on every available wall or door space.

Christmas had come to Mirassu.

"Where's the list with all the outdoor decorating that needs to be done?" She shuffled the papers that were laid out all over the wine bar. Rather than working in the office, she liked being right in the middle of all the action. Where she could watch everyone, and make sure they were doing what they should be.

Everything. Had. To. Be. Perfect.

"Right here." Eric found a yellow lined piece of paper and handed it to Brooke. "What do you need me to do?"

"Get me some Valium?" Brooke asked. "No? Fine. Then why don't you go double check our inventory? I want to make sure we have enough of the Pinot."

"Right." Eric took off in the direction of the wine cellar.

The worst thing that could happen would be to run out of their new line. She'd test tasted the latest crush, and it was quite possibly some of the best Pinot she'd had in a long time. Velvety smooth with a hint of apple. It could wind up being the new Mirassu's signature label, if all went well. It might even win the next private label contest. That would kill George.

Judging by the response from the invitations, half the town would be here on opening night. Including George and Chelsea. Too bad. Brooke hadn't seen how she could neglect to invite them, but hoped that they'd have the decency to decline. No such luck.

So she'd have to mingle with her ex and his fiancée for the first time since the night they'd announced their engagement. The same night she'd insulted George and quit on the spot. Not exactly her proudest moment. She didn't want Billy to know about that night, and there was no telling what George or Chelsea would let slip. Her plan was to keep Billy and George apart as much as humanly possible all evening.

Billy. She found that she wanted to be the kind of woman he thought she was. The kind of woman he seemed to see when he looked in her eyes, studying her, like he couldn't quite believe she was real. This morning she'd woke to find him staring at her. Thankfully not in a creepy stalker way.

Still, she'd hit his arm. "What? Okay, goofball. Stop staring. Have you never seen a woman sleep?"

"Can I help it if I enjoy it when you're quiet? Which is only when you're sleeping."

"Brat."

At which point she'd climbed on top of him and showed him how loud she could get. He'd wound up covering her mouth that time. Afterwards, she'd drifted to sleep again, only to wake up and find him gone. He left her a note saying he had a meeting with Coach.

She didn't understand why he wouldn't come out and admit how much he missed baseball. It had to be a guy thing. And the reluctance to talk about feelings, definitely something she understood. But there had to be a way he could keep his status as a former baseball superstar and also coach high school baseball. Yeah, in the wide world of sports it might be considered a step down but so what?

Brooke's cell phone rang and she checked the caller ID. No time to talk to anyone that wasn't of utmost importance. But it was Ivey calling again, for the third time in as many days.

"Hey," Brooke said as she picked up the phone.

"You picked up! I was getting ready to leave another voice mail. You do remember me, don't you? Ivey Garner? Your bff?"

"I'm a bad friend. I'm sorry. It's crazy, getting ready for opening next week. So many things to do."

"So delegate."

"I am, but—"

"Wait. Don't tell me. You want everything to be perfect."

"Well, okay. Sue me. It does have to be perfect." Billy depended on her, and she wouldn't let him down. Not when he made her feel so— so— what was the word?

"Some little thing is bound to go wrong. Go with the flow, enjoy it. Everyone is talking about this. It's going to be great, no matter what."

"George and Chelsea are coming."

"No."

"I had to invite them. But I didn't expect them to come."

"That's ballsy of him. Do you think he'll be a problem?"

"Nah, I got it. If he tries anything, I'll kick him where it hurts." He wouldn't ruin this day for Billy, Pop, and Eileen. Even Scott and Wallace were excited.

"How are things going with Lover Boy?"

Brooke felt herself smile. "Good." So good. She didn't have words for how good. Fantastic, maybe.

"Uh-huh. Care to elaborate?"

How did a girl say it exactly? Without sounding like an idiot? *He makes me feel — wanted. Safe.* "I'm not sure how to explain it. I— he— he's so—"

"Oh for the love of Pete, Brooke, you're in love!"

"No. I'm not." Why did her face suddenly feel like someone had lit a match next to it?

"You fooled around and fell in love," Ivey said and started singing the song.

"Stop. Don't be stupid. How can I be in love? It can't happen. It just can't." First Eileen, now Brooke. All around, women dropping like flies. Well, she couldn't do it. She wasn't naïve like sweet Eileen. No, Brooke had her mom to remind her that the Miller women were unlucky enough. And if Mom wasn't enough, Brooke had a string of failed relationships to drive the point home.

"It's about time you fell in love. I was beginning to think you might have a missing gene."

"I don't have a missing gene. Can I help it if I got an early education in what not to do? My parents taught me well."

"Good, then you'll just avoid those mistakes."

"Falling in love would be the mistake." She only wanted to enjoy this time, as long as it lasted. It might go down as the single most erotic time of her life.

"You don't believe that," Ivey said. "Look at me and Jeff."

"Sure, when you want to talk about young first love. That's powerful."

"Stop with the first love thing. So what if you didn't meet someone in high school? Not too many people did. What if this is your first love?"

"C'mon, Ivey."

First love at her age? Didn't that usually happen when you were still so young you might as well believe in the Easter bunny than in the fact that two people were forever intended for each other? And yet, if she were being honest she had to admit that she'd always envied Ivey and Jeff— it was all so romantic. They'd been each other's firsts in every way. Five years apart, and they still loved each other because they'd never stopped. Le sigh.

Well, apparently she still believed in fairy tales. Just not for her. They were for other girls. Girls who cried, girls who liked pink, unicorns and rainbows. Girls like Ivey and Genevieve.

Not Brooke.

She didn't want to put a label on what she and Billy had. "So what, exactly, makes you think I'm in love?"

"Oh I don't know. Maybe it's the fact that you haven't talked about— it. At all."

"It?" Really, sometimes Ivey could be so vague.

"Sex, Brooke. You haven't talked about the sex. And you always liked to talk about it. Almost like a man, for crying out loud."

She hadn't talked about the best sex she'd ever had in her life? Seriously? Maybe it was because it felt too private, somehow. Which was strange because she told Ivey, her best friend since high school, pretty much everything. Why hadn't she told her about the mind blowing, exciting, and toe curling sex with Billy?

"I haven't?" Brooke squeaked.

Brooke was still trying to figure that out when Ivey spoke. "I think it's because this time maybe it's too special. You're not having sex, you're making love. It's different. Maybe it's because you fooled around and fell in love." Ivey started singing again. At least she had a good voice.

"Stop it!" Brooke laughed into the phone.

"So what is going on between you two?" Ivey pressed. "Can I have a relationship status update?"

"It's complicated." Brooke answered. And she wasn't kidding or being cute or trite. Complicated was how she'd describe Billy in a nutshell.

"He's not being honest with me. Something is going on, I can tell. He's not done with baseball, no matter what he says."

"What if he isn't?" Ivey asked.

"I'm not exactly jock girlfriend material." Fallon, his ex-girlfriend and ex-head cheerleader, now she was a jock girlfriend. Definitely not Brooke.

CHAPTER 15

Billy gazed over the balcony gazing at the land he'd once assumed would be nothing but trouble, and only a promise he'd made to the grandfather he adored. The vineyard looked beautiful this morning, bathed in the glow of the soft moonlight on the eve before their grand opening. His place.

Yes, this would work.

He'd finally calmed Pop down, and made him realize that his contribution to the family enterprise hung on more than an old frenemy's secret recipe. The old man had listened, and decided that singing to the grapes would make them sweeter. If it worked as he thought it would, he planned to write down his own secret recipe, songs and lyrics included. Fine with Billy. Even Brooke had accepted Pop's almost constant presence among the rows of vines. Every now and again Billy would catch her laughing with Pop, tossing that wild mane of hair, genuinely appearing interested in what he had to say. And every time something inside Billy's heart cracked open.

Shit, he had it bad. Who would have thought in a million years he'd wind up falling for Brooke Miller? He had, for one.

A long time ago. Ten years to be exact, from the first time he'd kissed Brooke Miller in his car after a Varsity basketball game.

All those years ago, he'd found her standing alone outside waiting for a ride, shivering in the cool January air.

"Hey, Bungee," he'd said. "Did you come see the game?"

She'd given him the Death Stare. "Are you kidding me?"

"So, no?" He grinned. So what, he'd enjoyed pushing her buttons even then. "They won."

"Oh joy." She shivered in her thin short sleeved black top and jeans. No jacket. She might not be anything like the cheerleaders he usually dated, but when it came to clothing it seemed to him that all girls were created equal. Ill prepared.

He slipped off his varsity jacket and offered it to her. "Here."

He might as well have offered her a rattlesnake for the way she looked at it.

He rolled his eyes. "Seriously?"

"My ride will be here any minute." Her voice shook a little, probably from the cold.

"Suit yourself."

A second later he caught her staring longingly at the jacket, and shoved it into her hands. "Thanks," she said, falling into it.

She was so tiny that the sleeves of the jacket hung well over her hands. "What are you looking at, Hotshot?"

"You. Is that a crime?"

"Where's your girlfriend?" She said the word girlfriend in the same tone one might say asshole.

"If you mean Fallon, we broke up."

"Oh yeah? Why? Is she not perky enough?"

Well, hell, why not tell her? "I'm going to Chicago State on a full ride and I guess she's upset I didn't ask her to marry me and come along." He shrugged. *Women.*

Brooke's eyes widened. He'd probably never seen her that animated before. "You're going to Chicago State?"

"Is that so shocking? My grades are good enough." He didn't appreciate the stupid label being attached to every jock.

Brooke shook her head. "No, it's just that's where I'm going."

"Yeah?" That wasn't a surprise, since Brooke might well be the smartest girl in the class of 2004.

Brooke nearly smiled at him. He hadn't seen her smile much, but the few times he had there'd been a strong pull of lust that followed. It didn't make any sense, but he figured he didn't have any control over those natural impulses. Teenage guy and all.

"Maybe I'll see you there." Brooke said, which shocked him.

But then again, college would be different and there wouldn't be all of the clear lines between cliques and groups of kids. That's what Mom said, anyway.

"Hell, yeah. We should make plans to meet up."

Brooke had been about to say something when the sky let loose with a cloudburst that had the few remaining stragglers after the game running for their cars.

"Come on," Billy grabbed Brooke's hand and tugged her along to his car.

Once inside the car, she turned to him, hair damp, black eyeliner smeared. Looking a bit like a drowned squirrel. "I said I have a ride."

"Yeah, well you can wait for them here." He handed her a few tissues from out of his glove compartment.

Brooke started wiping away at her face, and a funny thing happened. All the black eye make-up came off and underneath it all was a freaking knock-out. Who knew? Brooke had amazing hazel eyes— eyes that looked right through a person. How had he not noticed that before?

She caught him staring. "What? Did I miss something?" She pulled down the visor and blotted at her face.

"No. You just look much better without all that black shit all over your eyes."

She gave him a long look. "What do you know Hotshot? We can't all be cheerleaders."

"I know you're beautiful. Without all that shit on your eyes." There. He'd said it. The worst she could do was jump out of the car into the pouring rain. He pretty much had her now as a captive audience.

Brooke surprised him by laughing. "Tell me what you really think."

How was a guy supposed to let that opening go unchecked? "All right. I think you should let me kiss you. Right here, right now."

She stared at him, incredulous. "What's wrong with you? Is this some kind of a joke? Did you and your buddies come up with this one? Let's see if we can get Brooke to loosen up?"

She put her hand on the car door, even if the rain was still coming down in sheets.

He put his hand on her arm. "Don't go. You don't have to kiss me. Sorry I asked."

She sat back in her seat and those gorgeous eyes narrowed. "Why did you ask, exactly?"

He lifted a shoulder. "Because I'm a guy. And you're beautiful."

"It's not like I haven't been kissed before, lots of times. Ted Coffington kissed me last week."

He scoffed. "Then let me show you what a jock kisses like." Dammit, why couldn't he stop?

"Why? Is it different?"

She couldn't seriously think— shit, Billy, stop it. Stop messing with her. She could be your first friend at Chicago State. You could hang out and study together, maybe even a double date or two. But kissing her might change things. Maybe she'd get all hung up on him like Fallon.

Nah, not Brooke. Right? "I guess I'd have to leave it to you to tell me."

Silence permeated the inside of his car, and outside the rain softly pelted the roof of his car. Brooke gazed out at the dark smoky night, and then turned to him.

"All right. Let's give it a try."

Not in his wildest dreams had he ever expected she'd take him up on it. His palms broke out in a sweat. "Yeah?"

"Why not? But if you tell any one of your friends, if you tell anyone, Billy Turlock, I swear I'll personally castrate you."

"Well, let's not get ahead of ourselves." Plenty of time to talk about that part of his anatomy later. He hoped. "You're going to have to come a little closer."

"Why don't you come closer?" She narrowed her eyes suspiciously.

So far this was not going well. He didn't have a big car, but why did it feel like there were one hundred feet between him and Brooke?

But something in him, probably his hormones, took over and Billy eased his large body closer to Brooke erasing some of the distance, real and imagined, between them. At the same time, he reached for her neck, pulling her closer. He was gratified when she didn't resist and leaned in closer to him.

Truth told, he didn't hold out much hope for that kiss. Figured it would be a big fat zero and they'd both move on. He hadn't thought the one kiss would not be enough, but that's exactly what happened.

After the kiss, which did include some tongue action, Brooke gazed at him. "That wasn't so different."

It had been for him, but for the sake of saving face he had to agree. "Let me try again."

"Oh, nice try."

He'd grinned and pulled her close again. This time the kiss surprised them both. He could tell it had for Brooke, because she moaned a little and one hand reached for his hair. The kiss lasted long enough for Billy to get hard and all the windows to steam up.

When Brooke pulled back she'd said, "Okaaay. Enough of that."

Right. Enough of that, Billy had to agree. Much more and he'd be begging Brooke to get in the back seat with him. And that would definitely change everything.

Turned out Brooke's ride didn't show, so he'd driven her home himself. On the way they'd talked about Brooke's latest cause, Save the Whales or the elephants or the tigers. Who could remember now? Of course he'd promised to sign the petition, as always.

Also promised that they'd be in touch, so that they could make plans to meet up in Chicago. Brooke had smiled again, and the lust factor skyrocketed into the double digits.

"I was worried I wouldn't know anyone in Chicago," she said as she got out of his car. "Even though it is a jock, I'll take it. Good night, Hotshot."

"Night, Bungee."

But there'd been no Chicago State for him. Turned out he'd been spotted by a talent scout. When faced with the option of playing baseball in the minor leagues or going to Chicago to freeze to death, the option was a no-brainer to an eighteen-year-old man-child. Mom had tried to talk him out of it, telling him that an education was priceless. All the stuff one might expect from a parent.

He hadn't listened. More than anything he wanted to play baseball.

Brooke, naturally, had never been more than a second thought in his addled teenaged brain. Nor had any other girl. He'd been too caught up in his good fortune, the newspaper headlines, the pride of his town. He would play baseball for a living; maybe work hard enough to make it to the major leagues.

He didn't tell Brooke personally, but she'd obviously heard, just as everyone else in Starlight Hill. She'd never talked to him again.

Every now and again when he'd been in Chicago, it wasn't so much the University and missed opportunity that called to him but the girl he realized attended it. The girl whose one kiss forever held top billing in the marquee of his sex life, above girls who'd given him far more.

Talk about second chances.

He understood flings, having spent much of the past ten years with them playing front and center in his life.

It was convenient. Easy.

Brooke Miller was no fling. Not for him.

She fit him like his favorite glove. His family loved her as much as he did, clearly. And he was beginning to think that despite her occasional complaints about them, she did love his family right back.

Giancarlo's background check had returned and the man was practically a saint. So while he didn't want to think of what unsaintly thoughts had crossed the man's mind to want to marry Mom so quickly, Billy had to approve. He couldn't have picked a better man himself. Thanks to Brooke, his mother was the happiest he'd seen her in decades. And she'd stayed away from DateaDeusch.com.

Yet for the first time in his life, he wasn't sure what the girl in his life wanted. Brooke didn't seem to need him, other than for sex. While he was more than happy to provide an endless supply, he wanted more.

The jock and the anti-jock weren't even an issue any more. Despite what Brooke believed, he understood baseball had to be a part of his past. No matter how much he missed it. That part of his life was over, and one day it might be easier to go to the major league games and be happy for his friends and former teammates. Right now it only made his gut pinch with envy, a feeling he didn't much care to indulge.

Brooke hated athletes and what they tended to represent, yet she'd encouraged him to find a way to stay involved with the sport.

He wasn't sure what to make of that.

But with any luck she felt the same way he did. She'd want to take this to the next level— marriage, babies, the whole stinking bit. It had never in his life held such appeal.

After all, if she didn't have strong feelings for him, why would she risk a job she obviously wanted and needed by sleeping with him?

* * *

Brooke wasn't sure how she felt about the media when it came to opening night. They'd been falling all over themselves to get photos of Billy and coverage of the opening of the hometown hero's vineyard. Articles appeared in the paper as quickly as she could get a press release out. It made sense because it was a nice human interest story: retired pitcher returns to hometown and infuses the local economy. Several travel magazines had approached her regarding future articles, all of them focused on Billy. Free publicity.

Still, she wanted to limit their time and access on the night of the event. What if they caught a photo of her kicking

George's family jewels? Because she would in a heartbeat if he dared to do the slightest thing to sabotage this night.

"Brooke, where do you want these chairs?" Scott asked, carrying a couple of the folding chairs she'd ordered. If all the RSVPs were any indication, tonight they would need extra seating.

"Just take them through the kitchen, and Eric will show you." Brooke said, waving in the general direction.

She carried a clipboard with her lists, and yes, a damn list of her lists.

Scott smiled as he walked by. "Everything looks great."

"Thanks." She'd forgiven Scott for the faux pass of inviting Fallon to Thanksgiving dinner.

Turned out Fallon had played upon his sympathies, saying she was alone and without family. Scott, Brooke had just found out, couldn't seem to leave his missions on the fields of Afghanistan. He had the same need to fix people and situations that Ivey did. And since Brooke had long come to accept Ivey's idiosyncrasies, she figured she could do the same for the brother of the man she loved.

Whoa, where had that come from?

"Tell the truth, dear. Is this too much?" Pop, dressed in a three piece suit, touched his red and green Christmas bow tie.

"No, it's perfect." Pop was so excited, and she for him. This was also the culmination of his dream.

"I almost went for the one that lit up, and played Rudolph the Red Nosed Reindeer, but I thought you might not like that one. Gotta be classy."

"Good choice," Brooke said, grateful she'd dodged a bullet there.

Brooke had to admit this was so far turning out to be the best holiday season in decades, hands down. Even Mom had been unusually cooperative, not once asking how much this whole celebration was costing. Only happy and pleased to have received an invitation.

There would be no hint of tofu anywhere tonight, and Eileen hadn't said a word about it. Too busy planning her wedding, and Brooke didn't want to know what else was keeping her occupied. None of her business, and she didn't need that thought in her head.

And hey, at least they'd be making it legal soon.

Billy had taken to showing how grateful he was for her hard work in multiple ways every night. So much so that she was afraid he'd ruined her for any other man.

She'd come to the realization that Billy Turlock was every bit the man the entire town had adored. Even if she'd never cared much for following the crowd, she couldn't help it this time. He was the best man she'd ever known.

A good son, loving grandson, protective brother and friend. Maybe she should order a halo for him. Brooke smiled. Nope, no halo for that man. He was pretty sinfully delicious underneath and she was far too well acquainted with all that yumminess.

Like he'd been summoned, yummyness appeared front and center. Brooke did everything but salivate. He always cleaned up so well. Even with the typical long-haired baseball player style going on, he filled a suit like ink filled a pen.

He had on a simple black suit with a red tie, festive but understated. "Hey, babe. Where do you want me?"

In my bed stripped naked and feeding me chocolate covered strawberries, Brooke wanted to say. Instead she pulled her mind out of the gutter and glanced at her list. "You're meeting with the media first. More pictures, more interviews. I figured if we give them what they want maybe they'll leave early."

He walked past her, one finger softly grazing up her arm. He grinned when she shivered a little.

She didn't like broadcasting their relationship at the work place, despite the fact that it was common knowledge throughout the entire town since someone (she suspected Fallon) had outed her to Stephan's blog.

An hour later, when she was frantically going through the lists of her lists and one of them was missing (horrors!) Eric grabbed her shoulders and gave her a little shake. "Easy, girl. Everything is under control. You've done a great job. Time to go get changed since people will be arriving in an hour."

"An hour?" Where had the time gone? "Eric, that's too soon. I'm not ready. We're not ready. What if—"

Eric held a finger up to his mouth. "Shut it."

"But what about the wine? The new private label Pinot we bottled? What do you think?"

Eric nodded. "I think you need a bottle for yourself right now."

"Funny."

"Seriously, Brooke. You hired me, and I know you trust me. So stop being a control freak and go get glammed up!" Eric turned her and pushed her in the direction of her cottage. She wound up face to face with Gigi.

"Hello, Brooke." Her tone was velvety smooth, the sound of a black panther if it could speak.

Brooke startled a little. "Uh, hello Gigi. You're early."

"Of course I am. You didn't think I'd let Billy handle the press junket on his own today?"

"Well, he is a grown man." Hated to point out the obvious, but sometimes Gigi needed a reminder.

"A grown man who has been known to throw a punch when some stupid reporter said the wrong thing. He needs me, Brooke and you should have thought of asking me to handle all of this for the opening." She put one hand on her hip and tossed that meticulous every-hair-in-place pageboy hair.

"I'm sorry. I didn't want to bother you. All we have is the local press. We have one small town paper. The Chronicle sent one photographer. That's it." The last two words were said on the edge of the last breath Brooke had left.

"Calm down."

"I am calm." Was that her heart making a loud thumping sound in her chest? "Maybe I should sit down."

"Yes, maybe you should." Gigi said.

"No, I can't sit down. I have to go change." She brushed by Gigi and didn't stop until she heard the sound of a black panther speaking again.

"Brooke?"

Brooke took a deep breath, stopped and turned, ready for the onslaught. Maybe they could do the figurative knock down drag out now, before she put on her nice dress. "Yeah?"

"You've done a fantastic job."

"Oh. Thanks." Well, she wasn't expecting that. Kindness from Cruella. She'd take it.

An hour later, Brooke was showered and frantically trying to find her red slinky dress. The one that had been in her closet a few minutes ago. Finally, she located it hiding behind a black sweater. Why couldn't she calm down? Something – nameless – seemed to be clawing its way up her throat.

Brooke pulled the festive red dress with a sweetheart collar off the hanger.

And why wouldn't she be nervous? The last time she'd thrown an event, she'd lost both her boyfriend and her job in one night. Lost her head and nearly trashed her career. She'd always kept such a close lid on her emotions that every time they came rising to the surface the way they had that night— she just didn't know what to do with them. She usually wound up exploding.

Venting, Mom had called it once. She'd said that Brooke

needed to learn how to 'vent' better. Let the steam slowly hiss out of the teapot instead of come spewing out in a big cloud of steam that would be bound to burn someone.

She unzipped the dress and stepped into it.

But that's why she had a Harley, the skydiving, the bungee jumping. Venting on steroids. Only thing, she hadn't had any time for those pursuits lately. Which might be the reason she currently felt like screaming.

Instead, she'd willingly participated in the one thing she swore she'd never risk: her heart. She wasn't ever supposed to risk that part of her anatomy, dammit. Bones would break and heal, but a broken heart was never the same.

That's what had happened to Mom – after the divorce, she'd never been the same. Quit her high powered law firm and moved to an organic farm that might as well be a modern day commune. Dad told everyone who would listen that she'd had a nervous breakdown, and Brooke wondered if it could have been true. But for the most part Mom was perfectly lucid – if a little too passionate about trees. But the divorce had ruined her, both financially, and emotionally.

Brooke couldn't let that happen to her.

That's why she'd tried to control everything in her life, and succeeded for the most part. Yes, she'd risked her job with George – dating her boss – but she'd never risked her heart. No, he'd never come anywhere near that muscle.

Since she'd met him again, Billy had waged a slow and steady battle for her heart. He'd forced her to give up control, and damn if he hadn't made it feel good. Scary, but wonderful.

She'd tried so hard to control her heart around Billy, but she'd been kidding herself. Suddenly the near hysteria made sense, because she'd done the one thing she swore she'd never do. From the first time he'd kissed her ten years ago when it felt like the world had stopped spinning for a moment, she'd made up her mind that falling for Billy Turlock would be craziest thing she could ever do.

And damn if she didn't feel certifiable.

* * *

"SO, ANY TALK OF A COMEBACK?" One of the reporters asked.

A camera clicked and Billy blinked. "Guys, I just retired. No, there's no comeback."

Fortunately, no one had to know that he still felt like he was missing a limb. Still walked around wondering what he'd do with himself for the next thirty years, because it wouldn't be baseball any more.

So far he'd fooled everyone with the belief that would be fine with him. Except for Brooke, since she'd always had that way of looking right inside him. She could tell something wasn't right. He hadn't told her anything because he didn't even want her to know. What man wanted the woman he loved to know that he felt like half a man?

That he wasn't sure anything other than baseball would satisfy that hole inside his heart? The smell of the grassy diamond field, the worn leather of his favorite glove, the swish sound of the ball as it left his hand at ninety miles an hour.

"Excuse me, boys." He turned to see Gigi had entered the room and announced her presence.

Great. He might have known she'd be upset that he hadn't asked her advice for this press junket, so she'd arrived early. "Everyone say hello to my publicist, Gigi Rosenberg."

She sidled up next to him. "Hello, stranger. This seems like an appropriate time and venue to make this announcement. I haven't even talked to Billy about this yet." She put a hand on his shoulder.

Gigi realized he didn't like surprises. He gave his best grin through a stiff jaw.

"Billy Turlock has just received an offer from Fox Sports."

More bright camera flashes, and an outpouring of questions from the reporters:

"I thought you were a vintner."

"Does this mean you'll leave Starlight Hill again?"

"Will they make you cut your long hair?"

"What's the salary?"

"Will you accept the offer?"

He glared at Gigi. This was not the kind of news he wanted to hear about in front of an audience. She knew full well how he felt about the talking heads. He wasn't one of them, and never would be. Apparently she thought that he might not be able to refuse in front of an audience.

His place was still on a baseball field, if only he could find a way to do it. Maybe Brooke was right. Maybe coaching high school baseball wasn't the craziest thing in the world.

"One question at a time, folks." Gigi waved her hand. "Billy has hardly had time to absorb the news himself. But I think we can all agree, this means that Billy Turlock's star power is still alive and well. You haven't seen the last of him in baseball."

Brooke walked in at that moment, a vision in a red form fitting dress. She'd obviously heard the tail end of the statement because her eyes were wide open and questioning. Vulnerability showed in her hazel eyes, and he was transported back to a single night so many years ago. A surge of tenderness kicked him so hard in the chest he considered checking his pulse.

"Excuse me, but I have to borrow Billy as the Cub Scouts have arrived on Santa's float. You're welcome to stick around if you like, but the rest of the evening will be all about wine. No more baseball talk."

Billy felt a grin spread across his face. Brooke had a way of doing that to him – of changing the face of the landscape. Instead of quick sand beneath him he distinctly felt solid ground. Somehow she managed to center him. To be his compass.

She returned his grin with a shy smile of her own – his girl, despite the wild nature beneath – was more vulnerable than she wanted anyone to know. Needier than she'd ever admit.

Once he and Pop had taken at least a dozen photos with Santa and his sleigh and the parade boat took off to make its way through the rest of the town, they were officially in business.

"Well, Pop, we did it," Billy said.

Inside, Mom and Giancarlo were holding hands and smiling ear to ear. That's what he liked to see. Chaste behavior from his Mom and her fiancé.

"Oh Billy, I'm so happy, darling. Pop finally has his dream." Mom said, hugging him. If he wasn't mistaken, her eyes were misty.

Giancarlo shook his hand, patting his back. "Well done, son. We can never, in my opinion, have too much wine."

"I would have to agree." From behind him, Billy heard an unfamiliar deep voice.

Turning, he saw a man he didn't recognize.

"George," Giancarlo said without a hint of warmth.

"Have we met?" Billy extended his arm to the man he realized must be George Serrano.

"I don't believe we have, even though we have so much in common." The man shook Billy's hand like a dead fish. "George Serrano. And this is my fiancée, Chelsea."

A tiny brunette who didn't look old enough to drink stepped forward. "Oh my gosh, Billy, my dad is like your greatest fan."

"Always nice to hear." Billy couldn't put his finger on it but something about this man set him on edge. Made him stiffen like nails on a chalkboard.

"We're anxious to taste your first vintage. You probably know Serrano's won the label three years in a row—"

George was stopped from tooting his own horn when Brooke appeared at Billy's elbow, pulling at him. "Sorry to interrupt, but there are some people I want you to meet."

He couldn't help but notice the tension in the air, charged and amped the moment Brooke interrupted. George stiffened and looked like he'd swallowed poison. Something definitely going on. But he'd already long suspected that the two hadn't parted well.

He caught himself enjoying the small display of PDA when Brooke perhaps unconsciously held on to his hand longer than necessary and pulled him in another direction.

Seemed like a hundred different directions. Other vintners and restaurateurs coming from San Francisco, most lamenting the price of a good wine. Business owners in town, wishing him success.

Billy saw and heard Pop make his way around the party on his own, imparting wisdom as only he could do. Letting everyone who would listen know that he hadn't needed his frenemy's help after all, thank you very much. Singing to the grapes was the key to a good vintage.

All in all, it was a great turn-out. The room filled to capacity, Eric and the others pouring, selling at times by the case. Who knew people would be willing to pay so much for a bottle of wine?

Brooke Miller, that's who.

This – their entire success – was due to her hard work. Early on he'd made the decision to cede control to her and he hadn't regretted it for a moment. Thanks to her hard work, there was every possibility that they'd be out of the red soon and he wouldn't be forced to take the sports casting job.

Maybe he could coach the local team, or open the pitching clinic he'd dreamed about one day. Gigi and all her talk of diminishing star power and returns be damned.

Brooke was right. This didn't have to be an all or nothing proposition.

He caught Brooke staring at him from across the room, engaged in a conversation with Ivey and Jeff. Those two were so in love they could hardly keep their hands off each other.

If it were up to him, that would be him and Brooke. He didn't care what anyone thought. But he had to respect her wishes, and he understood why as a woman she wouldn't want anyone thinking she'd done anything improper to get the job. Nothing like wrenching his heart out of his chest and holding it for ransom.

Nothing like that.

"Hey, so where's a man to find his Scotch?" He turned to see Wallace had arrived. The lone wolf again.

No one understood why. Billy had watched, at times with a twinge of envy, the way Wallace turned female heads when he walked into a room.

"No Scotch tonight, bro. Drink up from the vine. Go on, the water's fine." Billy slapped his brother's back.

"Yeah, yeah. Have you seen Scott? I'm going to make sure he doesn't force me to drive him home tonight."

Billy had, and he pointed in little brother's direction. Currently Scott appeared to be hamming it up with Melinda, whom Billy hadn't even seen come in.

Thankfully Scott had listened, and not brought Fallon. Billy had expressly told him not to. The last thing he wanted was for anyone to make Brooke feel uncomfortable tonight, or any night.

Genevieve approached with a tray of items Billy hoped

he'd be eating in heaven if he ever got to walk through those pearly gates.

"Bacon puff?" She asked, more to Billy than Wallace.

"You don't have to ask me twice." Billy took a bite of bacon encrusted joy.

He wasn't sure how Wallace, who had once eaten an entire pound of bacon by himself, could resist. But he was, barely glancing in Genevieve's direction. She, for her part, was doing a great job of acting like she didn't notice the tall man standing right next to her.

The one every other woman in the place was practically salivating over.

Yeah, definitely something going on there.

"Genevieve, would you marry me and cook this for me every morning?" Billy joked. Flirting felt safe, since Genevieve knew well that he and Brooke were an item.

"Oh, Billy!" She elbowed him and kept walking.

"All right, what was that about?" Billy asked when she'd walked away at a safe enough distance.

Wallace scowled. "I'm going to renovate her bakery. I put a bid on it last month."

"Great. That means you'll be around for a while. But you don't look happy about that."

"Should take me about a month or two, but not the way she keeps changing her mind. Some people think they understand construction when they should stick to baking."

"Careful, bro. That sounds a little caveman-like." Billy pointed out.

"Does it? Well, hell. I can't help it." Wallace walked away towards the bar, and joined Scott, presumably to try some of the vintage.

Gigi was speaking animatedly with Melinda – that had to be an interesting discussion, as he couldn't imagine to two more different women.

Mom was still gazing starry eyed at Giancarlo. Fine, someday he would get used to that.

Brooke flitted about, smiling, pouring from behind the bar when needed, and making him ache a little bit. He wasn't sure if he would ever get used to that feeling.

Eventually the crowd began to thin, and Billy looked forward to the end of the evening. He wanted Brooke in his arms again like he wanted another one of those bacon puffs. All of these people would have to leave before that could happen. He'd kick them out personally, but that couldn't be good for business.

Suddenly the young-looking woman he'd seen earlier, Chelsea he thought it was – stood at his elbow.

"I'm sorry Billy, I know I'm not supposed to bother you, but could I get an autograph? It's for my dad."

"Sure," he took the piece of paper she'd pulled out of her purse. "How old are you, sweetheart?" She looked twenty if a day which made her engagement to George, who looked to be at least thirty-five, a little sketchy.

"Oh I'm older than I look," she said without answering the question.

"Right." He handed her the autograph. "I hope you and George enjoyed tonight."

"We did." George showed up behind Chelsea, who quickly stuffed the paper in her purse. "But I'm not sure you have a prayer of taking that ribbon away from us."

"We'll see," Billy said.

"Well, hiring my former general manager won't be enough. My family's been in this business for decades."

"Yeah. Well, we all have to start somewhere. Don't we?" He gave Chelsea a lazy grin, to piss George off.

It worked. She blushed, and George grew red for a different reason. "Well, this isn't the American baseball league. This is where the real men play, not long haired jocks who never graduated from college. It must be nice to be a millionaire for throwing a ball around in a sandbox."

"George! What are you doing?" Chelsea pulled on the jerk's arm, and he pushed back so hard he nearly knocked her down.

She rocked a bit on her high heels, and Billy reached his arm out to steady her by the elbow.

"Be quiet. The men are talking," George said.

Billy felt his gut tighten and his hands curl into fists. This was so not good. The guy was goading him, and he couldn't let him win. Not like he hadn't been in the scenario before. He'd learned the hard way to keep calm. Take deep breaths and remain professional.

He tried again, forcing a grin. "If you push that little girl again I might have to escort you out of here."

"I barely touched her. I love Chelsea. She's going to be my wife." George put his arm around her. "She's a sweet girl. Not like Brooke."

"Excuse me?"

"Didn't you know? Yeah, Brooke and me. We were together. Guess she has a thing for the boss. The girl gets around. Don't think you're special or anything."

Later, he'd probably wonder how his arm now worked independently of his brain. The arm he'd trained for years. The same one that pitched a ninety mile an hour ball and a curve ball that wasn't half bad. It wasn't listening to him now, but there was no time to reason with it. Like it belonged to a stranger, his arm found itself reaching for George's collar.

And that's when all hell broke loose.

CHAPTER 16

For the first time in decades, Brooke began to believe that the curse of The Holidays had been removed. Otherwise, how was it that everything tonight had run so smoothly?

The wine flowed plentiful, the appetizers were a huge hit, and they'd sold out of what would obviously be their most popular wine: the earthy nutty Merlot that slid down a person's throat like wet silk.

She'd kept George and Chelsea occupied, having had Ernesto take them for a long and bogus special invitation-only tour of the vineyard, the wine cellar and the bottling room.

Everyone had seemed to enjoy the evening, and from the looks of it they'd sold a lot of wine. The crowd had thinned, but all in all she could say the event had been a resounding success. She'd kept her cool, kept her emotions in check, and controlled the outcome. Always the key.

In fact, the first concern of the evening came when Brooke heard Gigi scream Billy's name. The sound caused her to turn in that direction, and that's when she saw Billy, dragging George outside by his shirt collar.

Chelsea followed two steps behind Gigi, who waved her arms around, frantically trying to get Billy's attention. "Stop!"

"Uh-oh," Eric said. "This is bad."

Brooke didn't think, only ran towards them all. She didn't make it before Wallace and Scott were out the door, their faces reflecting the appearance of soldiers headed to war.

Not good.

Brooke hurled her body out the door, feeling her breaths come out in short little desperate spurts. "What's going on?"

Outside, Wallace and Scott flanked Billy, who could be heard saying, "I was about to teach this gentleman some manners."

"Why can't we all sit down and talk about this like civilized citizens of the world?" Gigi said.

"We could," Billy said sounding gritty and rough, "But some people don't know how to be civilized."

Brooke shoved her way to the front of the melee. "What's going on here?"

"George was leaving. Say goodnight." Billy let George go with a slight shove.

George smoothed over his Italian suit, probably one that cost a year of her salary. He glared in Brooke's direction.

"You picked the wrong man, Brooke. If you wanted a jock you should have said so." He turned to Billy. "You might pitch a ball at ninety miles an hour but let's see you build up a winery from the ground up. Oh wait, guess you didn't need to. You're a millionaire. You take my best people. But it won't be enough."

"He didn't take me, I quit. Remember? You should leave now," Brooke said through a shaky breath.

Billy moved forward but he was stopped on either side by

Wallace and Scott. "Listen to her. A ball isn't the only thing I can hit out of the park."

George finally walked away, Chelsea running behind him.

"What was that all about?" Gigi demanded. "I want an explanation."

Brooke was so afraid she knew exactly what it was all about. Billy hadn't even looked at her for the past few minutes. He knew.

George had told Billy about the two of them, and who knew what else he'd said. Not that it would matter to Billy, because he had to know how she felt. It was different between them, special. She kept trying to meet his eyes.

"Does it matter?" Wallace interrupted. "If I know my brother, he didn't do it without a damn good reason."

"I sure hope so, because this calls for some damage control. We need to spin this and get ahead of it. I'll make some calls." Gigi turned and walked back inside, glaring at Brooke.

Brooke stared at Billy, who finally met her eyes. The eyes that told her so much were shut down now. She couldn't hazard a guess as to what he was thinking or feeling. But her first guess? Not good.

Brooke's heart started to shiver in her rib cage. The curse of The Holidays appeared alive and well. Her stomach took the Christmas dive it remembered so well.

Gigi turned at the door. "Are you two coming? Let me rephrase that. Brooke and Billy, you two are coming with me."

A few minutes later, they were both seated on the couch in Billy's living room. It felt like there were one hundred feet were between her and Billy and not a few inches.

"Are you okay?" It was the only thing she dared ask.

"Yeah."

Funny, because he did not look okay. He looked the

furthest from okay that she'd ever seen. Happy-go-lucky Billy, who loved everyone and had a ready smile at a moment's notice. She'd ruined that. "Billy, I—"

"Not now," Billy said, then leaned back and took a deep breath, shoving a hand through that long hair.

She'd ruined everything again, her special talent during The Holidays. Disaster and ruination followed her at this time of the year. And even with her failed track record with men, she was about to lose the best one. Because she didn't deserve him.

Gigi hung up the phone. "Disaster averted. At least no press was there when you lost your head. How many times have I told you to count to ten?"

"I counted to a hundred," Billy said with a scowl. "He asked for it, believe me."

"I believe you. That brings me to the two of you. Hate to say I told you so."

"Then don't," Billy said. "This continues to be none of your business."

"But—" Gigi began.

Billy got up. "Sorry I lost my temper. Thanks for your help. Good-night."

With a hand on Gigi's back he led her to the front door. "We have so much to talk about. The offer by Fox Sports—"

"Brooke and I have to talk and we need some privacy."

For once, Brooke wished Gigi would argue more and stay a little longer. But she didn't protest as she threw a pointed look at Brooke (because this was of course her fault). "I'll call you tomorrow."

Billy shut the door and didn't move for a minute, his back still facing the door. Then he turned to Brooke. "I want to know how you wound up with a man like George."

Stupidity? Lack of options? Loneliness? She didn't know which one to say first. "Tell me what he said to you."

"No," he moved towards her. "You tell me what's true."

"I did have a relationship with him for a while, it's true. Because I was stupid and lonely. He was there."

"So— convenient?"

"Yeah, I guess. And did I mention stupid?"

"Is that what this is? I'm convenient?"

"What? No Billy, you can't honestly believe that. Nothing about you is convenient."

"How's that?"

"Well, you know what I mean. You're a jock. What do we really have in common?" Other than the fact that for reasons she couldn't quite understand everything in her world righted itself when she was in Billy's arms, the facts were that they were not exactly cut from the same cloth. They didn't have a whole lot in common other than the fact that they both loved this town, this vineyard. His family. Yes, she loved all those crazy people.

Billy sighed, reached for a hair tie and put his hair in a ponytail. She'd also never dated a man with long hair before, but Billy had such a rock star look when he pulled his hair in a ponytail that she nearly came every day he did it.

"Do you know the last time I was in a fight over a girl?"

They'd fought over her? Why did she feel like such an idiot? Why did she feel humiliation clogging her throat? "I don't know. High school?"

He met her eyes. "Try never."

Never. As she suspected, she brought out the worst in him. Brooke Miller, angst instigator.

"Sorry," she said with an exasperated sigh. "Sounded like Gigi was kind of used to this."

"I've lost my temper a handful of times with the press. Never over a girl."

She stood up. "I'm sorry. You didn't want to believe me,

but I must be cursed. It's The Holidays. I tried to warn you, but did you listen?"

He laughed and her heart broke open a little bit. "How do you feel about me, Brooke?"

Was this a trick question? She didn't quite know how to answer. If she told him the truth it could be a trap. It could be he sought some reassurance that she wasn't making her way through all the vineyard owners in town. Hello, humiliation. Why oh why had she ever taken up with George?

"How do I feel about you?"

"You heard me. Is that a tough question?"

Why would he ask her this right now? "What did George tell you?"

"Is that going to help you answer my question?"

"No. But I want to know."

"And I asked first."

"Fine." She took a shaky breath and smoothed the skirt of her dress. "I lo—" the word love stuck in her throat. Love meant misery and disaster. Broken promises and hearts. She didn't want to love him. "C'mon, you know how I feel."

"I need to hear it." He grinned and her heart broke open a little bit more. That's what Billy managed to do her. She didn't like it one bit. It was so out of control, and control was the only thing she had left.

To her horror, her eyes started leaking. Not possible, because Brooke Miller didn't do tears. But even so they were flowing out of her eyes. Salty, big, wet and floppy tears.

She caught one with her mouth, and wiped another one away with her hand. "I— I really—"

"You can't say it, can you?"

Of course not, because saying it out loud would make it true. Then she'd be sunk like the Titanic because loving him was the biggest risk she'd ever take. And she'd hurt a lot worse than a few stitches, broken bones or concussions. You couldn't heal a broken heart. She'd seen that first hand.

Then he was next to her, folding her into his arms. "I didn't think you could cry, Bungee."

"I can't." But dang if she wasn't doing a bang-up imitation of it. She buried her face in his warm neck – he smelled so much like a man. Her man.

Her mascara had to be smearing, and she probably looked like a raccoon, but Billy lifted her chin, like he might actually appreciate the raccoon look. "Let me tell you how I feel about you, then."

"Um, okay." She hiccupped. How did women manage this crying thing?

"I don't care about your past. We both have less than illustrious histories. All I care about is you. I know I let you down once before—"

"That was so long ago. No big deal."

He tugged on a strand of her hair. "It is a big deal. I should have told you I wasn't going instead of having you hear it from everyone else."

"But you didn't owe me anything."

"Maybe not, but you were a friend. I could have done better. I'm trying to do that now. I never forgot that kiss I talked you into—"

"Oh please, you didn't talk me into anything. I wanted it too."

He grinned. "We were too immature. Not too young to realize we had a connection, but too young to understand it was a once-in-a-lifetime kind of thing."

She was in so much trouble because she realized he was right. No one else had ever come close to her heart which made it easy for so long to keep things light. No commitments, and no heartbreaks. She'd met the right man when she was seventeen years old but he hadn't become a part of her life again until ten years later. A long time to wait, and she'd never been good at waiting.

"Being with you is the only time I feel like I can breathe. I used to live and breathe baseball 24/7, and you're right – I miss it. But when I'm with you none of that matters because you fill me up. I love you, Brooke. I want it all with you – marriage, babies. I wouldn't mind getting you knocked up right now." He kissed her in that bone melting way of his, reaching right into her heart.

She couldn't help but arch her body into his kiss, while her thoughts ran wild. *Not this. I can't do this forever love thing. It doesn't work. He's going to hate me before long. We're too differ-ent. Besides, I'm not the marrying kind. Not the girl you take home to Mom.*

After a few moments, she put her hands up against his solid chest. She'd have to lie like a rug, but in the end it would be for the best. "Here's the thing. I don't love you. I wanted a good time, and that's what we have. I don't want anything else. Why do we have to ruin it by talking about a fantasy?"

He blinked his surprise. "A fantasy?"

"Love and marriage. You and I both know it doesn't last. Look at your parents. When's the last time you saw your Dad? Probably around the last time I saw mine. It's been years. It's crazy to get married. Half of all marriages end in divorce. Do you want to be part of that statistic?"

"That wouldn't be us."

"Don't you think that's what they all thought? Do you want to do that to a child? Force them to split their time between two parents who can't stand each other anymore? Do you?"

"Brooke—"

"Can't we just stay like we are? I like what we have, just the way it is."

"That won't be enough for me." That green eyed gaze assessed her. She didn't see hurt in those eyes, but only a rock-steady assurance. He was so certain that she loved him back.

That pissed her off. Stuck up jock. "It will have to be."

He didn't say another word, but walked towards his front door and opened it. "Good night, Brooke."

"Good night?" But he couldn't be kicking her out. Didn't all guys want a no-strings relationship? Why did she have to fall for the one guy who didn't?

"It's been a long day, and we both need our rest."

Yes, but usually they rested together. Her head in the crook of his neck, his left hand on the small of her back. She rubbed up against him. "I'm never that tired. Let's go to bed and forget about all this."

"I can't." He made no move in response to her, but just stood there holding the door open.

Well, she wasn't going to beg. Not yet, anyway. "You can't or you won't?"

"All right, I won't." He stared at her, not at all apologetic. So he was going to punish her. Punish her for being the level headed one, the one who would save him from the alimony and child support due to her in a few years. This is the thanks she got.

"Fine." She brushed by him on the way out, hoping he'd reconsider.

He didn't. The door shut behind her and she stared at it for a moment. This role reversal couldn't be happening. The fabric of the universe had been torn in half somehow.

She couldn't stop crying, either, as she fumbled for the door to her little cottage. Inside, the cottage wasn't all that dreamy anymore. Not like Billy's place which for the life of her had started to feel like home. That had been her first mistake. Spending too much time over there, allowing him to suck her in like a Hoover vacuum. What a fool she'd been. She couldn't tell him the truth because she didn't want it to be the truth.

She didn't want to love him. Not with this ache that wouldn't go away.

A long time ago, she'd felt that ache for him, but eventually it had gone away. Out of sight, out of mind. Every once in a while she thought back to the night when they'd kissed, when in that one moment she'd embraced a kind of stupid-girl hope. Maybe she and Billy would date in Chicago, out of the confines of small town life and the roles they'd each been assigned. In Chicago she could be more than Brooke the button-pusher. She could be Brooke, Billy Turlock's friend. Maybe even someday something more than that. She'd made the grave mistake of planning, of hoping for something better. For somebody like him. If not him, then at least somebody like him.

But hope had returned a big fat zero. Billy Turlock would not go to Chicago. He would go to the minor leagues. She'd been nuts to think for a moment he cared enough to tell her personally. No, she'd heard about it like everyone else had. It was all anyone talked about for weeks. Hometown hero heads out for the big time. Next stop, the majors.

Now he said he loved her and she was supposed to believe that. Now he wanted her to trust him. Believe that he wouldn't let her down again and pull out the rug out from under her when she least expected it. Sure it was different. They were grown-ups now. It would hurt a whole lot more.

Brooke uncorked a bottle of Merlot. Another two fisted night of drinking lay ahead, because tonight The Holidays had delivered a knock-out.

* * *

BILLY TURLOCK HAD EXPERIENCED a lot of firsts in his life. The first time he'd pitched a no hitter: Oakland Coliseum 2004. The first time he'd bought a house: his mother's house, Starlight Hill, 2005. The first time the police were called for a baseball groupie that had holed up in his hotel room, insisting she would kill herself if he didn't marry her: 2008 (thankfully also the last time).

This newest first had come courtesy of the love of his life. The first time he'd refused sex with the woman he loved: Brooke Miller, 2014.

Yeah. He should drink to that, in fact.

He rummaged through the cabinets in the kitchen searching for his bottle of single Malt Scotch. He opened it, knowing full well it would upset Brooke and taking actual enjoyment out of that fact. Damn. The Scotch went down like it should: hot, burning a hole in his esophagus. Reminding him he had hair on his chest, and making him feel like he'd spontaneously sprouted a few more.

Brooke loved him. He knew that fact like he knew the order of the bases on the diamond. She was apparently so damaged that it was impossible to admit. Which slayed him as much as it pissed him off. Men like George Serrano might have had something to do with that. But before he pointed the finger, he had to remember that he'd let her down too. And forgiveness was apparently in short supply with his girl. Ten years ought to be long enough to let go of a grudge, but even if she said it didn't matter Billy wasn't buying it.

There was an insistent knock on his door and he opened it to find both brothers. "Hey."

"Are you alone?" Wallace, a couple of inches taller than Billy, looked over his head.

"Yep," Billy answered and waved Wallace and Scott inside. "Scotch?"

"You don't have to ask me twice," Wallace answered.

Billy poured his big brother a glass and handed it to him. They clinked and Wallace shot it down, grimacing. "Ah. Now I feel like a man. All that wine is too girly for me. And all the pastries from Genevieve's. Shit. It was so sweet in there I thought I was at a Nicholas Sparks movie."

"What? You didn't have the bacon puffs?" Billy asked.

"I did. Thought I'd died and gone to heaven," Scott said. "You gotta beer?"

"Here you go little brother." Billy reached inside the fridge and behind all the bottles of Mirassu white wine Brooke kept in there. Sissy stuff.

He handed Scott the bottle, then carried the Scotch with him to the couch, and his brothers followed.

"So— what was that all about tonight?" Wallace sat down and stretched his long legs out. He fixed Billy with his big brother stare. The one that meant he better talk now, because time was in limited supply and Wallace wasn't in the mood for stalling.

"George insulted Brooke." Billy scowled into his flask.

"Pay up, Wallace," Scott said.

"Man." Wallace reached for his wallet in the back of his pants pockets and drew it out. He laid out two twenty dollar bills next to him. "I bet Scott this couldn't be about a girl. Guess there's a first time for everything."

"That's because you don't know what I do. Brooke is different. Right Billy?" Scott leaned over and picked up the bills.

"She's different all right." Billy scrubbed a hand over his face.

"Where is she, by the way?" Scott asked, folding the twenties into his wallet with a grin.

"I kicked her out." All right, he was exaggerating but essentially that's what he'd done. And also it sounded a lot better than the truth.

Wallace plunked down his flask on the coffee table with a loud thump. "You defend a girl's honor and then you kick her out?"

"Isn't that kind of self-defeating?" Scott asked.

"Let's just say she didn't appreciate my actions as well as I'd hoped." Billy poured himself another shot.

"I see. So she's an 'I can take care of myself' type and I don't need you Alpha males starting up shit?" Wallace scowled into his drink.

Something didn't feel right talking about Brooke, brothers or not. Also, he wasn't going to pour out his heart. He'd already done that with his girl and he sure wasn't going to do it with his brothers. The teasing wouldn't stop until next Christmas, and then only if he was lucky.

"Yeah."

"And?" Scott pressed.

"And I'm not talking about it." Billy slammed down the flask and poured again.

He glanced up to see Wallace and Scott exchange a look.

"It's worse than I thought." Wallace said. "This girl played hockey with your brain."

"No hockey analogies." Billy slammed back another shot.

"Wait a minute, Billy," Scott interrupted. "Before you get too sauced there's something I need to talk to you about."

"Now's not the time," Wallace gave Scott a pointed look.

"What is it?" Billy poured another shot for Wallace, who just stared at it and then back at Billy.

"Well, you know your ex-girlfriend, Fallon? I didn't really tell you the whole story. Here's the thing of it. She's in trouble, and she needs money," Scott said.

"There it is," Wallace said, throwing up his hands.

Billy groaned. Everybody always needed money from him. At least Fallon wasn't trying to lie about having had his illegitimate child. Wait. Or was she? His brain was a little foggy but crap, he was scared for a minute. He didn't want to have a family with Fallon.

"Wait. Why does she want money from me?" He became vaguely aware of Wallace moving the bottle out of Billy's line of vision.

"She's going through a divorce and fighting a custody battle with the ex. She's afraid to lose custody." Scott lifted a shoulder.

Billy threw back his head like this was the worst news he'd ever heard in his life. Malt Scotch had a way of making him feel everything a hell of a lot more intensely. "How much does she need?"

"I don't know. You'd have to talk to her about that. I just said I'd swing it by you. Also, if you could get her a job too, that would be great."

What was he, some kind of magician? If he were, he'd waste no time in materializing Brooke in his bed right now. He might have been a bit hasty earlier, come to think of it. He let out a slow even breath and pinched the bridge of his nose. "Money. A job. Anything else?"

"No, I think that would do it." Scott grinned, taking a gulp of his beer.

"What does she do for a living?" Wallace asked.

Scott shrugged.

Billy could hire her at the winery. It would upset the hell out of Brooke. But even now, he couldn't do it. What a sap. "Maybe she can clean my house."

Scott turned in a semi-circle. "But your place is immaculate."

"That's because of Brooke," Billy said, rubbing his eyes. Suddenly he was exhausted. "But I plan on trashing the place from now on."

"Oh. Well, then." Scott said, putting his beer down. "This seems like a good time for me to exit. I told Ma I'd stop by.

Later, bro."

Scott let himself out the door, but Wallace didn't move. Billy closed his eyes for a minute and when he opened one eye he found his big brother staring at him. "What?"

"Are you okay?"

"Yeah. A little tired." No one needed to worry about him. He was going to be fine. He just had a lot of decisions to make, but he'd make them in the morning with a clearer head.

"I've never seen you like this over a woman."

Well, she wasn't just any woman. She happened to be *the woman* but what did Wallace know about it? Anyway, it was none of his business. "You've never seen me like how?"

"Like someone hit you over the head with a baseball bat. Or like that time you actually did have a concussion and we had to run you to the hospital."

"Get real. I'm fine."

"What about Fox sports? Are you going to take that?"

The last thing he wanted to talk about. He had been about to tell Gigi to turn the whole thing down, but maybe what he needed right now was some distance from Brooke. Give her some time to think things through. The winery could run without his help. Brooke obviously didn't need him. "I don't know."

What he did know scared him a little bit. He wanted Brooke, and a bunch of children by her. Maybe their own little league team. But it had been his misfortune to fall for a girl who didn't trust the whole institution. Probably should have checked that out first.

Problem being, he'd had no idea he'd ever wanted those things until Brooke.

CHAPTER 17

*B*rooke spent Christmas day at the farm. She and Billy hadn't so much as cuddled in twenty days and five hours, but who was counting? They hadn't split up, not technically, but Brooke certainly recognized the avoidance method. She'd never said she wanted to break up, but she guessed a man like Billy Turlock couldn't let his ego take a beating like the one she'd inflicted. He'd take it personally, and not understand there was something wrong with an institution that had such a high rate of failure.

Before he'd left for a children's charity fundraiser he made a point to tell her that they would talk on the 25th when he got back. Eileen had invited her to the Turlock family Christmas, but it was only fair to spend the day with Mom since she'd spent Thanksgiving with the Turlocks.

She would miss everyone, but it wouldn't be the same without Billy. Anyway, she wasn't exactly filled with Christmas good cheer and love for her fellow man. But Mom had seen Brooke in every one of her foul moods and still loved her somehow. Probably because it was in the Mom contract.

The farm actually looked festive this year – there were fairy lights strung between the trees (solar, of course) and the sharp smell of pine permeated the air. They usually planted a pine tree outside every year, this one being no exception. No tree inside, because that would be murder.

Inside the smell of a roasted turkey (organic Mom said, from the farm next door), cinnamon, nutmeg and spices.

Looking around the table at dinner, Brooke realized that Mom's unorthodox collection of hippie friends felt a little bit like family. Sure, an odd conglomeration of quirky characters who didn't have any blood connection to her. They kept their distance for the most part, and inquired politely about her life while staying on the outskirts where she wanted them to be. Not like Billy's family who was all up in his business and life.

Wonder what Eileen had made for dinner?

"Would you pass the goat milk, dear?" Mrs. Deering asked at the dinner table.

"Sure," Brooke passed the little dish that must have come from Dolly's nipples.

"I always like to make sure that Dolly's contributions to dinner are used up." She took a swallow of the milk, made a face and put it down.

Brooke picked at her dinner. Strange, because it was by far the best food she'd ever had at the farm and yet she had no appetite.

"Are you all right, Brookie?" This was from Al, an odd man she'd long suspected might have a crush on Mom.

"Yeah.Fine."

"Well, you don't look fine if you don't mind my saying."

"I think she does mind," Mrs. Deering said. "What kind of a thing is that to say?"

"Look at her. She's too thin. And also, she looks pale. Melinda, what do you think?"

"Al, she's been working hard. Let's give her a break," Mom answered.

Brooke didn't have the energy for their concern. Maybe some sugar would cheer her up. "So what's for dessert?"

"Ah! Now you're talking." Melinda got up from the large farm table and trotted into the kitchen. She came back with pie. "Pumpkin cheesecake. Your favorite."

"Wow, thanks, Mom," Brooke said without enthusiasm. She picked at the filling, leaving most of the crust.

Of course, no one at the farm believed in buying presents because that signified excessive consumerism. For once, Brooke couldn't care less.

Mom had knitted her a sweater in colorful autumn colors. Mrs. Deering made cards for all of them. Al had whittled Brooke a heart out of wood. She touched the smooth edges of the heart. A lot of work went into whittling. She'd had no idea the man was so talented.

"Thank you," Brooke said to all the gifts. "I brought you all some wine."

"Of course you did," Mrs. Deering said.

She circled around and handed over Mirassu Merlot, Pinot, Cabernet, and Chardonnay. Of course the wine reminded her of Billy.

"So Brooke, when do you think you'll settle down and bring some lucky guy around to meet us all?" Mrs. Deering elbowed Mom.

This was of course, the running joke every year. Brooke would always quip that no man alive could handle or tame her. Everyone would laugh loudly and say "You got that right" and that would be the end of it.

Ahead of time, everyone began giggling in anticipation. Brooke couldn't laugh this time, and for some reason, she burst into tears.

Al stood up so fast that he knocked his chair over and

nearly fell into the fresh organic cranberry sauce. "What's wrong with her?"

Mrs. Deering came to pat Brooke's back. "What do you think, idiot? She's crying. Obviously she's upset over something you said."

"Something I said? What did I say?" Al asked.

"So now you've got short term memory loss? You should try some of my flax seed oil."

"Really, Clara? You want to talk about my memory when Brookie is crying? What's wrong with you? And who forgot to turn off the stove last week?"

"Stop it," Mom said, rubbing Brooke's back and handing her some tissues. "I think I'd like to talk to Brooke alone."

This was so out of control. Brooke couldn't stop or get a hold of a breath. Al and Mrs. Deering left the room and Brooke sort of slid off the chair on to the floor. Felt kind of cool down here, but there were crumbs everywhere. Did anyone ever clean this floor? She would ask, but she couldn't breathe.

Mom didn't say a word for a minute. "I'm going to let you cry. You need it. And no one should stop you. Don't worry, I'm fine with it."

But when Brooke didn't stop, Mom took her hand and raised her up off the floor. "You'll be more comfortable on the couch."

The couch was soft all right, being made from the coat of one of Dolly's friends, Lana the lamb. So soft that Brooke sunk into the middle. Now she struggled against a sofa that would swallow her whole. After a little while the sobs became hiccups. Finally this torture would end. Really, how did women do this? Crying took so much energy. Energy better spent doing...anything else.

"I'm sorry about this," Brooke said to Mom's pale face.

"What's wrong? You haven't been yourself all day. You

didn't even roll your eyes when Mrs. Deering mentioned the super algae she's selling now. And you haven't mentioned the lack of a tree inside once this year."

"I guess I'm having some residual Holiday issues. You know, from the divorce."

Mom narrowed her eyes. "I can always tell when you're lying. Does this have anything to do with Billy?"

Brooke hiccupped. "Maybe. He wants to have babies, and all that crap I said I'd never do."

"Oh dear. And what did you tell him?"

"I couldn't tell him I love him, so of course he won't talk to me now. Because he's used to getting his way. He's a spoiled brat." Except she didn't believe that anymore. Did spoiled brats put their mother's suitors through a background check? Spend Christmas Day in the children's cancer ward? Buy a vineyard to make his grandfather happy?

"Or maybe he's hurt that you don't feel the same way. You do love him, don't you?"

Maybe Mom was right. He was hurt. "I guess."

"You— guess?"

"Fine! I love him with the heat of a thousand suns! I love him like crazy! What else do you want me to say?"

"I want you to tell me what you'd do if you weren't so afraid."

"Afraid? Me?" Mom had to be talking to someone else in the room.

"It's been hard to keep my mouth shut, but you can't go around jumping out of planes to show everyone how brave you are. The real courage is in the everyday living. The single mother who wakes up every morning and takes care of her children, hoping someday it will get easier. Not giving up on love just because sometimes it doesn't work. Oh honey, I'm so sorry about me and your Dad. We held on too long, because I tried so hard to make it work."

"It's okay, Mom. The divorce ruined you, but you bounced back. Sort of."

"What do you mean the divorce ruined me?"

"You had a career and after the divorce you lost everything. Came to live at this farm to sell shampoo. I'm sorry Dad did that to you. I never told you that before."

"Is that what you think? The divorce didn't ruin me, honey. I took him to the cleaners. Believe me, I got my share."

That didn't make any sense. "Then why do you live here?"

"I want to live here. This is what I wanted for my life. It's my choice. And by the way, this is my place. My farm. My land."

"Yours?"

"And someday it will be yours."

"But —why didn't you tell me?"

"You never asked. I assumed you knew."

"But all these people who live here – do they pay you rent?"

Mom laughed. "Oh no dear. They're my friends. Some of them need a hand up, and I give it to them. I choose to surround myself with people who think the way I do. I've got something to share with the world, and I'm not greedy. Not anymore."

"How – how did you manage to get all this land? How did you get Dad to pay you that much money?"

"Remember that I was once a damned good attorney. I negotiated a structured settlement – he thought he was getting a bargain, but in the end the stock he had to fork over was worth a lot more a few years later."

For the love of Pete, her hippie Mom was a financial genius. "You bought all this so that you could make shampoo and farm organic?"

"So that I could create the life I wanted for myself. I'm surrounded by people and things that I love, and I'm happy.

Family looks different depending on your point of view. We're a little family here. And of course, there's always a place for you should you ever want it. But I always had a feeling you would create your own reality."

"I did. I created a reality which works as long as I'm in control."

"I see. If you control it, then you don't have to be afraid. So you're brave when you're in control of your risks."

Or maybe when she'd fooled herself into having control. "I didn't want to fall in love. Especially not with a jock."

"But you did. And living your life in fear is not a good place to be. Love is a better place to begin."

"But what if I don't want the things he wants? Why can't we just stay as we are? Everything was so good."

"Because we don't get to stay still, Brooke. That's not how it works. You don't want to grow cobwebs, do you? But if you're not ready to get married, why don't you just tell him how you feel? I'm sure he'll understand. If you love him, you need to tell him."

Sure. Why hadn't she thought of that? Telling him how she felt would definitely buy her some more time. And honestly, he already knew so it wouldn't come as a big surprise. But at least he'd know that she wanted to love him. She wanted to stop holding it inside where it would slowly chisel away at her soul.

Who knew Mom could be so wise?

Billy would be back later today, and she had to see him. Had to tell him she had crazy love for him. A jock. Apparently God had a sense of humor after all.

So she loved a jock that had made millions playing ball. That same possibly over privileged athlete was the kindest person she'd ever known. He gave back to the community, and loved his family. He tried to keep his giving secret, but she'd happened to see some of the cancelled checks. And even though it meant being away from family at Christmas, he and Pop were visiting the children's cancer ward in LA.

But tonight, he'd be home.

Brooke showered, and later took her time applying her make-up so she could look her utmost best when she told Billy how much she loved him.

"I love you," she said to the mirror as she flicked on some mascara. "I love you, Billy. I love you, you idiot. I love you, dummy."

Neither sounded right. She couldn't make it light hearted just because that would make it easier. No, she had to get this right. Perfect.

She turned in the mirror. "Here's the thing. I think I love you."

Wow, no. Think sounded less than committed. I'm sure I love you. No. Sounded like a valley girl. Was there time to rent a romantic comedy and see how to do it right? The grand gesture – that's what she needed.

A big, humongous grand gesture. Except that was usually done by the man. Not that she wasn't ready to throw away conventions, but she didn't want to buy the ring for crying out loud. No, and anyway they weren't getting married. They were just going to take it a step at a time. She'd tell the big guy she loved him, and ask whether he would mind slowing things down a tad. Remind him they already had an upcoming wedding in June.

Brooke had worked herself up to the point that she was nearly out of breath when she completed her outfit with her favorite riding boots. She'd decide to dress for understated sophistication when she told Billy how much she loved him – in her favorite pair of jeans and the clingy black sweater he loved.

Around seven she glanced outside and from the very corner edge of the house she saw lights on and movement inside the manor house— he was home early. No time for the movie.

You can do this.

She shut the door to her cottage and bounded up the short steps to the main house. *I love you.* Best to go for simplicity when in doubt. And better to do this before she chickened out.

What's the worst that could happen?

Apparently the worst that could happen was seeing the ex-girlfriend of the love of your life locking his front door. "Fallon."

"Oh, Brooke. I didn't hear you."

"I guess not. I can't say that I'm shocked."

Fallon put up a hand. "Hold on. Don't get carried away."

"Forget it, no big deal." Even though, unfortunately, her cheeks felt like a flaming torch had been placed on each one. "An ex-cheerleader and a jock are a much better match."

Brooke turned to leave, but Fallon screeched from behind.

"Wait! Wait, you idiot!"

"What did you call me?" Brooke stopped and turned in her tracks.

"I had to get your attention."

"Well, now you've got it."

"Look, Billy hired me to clean his place. I need a job and there's not much I can do."

"I'm supposed to believe that?"

"Believe it. Remember, I didn't go to college. I got married right after high school. And anyway why would I lie to you? If I were with Billy I'm not the type to keep it quiet."

That much was true. She'd lord it over Brooke.

"He hired you to punish me. That's what he did."

"No, he hired me to help me. Because he's the greatest guy

I know. Don't blow it with him like I did years ago by being jealous."

"Or maybe he didn't want to get married at seventeen."

Fallon rolled her eyes. "I don't know why you still have such a huge chip on your shoulder. Why don't you like me? This isn't high school anymore."

"Who said I don't like you?"

"Seriously? Look, you're the one that went to college. I didn't. I have a kid and an ex-husband that says I'm a bad mother. Maybe he's right, but I'm doing everything I can to get my baby back. Even clean the house of the local millionaire. My ex-boyfriend. You have everything now. You have a great job, and people respect you. Stop acting like you're auditioning for Rebel Without a Cause because I'm sick of it. He wants you, and I'd give anything to be you right now. But I'm not."

Brooke didn't know what to say to that so she didn't say a word. Stood there staring at the gorgeous, tall ex-cheerleader, the most popular girl at Starlight High. She envied Brooke.

"Were you coming here to tell him something?" Fallon asked softly.

"Yeah. I have some news. And I thought he might like to hear it."

"Well, his plane gets in at San Francisco in an hour. If you hurry, maybe you can meet him in baggage claim."

For once, Fallon had a good idea. This could be her grand gesture. "Ok. Thanks."

Brooke rushed to the cottage to grab her leather jacket and the keys to her Harley, and she was off. The weather was dry though chilly, a good night ride. The Harley would calm her down and get her mind on track. Maybe Fallon was right. Without realizing it, she'd fallen into long ago set patterns the moment she'd seen Billy again. She'd been thrown back to that time when she didn't feel like she belonged, nor did she want to.

But everything had changed now. She loved Billy Turlock, and he loved her.

She was still trying to get over the shock of being envied by one of the most beautiful girls she'd ever known when traffic stalled along 101. The wind at her back, Brooke throttled the Harley and it made a resultant sound that reflected her thoughts. Powerful.

Mom hadn't been ruined by the divorce. She'd told Brooke about an inheritance she hadn't even known about. While it might have been better had Mom not kept that to herself all these years, it didn't matter anyway. Mom hadn't been ruined. She'd bounced back and created the life she wanted. It didn't look like what anyone else expected, but somehow it worked for her.

Maybe Brooke could do the same. Create the life she wanted, even if it might not look anything like what she'd thought she once wanted.

And even if she wasn't ready for marriage, she was finally ready for love.

If only she could get rid of the stomach crushing fear that surrounded love. An almost certain feeling that disaster would ensue.

Mom asked what Brooke would do if she were no longer afraid. For so long she'd tried to risk everything but her heart that she wasn't even sure what it might look like. Not to be afraid to love. Like Billy, who'd been burned so many times but still kept trying.

He was the brave one.

Brooke rode up through traffic, splitting lanes. She probably should have taken another route, but too late now. If she didn't hurry she'd miss Billy altogether. Sure, she'd see him at home but that wouldn't have the same effect. This was going to be her grand gesture.

She wanted to see his eyes when he saw her waiting for him – wanted to see those eyes tell her what they'd been telling her all along if she'd only listened.

"I love you," he'd said. She couldn't wait to tell him that she loved him too. Even if it scared her a little bit. She'd been scared the first time she jumped out of a plane, too. It was part of the thrill.

Like Mom said, facing fear is what made her brave.

Next stop, conquering the dark, which was nothing more than the absence of light according to Einstein.

Traffic sped up as she approached Marin, and Brooke shifted and turned in to the left commuter lane.

The car came out of nowhere, side swiping her, and knocking her clear off her Harley. She flew across the lane, wondering how she could stop her forward momentum, reaching out an arm helplessly. She felt it twist unnaturally, followed by a hot and searing pain.

I'm going to miss his flight, Brooke thought, as everything around her faded to black.

CHAPTER 18

The plane was two hours delayed, and Billy was fed up, tired and in no joyous mood.

"Merry Christmas! I'll have your best Cabernet Sauvignon," Pop said to the stewardess in first class. "What do you carry?"

"I've no idea, sir. It's in a box, if that helps," The annoyed woman said.

"Horrors! You should carry Mirassu wine on these flights. We sing to the grapes. Makes them sweeter," Pop continued, and Billy began to wonder if he'd stop talking sometime this year.

He checked his emails. Nothing from Brooke, not that he'd expected anything since they'd been avoiding each other. He had another email from Fallon, telling him she'd left the key under the mat and thanking him for the loan. Again.

Well, if having money didn't mean you could help your friends and family, then what good was it anyway?

Pop finally let the exasperated stewardess go, and turned to Billy. "Is something going on with you and Brooke?"

He hadn't seen the point in telling Pop, who clearly adored Brooke. "Why do you ask?"

"Every time you two are in the same room together you try too hard not to look at each other. And sooner or later one of you fails and then acts like they've stared directly into the sun during an eclipse."

He'd noticed far too much. "We had a disagreement."

"Ah. What about?"

"I thought she should marry me, and she disagreed."

Pop laughed. "Say what? You asked the girl to marry you?"

"Not exactly." Billy stared straight ahead and ignored the young stewardess who smiled at him and licked her lips.

"Young people. What does that mean?"

"I told her how I felt. I love her, and she doesn't feel the same way. And now we have to work together."

"Son, you can't convince me that girl doesn't love you. She's crazy about you."

"She has a funny way of showing it."

"It must have been hard for you, hearing no for once in your life."

"Excuse me?" He'd heard the word 'no' plenty of times in his life.

No, your dad won't be at the game.

No, you weren't our first choice in the draft. But you'll do.

No, you're not starting this game.

No, another surgery won't do it. The shoulder is too damaged.

He hadn't experienced a lot of rejection in his life, but the few he had really mattered. And now this. Brooke, the only woman he'd ever wanted to spend the rest of his life with.

No, Billy. I don't love you.

"You've been lucky most of your life. Blessed, even. You even left baseball out on top. Yeah, the injuries were a shame but you had a good run. And you've always been a looker.

Probably lost count of the amount of women you've said 'no' to, and now one of them says 'no' to you. It's got to be hard." Pop chuckled.

Not funny. "Yeah, it isn't pleasant."

"So what kind of ring did you get her?" Pop asked, clicking his seatbelt.

"Ring?"

Pop's jaw gaped open. "Boy, don't tell me you didn't do it up right."

There hadn't been time for a ring. Figured they'd do that later. What was the big deal, anyway? "If you're asking if I got down on one knee, then no."

Pop shook his head. "This is what it's come to. You need to hear about romance from an eighty-year-old man."

"Uh, no. I don't. But thanks just the same."

"You may not need help getting the ladies, but you do need help with this. I blame myself. When your Dad left Eileen, I said I'd do my best to be there for you boys."

"And you did. We have no complaints."

"But I failed in the romance department. You had a gift for sports, and I nurtured that. But I should have told you about love. Should have warned you about the women that might come after you for the wrong reasons."

"Mom did, and Gigi finished the job."

"Ah Gigi, but she didn't tell you much about the women who wanted you for the right reasons. Did she?"

"No." They'd never talked about it because it wasn't business. Seemed as far she was concerned there were no women who would ever want him for the right reasons. And he'd never before this moment realized how insulting that was.

"When you meet the right woman, you need to court her. Put a little romance into it. I don't mean flowers and candy, though that's fine. I mean make her realize she's not one of many. Know what I mean?"

"I did that." At least, he thought he had.

He'd made it clear to Brooke. Who hung on to a long expired membership card for ten years because it reminded him of the one girl he'd never stopped thinking about? He shouldn't have to apologize for his history, for wanting to do the right thing when he thought he'd gotten Denise pregnant. He'd never offered her a proposal because it was more of a business agreement. They'd both agreed it was the right thing to do.

Damn, he'd failed Brooke. He should have had a ring, at least should have bent the knee.

"So you asked her to marry you?" Pop asked.

"I didn't come right out and ask. It was more like I said I wanted to have all that with her – marriage and babies."

"Babies?" Pop choked out. "Where's the fire, son? At least let's have a wedding first."

Billy shook his head. "It doesn't matter. She's not interested in any of that."

"Maybe she's not ready now, but she will be someday. You have to decide if she's worth waiting for. And if you love her, my guess is that should be a yes."

He did love her, but this kind of love meant commitment. Facing fears. If she couldn't meet him halfway, he didn't know what he could do with that. She could fall out of airplanes and bungee jump off a bridge but loving him was too much of a risk? He wasn't buying it.

He was no stranger to fear, even if he'd been reluctant to admit it. Worried he'd never throw again. Fear had settled inside his soul for a while, and built a stronghold in his heart. Only his family, Gigi and his coach had managed to pull him out. Three more surgeries had followed, and then the news that nothing more could be done. That he'd reached the end of his fairy tale.

And until he'd met Brooke, he'd believed that. He'd

assumed he would bide his time pretending to care about a vineyard. Until she made him care.

When he got home, they would talk. It couldn't be avoided any longer if they were going to work together, and live so near each other. And if nothing else, he'd tell her he wasn't going anywhere.

Before boarding the plane, he'd made the call to his agent. A big pass on the sports casting job. He'd called coach, and told him they'd work something out with the coaching job. The man had been ecstatic, and nearly sobbed on the phone.

Billy had a vineyard to run, a little patch of land where he'd grown accustomed to seeing the sun set every evening. But baseball would never be completely out of life or his blood. Brooke, more than anyone, had helped him realize it. And if it meant for now he'd coach high school baseball, that's what he would do.

When they landed thirty minutes later at SFO, Billy turned his phone back on. A flurry of messages waited for him, none of which he wanted to see.

"Call me when you land." A text from Scott.

"Brooke has been in an accident." From Mom.

"St. Francis Hospital." From Scott. "Headed there now."

"What's wrong?" Pop asked, grabbing his arm.

Clearly, the news showed on Billy's face. His stomach had dropped to the soles of his feet.

"It's Brooke. We're going to the hospital."

* * *

SOMEONE WANTED Brooke to wake up, but she couldn't. Not now when the dream was so wonderful.

In her dream she wasn't afraid any more. The baby was cute, too. She looked to be around one and had Billy's eyes.

Like her father, she loved to smile. Everyone adored her, but none more than Brooke.

"Wake up."

I'm a Mom, Brooke thought, but fear didn't come into the equation. Only a love that reached far beyond fear. Love that made fear a chump.

"Brooke, please wake up."

"I don't want to," she managed to mumble.

She floated on air, sucking up all the happiness in the atmosphere. Feeling sorry for all the people in the world who weren't her.

When she finally decided to open one eye it wasn't because anyone had asked. Her arm hurt as though a wild rabid animal had chewed on it, and before she could get back to her dreams she clearly had to do something about that. Also, her mouth was so dry that a drink of water would be nice.

"Oh," she heard someone groan. Possibly it was her. Ouch. Correction, her arm felt as though someone had lit it on fire, ripped it off and then tried to sew it back on. Someone cruel and inhumane. Her legs too felt sore and bruised.

Her other eye opened to bright light, a comforting site.

She recognized the first thing in her line of site— a full head of dark brown hair lying on her stomach. Fortunately, she'd know that head anywhere. She lifted her left arm, the one that didn't hurt, and ran her fingers through his hair. *Billy.*

Then she remembered it all— the drive to the airport in traffic, the lane change, the accident. Flying and landing. Not much after that, but she did seem to remember some screaming in the Emergency Room. Quite possibly coming from her also. They'd hooked her up to an IV and she didn't remember much after that.

She had a cast on her right arm. Great.

Billy shifted, lifted his head and grinned. "Finally." He ran a hand through his hair, pushing it out of his eyes. He smiled and her heart did a silly ping followed by a somersault. Her heart had become a genuine acrobat.

"Were you the one who wanted me to wake up? I was having a great dream." She would like to get back to it but she needed water first.

Billy read her mind and had a straw to her lips. "Here."

She took a sip, and then groaned. "My arm really hurts. Kind of bad. Strike that. Horrible. That's the word I'm looking for."

"That makes sense since you broke it. A compound fracture. You had surgery."

"Oh, right. Now I remember. When I saw the bone sticking out of my arm I think I might have screamed a little. How long have you been here?"

"Since Pop and I landed yesterday."

An entire day had passed? It wasn't Christmas day anymore, but The Holidays seemed to be the gift that kept on giving.

Brooke shifted and her arm hurt even worse. "That was yesterday?"

"Yeah. I've been here all night. They tried to kick me out." He grinned again, and her heart flipped in the now familiar way.

"They wouldn't do that. How many people wanted your autograph?"

"Well, two or three but then they left me, I mean us, alone. For the most part. They've been coming in all night to check your meds. You probably need more of that, don't you?" He glanced at the IV.

"Where's my Mom?" Brooke didn't want to worry Mom, but she should probably be told.

"She's been here all night as well. I sent her home only a few minutes ago."

Then she remembered the rest. Trying to meet his plane at the airport. Failing big time.

"I have to tell you something."

They both said it at once.

"You go first." She understood that he'd been waiting. Asking her to wake up, she had to assume because he wanted to say something important. She wouldn't blame him if he'd changed his mind about her, since he'd had the misfortune to fall in love with a complete idiot. Someone who didn't recognize the right man when he was right in front of her.

"Listen—" He began, but was interrupted by Eileen, who walked in with Giancarlo.

"My dear," Eileen reached over, nearly shoving Billy out of the way. "What on earth happened?"

Following her were Scott, Pop, and Wallace, bringing up the year. The entire Turlock clan in her hospital room.

"I had an accident." Wasn't that obvious?

"Your Harley looks totaled," Scott said. "Sorry about that."

Brooke groaned.

"At least she's not totaled," Eileen said, straightening and tucking in Brooke's bed sheets.

"Thanks for coming guys, but we need to let Brooke rest," Billy protested.

"We brought some flowers," Wallace came forward with a large vase of yellow mums and put them on her nightstand.

"Thanks," Brooke said with a forced smile.

"How did this happen?" Giancarlo asked. "And why do you ride a motorcycle?"

"That's what I'd like to know." Eileen said, filling her glass with fresh water from the plastic pitcher. "They're dangerous. I don't allow my boys to ride them."

"Right." The boys answered like a chorus.

Brooke stifled a laugh, and that hurt. She happened to know all three boys had motorcycles they rode occasionally.

"Please, Eileen. You can't tell grown men what to do." Pop waved Eileen out of the way, and sat on the edge of Brooke's bed. "Now I want you to know we'll take care of everything while you're recuperating."

She hadn't thought about that— exactly how long would she be recuperating? Even though it was her right arm, maybe she could figure out a way to work with her left one. Or one of those dictation programs for any emails she'd have to send out. No, she couldn't be out of work for weeks. "Uh, you will?"

"We'll take it from here." Pop patted her shoulder gently.

She was digesting that information, thinking what an idiot she'd been to risk life and limb for a cool ride, when Billy was at her elbow. "Time for everyone to file out of here."

Scott and Wallace didn't need to be asked twice, and Pop and Giancarlo brought up the rear.

Eileen took Pop's place on the edge of Brooke's bed. Then she turned to Billy, who was staring at her. "Oh. You don't mean me, also?"

Billy helped his mother rise from the bed. "Please. I'd like to be alone with Brooke."

"Fine," Eileen said. "But I'll be at the house every day helping out. Don't worry about a thing, Brooke. I'll bring all your meals. Believe, me, after a while you won't miss your taste buds. And best of all, it's healthy. You'll recuperate faster."

"All right, Mom." Billy led her to the door.

Alone with Billy. At last. Too bad everything hurt. She'd come here by way of an ambulance, and she didn't want to think about the bill. Another thing. Brooke was in a private room. That had to be costing her a great deal, and even though thanks to Billy she had great insurance she'd probably have to dig deeply into savings for her deductible.

"How long do I have to be here and how much is this going to cost me?" Brooke asked.

"Just another day. Don't worry, I'm paying for everything."

"No, Billy—"

"I asked them to put you in a private room. Believe me, you don't want the co-pay for that."

Billy had just reached her side when the nurse walked in. "Excuse me," she said to Billy, as if wielding her power like a battle ax, "You'll have to leave for a few minutes."

Billy scowled at the nurse as though he was about to protest, but then he turned to Brooke. "I'll be right back."

When he'd left, the nurse whose name tag read 'Renata' turned to Brooke. "If you want him to stay out I can make it happen."

"Why would I want that?"

"Well he's been here all night. He wouldn't leave, and honestly I'm no baseball fan so I was about to kick him out. Unfortunately Dr. Harrison loves the Sliders." Renata sighed, overcome with woe apparently.

"Yeah, I'm no baseball fan either." Brooke squirmed a little as Renata checked her IV line.

"What are you doing with a man like that?"

Brooke wanted to ask if perhaps the kind nurse should have her eyesight checked. But it wasn't just his looks. It was — him. Jock or not. He was one of the good guys, even if it had taken her the better part of ten years to realize.

"He's not a ball player anymore. He owns the Mirassu vineyard in Starlight Hill."

Renata slipped the blood pressure cuff on Brooke's good arm and started pumping. "Is that right? Well he's an odd duck, that one. Wouldn't let me shut the lights off all night long. I know baseball players have their quirks, but let me just say right now that was a strange one."

"He wouldn't let you turn the lights off?" Something inside Brooke's heart bust open.

"Said you needed the light. Right. I asked him if he was aware that your eyes were closed. You know, athletes are not always the sharpest tool in the shed. But he insisted."

He insisted. Because he knew how afraid of the dark she'd been, knew she still slept with a nightlight even with his big capable body right next to hers. Might have realized after the accident she didn't want to wake up in the dark and in strange surroundings.

"Hmmm. Your heart rate is a little higher than earlier. You feeling okay?" She asked as she slipped off the cuff.

Better than ever, actually. Except, of course, for the road burn, scratches and broken arm.

"I love him. Big time." Had she just said that out loud? From the dumbfounded look on Renata's face, Brooke had.

So what if the first person she confessed this too was a nurse she might never see again? She was working up to telling the man himself. This was like a running start. A rehearsal. A dry run.

"I don't know why patients feel like they need to unburden themselves to me. I have that kind of face, I guess. Fine. He's a good looker. I'll give you that. Although the hair? Maybe a little too long. Get a haircut every now and then. Even men get split ends. But try telling them that. Anyway, is that kind of man really the settling down type? Now think about it."

"I'm the one who's not marriage material."

"You?" Renata didn't seem to buy what Brooke was selling.

That was okay, because things had changed. "I wasn't, but I am now. He loves me and I love him."

"Well. Maybe the kind of love that can be a little suffocating."

"Not to me," Brooke said and for the first time in her life she meant it.

Every relationship had fizzled out in the past, and she'd walked away if a guy got too serious. Often too serious meant wanting her to meet his family, or vice versa. She'd been strangling from the inside out. She'd always thought it had to do with the fact that she wasn't cut out for long term, not that she'd just never met the right man.

But of all the times to declare her love for the man, this had to be the worst. In a hospital bed, banged up, with a broken arm.

At that moment, he walked through the door.

"Looks who's back," the nurse said without enthusiasm. "You're like a rash."

"I'm going to go out on a limb and take a guess that you're not a big sports fan." Billy said with his amazing smile.

"You guessed right. I'll leave you two alone," she said as she fiddled with the IV again. "You should be feeling less pain in a minute or two. Might even sleep some more if *someone* would let you."

When she left the room, Billy lifted a shoulder. "Hey, you can't win `em all."

"I'm sorry about that. I guess she doesn't like ball players."

"Like someone else I used to know," Billy said as he reached her bedside.

Her heart melted a little bit more. Pretty soon her heart would slide right out of her, nothing but a gooey mess on the ground. "I remember her. I didn't really like that girl. She wasn't just afraid of the dark. She was afraid of letting anyone too close. Especially boys that she shouldn't like, but somehow did anyway."

"You liked me?"

She thought maybe she might be blushing because her face felt hot. "C'mon, Billy. Everybody liked you. You're hard not to like."

He glanced in the direction of the closed door. "Some people manage just fine."

She'd give him that. "I need to tell you something."

He squeezed her good hand. "You were going to let me go first."

"Oh, right." She'd waited this long, she could wait a few more minutes.

"I'm sorry. You were right. I pushed you too hard, too fast. I want things to stay the same too. Whatever you want. I just can't lose you." He was threading his fingers through hers, and good grief, the soul-catching gaze in his green eyes. *Billy, the soul reaper.* How could anyone resist him? Certainly not her.

Her hardened heart had barely resisted him ten years ago.

She yanked on his hand pulling him even closer, letting her fingers slide through dark hair. How had this hair ever seemed too long before? It happened to be the perfect length. "You're not trying to back out on me now, are you?"

He looked confused. "No— wait. What?"

Brooke sighed. "I had it all planned out. I was going to do better than this. For one, I wasn't going to be in a hospital bed. I didn't plan on this cast, on my right arm no less. And I probably don't look as good as I did when I was practicing in the mirror."

Even more confusion. "What mirror?"

"Never mind." She shook her head. Ouch. Well, couldn't lose her nerve now. What if she'd broken more than her arm? What if— she didn't want to go there. "Here's the thing. I think you already know this, but I love you like crazy."

"Yeah?" Wow. Her favorite smile. Full throttle.

"Crazy love. Are you ready for that?" The man deserved

fair warning. She wasn't sure what crazy love would look like, but it would probably involve spending a lot of time together and being a little bit jealous. She'd work on that.

"I want crazy." He kissed her hand.

"You say that now, but are you sure? My kind of crazy means Fallon can't clean your house anymore."

"Actually, that makes sense."

"So I'll find something she can do for me at the winery." Under Brooke's supervision. Too bad that she didn't trust ex-girlfriends who had admitted they were jealous. "I know you want to help her."

"But you come first with me."

Tears formed in her eyes, making it hard to see his face through the blur. Love had turned her into a first class wimp. "Tell me that you still want to marry me."

"Any time. Any place. I mean it."

"I was worried you'd changed your mind."

"Why? Because you like to challenge gravity every now and then? You think a little thing like that is going to scare me off?"

"No, because I'm a coward at heart. I couldn't tell you when you needed to hear me say it. But I was on my way to tell you yesterday, when I had the accident."

"I made my own mistake, Brooke. I shouldn't have brought up getting married like it was the way to end an argument. If you don't mind, I'd like to try again."

She smiled and damned if her face didn't hurt too. "I think we both need a second chance."

CHAPTER 19

Brooke wasn't sure how long she'd been asleep when hushed voices woke her up. Hands down, the hospital was the worst place on the face of the earth to get a decent night's sleep. She couldn't wait to get home.

"Which does she like best?" A woman asked, sounding oddly like Mom.

"Personally, I like her in red. It is the season."

Was that – Eileen?

"This is her favorite," Ivey's small voice said.

Brooke opened up one eye. She wasn't dreaming this. Mom, Eileen and Ivey stood just inside her hospital room holding up dresses.

"What's going on?" Brooke asked. "Is there some discharge dress code I'm not aware of?"

She was scheduled to go home today, both the doctor and the nurse had said. They'd already held her an extra day out of an abundance of caution. Plus, Billy had promised. Her last memory before she'd drifted off to sleep had been of him, just sitting next to her holding her hand.

"Good, you're awake," Eileen said moving toward her bedside.

The others followed her. "Do you prefer the red dress or the black one?" Ivey asked. "I said the black one, but it is Christmas time."

"Can't I just go home in jeans?" She wasn't exactly feeling glamorous.

"Believe me, honey, you're going to want to look your best in a few minutes," Mom said.

"I brought your make-up," Ivey said. "Do you want me to help you put it on?"

Considering she was right handed, the answer was obvious. But why did she need to wear make-up? Brooke sat up a little straighter. "All right, what's going on?"

She caught Eileen, Mom and Ivey exchange a look.

"There might be some photos taken in a few minutes. And I figured you'd want to look your best," Ivey said.

Brooke's heart sped up into the stratosphere. She hadn't asked if anyone else had been involved in the accident. What if there was a press conference? "Was someone else hurt in the accident? I thought it was just me."

"Oh no, dear. This is good news," Eileen said. "The best. Just please listen to the women and do as we say."

"You won't regret it," Mom said.

"The shoes!" Eileen said. "I almost forgot."

"I'll come with you," Mom said following Eileen out the door.

For the first time it occurred to Brooke that Mom and Eileen had a lot in common. One loved healthy food, the other one the ground that provided it.

Ivey came at Brooke with the mascara wand.

"Put away the wand, and nobody gets hurt." Brooke said.

"Just let me do this and stop asking questions," Ivey said with a pout. "I've been sworn to secrecy."

Brooke sucked in a breath. She remembered bits and pieces of her conversations with Billy. He wanted a second chance. He wanted to ask her properly. Could this have anything to do with it? She was beginning to have suspicions.

But why now? In her hospital bed?

But would she argue the point? She wasn't picky about the location or the proposal. It just had to happen, the sooner the better, so she could say yes. Hell yes. "Put it on, and make sure it doesn't clump."

A few minutes later, Brooke sat up on the edge of her bed. Her hair and make-up were done to perfection. She wore her red dress and black stiletto heels and felt a bit like a Christmas card come to life. She tried not to think about how the holidays had never been particularly good to her.

Maybe this year would be different.

Eileen, who had been alternatively staring out the window and pacing the bedroom floor finally waved Brooke over with a smile.

"Brooke, come see this."

BROOKE KICKED off the heels and shuffled over to the window, Mom and Ivey flanking her on either side. Several stories below, a smattering of cameras were pointed at a microphone stand. And the man behind that mike was none other than Billy.

He looked heartbreakingly handsome in casual jeans and a Sliders jacket.

Ivey flicked on the TV set and Brooke turned to see Billy on the local channel.

"Do you have an announcement to make?" someone shouted.

"What's this about, Billy?"

Billy smiled. "Thanks for coming. I have decided to pass

on the sports casting offer from Fox Sports with regret. Instead I'll be coaching the high school baseball team, the Starlight Hills Panthers. The place where I began. And of course, I do own Mirassu vineyards as most of you know. But starting next month the place is under a new name. It's going to be called Brooke. Brooke's Wine. That has a nice ring to it."

Brooke's heart dropped. She didn't want the place named after her. Yes, that was kind and generous but what about her marriage proposal? She tried to smile but her eyes grew watery and she leaned a little bit on Mom. "That's sweet. This is a surprise."

The press would probably want photos of her and it was a good thing she looked presentable. As long as she could keep the tears in check.

Anyway, there would be plenty of time for a proposal later. She needed to get a grip.

"And guys, I know the media and I haven't always had the best relationship, but if you could help me out here. You see, my girl doesn't much like the holidays. I wanted to change that this year."

Brooke's knees grew weak. Someone that looked suspiciously like Stephan brought out a giant blown up photo of the one on Stephan's blog and handed it to Billy.

Written on the photo in large and bright red letters were the words:

"Would the woman in this photo please marry me?"

That's when Billy looked up as if he'd marked her window and knew her exact location. Smiling, he turned the sign up to her. Cameras clicked and reporters fired out questions. Brooke couldn't hear any of them over the buzz in her brain.

Mom squeezed her shoulder. Ivey sobbed.

Eileen cried out, "My son is such a romantic."

"Does this window open?" Brooke asked. First things first. How could she say yes through a closed window? "Ivey, help me open this window. Quick!"

Ivey shoved the window open, but Billy wasn't standing in front of the mike any longer.

As if he'd anticipated her questions, the TV news camera zoned in on one reporter.

"Ladies and gentlemen, sports fans everywhere: Billy Turlock has entered the hospital building. I've sent a runner behind him and I'll be giving you a play by play. Stand by, please. We've all watched Billy's career, but I think it's safe to say this is the most important pitch of his life. Will she or won't she, folks? Aaaaaand he's on the second floor. Sprinting down the hallway, my runner tells me. Still carrying that huge sign. What do you expect? He's an athlete. And I'm willing to bet Billy has just thrown one of his famous fast balls tonight. Sailing across the plate at 98 miles an hour straaaaaight into the catcher's glove."

"I feel like we're at a ball game," Ivey muttered then suddenly grabbed Brooke. "Put your heels on! He's coming!"

"I don't need my heels. So what if I'm short," Brooke said as she moved away from the window.

She had to catch her breath. Billy was going to do this right here, right now, just two days after Christmas.

She heard a nurse down the hallway. "All right, I'll allow this foolishness but no way is that man going in with you. And give me that ridiculous photo."

Suddenly the reporter on the TV channel stopped talking and scowled into the camera. "We'll be back after a word from our sponsor."

Then Billy was inside the door, and she stood frozen to the spot. She probably couldn't move an inch if a hurricane came through her room and her heartbeat banged against her rib cage hard enough to wake the dead.

"Hi," she said to the whirlwind that was Billy Turlock. If she didn't love him so much she'd hate him for not even looking winded.

"Wow, you look beautiful." He sounded surprised. Was he seriously going to propose with her hospital gown on? *Men.*

She threw a grateful smile in the direction of Mom, Ivey and Eileen. Then she turned back to Billy. "Yes!"

"No, wait a minute." He fished in his pants pocket.

"Too late. You can't take it back now," Brooke said.

He flashed the full throttle grin and dropped to one knee. "I've been a lucky man most of my life, but I think the luckiest day of my life was when I bought the Mirassu vineyard. Not because I got a deal on a great piece of land but because it led me to my real treasure. I don't much care for wine, or money, or even baseball if I can't have you there with me. Would you marry me?"

Brooke stared at Billy's now open palm. In it was a beautiful solitaire diamond ring. "Yes, yes! I'll marry you!"

Billy slipped the ring on her finger and thank goodness her left arm wasn't in a cast. It slid right on like it had been sized for her. "I love you, Brooke."

"I love you," she whispered, relieved she could finally say it and no longer be afraid.

In the next few minutes the room became filled with the rest of the Turlocks— Pop, Wallace, Scott. Even Giancarlo appeared, joining Eileen's side.

Pop uncorked a bottle of champagne. "Hot diggity dog! Let's celebrate!"

The holidays would never be the same again.

Billy threaded his fingers through her left hand, and Brooke turned to see all the smiling faces in the room. Pop grinned ear to ear, Wallace for once looked interested, and Scott was pounding Billy's back. Ivey was sniffling and smiling, Mom was pulling a tissue out of the nearby box, and Eileen was openly weeping in Giancarlo's arms.

There were a whole lot of people in the room for one proposal. But she wouldn't have it any other way. She squeezed Billy's hand.

This was a family affair.

ALL OF ME

CHAPTER 1

ot a good sign.

Instead of being ushered to HR to sign employee paperwork and W2 forms, Ivey Lancaster had been sent to the medical director's office.

Probably some minor mix-up with the paperwork. By now they'd received the glowing letter of reference from her mentor, Babs Holiday. Ivey was more than qualified for the midwife position at the new women's center.

Deep breath. *You've got this.*

Finally, Dr. Lillian Walker strode into her office.

"I apologize, but I'm running behind this morning." She shook Ivey's hand. "We're on my son's third babysitter. He's four, and the master of his universe. In other words, he's going to grow up to be a surgeon." Lillian sat behind the futuristic-looking stainless steel desk, drew in a deep breath and leaned back in her chair.

Uh-oh. "Is something wrong?"

Lillian picked up a file, stared at it, and put it back down. "You could say that. This morning I found an orderly and a nurse in a closet, and they weren't looking for supplies. Dr.

Harrison has taken an ill-timed vacation, since his wife threatened that if he didn't come along she'd go by herself and not come back. So I'm short staffed again. And then there's this desk. Who ever heard of a desk without drawers? It's beautiful, but why do I feel like I'm Uhura on Star Trek? I'd like to strangle the designer."

Ivey wished she could help, but she had her own problems. Aunt Lucy had a broken leg, and she'd be waiting at home right now. Wondering if her niece would get the job. So if Lillian could get on with it that would be nice.

"And then there's the women's center, and the midwife position." She scowled.

Directors scowling: another bad sign.

Ivey tensed at the overpowering scent of Lillian's lavender perfume, causing a sudden memory of Mom. On a good day, Mom had always been in Ivey's corner. On a bad day, Mom couldn't find the corner.

But this didn't make sense. Lillian had practically promised the job to Ivey, and she'd done well in all the interviews.

"It's not you," Lillian said.

Great. Could any good news start out that way? "So there's a problem."

"You guessed it. I've run into some objections from the obstetric doctors on staff." Lillian sighed and tapped a manicured nail on her desk.

This didn't come as any big surprise. Ivey had dealt with territorial doctors before, but Lillian had filled her mind with thoughts of a progressive hospital. "But you said ..."

"I know, and I'm sorry, Ivey, but I can't hire you. I can't hire anyone right now. The work requisition has been held up due to the doctors' objections. They went to the board. Behind my back." Lillian's lips were a thin, straight line.

"I thought—"

"Think about what it's like for me as medical director of this hospital. The first female director. Our small hospital has been overwhelmed with budget cuts—"

"But this is why you would save money with the midwifery program. The hospital can save money when a midwife delivers a baby," Ivey said, but suddenly the problem dawned on her like a pink zebra in the room. Doctors, pressed between onerous HMOs breathing down their backs and struggling hospitals, felt their livelihoods threatened. She'd heard this story before.

"You can imagine how well it went over with the doctors on staff. I only have three of them on the L&D floor. It's hard enough to keep them here. Malpractice insurance costs, rising health care costs, and now the Affordable Health Care Act." Lillian waved a hand in the air.

Ivey sank in her seat. "I see." Until this moment she hadn't realized how much she wanted the job. She'd gotten used to being home again, among the hills and rambling vineyards of Starlight Hill in Napa Valley. Aunt Lucy constantly complained about its appalling lack of nightlife, but Ivey loved the quiet and the time to reflect. She'd been gone too long, kept away mostly by memories too tender to face even after all this time.

But she was back now, and that said something. It said Ivey Lancaster was ready to move on and make a life.

Now she'd have to find Plan B. Damn doctors. "Thank you for your time."

Ivey started to get up, but Lillian spoke again. "Unless, and I can't ask for this—" Lillian's steadfast brown eyes settled on Ivey.

"Unless what?"

"Unless you like a fight."

As it happened, Ivey had been fighting for one thing or

another most of her life. Did she like a fight? Yes, but only if she could win.

"I like a fair fight. And I especially like to win." Might as well put it out there.

"I thought so. I'll be honest. I had a feeling it would be difficult to get this idea past the doctors. But it's time for some changes around here. And I saw something in you I didn't see in the other candidates. You don't give up easily, do you?"

A person with dyslexia didn't get through life without engaging in a metaphorical fight or two. Or three. "True."

"If you'll help me, I believe we could make this vision of ours a reality. Since the doctors' objections, the board has arranged for a subcommittee to oversee the decision. They've appointed one doctor to represent them, and I'd like to appoint you."

"*Me?*" She was a midwife, not a committee member.

Every time she'd had to make a presentation in school she'd clammed up. It had meant PowerPoint slides and reading out loud, and with her dyslexia, that was not a good time. She'd finally memorized every last word so that she wouldn't have to rely on any reading.

The whole idea was out of the question. "Sorry, I'm not a good speaker."

"You won't have to present. It's simply a written recommendation to the Board. What I need is someone who believes in my vision—someone who shares it with me."

"I see your point, but I'm not sure how I can help."

"I want our new women's center to eventually have a staff of midwives available. Women who have low-risk pregnancies deserve that choice, don't you agree?"

"Well, of course I agree." But that wasn't the point. The point was she wasn't going to be on any committee, sub- or otherwise.

"Thank you! You won't regret this. The doctors have appointed a first-year resident to the subcommittee. Some requirement by one of the benefactors. Don't ask me why, but surely the two of you can get along and come to some sort of compromise. You're both young, so you'll be flexible." Lillian stood up.

"But I—" Wait. When exactly had she agreed to do this?

"Follow me. I'll find the resident they've appointed, and maybe the two of you can arrange the first meeting."

She hadn't agreed to anything, and yet why were her feet following Lillian?

Lillian led her to a conference room and waved towards a chair. "I'll be right back once I find him. He's an ER resident, so if he's here at all, that's where he'll be. Sit tight."

Ivey didn't sit. She'd rather stand, thank you. Pace, more like it. She might pace her way right out of this conference room and right through the front doors of St. Vincent's Hospital. Hop in her SUV and drive back to the Vineyard Cottages where Aunt Lucy would be waiting.

But she did want this job, and the fact remained that a first-year resident wasn't going to be all that intimidating. No, she could handle him. Then the door opened, and Ivey's world shifted off its axis. She dropped into a chair before she fell down. This. Wasn't. Happening.

"What are *you* doing here?"

Jeff Garner should not have walked into the conference room like he had any business being here. He was supposed to be away in another state, completing his residency.

He met her eyes. "I was going to ask you the same thing. I'm here for a subcommittee meeting."

"That's not funny."

"Good, because I wasn't trying to be." Jeff took a seat on the other side of the table. As far away as he could get from her, because he was good at that. Interesting how some things never changed.

"Why aren't you in Maryland?"

"Because that would be a hell of a commute." He leaned back in his seat.

"Funny. So I guess you're no longer doing residency in Maryland."

Lillian breezed in. "Oh good, you've met. You two are the chosen subcommittee to meet and make a recommendation to the board on whether the women's center will add midwives to the staff."

Ivey stood. "Excuse me."

"Is there a problem?" Lillian turned to Ivey, eyebrows arched with the classic there-had-better-not-be-a-problem-because-I-trusted-you look of a superior.

Ivey glanced over at Jeff, who was smiling. *Yes, there's a problem. I didn't agree to this. Especially not with him.*

"Not at all." She couldn't give him the satisfaction of knowing he upset her that much.

"When do you need us to report back to you?" Jeff piped up.

"How about in one month? That should give you enough time. I'll give you two a few moments to get acquainted." Lillian left the room and shut the door behind her.

Get acquainted. That was a rich one. She was so well acquainted with her ex that she knew how many freckles he had on his back. And that would definitely not help her right now.

Jeff stared at his smart phone. "One month. That's doable. I'll give up sleeping."

Ivey snorted. She guessed she was supposed to feel sorry for him. Well she didn't. "This isn't going to happen. You and I can't work together. It's asking too much."

She thought she could see Jeff's jaw tighten, nearly imperceptibly. A chink in his armor. "I'm fine with it. We're both adults and professionals."

Except that right now she didn't feel much like an adult, because somehow Jeff made her feel like a sixteen-year-old again.

"You're right. If you can handle it, so can I."

"Good." His pager went off. He glanced at it and then stood. "Let's reconvene again tomorrow?"

"What time?" Ivey asked, as he moved towards the door.

"You pick the time. I pretty much live here."

"Okay. How about nine?"

"Fine." He walked out without a backwards glance.

Ivey swallowed. No big deal. She could handle this unfortunate turn of events.

But it didn't help that Jeff looked better, somehow, than she'd remembered. He'd grown into a man, cords of muscles in his forearms. Not tall and lanky anymore. Now his muscles had muscles. His dark brown hair was no longer long and unruly but closed cropped. Although some things never changed—he still had the same panty-melting gaze in his whiskey-brown eyes.

Those eyes had once regarded her with desire and tenderness, but now they only reminded her that they were virtually strangers. No matter. He might have a stare to melt glaciers in the Arctic, but it wasn't going to have any effect on her. She wouldn't let it.

CHAPTER 2

*J*eff ambled down the corridors of St. Vincent's, dodging orderlies and nurses on his way to the ER, acting like it was any other shift. Pretending he hadn't coaxed his heart back down into his chest cavity where it belonged. Asked it to please resume its regular rhythm.

He worked his ass off for this hospital, and when some lofty admin-higher-up had issued the command that he would represent the doctors on the subcommittee, he'd cringed and hoped for the best. Seemed to be all he did these days.

But then he'd walked into the room and seen Ivey, and just like that, it was five years ago again, and he'd come back home on break from medical school to find she'd left town to meet up with some idiot she met on a dating service.

He'd done his best to pretend that she wasn't even more beautiful than he remembered, and he had a pretty good memory. A sultry version of Snow White, with her espresso-colored hair and blue eyes. He found himself wondering if she'd wound up with the dating service guy. Maybe she'd married, and had kids with that loser. Kids that were supposed to be Jeff's.

Hopefully he wouldn't run into the man, because Jeff wasn't sure he could hold back the resentment he felt towards someone who had romanced his girl with a freaking computer while he'd been away at medical school.

Not that he should give a damn.

Dr. Stewart met him in the elevator, and hopped on at the last minute. "I heard you got put on the subcommittee."

"Don't know how that happened. I'd like to sleep sometime."

"Interesting. So you don't know. Well apparently one of the benefactors behind the women's center insisted that it be you. Why do you think that is?" Stewart eyed him with suspicion.

"Just lucky, I guess."

"I can count on you to let me know what kind of progress you're making?" Stewart was the head of obstetrics and had his own agenda when it came to the hiring of midwives on staff.

Come to think of it, they'd likely picked Jeff because he had no skin in the game. And that had been true until he'd seen Ivey. Now he didn't even know what to think. Probably because he'd been on his feet for twenty-four hours. Thinking had become difficult, and sleep a distant but fond memory. Fortunately his shift was at an end.

"I'll let you know." Jeff stepped off the elevator and onto the ER floor.

"There you are," Donna, the ER nurse, said. "I've got Frank in bay two."

He stopped moving, not an easy thing to do on the ER floor. "Again? That's the second time this week."

"You know Frank," Donna said from behind the nurse's

desk. "You're his favorite. But don't worry, Dr. Lewis has already seen him. Frank wants to say hi."

"After this, I'm going home. If I can remember where that is." Jeff made his way to the bay and opened the curtain. "Hello, Frank. What's it been, three days? You doing okay?"

"That depends on whether you think oxygen is a good or a bad thing." Frank sat up straighter on the cot.

"It's a good thing, and you know it." Jeff checked Frank's vital signs. As usual, Frank was the healthiest elderly man he'd seen in his ER. But the man insisted he had a heart problem and a breathing issue. And on Fridays, a skin condition.

"That's what I thought. So when I can't breathe, that's a problem."

"You breathe fine, and I think I've proven it." Jeff had tested his oxygen levels countless of times.

Frank coughed. "You should check my heart this time."

"What's wrong with your heart this week?" His vital signs showed a steady and regular heart rate, better than Jeff's had been a few minutes ago. The EKG looked good.

"I was sitting down watching cable television earlier, and suddenly my heart rate shot up into the stratosphere. I swear it must have been two hundred."

"Two hundred?" That would be a concern if it were true, but Frank's heart had never gone over ninety when he'd been in the ER. "What makes you think it was that much?"

"I don't know for sure, but when the young lady took her top off I remember thinking, 'For the love of Pete, those can't be real,' and that's when my heart started to gallop like a bunch of horses off to the races. The world is a strange place, Doc."

Jeff would have laughed, but he didn't have one in him today. "All right, Frank. Maybe stay away from the porn channels."

"You think that's it? Can I get a prescription?"

"You don't need a prescription, you need advice. Here, I'll write it on my pad if that makes you feel any better." He scribbled instructions to avoid porn, and tore it off. "Here you go. Have you seen your regular doctor? Last time you were here I asked you to make an appointment for follow-up."

"Nah, that doctor reminds me of a toddler. I'm afraid to let him touch me. Where did he get his diploma? The Romper Room?"

Jeff sighed. "Frank, there's only so much I can do for you here."

"You talk to me, and that's more than anyone else does."

Jeff faced Frank and used his official doctor voice. "Make an appointment with your regular doctor."

"All right, Doc. I'll try to get in to see him. But I'll be back if it doesn't work. Or if I get the rash back."

"And I'll probably be here."

"Right. Where else would you be?"

As he undressed in the locker room, he thought about the fact that Ivey knew where he'd originally been accepted for residency. But if she'd been keeping tabs on him—which he found . . . interesting—she'd missed an update on the past year.

When news got around to his family that he'd been recommended for a resident position at St. Vincent's, they'd waged a campaign for his return to Starlight Hill. Granted, he hadn't been back for much more than a short visit in the past few years, but his niece and nephew Becky and Liam were getting older, and his sister Ali wanted their only uncle around more often. Little did she know someone would have to be injured to see much of him.

He supposed it made sense that Ivey was back for a visit, but applying for this job meant she wanted to stay. Maybe things hadn't worked out with Computer Guy. Or maybe they'd worked out great, and for all he knew they'd moved their family to the best small town in Napa Valley to raise a family.

He didn't know and neither should he care. All he wanted now, besides a few hours of uninterrupted sleep, was to get through this punishing residency and secure his future. He hadn't been through eight years of school to give up now, even if at times he wondered if he was doing any good at all.

At St. Vincent's he'd become accustomed to the regulars, Frank being one of them. There was also the usual quirky small-town mix he'd come to expect——people he'd literally grown up around, like Ed, the accident-prone owner of the hardware store in town; the occasional migrant worker who'd met with the wrong end of a shovel; Marci, the hypochondriac; Eleanor, the pack-a-day smoker who insisted that he "do something" about her diabetes but refused to quit smoking or watch her diet; and the occasional wayward teen with alcohol poisoning.

Frank concerned him the most. It didn't take a psychiatric consult to see that the man was lonely. Jeff wasn't supposed to concern himself with how his patients did after they walked out the doors of the ER, once he'd pronounced they weren't in imminent danger of death. But he couldn't help being protective of Frank, who lived in assisted living and took too many trips to the ER.

Sooner or later, Jeff would need to get to the bottom of it.

* * *

IVEY UNLOCKED the door to Aunt Lucy's condo with shaking hands, closed it quickly, and leaned against it as though she could barricade herself inside from the rest of the world. The world in which Jeff lived in Starlight Hill again, breathing and eating and sleeping and Lord only knew what else.

And still looking too good.

One thought immediately sprung to mind: *I'm going to have to tell him.*

"What on earth?" Aunt Lucy stared from the couch where she lay splayed among magazine issues of *People*. "I saw a girl with the same expression you have on your face right now, but she was running through the woods from a madman who had an ax."

"I thought I told you not to watch those kinds of movies." Ivey walked to the TV and shut it off. She was the only one who could handle crime shows, and Aunt Lucy needed to stick to a steady diet of romantic comedies.

"Well thank goodness you're back. It itches again." Lucy shoved a pencil deep into the cast that covered her from knee to toe, thrust it up and down, grimaced for several seconds, and then sighed.

Ivey winced. "I don't think you should put a pencil down there."

"When you break your leg, you can talk. Lordy, when I get this cast off next week, I might kiss Dr. Stein."

"Please don't." Hadn't Ivey endured enough embarrassment when Lucy asked the doctor how a woman could have sex with a cast on her leg, and if he could recommend what position might work best?

"I'm kidding. He's not my type."

Not at all. Unfortunately he was at least thirty years older than her type, which lately tended towards thirty-something unemployed men. Not a bad thing, except for the fact that her aunt was fifty-eight.

The problem was that Aunt Lucy's priorities had changed when she'd won the California lottery ten years ago, and now she seemed determined to suck the marrow right out of life.

When she'd phoned about the broken leg she'd suffered skiing in Vail on the constant vacation she called her life, Ivey rushed back from Los Angeles to help. Aunt Lucy had once helped Ivey during a difficult time, and at least now she could pay back her kindness by tending to her every need. Even if every one of those needs was getting on Ivey's last nerve.

"How did it go at the hospital? Did you get the job?"

"No. I've been put on a subcommittee with one other doctor. Together we're supposed to come up with a recommendation for the board next month." Ivey grabbed a soda from the fridge and held it for a second against her flushed cheeks. Then she plopped down on the couch next to Lucy.

"A recommendation for what?"

"Whether they should even hire midwives for the women's center. I guess some of the doctors have objections."

"Oh they do, do they? Well la-di-da. So who is this doctor you're going to be working with?"

"Jeff Garner," Ivey said flatly, hoping she'd successfully removed every ounce of emotion from her voice.

Aunt Lucy's eyebrows went up to her forehead, and that was hard to do with all the Botox. "Oh. Oh, dear."

"Yeah."

Aunt Lucy fanned herself with the latest edition of her movie star magazine, and a picture of a smiling Brad Pitt and his arsenal of children waved in Ivey's direction. "It's for the best. Time you told him everything."

"No! It's not."

"He has a right to know." Aunt Lucy had always believed that, but she'd supported Ivey's decision.

"What do you think I should tell him? Hey, Jeff, five years

ago when I left town I was pregnant with your baby. Thought you should know. So have a great day."

"I never said it would be easy."

"I don't need to make enemies at the hospital, and he'll hate me."

"Or it will finally make sense to him that you took up with someone on the Internet and left town like you had something to hide. I wish you'd come up with a better story than that one. Everyone in town talked about you for weeks. Took sides and made me crazy. What a ditzy move that was."

Ivey threw her hands up in the air. "Why is it so crazy to believe I met someone on an online dating service? Hundreds of millions of people have found love there, or so the commercials say. And that's where I met Joe."

"Joe? I thought the name you made up was John."

"Don't you think I can remember the name of my own fake boyfriend? It was Joe. I've always liked that name. Joe's always a good guy. You can count on Joe."

Aunt Lucy shook her head. "You better make sure you keep that name straight if you want to keep up this ruse."

"I don't need to talk about Fake Joe. It didn't work out."

"If Jeff's like most men, the last thing he'll want to do is talk about your ex-boyfriends. Fake or otherwise."

"I'm not going to talk to him."

"How will you communicate? Sign language?"

"No. I'm going to get off this subcommittee." Ivey stretched her legs out on the couch. "It's the only way, so that's what I'm going to do."

No way would Lillian make her do this. She'd be there bright and early tomorrow morning and explain everything. Maybe even throw in a little tear or two. Those weren't all that hard to call up when she thought about the past and how badly she'd screwed everything up.

"I don't think that's a good idea. If you want this job, fight for it. Don't let him chase you out of town again."

"He didn't chase me out of town. I went willingly."

"Because you didn't want to be a glitch in his schedule. Well, Missy, it took two to make that baby."

"You don't have to tell me that." As it so happened, she had a distinct memory of the event, and she definitely hadn't been alone. Not that she wanted that image in her head right now.

But Aunt Lucy did have a point. She wasn't going to go anywhere, not this time. If it would be difficult for Jeff to have her stay in town, too bad. She was not going to accommodate him anymore.

"I want the job. It's not that. I only want off the subcommittee."

"Fine. But what's he going to think about that?"

"You know what? I don't care."

With a little more effort, Ivey might be able to convince herself of that.

CHAPTER 3

$\mathscr{E}$ight hours of fitful sleep were not enough, especially when Ivey had invaded half of Jeff's dreams, but they'd have to do.

Still, when he opened the door to the conference room at precisely nine o'clock the next morning, he'd half convinced himself that yesterday had been a nightmare. He wasn't really going to be on this subcommittee with his ex-girlfriend-slash-first-love.

But no, she was here. Not a figment of his imagination. He rubbed an eye with the back of his hand, more exhausted than disbelieving.

"What's the matter? Didn't sleep well last night?" Ivey looked up at him from her seat at the long conference table.

"Something like that."

"None of this bothers me, in case you were wondering. I slept like a baby."

"You always did. More like the dead, actually." He took a seat. "You shouldn't see me as the enemy. I'm the sucker that got appointed to this. I honestly don't care what happens with the women's center. They could hire a fleet of clowns and I wouldn't care."

Ivey eyed him with the Death Stare. "Are you comparing midwives to clowns?"

Yeah. He should have thought that off-the-cuff comment through a bit better. Blame it on the lack of caffeine, because there wasn't enough in the state to keep him firing on all cylinders.

"No. I've always liked clowns." Sue him. He couldn't resist.

Ivey stood. Today she wore a white ruffled top that went up to her neck, and her long hair in a tight bun. If it wasn't for the pencil skirt, she'd look like a prairie woman. And what was up with that?

"Let's go."

"Where are we going?"

"We're going to talk to Lillian. I'm going to tell her I can't do this, and I want you there when I do it."

"What can I say? I'm honored." He held the door open, and followed her out, trying like hell not to check out her ass while he did. Epic fail. Dammit, even dressed like Dr. Quinn Medicine Woman she managed to arouse him.

Which would mean he'd stepped into a time machine, because that shouldn't be happening.

Usually the hospital smelled like antiseptic and on a bad day in the ER like blood, but at the moment all he could smell was Ivey. Standing near her in the elevator, he swore he could smell the soft scent of vanilla. Did she still wear the same body spray he'd bought her years ago? The one that tasted as good on her as it smelled?

"It doesn't have to be like this," he finally said after a few more minutes of silence. Maybe they could at least put up the appearance of friendship.

Her shoulders seemed to relax an inch or two below her

ears, but then she looked at the floor. "You were supposed to be in Maryland."

"Sorry to disappoint you."

"I didn't mean—" She stopped midsentence. "Look, my Aunt had an accident and she needed me. I didn't know you were in town. Then this opportunity came up."

"You should take it if that's what you want. Couples break up all the time, and it doesn't mean one of them has to leave town. That was your choice."

She seemed to swallow hard at that. "I'm aware of that."

The elevators doors swung open, and Ivey continued walking towards Lillian's office, so he followed. If she wanted off this committee, they'd probably appoint someone else. Meanwhile he'd be stuck with the responsibility. Hopefully the new subcommittee member would be a man. Or ugly.

Ivey knocked once on Lillian's door, then hesitated and knocked again.

Lillian opened the door, tissue in hand. "Come on in."

It appeared that the medical director had been crying. Her eyes were red and her cheeks blotchy. But that couldn't be, because there was no crying in medicine. Only patients were allowed to cry. Sometimes.

So far this day was not shaping up to be any better than the last forty-eight hours.

"Is everything okay?" Ivey asked.

"Wonderful. I just have something in my eye. I'll need to find a new babysitter though. My son hid the babysitter's dentures. I could barely understand the woman when she called to quit on me. This is the third babysitter we've been through. Did I mention that? But you don't need to hear my problems. What can I do for you?" Lillian sniffed into her tissue and offered them a brave smile.

Jeff turned to Ivey and didn't say a word. It was for the best that he remain mute.

"I wanted to tell you that—" Ivey began and then stopped. Glanced at him.

For help? Really?

"Yes? What is it?"

Ivey let out a breath. "I'm going to enjoy working with Dr. Garner. I think we'll make a good team."

The director sighed deeply. "That's what I like to hear. Finally some good news. You've made my day."

On the way back down in the elevator, Ivey pointed a finger in his direction. "Not a word. It's hard for a working mother to find good child care. Besides, we can make this work, can't we? If we sit on opposite sides of the table and divide up the work."

Funny how Ivey behaved, when she'd been the one to leave him. Suddenly he'd had enough of her games. "Explain why you're so pissed when you're the one who broke up with me."

"That's good, Jeff. Are we now going to rewrite history? Let's go ahead and get rid of the Vietnam War while we're at it. *You* broke up with *me*."

"Speaking of rewriting history, you just did that." He stepped off the elevator and walked briskly ahead of her to the conference room.

He opened the door and stood aside for her. Ivey started to walk through, then stopped. She took a deep breath and then gave him a long look with those blue eyes that sometimes looked violet, depending on the light. "Before we walk in there, we have to agree to leave our personal lives outside. That's the only way I'll do this."

"You got it."

"Good." Ivey walked to the conference table and opened her tablet. "Let's get started."

Jeff went ahead and pretended that magical pixy dust had settled over them the moment they crossed the threshold. For the next two hours, they talked birth statistics, labor and delivery, and emergency C-sections. Ivey's cheeks got a little pink every time they discussed a woman's pregnancy and risk factors, a bit strange for someone who claimed to be a midwife.

"I'm sure your part in all of this is to sway the board that it might be best to keep midwives out of a hospital," Ivey said, tapping away furiously on her tablet.

"Wrong again." He leaned back. "My part in all of this is to remain objective and give an honest recommendation."

And he would try like hell to remain objective, even if all he wanted to do was take her home and show her how much he'd missed her. Then do it all over again.

She arched a brow. "And you think you can do that?"

Maybe. Probably. Oh hell. No. "What part of 'I'm not the enemy' do you not understand?"

Ivey shook her head. "Sorry."

"Dr. Allen Stewart." She should know the name of her real enemy, and it wasn't Jeff.

"Who?"

"He thinks the hiring of one midwife is the beginning of a long, slippery slope in which he ends up destitute on the side of the road."

"He's not any different than most doctors I've known."

"How long have you been a midwife?" He changed the subject, hoping she wouldn't notice he'd taken a tangent leading toward the personal. In the past, biology had never been her strong suit, unless you counted the time they'd spent in the bedroom.

"I worked as an apprentice midwife for Babs Holiday, and for the last two years I've been on my own."

"Why not work as a home birth midwife?"

"I want to work in a hospital. We need to stop acting like doctors and midwives are mortal enemies and learn to work together."

"It's not going to be easy. And Stewart is a hard-ass."

"So you don't think I can handle him?"

"I didn't say that." Jeff didn't like this little semi-friendly exchange. It was easier to keep the emotions bottled up and tamped down tight where they couldn't bother him. Right now they were rising to the surface and annoying the hell out of him.

Just because he was lonely and couldn't remember the last time he'd been laid, it was no reason to take up with the ex.

Ivey shut her tablet. "Why don't we end for today?"

"Good idea. My shift starts in an hour, so I'm going to grab lunch."

"Another long shift?"

"Yep."

Right about now, Ivey would be counting her blessings that she hadn't wound up with him. Maybe whoever she'd wound up with could give her more than two hours a day of his time. "At least you'll know where to find me."

"Right." Ivey glanced up at him, the hint of a smile on her lips. "Will you be in the cafeteria? I mean, in case I need you. To ask you a question."

"No, I won't be in the cafeteria because that would be crazy."

He'd be heading to Em's. She made the most succulent pot roast he'd ever tasted, and he'd grown accustomed to the fact that a home-cooked meal waited for him every night he could make it to her kitchen before closing time. Even though there hadn't been many of those nights lately.

"That bad, huh?"

He hesitated for a second, and then hormones won the

day. Again. "You should come with me. I'll show you the best place in town to eat."

Her forehead wrinkled. "No, that's all right."

"What's the big deal? We could catch up. Since we can't speak about anything personal when we cross the threshold."

Damn, he hated the fact that he wanted to be with her even for a few more minutes. Maybe some place where she'd loosen up a bit. This whole prairie woman look wasn't the Ivey he remembered.

She clutched her tablet. "Why do we have to talk about anything personal?"

"We don't. But we were friends first, and if nothing else we could be that again." What the hell was wrong with him? This was Ivey. Ivey who left him right at the toughest time of his life. He should be pissed.

Except for the fact that what she'd said earlier had brought back an old memory he'd long buried. First year of med school he'd been drowning. He knew the stats for first year students. So did Ivey. The dropout rates were astronomical, and he couldn't join those ranks. Not with how much his middle-class parents had sacrificed to help put him there. He and Ivey had managed a long-distance relationship for four years of pre-med, but that first year of med school she'd become unbearably clingy and needy.

So yeah, he'd told her he wanted a break. He hadn't expected she'd listen so well. Interesting how he'd rewritten that in his mind, mostly because from the time she'd been sixteen Ivey had always been his, and he'd never expected that to change. He'd thought she might back off and let him breathe a bit. Let him come back to her, because he always would.

Hadn't quite worked out that way.

"Friends? You and me?" Ivey asked.

Why the hell not? Stranger things had happened. He'd seen them firsthand in his ER.

* * *

IVEY AND JEFF could not be buddies.

On the other hand, he was the only other member on the subcommittee, and he could exert a deep influence on the other doctors. Someone had put him there because they trusted his judgment. And if she wanted this to go well, it would be important to have Jeff on her side.

Like old times.

And he had asked her out to lunch. Not a date, just friends. He wanted to show her a decent place to eat near the hospital. Something he'd do for any colleague.

"Well, what do you say?" He was still waiting for an answer.

"All right," she said, because she'd always had impulse control problems around him.

She hadn't known what to expect, but it wasn't to walk. Still, she slipped her tablet in her bag and followed Jeff's long strides. Across the street from the hospital and two blocks to the east stood a little diner Ivey remembered all too well.

"Mama's Kitchen? I remember this place," she said as he held open the door to the diner.

"Under new ownership. I heard that Em and her husband Si took over about three years ago. I'm a regular."

Good thing the place was under new ownership because the old owner, Mr. Peterson, was a sixty-year-old man who hated kids. He'd inherited the place from his mother, the original Mama. The man hated teenagers in particular, and when she and Jeff used to come in here and sit at the booth in the corner, he would yell, "Let me see some daylight between you two!"

The aromatic smell of coffee, sizzling bacon, and burgers permeated the diner. No doubt about it, this place smelled like a mother's kitchen should, as long as the mother didn't care about cholesterol and calories.

"Hey, Si, would you look who's here." The woman who greeted them had short salt-and-pepper hair and earnest blue eyes.

A ponytailed man Ivey assumed was Si ducked his head through the kitchen partition, bumped it, and rubbed his forehead. "Damn this thing. What did you say?"

"I said your favorite doctor is here," Em shouted back at his puzzled look, then waved him off. "Never mind. He can't hear me back there."

They followed Em to a booth, and before they sat down, Jeff introduced Ivey. "She used to come here also."

"Ah." Em leaned down and rubbed Ivey's shoulder. "Don't worry, dear. That blue ribbon is long since gone. You'll find I'm apolitical in every way. I love everyone as long as they eat."

When Em walked away, Ivey couldn't help but ask. "What blue ribbon?"

The menu suddenly seemed of deep interest to Jeff, a man who by his account should have it memorized. "After we broke up, some of the business people in town took sides. Those who liked me hung blue ribbons in their establishment. Those who liked you put up pink ones."

He looked so serious, and that's what kept her from laughing. "Is that supposed to be a joke? I'd forgotten about your weird sense of humor."

He continued reading the menu as if it were a medical journal. "Mr. Peterson put up a blue ribbon, but that was before Em bought the place. She took it down."

"Aunt Lucy mentioned something about people taking

sides, but I thought she was exaggerating as usual." Blue and pink ribbons? Had the whole town gone mad together?

"How many pink ribbons were there?" It would be nice to know who her real friends were.

He met her eyes. "I didn't count. I thought it was as ridiculous as you do."

"But Mr. Peterson had a blue ribbon. He always liked you better."

"You were the one who used to practically sit in my lap every time we were here."

Ivey felt flushed at hearing the truth stated so matter-of-factly. Even if Jeff had never protested the seating arrangements. "Mr. Peterson was a misogynist."

"Everyone's over it now. But I wouldn't go into the hardware store on Main Street."

Ivey let out a deep sigh. Everyone had held it against her for leaving town for a man she met online, but it had turned out to be the best place to find a fake boyfriend.

Em came and took their orders. Without the menu, Jeff turned his full attention on Ivey. "So how's lover boy? John, was it?"

"Joe." Why couldn't anyone get his name right? Even imaginary fictional characters deserved a little respect.

"Are you sure?" Jeff narrowed his eyes. "I'm pretty sure it was John."

"Thanks, but I think I know the name of my ex-boyfriend better than you do."

"Ex?"

Ivey played with the edge of her napkin. "It didn't work out. Next subject."

Why had she ever agreed to leave the sanctuary of the conference room where they'd agreed not to discuss personal stuff? It was a trick, and she should have seen it coming. Damn Jeff and his perfect build, smoldering eyes, and aesthetically pleasing jawline. If he didn't stop talking about the past, she might be rearranging that perfect face so that he would need to see one of his colleagues for a little rhinoplasty.

Em brought out their burgers and sweet-potato fries. They'd both ordered the same thing.

"How are your parents? And your sister?" If he wanted to talk personal, two could play this game.

"My parents moved to Oregon a couple of years ago. They come down every year for the Grape Festival. Ali lives in town with her husband Bob and two kids."

"Two?"

"Becky is four and Liam is two."

Ivey took a gulp of water and swallowed hard. She should have never opened up this line of discussion. "So what about your love life?"

He gave her a long look. "What love life?"

"You asked about mine."

"I don't have one. The hospital is my significant other."

"Ah, the life of a resident."

"Only the highly tolerant need apply."

While it was difficult to believe that someone who looked like Jeff didn't have the nurses in a tizzy every day, it was possible that he'd try to keep his personal life and business separate. Though not likely.

"So what happens if the board decides against hiring a staff of midwives?" Jeff asked between bites.

"You mean after our subcommittee's powerful recommendation that they do?"

He grinned and bit off a french fry. "Of course."

"I suppose I don't get the job."

"And then what?"

She hadn't thought that far ahead, having always been a fly-by-the-seat-of-her-pants type. But she wanted to stay, despite the news of the pink versus blue ribbons. Maybe she'd find out who'd had a pink ribbon displayed and thank them for their support.

"I'll find another job."

"You won't leave town again?"

"I won't. Why would I?"

"I don't know. You have a history of leaving when you don't get your way. I break up with you, and you leave town."

"Oh so you admit it now."

"I remember saying I needed a break. I was trying to get through the first year of medical school. But I was already out of state, so I don't see why you had to leave."

Because then everyone would have seen her pregnant body, and in this town of blue and pink ribbons Jeff would have found out. The first person to see her throw up would have phoned him and probably given details as to where she'd been and what she'd eaten before she threw up.

"The reason I left town was because Joe was in LA, and long distance relationships don't work."

Jeff leaned back in his seat. "You mean John."

Ivey resisted the urge to pound his gorgeous face and hit the table instead. "Joe, dammit."

Jeff grinned. Fine, she'd let him have his fun. She still needed him to be on her side.

"We managed to have a long distance relationship."

"And look how well that worked out." Ivey picked up a french fry.

Jeff had a funny look on his face, his eyebrows arched and a smile tugged at the corners of his mouth.

"What's so funny?" That's when she realized she'd reached for a fry off of his plate instead of her own. Ack. She dropped the fry and drew back her hand like a snake had bit it.

"That's all right. You can have my fries." He pushed the plate in her direction. "Force of habit. The last time you and I ate together we…shared more than fries." He gave her a wicked grin.

She pushed the plate back. "I don't want your stupid fries."

"C'mon Ivey, you know you want some." He pushed it back in her direction.

She didn't like that penetrating look in his eyes. The air between them charged and electrified. The overwhelming knowledge that despite everything, they weren't quite done with each other.

But they had to be. Ivey pushed the plate back. "That's where you're wrong. I'm done."

And she had to remember that.

CHAPTER 4

One week later, Ivey had quizzed Aunt Lucy thoroughly and found that the fabric store and the hair salon Lucy used to run both had pink ribbons displayed proudly for a time. Even the bookmobile (Ivey was a regular) had a pink ribbon. The vintners had fought hard to stay out of it.

Somehow Ivey recovered from the french-fry stealing incident in which her hand had subconsciously gone where it shouldn't have. She couldn't have that happen again. Couldn't have her hand touch that gorgeous head of thick brown hair, or let it graze the stubbly jawline. No. Couldn't have that.

Aunt Lucy's screechy voice pulled Ivey from her thoughts. They were at the doctor's office, and Lucy's cast had been removed.

"Six long weeks! You have no idea how difficult this has been for me. I haven't gone this long without sex since—well, I can't remember when."

While Ivey prayed the ground would open up and swallow her whole, Dr. Stein ignored the comment and continued to examine Lucy's x-ray. "The bone healed nicely. You're quite lucky. We can't always expect that in a woman of your age."

Ivey sucked in a breath. *Oh no, here it comes.*

"'A woman of my age'? What is that supposed to mean?" Aunt Lucy asked.

Dr. Stein seemed oblivious to his slip. "I mean that as a woman ages, osteoporosis sets in, and bones tend to take much longer to heal."

Aunt Lucy slipped off the examination table. "Well I don't have any of that osteo stuff. I'm in great shape."

"I'm sure you are," Dr. Stein said.

The poor man had no clue.

"When should we schedule her follow-up?" Ivey kept track of Aunt Lucy's appointments in her notebook, and she pulled it out of her purse, ready to make a note.

"Never! I'm done here. Good day." Aunt Lucy gathered her Coach purse from the chair and stopped at the door. "Are you coming, Ivey?"

"I'll be right there." She had to make her apologies to Dr. Stein and find out about follow-up care. Even if her aunt wanted to ignore follow-up, Ivey knew how important it could be to a full recovery.

After speaking with the doctor, she asked the front office receptionist to send a reminder of the six-month checkup. What on earth would Aunt Lucy do without Ivey's help?

Next she had to go find Jeff and schedule their next meeting. They hadn't met since last week—a good thing since she'd needed a little bit of time after the french fry incident. But he was the other half of the subcommittee, and if she couldn't convince him to go along with her recommendation, she wouldn't get far.

Aunt Lucy had already walked out of the reception area into the hallway of the clinic attached to St. Vincent's

Hospital and now giggled into her phone. She had to be speaking to a man.

Ivey marched toward her aunt, who still made googly eyes into her cellphone. Good grief. Aunt Lucy finally got the hint and wrapped up her phone call.

"That was Antonio. He misses me. Hoo boy, that man has the sexiest accent I've ever heard."

Ivey inwardly cringed at the mental picture of Lucy and Antonio and then felt guilty. After all, Aunt Lucy deserved to be loved.

"I have to go find Jeff—I mean, Dr. Garner, so I can schedule our next meeting. Will you be okay? It won't take long."

"Of course, dear. I'll call Antonio back. We've gotten pretty good at phone sex."

Ivey whipped her head around, grateful no one had been close enough to them in the hallway to hear her aunt. "Umm, okay. I'll meet you in the car?"

Ivey handed her the keys and hoped Lucy would take the hint. If she insisted on having phone sex, at least she could spare everyone within earshot.

Ivey had only begun to get the layout of the hospital and took the elevator down to the first floor where the emergency room was located.

As she approached the reception desk, a tall and slender redhead turned towards Ivey. Her name tag read *Donna—triage*. "How can I help you?"

Ivey introduced herself and explained that she was looking for Dr. Garner to schedule a meeting. "Is he around?"

"I just got on shift, so I'll need to check." She went through the double doors leading to the restricted area.

"Pssst."

Ivey turned, and an elderly gentleman smiled in her direction. "Did you say something?"

"I'm here to see him too. And I've been waiting a while. Name's Frank Sullivan," he said, sticking out a frail hand.

Ivey sat next to him, and then the Florence Nightingale in her took over. "Are you feeling all right? What's wrong?"

"It would be easier to tell you what's not wrong." Frank tapped the side of his head. "Nothing wrong up here, that's for sure. Everything else, the warranty has worn out."

Endearing and cute. "I'm sure the doctors here can help you with whatever has, uh, worn out."

"Dr. Garner can. He has the magic touch. Every time I come here, I see him."

"Every time?" The statement implied he'd made multiple trips to the ER, and for his sake she hoped that wasn't the case.

He nodded. "He's always here, so it's not a problem."

"Yeah, that's what I heard."

"And what are you here to see him for, dear? You look healthy enough, but sometimes it's hard to tell." He cocked his head to the side.

"No, I feel fine. We kind of work together, and I need to talk to him."

"You're a nurse? Or a doctor?"

Ivey straightened a little taller in her seat. Frank hadn't automatically assumed she was a nurse. "I'm a nurse midwife."

"They certainly are turning out pretty nurses these days." No sooner had Frank given her his compliment than Jeff and Donna both came through the double doors.

Jeff had a stethoscope around his neck and bags under his eyes. "Hey."

Ivey couldn't help a tiny twinge of sympathy for him. "I should have called you, but then I realized I don't have your phone number."

"Pssst, Doc, I would remedy that if I were you," Frank said from his seat.

"Yeah. Thanks, Frank. So what's up?" Jeff took a step toward Ivey, as though he'd give them a modicum of privacy.

"I want to schedule a time for us to meet with a local midwife in town. What's a good time for you?"

"I'm here most of the time."

"We'll need to go to her. Why don't I meet with her, and then I'll report back to you. Next Monday?"

"Doc, I 'm going to need some fluids today, I think," Frank interrupted from behind them.

"I've got to run. See you then." Jeff moved to give Frank a helping hand. "Donna, let's get Frank checked out. Talk later, okay Ivey?"

"Nice to meet you, Ivey," Frank said as he shuffled away. "Be sure to leave your phone number with the doctor."

"Excuse me?" Ivey asked.

Frank stopped walking and turned toward her, then spoke loudly as though she might have a hearing problem. "I said leave your number with the doctor. Then maybe you two could go out some time."

"Frank," Jeff said in a warning tone.

"Well, Doc, you're here every time I come and you don't see a problem with that?"

Jeff didn't reply, his quicker pace being the only indication that he'd heard anything at all. They both walked through the double doors, leaving Ivey standing alone, wondering if Jeff wanted her number and why she should care.

* * *

"Italy?" Ivey couldn't believe her ears. Aunt Lucy's cast had been off for four days, and she had already made plans to leave the country.

"I have to do something to celebrate the end of being cooped up for six weeks." Now that she was mobile again, Aunt Lucy used the energy to pack her bags. "And Antonio has rented us a villa in the Italian countryside."

"But we were going to start having fun. I was hoping you'd stay." Ivey fought to keep the desperation out of her voice, but the last thing she wanted was to live in this extravagant condo alone.

"It's time for me to move on. The leg slowed me down for too long. Anyway, you stay here and get that job you wanted. The women's center has been a long time coming, and I know you'd be great for the job." Aunt Lucy laid her minx coat gently in the suitcase. She tossed her last pair of Jimmy Choos into a suitcase dedicated only to shoes and then threw sweaters into another one.

"What if I forget about the job? I could spend every day with you. Would you stay then?" Okay that was desperation talking. Ivey wasn't going to give up the job and stay home and have one long slumber party.

"Oh honey, you don't have to do that. I'm still hoping you'll come to your senses and get back with your ex."

Oh, sigh. Would Aunt Lucy ever give up? "That's not going to happen."

"Are you sure?"

"Yes, and stop looking at me like that. I didn't come back here for him. I came home because you said you needed me."

"And I thank you for that. But you might want to ask yourself why you want to stay—you could get a job anywhere else. Maybe you did want to come back, and I gave you the perfect excuse."

No, she wasn't staying for him. In fact, he was the hardest

part of staying here, since every time she looked at him she hurt a little bit. "We never did see that movie—the one with your favorite actor—umm, what's his name?" Ivey couldn't even remember now, as panic set in.

"I'll wait till it's on DVD." Aunt Lucy waved her hand. "You'll be fine. You can stay here. It's not far from the hospital, so it's convenient if you ever wind up getting that job. I've still got my money on you. You can do this."

The last suitcase packed, Aunt Lucy marched to the kitchen where she used the phone to call for a taxi.

"Do you really have to leave tonight?" Ivey would have liked at least a day to get used to the idea.

"I've been cooped up in here for too long."

"You didn't even spend any time in the town itself. There are beautiful vineyards right here and people come from all over the world come to see them."

"You don't have to tell me. I lived most of my life in this little town. I talked Ben Cartwright into buying this condo so I could visit. They say you should never forget where you came from."

Aunt Lucy pulled out her compact and outlined her lips in fire-engine red. Presumably so that people would see her lips a mile away. Then she put her hands on both of Ivey's shoulders, the most affection she'd demonstrated in weeks. "I'm not like you and your mom, honey."

There it was again. Ivey hated it when Aunt Lucy brought her up or compared them. "I'm not like her either."

"Nonsense. You're so much like your mother. Oh, I miss her. She never wanted to leave the town where she met and fell in love with your father. Something about putting down roots. I could never figure her out either." Aunt Lucy shook her head and dug in her purse again.

But Beth Lancaster had made a habit of ruining people and relationships, and Ivey had gone behind her fixing what she could. Making excuses for mom, cleaning up the chaos. Protecting Beth from the nasty rumors. Unlike Mom, Ivey couldn't even drink a sip of alcohol without being inebriated, but that didn't seem to matter. When she looked in the mirror she still saw Beth Lancaster's dark hair and blue eyes gazing back.

The phone rang and Lucy picked it up. "Could you come up and help me with my bags?" She hung up and turned to Ivey. "Don't look so sad, dear. You have my cell phone number, and you can call me any time. And stay here as long as you like."

"But this place is too big for me."

"Then find someone to share it with. I know who that someone should be." Aunt Lucy squeezed her hand and then opened the door for the driver, waving him towards the bedroom.

"Stop. Why do you keep bringing him up?" Couldn't Lucy see how much it hurt? Did she have to spell it out for her aunt?

"Ask yourself why I would want to come back to this god-forsaken town to recuperate when I could be anywhere in the world?"

"I thought it was because this is our home town. You grew up here, so did mom. So did I. We have good memories here."

"Honey, I wanted to bring you back the minute I heard your old beau was back in town and the hospital would be building a new women's center."

"You asked me to move in so you could play matchmaker?" And she'd imagined it was for her great nursing skills.

"Every two months someone in this town asks me for money. But when they came to me for a donation to the women's center, you better believe I gave them a sizeable one. Enough to call myself a benefactor. Doesn't that have a nice ring to it?"

"You—you did this? You're the one who wanted Jeff on the subcommittee?"

"Why not? You two needed a little push, is all. More like a big fat shove."

Ivey had left a fledging practice as a home-birth midwife. She'd left a decent apartment and friends so she could rearrange her life to take care of Aunt Lucy. Because she'd asked.

"I can't believe you did this! Undo it right now. Call and tell them you changed your mind." Ivey handed Lucy the phone.

"I will do no such thing. I don't mind telling you, you were one silly girl to let Jeff go. By now you'd be married with two or three little ones. Isn't that what you always wanted?"

And Jeff would have dropped out of medical school. He would have married her out of obligation, not love. Maybe they'd be happy, and maybe they'd be miserable.

"You can't do this to me."

"I can, and I did. You can thank me later." Aunt Lucy patted Ivey's back.

The driver stuck his head in the door. "All ready, ma'am."

"When will you be back?" Ivey managed to squeak out.

"I'm not sure. It could be months if all goes well. I'll be in touch. And I'm going to buy you a new car. No arguing. That old SUV is about to give out on you. Pick out what you want and I'll pay for it. Walk me outside?"

Ivey walked Lucy to the curb and watched the taxi cab become a smudge of yellow in the distance. She swallowed the lump in her throat and the memory that came back. Leaving seemed to be a pattern with Aunt Lucy.

In Los Angeles, Lucy had found a little cottage for Ivey to

rent. Not that she had ever spent much time there with Ivey. After Lucy had made sure Ivey had enough money to stay for the remainder of her pregnancy, she'd murmured a few choice phrases about Gloria Steinem and the sacrifices women had made so that Ivey wouldn't have to hide a natural event and then taken off on her next adventure.

But Ivey wasn't hiding because she was ashamed. Not exactly.

She would take care of their baby, and within three years, once Jeff was done with medical school, she'd let him know. Then he could decide for himself if he wanted a relationship with their child. He'd probably be a little bit mad, Ivey figured, but in the end he'd see her sacrifice was noble. He'd see she'd done it for him. So that he could keep going forward without interruption. So that if they wound up together, it would be for the right reasons.

But it hadn't quite worked out. There was no point in rehashing the past now, bringing up old wounds and mistakes to examine them under the harsh bright light of today.

No point at all.

CHAPTER 5

$\mathscr{B}$y the evening after Aunt Lucy had gone, Brooke had already invited Ivey to a wine-tasting event. Brooke ran Serrano's, one of the more popular wineries in town, and recently she'd been so busy with their booth at the Grape and Wine Festival that she suggested Ivey join her at the winery so they could hang out. Ivey didn't drink, but Brooke Miller was her best friend and a person didn't grow up in Napa Valley without learning how to swish and spit. Wine tasting events and the annual festival were as much a part of the landscape of Starlight Hill as the river that ran through town.

Ivey, for her part, wondered why Brooke hadn't thought it important to let her know that Jeff was back in Starlight Hill. A little heads-up might have been nice. Not that Ivey would have let his being back in town keep her away from helping Aunt Lucy. That would have given him too much power.

However, his being in town was one matter and working with him on a subcommittee another. Her teeth hurt thinking about it. The last person she wanted to discuss pregnancy matters with. It didn't help that his eyes seemed to glaze over every time they talked about high risk versus low risk. Unless maybe he was as exhausted as he claimed.

His supposed exhaustion hadn't stopped him from checking her out. Yeah, she'd noticed. Several times she'd glanced up from her notes to find him staring. Never even bothered to hide it. And she was done walking in front of him. She could literally feel his eyes like lasers trained on her assets.

No, she wouldn't go there again, to a relationship that failed because Jeff didn't have time for one. And he still wouldn't, not with his resident's schedule. She'd bet a lifetime's supply of chocolate on that fact. Besides, he liked to plan everything and Ivey loved surprises. Adventures. Flying by the seat of her pants. Living life without regrets.

Brooke was behind the wine bar, wearing long dangly turquoise earrings, and a colorful bracelet in the shape of a snake hugged her bicep. Back in their high-school days, Brooke had worn her naturally blonde hair dyed black to match her mood, but now she was back to her blonde bombshell look.

"Hey, I'm here." Ivey sidled up to the bar. "And I'm not tasting."

"No kidding." Brooke of all people understood Ivey's aversion to alcohol. It wasn't that she judged others, but ever since Mom's accident, Ivey didn't drink on principle. Which made living in Starlight Hill ironic.

"Hey, Eric, I'm taking a break. And don't give me that look. I'm not even supposed to be pouring." Brooke waved an arm in a young man's direction.

"I thought you ran this place," Ivey said, following Brooke, who carried one glass of wine with her.

"I do. Which means I have to pour when we have an event and we're short staffed. Like today. We're bringing in a new line of Cabernets that have a woodsy, nutty—you don't want to hear about this, and I want to hear about the job at the hospital. Did you get it?" She sat at a table and Ivey joined her.

"No. But here's the good news. I've been put on a subcommittee with a resident." Ivey explained the details.

"Well that sounds promising."

"Maybe. Except that Jeff is the resident."

Brooke froze. "Uh-oh."

"I'll say. I didn't even know he was back in town."

Brooke might have picked up on the accusatory tone in Ivey's voice. "Hey, sorry if I forgot to mention it. Life gets busy, ya know? Besides, I'm sick of you acting like you should be wearing a scarlet letter."

"I'm doing no such thing!"

"The hell you aren't. There's nothing to be ashamed of."

"I know that." It wasn't shame that had kept her away but more like a seismic change of plans.

"Think you can work with him on this subcommittee?"

"So far he's actually been kind of nice." As long as she didn't count the midwives-as-clowns comment. "Even admitted that he broke up with me."

"The break." Brooke held up two fingers like air quotes.

"I'm going to make sure that we don't talk about anything too personal. He's already asked about Joe, only he calls him John to annoy me."

"It's almost like maybe he thinks imaginary Joe isn't real. Crazy." Brooke rolled her eyes.

Something pinged deep in Ivey's belly. "He's on to me? You think?"

Brooke shook her head. "I don't know if he would give it much thought."

"Don't look now, but your dislike of Jeff is starting to show."

"Oh yeah? Well I wasn't trying to hide it." Brooke had loyalty down to a science, but then again she'd resented the fact that Ivey and Jeff had been a couple all through high school when Brooke had remained single. Not through lack of options, which was a mystery Ivey still hadn't cracked.

"I'm afraid I'll break down and tell him everything. It'll come flowing out of me."

"After all this time? No, forget it. You need to stem that flow and keep your mouth shut tight." Brooke touched her lips on the word tight. "That's your business."

"Aunt Lucy doesn't think so. She still thinks he has a right to know."

"Lucy isn't exactly the authority of all things relationship-wise. Which husband is she on now? I lost track."

She had a point. Aunt Lucy had been through four husbands, three of them since winning the lottery. Husband number four was under house arrest in New York, awaiting trial. What did she know about long-term relationships? "But she has a point. Doesn't she?"

"Maybe she had a point five years ago. You should have told him. You were way too honorable for your own good. He should have stepped up."

"He would have," Ivey said and then wondered why she was defending her ex. They'd had plans, and they didn't include a baby. He didn't want to get married until he was done with medical school. Having a baby would have sent him over the edge. Besides, had everyone forgotten he'd broken up with her? He didn't want her then, and she sure didn't want him to come back to her out of duty.

"As usual you made it easy for him. Like you do with everyone. Think about it. You didn't tell Jeff because he'd drop out of school, you left your job in LA to take care of your aunt, and now I'd bet my Harley that someone else talked you into being on this subcommittee. Who is it this time?"

Brooke had kindly left out all the times she'd covered for Mom. *I'm sorry, Mrs. Monroe, my mom can't come to the phone right now. She's got the flu.*

"All right, so what? I try to help people. I'm a nurse. What do you want from me?"

"I want you to bandage a cut or deliver a baby but stop trying to fix everybody and everything. For once, will you do what you want?"

"It's not that easy. When I look at him—I don't know, he reminds me of what I lost. I can't help it."

Brooke squeezed Ivey's hand. "But what do you want?"

"I want to stay. And I want this job." Saying it out loud confirmed it, and for once maybe she'd stay, even if it was going to make things more difficult for her, for Jeff, and the rest of the blue-versus-pink-divided town. Too bad.

"Good for you. Then take it. Fight for it." Brooke pounded the table with her fist.

Ivey startled. "Right."

A hard-looking man with his jaw dialed to crush strode up next to Brooke and put a hand on her shoulder. "I need to talk to you. Now."

"I'll be right back," Brooke said as she rose, then called out to her coworker: "Eric, I'm taking a break."

"Hey, how long are you going to be gone? You have to get me some help," Eric shouted from behind the bar.

"Ivey, do you mind? All you have to do is pour and look pretty. You can do it."

Great. She knew almost nothing about wine. "You're kidding, right?"

"I'll be right back," Brooke said as she led Ivey behind the table. "Eric, here's your help. Be nice."

Eric, who didn't even look old enough to drink, glanced at her sideways. "So. Who are you?"

"Ivey. Can't that man wait to talk to Brooke?"

He lifted a shoulder. "I doubt it. He's the boss."

That explained it. Ivey had never seen Brooke rush to please a man like that. She was probably working on a promotion. "Help me out here. What should I do?"

"Push the Cabernet, and you'll be fine." Eric handed her an opened bottle.

For the next twenty minutes offering Cabernet seemed to be enough as Ivey poured and smiled.

She recognized some of the locals, but most of the people here would be tourists. The wine train made a regular stop here, and it was that time of the year.

"My heavens, Ivey, is that you?"

Ivey turned to see Wynonna Pusini, the high-school cafeteria lady. Most everyone in town referred to Mrs. Pusini as the town's spinster. Aunt Lucy said every town had one. It wasn't fair, but the label seemed to fit. Mrs. Pusini was a spitfire Greek-Italian woman who didn't put up with anyone's shit, and that was the main reason, she'd once explained to Ivey, that she had no husband.

Ivey stood up straighter and poured a glass of the red. "Hi, Mrs. Pusini."

She had to be retired by now, and she wasn't alone. There was a gentleman with her, balding with a slight paunch, his arm protectively around Mrs. Pusini's waist. Well, well, good for her.

"This is my husband, Al." She introduced Al, who took his arm off her for only a second to shake hands with Ivey. "I got married last year. Can you believe it?"

"Finally someone had the good sense to catch you."

"That would be me." Al nodded.

"What about you? Are you and Jeff back together? Please

say you are. You wouldn't believe it, but I finally believe in happy endings." She held out her glass again.

Ivey poured her another taste. "No, we're definitely not back together. But we're friends."

"Bah! Friends? What kind of nonsense is that?"

Ivey blinked. Mrs. Pusini had had enough, and Ivey held back the bottle. That didn't make her too happy, if one were to go by the sour expression on her face.

"We don't all get our happy ending," Ivey said.

"Baloney. Look at her, Al. Isn't she pretty? What about your nephew?"

"What about him?" Al, bless his heart, asked.

"For Ivey. She needs someone. Isn't he about her age?"

"I think he's nineteen."

"Perfect!" Mrs. Pusini sang out.

Oh, for the love of Pete. "I'm twenty-five."

"Even better. You're a cougar." She cackled. Still smoked a pack a day, Ivey would guess.

She didn't like this new Mrs. Pusini. As Al pulled Mrs. Pusini along to the next tasting table, Ivey wondered if they still had a town spinster. Seemed like everyone was married or dating someone, if tonight was any indication. Except, of course, for her. She was the loneliest number.

Every town had a spinster. Could she be the town's spinster in training? Ivey wracked her brain for the last time she'd had a date. Back in LA, she'd given up hope on men. Seemed like every single one of them was either gay or an actor. But it was time to get back in the game. She couldn't take Mrs. Pusini's place. Someone else would have to do that.

Ivey bent over the bar and waved. "Mrs. Pusini, wait! I'll give you my number."

She waved back and smiled. Possibly she couldn't hear over all these talking, happy, disgusting couples. *Who are you kidding? You'd give anything to be that disgusting.*

When Ivey turned back to pouring, a gray-haired gentleman who had moved to the front of the bar startled her. He was also alone, Ivey noticed. Though maybe with good reason, as he had a stalker-slash-serial-killer vibe going on. It was in those dull, gray, empty eyes.

"Do you uh, want some of this?" Ivey offered.

He didn't hold out his wine glass but continued to stare. "What is it?"

Ivey swallowed, then smiled. Just pour and look pretty, right? "Wine. Red."

"That's fascinating, considering we're at a wine tasting event. Care to elaborate?"

"It's a—" Ivey turned the bottle in her hands, hoping she could decipher the label and it would tell her something. Anything. But Mrs. Hughes's second grade class came back to her in Technicolor. She'd never been any good at reading out loud or on the spot. Dyslexia forced her to take her time.

"Miss, do you know anything about wine?" The man looked at her as though he could see right through her and the charade.

Where was Brooke when Ivey needed her? And did Brooke realize the irony in this situation? She'd told Ivey to stop helping people and then set her up. Damn, and Ivey had fallen for it. When would she learn to say no? Hell no. Well it would not be tonight, because something about this man made Ivey want to run and hide, not suddenly grow a spine.

She glanced over at Eric who was busy schmoozing with ladies who appeared to have had more than enough wine already. "Of course I do, sir. This wine is, um, dry?"

He took a sip, swished, and spit in a paper cup he carried. Gross. No one else was spitting tonight. They were swirling and swishing. But this guy had to spit.

"You call this dry? Has this had any chance to breathe?"

Did wine breathe? News to her.

Brooke rejoined Ivey then, easing her slender body behind the table and taking the bottle swiftly from Ivey's hands. "Mr. Dougherty, so good to see you. I have a case of the private label Merlot you wanted in the back. But this is our new Cabernet . . . "

Ivey relaxed and watched Brooke do her thing. After Mr. Dougherty had been satisfied, Ivey grabbed Brooke's arm and squeezed. Tight. "Where were you?"

But Brooke didn't have to say another word as Ivey took a good long look at her friend—face somewhat flushed, hair messed up like she'd gotten out of bed—*what the?*

"Did you just—have sex?"

Brooke pulled Ivey aside and shushed her. "Okay, you got me. A little quickie in the back. Thanks for covering for me."

Ivey felt the red color of indignity spread straight down to her unpainted toenails. "You drag me into doing your job so you can get a little action? I thought you were working."

"I'm sorry. My brain said no, but the rest of my body doesn't understand English when I'm around the man. Look, Ivey, I owe you an apology."

"You're damn right you do." She'd never leave a patient alone for a quickie. Although, okay, her patients did have a way of reminding her that a few hours of bliss often amounted to five times the amount of pain.

"Okay, here goes. When you and Jeff—let's just say now I understand why you ditched me."

"I didn't—" Ivey stammered, but her face flushed because they both knew it was a lie. She'd ditched Brooke on more than one occasion for Jeff.

"Back then I didn't know what I was missing. I was an eighteen-year-old virgin, and I didn't get why you and Jeff couldn't stay away from each other. Well believe me, now I do. You should have told me how—and then when the guy—

how great it is when you both—Well, if I'd known how much fun you were having, I would have understood."

"Well, I—" She'd been in love, desperately and completely as only a sixteen-year-old could be.

Brooke laughed. "Okay, quit stammering. I didn't mean to embarrass you."

Eric called out again. "Brooke! If you're not here in two minutes I'll be handing in my notice. And this time I'm not kidding."

"Sorry, got to go. He quits once a week, and even if he is a pain in the ass, he's good at what he does."

Ivey didn't know why, but it felt like everything and everyone around her had changed while she'd stood still. Sure the hills were in the same place. The ambling country road into town peppered with vineyards every hundred feet: the same. But Mr. Peterson was gone (good riddance), Mrs. Pusini was married, Jeff no longer had his nose stuck in a medical textbook, and Brooke was behaving like she'd discovered butter.

Meanwhile, Ivey still felt like the twenty-year old who'd left town with big hopes, only to come back empty handed. She still had the nagging, pressed-down feeling that she'd done something wrong, something unforgivable, even with the best of intentions.

She stood for a few more minutes watching Brooke pour and laugh with the customers. A few minutes ago Brooke had been with her boss somewhere in the back having sweaty sex while everyone else sampled wine, clueless.

That single thought served as a segue for sudden thoughts of Jeff and sex. Sex with Jeff. The type of thoughts she didn't want to have in her head right now.

Stupid wine. She didn't even have to drink it for it to mess with her head.

* * *

"Mommy says you don't have a girlfriend."

"Nope. What about you? Boyfriend?"

"No!"

"Ah. You're married, then."

"I'm not married, you silly."

"Don't tell me you're divorced."

"No!"

"Don't worry, someone will come along."

"Ew! I'm never getting married."

"That's what you say now. Your mother used to say that too, and now look at her."

"Becky! Jeff! Dinner's ready."

"C'mon, squirt. It's time to make conversation with the grown-ups and make believe we're interested." Jeff caught four-year-old Becky as she leapt off the jungle gym and into his waiting arms.

"I can fly!"

"Yeah, yeah." He plopped his niece on the lawn and watched her skip up to the back porch and through the sliding glass door.

Seemed like she'd grown three inches and several IQ points since he'd seen her last month. He didn't see his family often enough, so it was probably for the best that he didn't have one of his own. Who had time? Unless he wanted to blame the five-foot-nothing fireball that had come back into his life. They'd had a plan. Marriage, kids, the house, dogs. Maybe even a cat if he was feeling generous.

Medicine was now his life. He had to keep reminding himself that some choices required sacrifice. Even if he felt he'd already sacrificed enough.

Ali, as usual, was worried about him. She'd already seen Ivey back in town and probably understood the effect that would have on him. Ali said it was because they'd never had real "closure," which sounded like the psychobabble word du jour.

After dinner, he helped his sister clear the dishes while Bob the Saint put the kids to bed.

"I've wanted to talk to you about someone," Ali said.

"You mean something." Jeff handed her a plate.

"No, someone. I met her at the park last week."

"No." Among all of her sisterly duties, Ali had become his dating service.

"She's a single mother of one adorable little boy. And a professional. She's a lawyer."

"Hate to repeat myself, but no."

"But why?"

"I don't do blind dates."

"But this woman is perfect for you."

Ivey was perfect for him, and look how well that had worked out. "Even worse."

"You're not making any sense. It's because of Ivey, isn't it?"

When it came to Ivey, it was true that nothing made sense. "I haven't let you fix me up for a year, and now you want to blame it on Ivey?"

"I thought I was wearing you down."

"You weren't."

"I hate that you're alone."

"I'm not alone. I have you guys. Scott, my roommate, even if he is gone half the time. And the hospital. Don't know if you heard, but we're engaged. Very happy together too. I'll make sure to send you a save the date."

"This isn't funny. You're a great guy, a real catch. And even if you are my brother, the word is that you're hot. I know, gross."

"Disgusting. It's not like I haven't dated. I don't have time for a relationship, in case you hadn't noticed."

"I noticed. But sooner or later you'll have time. And then what? Are you going to settle down with someone because the timing is right? It doesn't work that way."

She wasn't saying anything he hadn't thought of at one time or another, when he had time to think about personal shit. Which was about ten minutes out of every twenty-four hours. Yeah he was alone, and he hadn't planned it that way. He'd wanted to marry Ivey right after medical school. He figured his wife would put up with the long resident hours and near poverty like no girlfriend ever would. He'd taken a lot for granted.

"What about one of those computer matchmaking services?"

Jeff couldn't help the tick that formed in his jaw or the way his hands tightened around the glass he held. "You mean like the one where Ivey found her perfect match?"

His sister had the decency to look shamed. "Obviously she didn't, or she wouldn't be back in town, single again. That's what worries me. You two are going to gravitate back toward each other like magnets."

While that had a nice ring to it, he had his doubts. "Don't worry about that. She hates me. The way she sees it, I broke up with her."

Ali froze and stopped rinsing the plate midair. "That's because she doesn't know, does she?"

"And she never will."

One month after their fight, he'd made it through exams and headed home to Ivey. To spend the entire weekend in her arms and never leave the bedroom. He'd been too abrupt with her in their last conversation. One week later he'd regretted it, but instead of calling, he'd waited and hatched a scheme to surprise her. Gone by his parent's house to pick up his grandmother's ring. His idea of a compromise. Ivey would understand how he felt about her. There was no else for him, but he needed more time to put his career in order. He would propose, and they'd have a long engagement. Ivey would get the surprise of her life.

Yeah. Surprise!

"It's for the best that she never knows, believe me. You two together were too intense. Young love. Bound to burn itself out in time."

If that were true, why did he still feel like he was waiting for that flame to die out?

CHAPTER 6

"You can't be serious." Marissa Hartsell fixed Ivey with a look equal parts badass and college professor. Ivey was pretty sure that not a single one of Marissa's patients thought twice when she ordered them to push.

Even though her A Little Miracle office waiting room was filled with clouds of pink, blue, and white, Marissa didn't give off the same calming vibe. Ivey hadn't known what to expect, but it certainly wasn't this.

Marissa had managed to fit Ivey into her schedule two weeks after Ivey had phoned to ask for some time to talk about her midwifery practice. They were sitting on two chairs in the empty waiting room of the office converted from an old Victorian in the middle of town, and Marissa, from the looks of it, was not one bit thrilled by the idea of a staff of midwives at St. Vincent's Hospital's new women's center.

Ivey had explained the dilemma and her appointment to the subcommittee. She'd explained the doctors' objections to

352

the idea. This was where Marissa should get on her soapbox and have a tirade about the unfairness of it all.

"Why on earth would you want to work in a hospital?" Marissa asked.

"Because I want women to have the choice of a completely natural labor without any medical interference."

"In a hospital?" Marissa nearly squeaked out the last word.

"I realize it doesn't sound like the best place to avoid medical intervention, but—"

"It doesn't sound like it, because it isn't. That why we're here, Ivey." She waved around her waiting room. "Women do have a choice. We're part of one of the oldest professions, working with the most natural event in nature. Well maybe the second most natural event, not coincidentally arising from the first."

"But women don't even think about midwives anymore. They're trained to go to doctors, and the option isn't really ever presented to them. Not often enough."

"We've done a good job of getting the word out around here. But some women are always going to feel safer within the confines of a hospital." Marissa lifted a shoulder. "I can't help those women."

"Don't you think it would be best if we could all work together? Doctors refer low-risk cases to midwives, and midwives refer high risk to doctors?"

Marissa leaned back in her seat. "Ah, so you're a dreamer. You didn't tell me that."

Ivey sighed. This wasn't going well. She was supposed to meet Jeff in an hour so she could report on the results of the meeting. Only so far it didn't look like she'd have anything good to say. "Wouldn't this give new opportunities to midwives?"

"New opportunities to be subservient to doctors. Let's

face it, the hospital is their turf. They've earned it through hundreds of years of the establishment's rules. We've always worked in homes and places where women feel most comfortable. Let the doctors keep the hospitals. As long as they're in the same building, they'll never stop interfering."

Ivey hadn't expected to have this fight with a midwife. She hadn't been too surprised by the doctors' attitudes, but why couldn't Marissa see this as a new frontier?

"This is already being done in some hospitals in LA and other large cities."

"I've heard, and it's not working well, in my opinion. Too much medical intervention. Lots of fighting between midwives and doctors. Anyone who has ever been through labor knows that it's tough to get through it naturally. When the option is available for drugs and comfort, it's too tempting. Being at home removes that option."

Sounded like Marissa didn't have a whole lot of faith in women in labor.

"But what about complications?" Surely Marissa could see the need to be in a hospital for that.

"Ah, yes, for the five percent of low-risk women in labor who wind up having complications? Well that's when we transport to the hospital. But believe me when I tell you that I've never once had to take a patient to the hospital. That's because being at home reduces the risk of complications. Whenever pain relief is introduced, for instance, complications arise."

A half hour later, Ivey hadn't managed to make Marissa budge. When Marissa's next patient waddled in precisely at noon, Ivey felt as tired as the pregnant woman looked.

After introductions, Ivey prepared to leave, but Marissa quickly pulled her aside for one last parting shot.

"I wouldn't want to see you lose sight of what's important. A completely natural, non-medical experience for our patients. Anything less than that and we've robbed them of that joyful experience."

"Thanks for your time."

"Of course, dear. Anything for a friend of Babs. Why don't you think about coming to work for me here? I could always use an extra helping hand."

Ivey nodded. "I'll give it some thought."

She hopped in her SUV and it came alive with a pathetic effort, meaning she should have taken Aunt Lucy up on her offer to buy her a new car. The engine light had been flashing on and off for a while. That probably wasn't good. Next week she'd get it into the shop for a tune-up. Or a major overhaul.

For now, she needed to rethink everything. How was she ever going to convince the board to go along with hiring a staff of midwives? If Marissa's sentiment was the norm, she'd not only have a bunch of doctors angry for encroaching on their territory, but she'd also have midwives in a tizzy. And you didn't want to get a midwife in a tizzy.

Maybe she was going about this the wrong way.

Her SUV seemed to agree, as it made a screeching flappetty clackety sound. Ivey coasted off to the side of Merlot Highway. Perfect. Stranded on a sweltering August day. Wearing a white halter dress—obviously the perfect outfit for car trouble. She made the useless effort of pulling up her hood, always more of call for help than anything else. Like waving a flag of distress. Nothing under the hood made sense to her anyway.

With the hood up, she stared at the engine. Someone would stop and help. She should stand and look concerned. *Oh look, the thingamajig is broken. Dear me, I'll need a new whatchamacallit.*

Within a few minutes, she had her first stop. She didn't recognize the guy, so he might be a tourist. Then again, she didn't know everyone in town anymore. This guy looked like an auto guy, big and burly with a handlebar mustache. And probably no danger to her at all in the middle of the day.

"What's the trouble?" he asked.

"Ah, well. Not sure." Ivey looked down at the engine and shook her head. Like she'd tried to figure it out, but dang it, she was stumped this time.

She moved aside so he could look, but before he did he gave her a long look. "You're Ivey, aren't you?"

She tried to smile. "Do I know you?"

"Nope, but I know you." He rocked back on his heels. "I had a blue ribbon."

"Let me guess. You work at the hardware store."

He took a few steps back, shaking his head. "I work at the car shop. Bad luck for you that Dr. Jeff doesn't work on his own car. I'd help you, but I had a blue ribbon."

"Don't be ridiculous! Everyone took down their ribbons ages ago. It doesn't count anymore. Are you going to leave me out here? Where's your sense of decency?"

"Where's yours? Date a Deusch.com over a doctor, lady? Anyway, it's the bro code. Nah, tell you what. I'll call someone else to help you. Someone who had a pink ribbon." He ambled over to his truck and got back in.

It was official. Everyone in this town was shit-faced crazy. Certifiable.

"He broke up with *me!*" Ivey shouted as the guy took off.

Ivey stomped her foot, took out her cell and dialed Brooke. She was working, something about the first crush, but maybe she'd answer. No such luck, as the phone switched over to voice mail. Was Ivey really supposed to wait here until someone who had a pink ribbon showed up? Would the insanity ever end?

No other cars passed by in the next few minutes. It was the middle of the day in the middle of the week, and she wasn't going to stand around until someone meandered home. She was only a few miles from the hospital, and if she didn't get there soon she'd be late for her meeting with Jeff. Late to tell him that the women's center might have to be fully staffed by doctors, because no midwives would come near it.

Lillian wouldn't be thrilled. She'd given her a chance, and Ivey couldn't blow it now.

Ivey rubbed her forehead. She felt a headache coming on, and the heat didn't help.

Whipping out her cell phone, she thought about calling Jeff, but that would take him away from the hospital. Sick people needed him more than she needed a ride.

She'd walk. It couldn't be more than a mile or two.

* * *

SOME PEOPLE CHANGED their mind every ten minutes. Ivey now wanted more of his fries. She had that familiar longing in her eyes, so he pushed the plate in her direction.

"Have as many as you want, Little Face." He couldn't remember the last time he'd called her that, but she didn't even blink. Smiled and licked her lips.

And since when did she wear lingerie to the diner? How had he failed to notice she wore the same red lace teddy he'd bought her from Victoria's Secret so long ago?

Damn, she drove him crazy. Always had.

He wanted to kiss her more than he wanted his next breath, and for the first time in years they seemed to be on the same wavelength. She joined him on his side of the booth, threading her fingers through his hair.

"Ivey," he groaned.

She put a finger on his lips. "Shhhh."

That's when he heard the buzzing sound. It got louder

and louder as Ivey got smaller and smaller in his arms. "Wait. What's happening? Where are you going?"

When she disappeared, he woke up with a jolt.

Damn it. Sleeping on a cot in the doctor's lounge again. Alone. No Ivey anywhere in sight. Certainly not in his arms.

His cell phone was buzzing. "What?"

"Hey, Doc. It's me, Tim."

Tim? His mechanic? Jeff rubbed his eyes. "What's up?"

"Thought you should know. Your ex? She's stranded on the side of Merlot Highway. I didn't help her. Solidarity, bro."

What the hell? "Wait. Are you telling me you didn't help her because of the blue ribbon?"

"Yeah, and I feel bad. I was going to call someone, then I thought maybe you'd want to know."

"Tim, you should have picked her up."

"I can go back now. I'll do it. Whatever you say."

"Never mind. I'll go get her."

"By now someone else gave her a ride. Doc, she looked real pretty."

Jeff was almost positive she did, especially in this heat. Probably not dressed like a prairie woman today. The thought had him reaching inside his locker for his keys and grabbing a cold bottle of water from the fridge in the lounge.

"Anyway, thanks for calling me. You and I will talk about this later."

"Good luck. I really would like to get rid of the blue and pink ribbons. I have a lot of female customers that still won't talk to me."

"Yeah." Jeff thought they had gotten rid of them, but apparently Ivey's reappearance had dredged the whole thing back up.

"I'll be right back," he called out to the charge nurse.

He wasn't a mile from the hospital when he saw her in the

distance, walking slowly until she saw him pull to the side of the road. Then she picked up her pace. It made him smile.

"Get in." He turned the car around, and hung his head out the window as he drove behind her on the shoulder.

"I'm almost there. Sorry I'm late for our meeting, but my SUV broke down." She finally stopped walking, turned to him, and damn if she didn't look like she could headline a wet t-shirt contest. Sweat dripped down her neck and had soaked through her halter dress, leaving nothing to the imagination, not that he needed any reminders.

"I got here as soon as I heard." He stopped the car, and walked around to open the passenger door. "I've got air conditioning."

She tentatively moved toward the car, for which he was grateful because he didn't really want to throw her over his shoulder and drag her into the car.

Her hand went to her neck, dabbing at some of the sweat. "Thanks. It's getting a little hot out here."

Considering the trip computer in his car said the temperature was a balmy ninety-eight degrees, he'd have to agree. He felt stuck somewhere between anger with her for trying to walk all this way in the heat, and guilt that his car mechanic thought he'd been doing Jeff a favor.

Finally she climbed in the passenger seat and turned the dial up to Antarctica, pointing every vent in her direction.

"Drink." He handed her the bottled water. "Why didn't you call your aunt, anyway?"

"She's in Europe on vacation."

Ah, the constant holiday of the wealthy Aunt. "Speaking of your Aunt Lucy, why couldn't she use some of her bounty to get you a better car?"

"She offered. But I'm not going to be one of the people who are constantly taking her money."

Typical Ivey, always offering to help, never asking for any.

"She is your *aunt*."

She guzzled, then turned to him with a pout. "Your mechanic wouldn't help me. Something about the bro code. And the blue ribbon."

"Sorry. But he did call me, so his conscience must have been nagging at him." As well it should have. If it weren't for the fact that Tim was an excellent mechanic and Jeff was a doctor that shouldn't send people to the ER, he would have no compulsion with beating the shit out of Tim. Jeff could take him, too.

Ivey finished off the bottle, and as if she'd suddenly noticed that she was giving him a free show, she covered her breasts with her hands. "Oh. My. God."

He turned to keep from showing her his smile, and pulled out onto the highway.

"I guess you're enjoying this."

"Never."

"What did you tell everyone after we broke up? There must be some reason the entire town took sides. It must have been something you told them."

Of course she would blame him. "I didn't say anything at all. But I don't know, maybe I might have given off a certain vibe."

"What kind of vibe?" Her eyes narrowed.

That his heart had been ripped out by the seams? That he was a damn fool? He hadn't said a word, but he was pretty sure his face had said everything for him. "The bummer vibe?"

"This isn't fair. There are two sides to this story."

"There usually are. But you're the one who left."

"And you left me first. That's the part everyone seems to be missing, because you kept your mouth shut like a typical man! So I leave town and some people assume I'm the one who broke up with you?"

Yeah, she was really fired up now. Too bad he loved it when she got all heated and outraged. It didn't happen often enough. "That's usually how it works. And you told everyone that would listen that you'd met someone over the internet and were going to be with him."

"So because I try to move on with my life, I get the blame?"

"Forget about it. This is what people in a small town do. Entertain themselves with the gossip mill. You knew that before you left."

"But why do they have to pick on us?" She sighed and brought her hands down from her breasts. "It's kind of funny, in a bizarre way. Blue and pink ribbons."

"If it makes you feel any better, I think today's going to go a long way toward ending the problem."

"You do?"

"Think about it. Tim called me, and he knew I was coming to get you. He'll tell his wife, who'll tell her friends. And on and on."

"Right. They'll know that you and I aren't angry at each other, and maybe then they'll stop being mad too."

Jeff sensed an opening and he proceeded to drive the proverbial Mac truck through it. "The best thing you and I can do is show everyone in town that we're getting along. That we're friends again."

"Yeah. We better get the word out."

He nodded. "Having dinner with me might help too."

She whipped her head around so fast he worried about whiplash for a minute. "You and me? Not for real. That can't happen. We're not going there again."

"Going where?" Yep, he was going to do this. Watch her walk right into his trap.

"Sex. Getting back together. Do I have spell it out for you?"

"Wow," he said. "I'm flattered. But I was talking about dinner. You and your one-track mind."

Suddenly, absolute quiet from the passenger seat. But as his luck would have it, not for long. "I caught you staring at my boobs. Don't try to lie to me now."

"I'm a man, Ivey, and right now you're a wet-t-shirt-contest dream."

"Don't you dare stare at my boobs!"

He grinned. "Try and stop me."

She shifted her entire body away from him, facing the passenger side door. "I don't suppose you'd consider taking me home to change before we have our meeting."

Would he consider taking her home? This day was turning out better than he could have expected, but he was due back at the hospital. Eventually someone would page him.

He hesitated too long because Ivey changed her mind. "Never mind, actually. We shouldn't even bother with a meeting. Take me home."

This was a new turn of events. He'd never known a time when Ivey would pass up a chance to talk. And she loved talking about pregnancy. For his part, it was all rather disconcerting. Early on he'd decided to steer clear of obstetrics when he'd done that rotation and witnessed a woman in labor scream like a hyena. He didn't do screaming women.

He'd always assumed that one day he'd be a father, and until that time he'd have preferred not to think about it. No such luck with this subcommittee assignment. He was elbow deep in all the gritty stuff that happened between two pleasant events.

"Why aren't we going to bother?"

"I met with the local midwife I told you about—Marissa. Let's just say it didn't go well."

"Elaborate." He drove well under the speed limit, and

hoped she didn't notice.

Ivey turned to him. "It's not only the doctors that don't like the idea of midwives in a hospital setting. The midwife I talked to seems to think it's a crazy idea. The last place she wants her patients to be is in a hospital."

"Why?" Granted he hadn't specialized in obstetrics, but he understood and had studied how much could go wrong. It made sense to be in the hospital.

"Because this seems to be an 'us-versus-them' argument. I guess we're messing with thousands of years of tradition, and no one likes change. I thought I would get support from a midwife, because women who are too paranoid to give birth at home at least have another option."

"But again, why would women give birth at home when they could go to the hospital?" A stupid question, he was almost certain of it, but he dared to ask it anyway.

She blinked. "Haven't you been listening to anything I've told you?"

"Yeah. Listening." Mostly. Between, of course, the hard pulls of lust he felt every time she was in the room. But he could do more than one thing at a time, and he'd be willing to prove it.

"If you'd been listening, you would know that birth is a natural event, and it shouldn't be treated like a medical condition. The less intervention, the better. Unless absolutely necessary."

"You had me at absolutely necessary."

"Fair enough. It happens sometimes. Unexpectedly. We can't anticipate every problem. That's why I thought a good compromise would be the women's center."

"It makes sense. Why does the midwife object?"

"Because, as you said about your pal Dr. Stewart, she sees it as a slippery slope."

They sat in silence for a few minutes, then he spoke

because before long he'd be pulling into the exclusive gated condo her aunt lived in. It was the only one in town. "So what are we going to do?"

She turned to him, the light in her eyes that made him a goner. "We? Does that mean I've already convinced you, Dr. Garner?"

He couldn't help but grin. "Congratulations. I think we should make our recommendation that the board hire a staff of midwives and let them decide."

She stared out the window. "I don't know."

He didn't either, because he was afraid he'd left something unfinished with Ivey. And it wasn't because he was lonely, but because he'd been an idiot.

He wasn't quite done with being an idiot. He pulled up to the condo gate, and Ivey recited the security code, which he punched in. "So—dinner Friday night? We have to make it look good. Make it clear to everyone in town that we're friends and they can stop taking sides."

"Maybe," she said, uncertainty wavering in her eyes. That one look hit him square in the gut, because he could see the worry etched in her eyes. She didn't trust herself with him. "You mean you're not working this Friday?"

"I meant next Friday."

Ivey looked gratifyingly disappointed. "That's right. I forgot you're not spontaneous."

"Hard to be, with a schedule like mine."

Now she looked guilty. "Of course. I didn't mean anything by it. But should we? This Friday, next Friday. Neither one is a good idea."

They'd have to agree to disagree on that. This was one of the best ideas he'd had in months. "I promise I'll behave."

"You better. Seven o'clock." She wrenched herself out of her seat and fixed him with a look. "And don't be late."

He wouldn't dream of it.

CHAPTER 7

*W*ithin a week Ivey's SUV had been repaired and driven back to her home by none other than Tim, who might have suffered a crisis of conscience. He left a pink ribbon taped to the windshield, in case she had any doubts as to his apology.

Maybe Jeff was right. It was a matter of winning the hearts and minds of every misguided person. Sooner or later they'd see that Jeff and Ivey weren't interested in anyone taking sides, and the pink and blue ribbons would be a funny story she could tell her grandchildren someday.

Of course, they wouldn't be Jeff's grandchildren. It was too late for them, even though that fact seemed to make her a little bit sadder every day.

Recently she'd had the occasional random thought that maybe it could work this time. Maybe this time he'd realize how much he loved her, and—great, she was doing it again. No. Just friends, Ivey. Friends, and nothing more.

Jeff had left the hospital to pick her up simply because he'd felt guilty, and not because he still had any feelings for her. He would certainly not be willing to rearrange his life for her in any way, to get married because he loved her, whether the timing was right or not.

He would go where his career took him, because that was of primary importance. It came first in his life, and she was a selfish brat for ever thinking she deserved more. Someday he'd find an understanding woman who would put up with late nights at the hospital. And it wouldn't be her. She had to be done with all that.

She'd turned over a new leaf, and it was all Ivey, all the time. Numero uno, baby. Sounded horrible, but there it was. Brooke said it was a good idea anyway.

That's why she would do this dinner thing with Jeff tonight as he'd suggested. Because her own reputation was on the line, especially if she was going to stay here and make a life here.

When her doorbell rang on Friday evening, Ivey took one last glance in the mirror and then reminded herself it didn't matter a hill of beans what she looked like. Friends.

But when she opened the door, words failed her. Jeff was dressed in dark blue jeans and a white button-down, rolled up to his elbows. Casual but oh-so handsome.

"The security guy at the gate thinks your name is Iris."

"Oh," Ivey said as she snapped out of it. "Yeah, Ron does that."

"Ready?" Jeff asked, braced in her doorway.

She supposed she could let him in, but that wouldn't accomplish their purpose. They needed to be seen publically having fun, laughing, and being friendly. Definitely not kissing.

She grabbed her purse. "Let's go."

As Jeff's car passed the security gate on the way out, Ivey asked Jeff to roll down the window. She leaned across. "My name is Ivey. Ivey Lancaster. Not Iris. That's another flower. I'm Ivey with a V."

The man blinked. Jeff grinned, and as he rolled the window back up, he asked, "You're only now correcting him?"

"I didn't see much point to it. First I thought I'd be a short-timer around here. And after a while, it got awkward. I didn't want to embarrass him. He's been saying it wrong for a while."

"You've got to stop doing that. Worrying too much about other people's feelings."

"Exactly. That's what that was all about."

They rode the short drive to the middle of town in silence. Jeff pulled into Giancarlo's Bistro.

"This is where we're going?" It was one of the highest-rated Italian restaurants in Starlight Hill, known for serving the best wines in the valley. Giancarlo himself was almost a legend in Starlight Hill, having raised some of the best-looking girls in town and earned lonely attractive widower status about ten years ago when he lost his blessed wife. But Ivey hadn't really considered Giancarlo's to be the heart of the rumor mill. And also, it was mostly a place for lovers.

"There's a method to my madness. There's a chamber of commerce dinner here tonight. And Giancarlo's daughter Sophia is home from college. She likes to talk. A lot."

"You've given this a lot of thought. Perfect." Leave it to Jeff to find the most expedient way. He had more brains in his little finger than she had in her whole head.

There was a reason he'd been class valedictorian, and she —hadn't been, not even close.

Jeff led the way, opening doors and making her feel like they were on a real date. She should tell him to stop doing that, but it might be rude. Not to mention that she was rather enjoying it. It reminded her that she hadn't been on a real date with a real man since—she couldn't remember.

Giancarlo greeted them. "Dr. Jeff. Ivey. To what do I owe this pleasure?"

Ivey sized him up—blue or pink ribbon? Hard to tell. "It's not a date," she blurted out.

"Right," Jeff added. "Just dinner. I have reservations for two."

"Follow me," the gentle Italian said as he walked them to a table near the back.

"Could we have something near the front?" Ivey asked.

Giancarlo then led them to a table in the center of the room. "Would this satisfy?"

"Yes," Jeff said, holding the chair out for Ivey.

"Sorry, Giancarlo. But we need to be seen," Ivey said as she took the menu.

"Ah." Giancarlo leaned in, then whispered. "By whom?"

"By everyone, of course."

Giancarlo simply smiled and nodded, then walked away. He was the kind of man who never questioned anyone's quirks, and for that she was grateful.

"Blue or pink ribbon?" Ivey asked Jeff, pointing behind her menu towards Giancarlo.

"Neither," Jeff answered. "He seemed to stay out of it, somehow."

"Bless him. So how are we going to do this?"

"Let's look happy." Jeff smiled, and he did look content. Didn't even look like he faked it.

Giancarlo brought them a bottle of white wine on the house, and after the ritual of sniffing and swirling had been accomplished, Ivey reminded Giancarlo that she didn't drink.

Still, when a couple she recognized walked past them, Ivey held up her glass in a mock toast with Jeff, who followed her lead. She smiled. Jeff smiled. The couple gave them an odd look and kept walking.

"Is this working?" Ivey asked uncertainly. For the first time since they'd walked in the restaurant, she took a nice long look at Jeff.

He looked relaxed. The furrow in his forehead eased, and he had on his lazy smile. She hadn't seen that one in a long time, and it so happened to be her favorite.

Maybe she'd done this. He was happy, free from obligations other than to his career. A doctor now the way he'd always dreamed and planned.

"Be patient," he said with that drop dead gorgeous grin.

Yeah well, she'd never been good with patience but always better at easing burdens, starting with Mama. Continuing with Jeff and their little bump in the road. Nothing had stopped his forward trajectory, thanks to her. Someday she'd tell him. But today would not be that day.

"Did you date anyone in LA after Joe?" Jeff asked.

Well. At least he got the fake name right for once. "Um, not really. I became a serial dater. No one special. And you?"

"Same. Although my sister keeps trying to fix me up. For the past year that I've been back, she hasn't really given it a rest."

Ivey squirmed. Yeah, she wouldn't be surprised. Ali had always been protective of her little brother, which meant that she probably owned a case full of blue ribbons.

"And I'm guessing that since I got back into town she's really stepped it up."

"Maybe." Jeff's finger trailed the edge of the butter knife. Ivey had never wanted to be a piece of silverware before, but at the moment she did. She had a sudden unbidden memory return of what those hands felt like on her skin.

"She seems to think you and I are like a pair of magnets." He met her eyes again, not for the first time tonight. But it was the first time that Ivey felt a tug deep in her gut.

She opened her mouth to speak, and a raucous noise

came from the direction of the banquet room. A large group was filing out, which meant that the chamber meeting was likely ending, and they would be walking right by her and Jeff. Perfect.

Ophelia Lyndstrom, owner of the fabric store, was the first to see them. "Look at these two! Together again. It does an old woman's heart good. This is wonderful. No more ribbons. I've seen enough ribbon to last me a lifetime. Enough already."

"We haven't had the ribbons in years. What are you babbling about now?" Kevin Morrison, the cigar shop owner, came up behind her, and when Jeff and Ivey came into his line of sight he scowled. "Not this again."

"Our town can't go through this again. What are you kids trying to do to us?" This was from Henry Brandt, owner of the only market in town.

This wasn't going as well as she'd hoped. Jeff's expression said that he felt the same way. "We wanted everyone to know they can stop the madness. Ivey and I are friends. No hard feelings. No more blue and pink ribbons, and no more divided loyalties."

"That's right, Henry. It's none of our business if these two kids want to get back together, break up, get back together. They could do it a hundred times and it still wouldn't be any of our business," Ophelia said, waving her hands back and forth.

The rest of the Chamber members had gathered around their table to stare, making Ivey feel like a sideshow sensation.

She heard whispered words:
"her fault…,"
"blue ribbon…,"
"doctor…,"
"online dating…,"

"not a lick of sense… "

Enough. Ivey stood up. "All right, you all. Jeff and I are friends, and that ought to be enough for all of you. And by the way, in case anyone's interested, *he* broke up with *me!*"

All eyes then turned to Jeff, who sat rubbing his jaw, a slight grin on his face. "It's true."

"You never said that." Ophelia didn't look happy. Score one for Ivey.

"And you didn't ask. Plus, it was none of your business." Score one for Jeff. Damn, a tie.

Some grumbling ensued, and within a few minutes the chamber members filed out of the restaurant, all one cohesive unit. Like a school of fish.

"Well I think we've got that settled." Now maybe she could enjoy her dinner.

"I do like it when you get all riled up." Jeff grinned, which did all manner of odd things to her stomach.

Their waitress sauntered over to them, and held her phone above her, bending down next to Ivey. "Selfie!"

Ivey was in the middle of the word *no* when the young woman snapped the photo.

"That was awesome. Okay if I put this on the Facebook page?"

"Ivey, this is Giancarlo's daughter Sophia. Remember I told you about her?" Jeff threw Ivey a pointed look.

"Oh right. Sure, put it on Facebook and Twitter, everywhere. Let's get another one, maybe one without my mouth open." Ivey brushed back her hair, smoothed down her dress, and sat up straighter.

"Dr. Garner, you get in there too." Sophia motioned to Jeff.

No need to do so, because he'd moved in closer without having to be asked. Ivey could already feel his warm skin next to hers, and he'd casually slipped an arm around her shoulder. Once that arm had been like a second skin, but now the sheer strength of it made Ivey feel like she had a barbell on her shoulder. She stiffened, aware that Giancarlo was looking on, smiling. Enjoying this little show they were putting on. Because that's all it was, a show.

Sophia snapped two or three photos, and when she was done, Jeff's hand slid down Ivey's shoulder to her waist, like it had any business being there. Maybe announcing their friendship to the town was a great idea, but it might be a whole lot better if he could stop looking at her like she was his dinner.

"Are you trying to cop a feel?" She shifted away from his touch.

He lifted a shoulder. "Trying to make it look real."

Right now this was all beginning to feel a little too much like a walk down memory lane. But she wasn't going to take that stroll again. Been there, done that.

Survived him.

But how nice to be out with a man who didn't want her to run lines with him or ask her whether she thought it was a wise investment to have his teeth capped.

Giancarlo brought their orders, and it felt good to be with someone who wouldn't question why she didn't drink. Who chose not to drink either, not because he had to, but maybe because he understood. He knew her history.

Jeff knew about Mama and her drinking. All about the accident that had claimed her life and thank God no one else's. He also knew that Ivey not only couldn't hold her liquor, but that after the accident she simply refused to drink on principle. And even though he didn't share her feelings, he respected them.

"It's actually nice to have dinner with someone who doesn't want to recite lines with me later."

Jeff quirked an eyebrow. "Actors?"

"All of my serial dating involved men who either were actors or on the way to becoming actors. I've had many different roles, I'll have you know. Unfortunately, mostly I've played criminals. Cop shows, you know, they're so popular. I've been a detective on the take, a hooker, and a junkie."

"So playing against type."

"My dates always had the best lines. It got old after a while. But I did have other, far more pertinent influence on the actors of today."

"Like?"

"To cap or not to cap teeth? To wax or not to wax the chest hair?"

Jeff winced.

He happened to have the best kind of man's chest in her opinion—a light sprinkling of hair, not too hairy and not too bare. Like Goldilocks's bed—just right. He'd never wax his chest. If he ever did, Ivey would know for certain that hell had frozen over.

He looked at her now, those brown eyes assessing her, making her feel emotions she didn't want to feel and have thoughts she didn't want to have.

Like what a great kisser he was, taking his time and savoring every second. Taking his time with—everything.

"So did any of these guys get work?"

Ivey cleared her throat. That's right, they'd been talking about her dates. What kind of a woman babbled on incessantly about who she'd dated in the past? A woman who didn't know how to behave on a date any more, that's who.

"I think so." Subject change, quick. No more talking about failed serial dating and men who were more fascinated with themselves than they were with her. What a fine way to advertise. Not that she was here on a date.

Friends, Ivey. Friends.

* * *

Jeff kept the smile in place, even if he didn't want to hear about the idiots Ivey had dated in LA. Not exactly the best conversation if they were on an official date, which they weren't. All the wishing in the world wouldn't make it true.

Even if he couldn't keep his eyes off Ivey, who was far more delicious than anything on his plate tonight. That said something, since Giancarlo cooked the best pasta carbonara in the valley, hands down.

Ivey. He had a distinct memory of what she felt like in his arms—soft, but pliable with heat. Not shy and retiring like she looked by her outward appearance, always dressed in sundresses and jeans like the girl next door. No, with him she'd been bold and self-assured. Wild and uncensored. Angel and Vixen.

They were good together, and if she hadn't left town the way she had, today everything in his life would be different. But by now he understood that he couldn't control all outcomes. Not in the hospital, and not in his personal life. Some things were left to chance.

"Ready?" He pulled out his wallet.

"We'll split it," Ivey said, obviously wanting to make it clear this was no date. Just two friends going Dutch.

"No. This was my idea. Remember?" He stayed her hand, so soft and small under his, and man, it felt so good. The first time he'd touched her since she'd come home, and it only reminded him that he wanted more. Much more.

Bad idea, because she was looking at his hand over hers like she'd come upon a bear in the woods. Alone and helpless, like freaking Bambi.

"Okay," she said slowly. "You win."

If only that were true, but they were talking about the check.

In a few minutes he'd be dropping Ivey back off at the place where Ron the security guard couldn't remember her name. Then he'd go home alone to his lonely bachelor pad. Now that Scott was off touring a baseball series with his brother Billy, he had a lot of quiet nights ahead of him.

It seemed a little odd to see the Channel 7 television van pulled up outside of the gated entrance, a newscaster speaking into a microphone.

"That's strange," Jeff said as he punched in the code he'd memorized.

Ivey held a hand to her mouth. "Oh no. I hope he hasn't finally killed her."

"Killed who?"

"Mr. Alfonso. They're our neighbors, and I've heard him yell once or twice that he's going to kill Mrs. Alfonso. Am I going to be called to the trial? I'm probably going to be the witness that says 'yes, Your Honor, I heard him say he would kill her.'"

Apparently Ivey's dates were not the only ones with a flair for drama. Maybe it had rubbed off on her with the actors and scripts. Because Mr. Alfonso was an over-excitable Italian who wouldn't hurt a fly, and Jeff would bet those threats were Mr. Alfonso's misguided idea of foreplay.

"Ivey, he's an usher at St. Catherine's. And this is Starlight Hill."

She turned to him. "But murders happen everywhere. I see it on TV every Friday night."

Jeff slowed down at the gate, where the guard wasn't his usual stoic self. "Miss Iris—"

"It's Ivey!" she shouted back to him. "What's going on? Why are all those reporters in the front? Who got hacked up or shot?"

That's it. Definitely too many crime shows. She ought to go to the nearest drug store and pick up a pack of cigarettes because they were the only killers he ever saw around Starlight Hill.

"No one got killed, Miss," the security guard said, maybe finding it safe to not even attempt the name this time. "I'm sure it's all a big mistake. But they're waiting for you upstairs."

"For me?" Ivey drew a shaky hand to her throat, and for the first time since she'd been back, every protective cell in his body resurrected itself. This was Ivey. Ivey, who regardless of the way she behaved in the bedroom with him, was a freaking Girl Scout.

"Who's waiting for her?" he asked.

"The men from the FBI."

*J*eff still didn't think Ivey had calmed down enough when they were inside the condominium, waiting for the elevator.

"Did you hear that? The FBI!" Maybe out of old habit, she leaned into him.

He snaked a supportive arm around her waist. "Calm down. It's a mistake. That's all it is."

"A mistake." She repeated, her eyes glazed over.

"Let's go up." Jeff more or less led Ivey into the elevator and up to the second floor.

There were indeed men in distinctive black suits with badges. No yellow caution tape. But a sign on the front door read: *Seized by Order of the United States Government.*

The audible gasp from Ivey meant she'd read the sign as well.

A gray-haired agent stepped up to them, showing his badge. "Are you Lucy Cartwright?"

"No, that's my Aunt. Is she okay? What's happened to her?" Ivey clutched Jeff's hand.

"Nothing, ma'am. As far as we know she's fine. This property has been seized for payment of debts owed to investors by a Ben Cartwright."

Jeff squeezed Ivey's hand. Everyone in town realized Lucy's last husband was under house arrest in New York City. The story Jeff had heard was that he'd been indicted in a Ponzi investment scheme. But if Lucy thought she'd walked away with this asset in their divorce, she'd obviously been mistaken.

"Didn't Lucy Cartwright obtain this property in the divorce?" Jeff asked the man.

"It's a common trick to pass over assets that way, but Cartwright's not getting away with it." The agent handed over paperwork to Jeff.

"If you've been staying here, we'll give you time to get a few essentials. But you need to be out of here tonight."

"Tonight?" Ivey squeaked out.

"Go find a hotel room somewhere. Maybe there's someone you can stay with."

"You might have noticed it's a small town and there are no hotels." These guys were starting to piss Jeff off.

The agent shook his head like it wasn't any of his problem. "Mr. Cartwright should have thought of that before he robbed his investors of their savings."

Yeah, Jeff got it. He didn't like Mr. Cartwright either.

"Those people need to get their money back, of course," Ivey stammered out.

"Well, this will barely put a dent in it." The man said abruptly and went to confer with the other agents.

Jeff pulled Ivey to the side. He hated to see her this way. Confused, hurt, frightened. Again, someone in Ivey's life had hurt her. First her dad, who'd left Ivey and her mother when Ivey was ten. Her mother, dying in another small-town scandal when Ivey was eighteen.

Even he'd let her down.

"Where am I supposed to go now?" The look on her face, like she'd been gutted, slayed him. Maybe because he deserved it, he punished himself with the thought she might have had the same look when he'd told her that he needed a break. A break from her. That's how she would have heard it, when all he'd wanted was a tiny respite from the pressures of all the responsibilities.

"You can stay with me."

After the words were out of his mouth, he couldn't believe he'd said them out loud. But if nothing else, Ivey's wide eyes clued him in that he actually had. Not the way he'd once pictured living with Ivey. It would have been better if she'd chosen to be with him instead of being rescued, yet he couldn't see any other solution.

"With you?" Ivey asked, her right eyebrow twitching. She'd probably had one too many shocks tonight.

"I have an extra bedroom for a while." It made perfect sense, as long as he didn't think about it too much.

"I'm not going to be your roommate."

"Great, because I don't need one. Scott Turlock is my roommate, but he's out of town for a few weeks. It's temporary, until you get the job and find a place of your own."

"I could stay with Brooke." She worried a nail between her teeth and stared at the men in black.

"Seriously?"

"Don't look at me that way. I know you two don't like each other, but she's still my best friend in the world."

He liked Brooke fine, though he realized the feeling wasn't mutual. Daredevils like her practically kept him in business, but he happened to know she lived in a complex of Victorian homes converted into studio apartments, and it gave new meaning to tiny. He'd looked at one of the apartments when he'd first come back. "That place is the size of a postage stamp. You'll trip over each other in the hallway."

"You've been there? To her place?" Ivey's face reddened.

She couldn't seriously think he and Brooke—was she jealous? "No, but I am an ER doctor and Brooke is—well, Brooke."

"Stitches?"

Thank God, she believed him. "Stitches, x-rays." He couldn't, and shouldn't, list all her injuries.

"She also has a boyfriend and I'd hate to be in their way. But wouldn't I be cramping your style, or love life?"

What love life? If she meant his sex life, that was one thing, but he hadn't had a love life for years. He was looking at the extent of his love life right now, and it was pitiful that he couldn't convince her to let him help.

"No, you won't be."

"It's not a good idea. I need wide open spaces when I'm around you," she added.

"It's not like you have a lot of choices."

"Wow. I've waited all my life to hear a guy tell me that."

"C'mon, Ivey. Let me help. Stay the night and we'll figure things out in the morning. You don't have much time to decide, because this offer is going to be rescinded in about ten seconds. And then what will you do?"

"I'll figure something out!" But she took another pointed look in the direction of the FBI. One thing you could say about those men was that they didn't look friendly.

"Yeah, and there is the park. Of course, the bench isn't very comfortable, and Burt won't let you sleep on it. I tried."

"Look, I don't want to be any trouble."

"Ten, nine, eight, seven . . . " He began the countdown.

"Would you stop counting?"

"Five, four, three . . . "

"Fine! If it will get you to shut up, I'll stay with you. Temporarily."

* * *

WHAT WOULD the good people of Starlight Hill think of her now? What would Jeff think?

By way of marriage, she'd been related to a Ponzi scheme investor, which was bad enough, but now she'd been kicked out of her home. Practically in the middle of the night. Fine, the place would be sold and some of the investors paid off. That was only right and expected.

But now a bright light pointed to Lucy's ex-husband and the last thing Ivey needed was that kind of an association. She was still repairing her image as a love 'em and leave 'em witchy woman.

Ivey and Jeff packed up her bedroom, throwing clothes in plastic garbage bags.

One phone call to Aunt Lucy later, and Ivey had one more reason to be annoyed with her Aunt. She'd ignored all the legal notices forwarded to her because she had no interest in keeping the condo anyway. She ended the phone call by reminding Ivey that this was a chance to reconcile with Jeff, but if she insisted on being stubborn she'd send her more money. Ivey hung up on Lucy, and didn't bother telling her she was indeed on her way to living with Jeff, but not in the way she would have preferred. No, she'd be his roommate.

How could she live with this man and not be tempted every single day?

With enormous willpower, that's how.

Jeff surveyed the bags they'd hauled out of the condo. "We might be able to do this in one load."

She'd left everything behind in LA, and her roommate Sandy was only too happy to sell it off on eBay. She was still trying to raise money to get her teeth capped.

"All the furniture was my aunt's." She frowned in the

direction of the men hauling out oil paintings, chairs, and a flat screen TV. "Except for this lamp."

Ivey touched the lamp she'd won at a midwife convention, her very first one in Atlanta. The pink, headless, and armless body of an ample woman, large breasts, swelled wide and engorged in the middle with the light portion of the lamp shining in the place of the womb. Quite possibly the ugliest thing she'd ever seen, but it held memories of her first professional achievement, and she wanted to use it in her own office someday when she set up her private practice. After first proving to the medical establishment that she wasn't a shaman.

"It's uh—interesting." The look on his face was a mixture of pure disgust and that ridiculously perfect grin of his.

"You don't have to be nice. It's hideous. But I won it, and it's supposed to be good luck."

"What is it, exactly?"

"A fertility lamp. And it should bring my future patients plenty of babies. Or at least a good laugh."

Jeff picked up the lamp, holding it at a distance as though he feared it might actually work. "If you say so."

"Don't worry, it's going in my temporary bedroom." She took it from him, and placed it in the trunk of his car.

Ivey sunk further down on the passenger side as they passed the camera news crew on their way out. If she wasn't careful, she'd wind up being the news story. "I can't believe this is happening."

"It's not your fault," he said, pulling out of the gated community.

"But everyone will think it is."

His only answer was an unintelligible mutter under his breath, and they rode in silence for the next few minutes. He probably wasn't pleased.

Neither was she, since this hadn't been the way she'd

pictured living with Jeff once before, when she'd casually asked him about married-student housing. He had made up some excuse about there being no room, and she got the message. *Not yet.*

She'd wondered if they'd ever get married. In the end he hadn't wanted to marry her, end of story. She'd been the high school sweetheart he couldn't shake. And now he probably didn't actually want her to stay in Scott's empty room, but he felt too guilty to turn her away.

If you weren't lucky or wealthy enough to own land in Starlight Hill, you were squeezed into one of about four small housing developments or one fancy gated community, built under protest according to Aunt Lucy. The city council kept a tight handle on progress, and not much had changed. As they drove, Ivey realized that she didn't know where Jeff lived. His parents had once owned a house in one of the newer tract neighborhoods in town. But now he turned down El Toro Street, and into what she and Brooke used to call Sweet U Lane. A smattering of pre-WWII cottage-style homes that were mostly rented by university students. The cool kids.

And even now, as Jeff pulled into the carport, Ivey noticed a group of girls hanging on the porch of the house right next door. Young, nubile girls wearing Daisy Duke cut-offs and guzzling beer. Basically Ivey's worst nightmare.

"Hey, Jeff," one of the girls called out. "Wanna beer?"

"No thanks," Jeff answered without a look in their direction when he unlocked the front door, carrying a bag of Ivey's clothes.

Ivey heard girlish giggles that trilled through the cool summer night air and followed them inside. "You can go with them if you want. I'll get settled."

He met her eyes. "I don't want to go with them."

Why didn't she believe him? Jeff was a single hot-looking

guy and those girls were not shy about showing how available they were.

Together they carried in the rest of her boxes and bags, turning down help from the girls next door, who, to their credit, did offer. Probably so they could get a little closer to Jeff, and maybe sniff out what was going on.

Jeff set the lamp down outside one of two identical-looking bedroom doors. "This is Scott's bedroom. I should probably go inside and make sure he didn't leave anything embarrassing lying around."

"Please do." Ivey set down a bag of clothes outside the door.

After a few seconds, he came out. "This room is cleared."

There was an uncomfortable moment of silence between them as they stared at each other, and then Jeff ran a hand through his hair and cleared his throat. "You should get settled."

Ivey carried her bag in the room and shut the door. The room screamed military, which made sense since Scott was in the Army. The small twin bed was neatly made, with all the flat corners one would expect. Setting a bag of clothes down on the floor, Ivey took a seat on the bed. How odd to be here in a place that reminded Ivey so much of the dorm rooms where Jeff had lived. Every room and door so similar they were almost indistinguishable from each other.

Back then, she'd also been a temporary visitor too. She'd acclimated to spending weekends in surroundings that screamed testosterone: girly posters, beer, stinky socks. But she hadn't minded because it meant sharing a bed with Jeff, and getting all his attention for a while. He'd taught her how to please him, and she'd become well versed in the art of distracting him from anything else but her. It was that need for him that drove her life back then, but she was not the same innocent girl anymore.

She had goals and a direction. Unfortunately life had taken a left turn again while she'd been ready to turn right. But she'd roll, as she had so many times in the past. On the other hand, Jeff had a penchant to schedule everything down to the last detail, and all this couldn't be sitting well with him.

* * *

THIS COULD GET COMPLICATED. He wouldn't mind complicated if it meant seeing Ivey naked, but that was a pipe dream. This wasn't part of any plan he could have imagined. Ivey living with him, her bedroom inches away from his.

A few minutes later, he'd changed and pulled a beer from the fridge when Ivey emerged from the bedroom wearing a tank top and sweatpants that read *bootylicious*. In case he'd forgotten, which he hadn't.

They simply stared at each other for a minute, and then they both spoke at once.

"Are you going to bed?"

"I'm going to watch some TV." Ivey headed towards the set and turned it on to the news.

Not a good idea. "Maybe not the news."

"There's nothing else on, and I might hear something about what happened tonight."

"Do you really want to?"

"Of course. I want to make sure they got the story straight. My aunt had nothing to do with this."

Curious, he waited to hear as well, and when they listened to a story about a boy who had figured out a way to recycle straws, Jeff had convinced himself that they'd skip the story altogether.

But no such luck.

"In other local news tonight, a Wall Street financial investor's home has been seized in an FBI sting."

"A sting?" Ivey cried out. "There was no sting."

They showed film of the newscaster at the scene, reporting on the few known details. Nothing Jeff and Ivey didn't already know. Then back to the talking heads, who seemed amused. Slow news day and all.

"I thought all they had in Starlight Hill were vineyards." The male anchor preened.

"Sounds like they've got crooks too. But even those are high-class." A light elbow to her co-anchor. A little chuckle.

Next, a large photo of Ben Cartwright and Lucy at their wedding. "Here's a photo of the couple in happier days. You know, Lucy Cartwright is a local who won the California lotto several years ago. It goes to show you, it's never enough." The male anchor shook his head sadly. This, obviously, was the news commentary portion of the show.

"For some people, it never is. But justice prevails, and tonight maybe a few unlucky investors are a little closer to getting back their life savings. Well, good night and sleep tight, folks." The female anchor winked.

Jeff turned toward Ivey, who hadn't said a word. She stared at the screen, mouth gaping. "Did you hear that? They lumped them together, showed their wedding picture for crying out loud, and made it sound like my aunt was involved."

He rubbed his forehead, feeling a headache coming on. "No they didn't. And no one will believe that."

"I'm going to call the station. This is irresponsible journalism. They might as well call it the evening rumors."

"You want to let it go. Let it die out. You'll only call more attention to the situation."

"I don't want people to think badly of Aunt Lucy. I know she's been married four times, and she probably has more fun than any fifty-eight year old woman should, but she's been good to me. And she's been good to the hospital too. That's something nobody knows. She's the women's center's main benefactor."

That got his attention. When he'd pressed, he'd been told that it was one of the benefactors who wanted him on the subcommittee. No explanation. Could that have been Lucy? "No kidding."

Ivey froze, then turned from him and snapped the TV off. "I shouldn't have said anything."

"She's the one that wanted me on the subcommittee, isn't she?" He would have a little fun with this tonight. And maybe someday personally thank Aunt Lucy, since he'd had more excitement lately than in the past year. "Maybe to get us back together."

"Why would you say that? My God, the ego on you! Are all doctors like this? Don't answer that. I happen to know they are."

She tried to get by him, but he grabbed her wrist. "Tell the truth. It will only hurt a little. It's like tearing off a band aid."

"I've said enough."

And maybe she had, because he had his answer. Aunt Lucy had played matchmaker, because somehow even she knew that they weren't done with each other. "Thank her for me."

"I will not."

"Then I'll thank her." He let his fingers trail up her arm and then back down again.

"I can't stop you." Her eyes didn't betray a single emotion, but he did feel her arm shiver.

Then his pager went off, because that thing had the timing of a metronome on crack. Reluctantly, he ended the standoff and went to find his pager on the counter where he'd unloaded it.

He recognized the ER's number, and called them back on his cell phone. "Dr. Garner. You paged?"

"It's Nancy. I thought I'd let you know that Frank Sullivan came in and he was taken up to cardiology. Apparently there's something abnormal on the EKG. I know how fond you are of him, so I wanted to let you know."

"Thanks. I'll be right over." He gathered his wallet, his keys.

"Don't you dare. You've already logged too many hours, and the board will have our hide if they hear about it. I shouldn't have called you. Donna was right. And you know how I hate it when she's right. Stay where you are, Doctor, or I'll be forced to take drastic measures."

He let out a breath. With all the extra shifts he'd pulled, he needed the break. But this was Frank. How many EKGs had he ordered, all perfectly normal? What had he missed?

"Fine. I'll drop by to see him tomorrow." He hung up the phone.

"Is something wrong?" Ivey asked from the couch. She had a book in her hands now, something that looked like a romance novel.

"Nothing," he lied. Something was wrong with Frank, and he'd missed it. Maybe because he'd been too tired, working too hard. Thinking too much about his own needs and whether the ER was where he wanted to land.

"You care about your patients, don't you?" This was said kindly, and took him by surprise.

"Does that surprise you?"

She smiled a little. "I wasn't sure how you'd do with patients. I've always known how smart you were, but not every doctor has the compassionate side of them fully engaged."

"I think they wind up being radiologists."

Ivey laughed. "We're not so different, you and me."

"Uh huh." Damn, he was tired. Not too tired to flirt with Ivey, but too tired to talk about what a great doctor he was. Or wasn't. The jury was still out. And he had an early call tomorrow morning. He took one last longing look at Ivey and made a snap decision. "Good night. I'm going to bed."

With any luck, he'd actually sleep.

CHAPTER 9

*I*vey blinked awake as the pale moonlight spilled from the overhead skylight. She jerked up, forgetting where she was for a moment. She'd fallen asleep on Jeff's couch. Her last memory was of fighting off sleep so she could read a few more pages. She'd almost finished the novel, and soon Melody and Bobby would be together again after all the trouble. They were meant to be.

She stretched and yawned. The digital clock on the kitchen microwave read four in the morning when she staggered towards her bedroom, eyes bleary and half-mast.

Once in her dark room, she fumbled for the bed and pushed back the covers. The bed seemed bigger than it had looked earlier. She snuggled into it, grateful for another few hours of sleep before morning.

"This is an interesting way of flirting," Jeff said from the other side of the bed.

What the hell?

"What are you doing in here?" Ivey rolled off the side of the bed and fell in a heap on the floor. "Oh, ow." This floor was so much harder than it looked.

"Are you all right?" He leaned over the side of the bed, shirtless. And who knew what else "less." In all their time together, she'd never known him to sleep in anything but a pair of boxers *if* he felt cold.

Ivey held up her hand. "No! I mean yes, I'm fine, and stay there! *Please* don't get out of bed."

But of course he hopped out of bed, flipped on the light and was next to her in seconds. "Did you hit your head? And why are you squeezing your eyes shut?"

I won't look, I won't look, I won't look. "I'm okay, you ninny."

"If you're okay, then open your eyes and look at me."

Please let him have some clothes on. She slowly opened one eye and then the other to find Jeff crouched next to her wearing a pair of dark boxer briefs. Okay, not so naked. But still. "I'm looking at you."

He gazed in her eyes intently—as if he'd lost his keys in there. "Where does it hurt?"

"Oh no, I'm not telling you that." He'd completely unnerved her with his penetrating eyes and his stupid sexy boxers.

"Don't be ridiculous."

"Let's put it this way: you're not touching where it hurts. Got it?" Her lower back had taken the worst of it, right next to her bottom.

"I'm getting you an ice pack." He was out the door before she could protest.

"Stop overreacting." She slowly rose from the cold hardwood floor and rubbed her butt. He had to stop behaving like a doctor and understand she could take care of herself. Nurse and all.

She made her way to the door only to find him blocking it, holding the ice pack in one hand. "But how did you manage to get the wrong room, Little Face?" He gave her a lazy grin as he leaned against the door frame. Her breath hitched when she heard his term of endearment. No one had ever called her Little Face before he did, or since.

"I was half asleep when I woke up on the couch. These two doors look identical. It was an easy mistake. And are you going to give me that ice pack?" She tried to snatch it out of his hands, but he was too quick for her and pulled it out of her reach.

"Maybe this is really where you want to be." He moved closer until he was only inches away, and she swore she could smell the minty flavor of his toothpaste.

She couldn't help but tremble a little bit, because he was so close, and dear Lord he was so gorgeous. The dimple on his chin. Words. Words would be good right now. "The—ice pack?"

"Yep," he said, but rather than put it in her outstretched hand, he reached behind her and held it right where it hurt. As if someone had drawn him a map of the area.

She jumped when his hand hovered near her behind. Exactly where he had no right to be, MD or not.

"Cold?" he asked.

But also pretty hot, if I'm being honest. She put on her best smile through gritted teeth. "Take your hand off my ass."

"Sure." He handed her the ice pack. "I don't recall inviting you in here, but you might as well stay."

"I might, except that I'm not." She shoved past him and closed the door quickly, unwilling to hear one more word out of his sexy mouth.

She'd never make this mistake again, dark hallway or not. Maybe she'd mark her bedroom door with a glow-in-the-dark sticker to be on the safe side.

She didn't know what upset her most, the fact that he'd suggested she'd done this on purpose, or the frightening reality that for one moment she wanted to stay exactly where she was and find out if those abs were as rock hard as they looked.

No, the only way this arrangement was going to work, the only way her heart could handle this, was if they both kept their hands off each other. And if tonight was any indication, it would be a challenge.

The next morning Ivey blinked awake and pulled the covers over her head. Under the covers she'd stay until she could be certain he'd left. Wandering into his bedroom was not the way she'd planned her first night as his roommate.

One way or another, he'd get the message that they couldn't do a round two of Jeff and Ivey. A second breakup and there might not be enough pink and blue ribbons in the state. Anyway, one kiss and he'd see inside her. And he wouldn't like what he found.

When in the silence of the morning she heard a lone dog barking in the distance, Ivey tiptoed out of the bedroom and into the bathroom. Sharing a bathroom was another challenge she hadn't thought all the way through.

She would have to remind herself to check the toilet seat on a regular basis, because falling in during the night would hurt almost as much as falling onto the hardwood floor. She rubbed her lower back. Despite the ice pack, it still felt sore and bruised. Much like her pride.

The bathroom was organized better than she would have thought for two guys. And it was clean. The medicine cabinet had two empty rows—he'd made room for her. Well. This could work if he continued to be so accommodating.

His thin row contained only deodorant, a razor, toothbrush, toothpaste, mouthwash, and a small almost-full bottle of men's cologne. No hair gel for his glorious hair. No hair spray. So in other words, it still took no effort to look that good. Ivey frowned as she pulled out her toiletries from the bag she'd left in the bathroom yesterday—hair mousse and gel, hair spray, make-up remover, body spray, razors, special teeth-whitening toothpaste, deodorant, and make-up. Before long her rows were full and she squeezed a few more items onto his row, hoping he wouldn't notice since he obviously didn't need the room.

After her shower Ivey towel dried her hair. She wiped the steam from the mirror, viewing the face of a determined woman. A woman who had plans, a career, a direction. So what if she'd been alone for the past few years?

She would be all right, as long as she could stop thinking about him. Last night had been humiliating enough, but thank heaven dreams were private. In her dreams she'd stayed in that bed with him and enjoyed every part of his hard body. Even now, her naked breasts quivered at the memory.

Ivey pointed to her reflection in the mirror. "Stop it."

She dressed and looked through the bare kitchen cupboards. There were a few cans of soup and not a single vegetable in the crisper. A nearly empty gallon of milk, and some kind of science experiment that might have been cheese at one time. Ivey started a grocery list.

The man was definitely household challenged. Although he wasn't challenged in any other way. Highly intelligent, educated, respectful, kind, with bedroom eyes, and thick brown hair that she wanted to run her fingers through. That any woman in her right mind would want to run her fingers through. Broad shoulders, strong arms, and large hands that knew how to hold a woman. She did remember that. Abs to die for, she'd seen those last night. Ivey sighed, and then sucked in a breath when she took a closer look at her grocery list. She'd unconsciously written down every one of Jeff's attributes right along with the food items. She tore up the list and threw it in the trash.

What are you doing, Ivey? Fantasizing about her ex, that's what. She had to remember that he'd left her because she wanted too much from him. And he hadn't been willing to give it. Didn't want to marry her. Even if he didn't know she'd been pregnant, the fact was he'd never changed his mind. Never called and said he was sorry. Never told her he regretted their fight. Not a single phone call, text, or email. Maybe it was harder for her, because she'd carried a part of him, and that had made it impossible to ever forget him.

But sometimes Ivey wondered if she were silently punishing him for something he didn't know. She couldn't hold him responsible for the things he didn't realize had happened, but some small and unreasonable part of her wanted to believe that somehow he should have known.

Her cell phone rang. Ivey recognized Marissa's caller ID and answered with a smile. "Have you reconsidered?"

"I'd like to talk to you about that. In person. Could we meet, maybe for breakfast?" Marissa sounded perky and excited. This had to be good news.

Ivey knew exactly the place. Sooner or later she'd have to face everyone after last night's broadcast. No better place better than Mama's to find out if she and Aunt Lucy were still welcome in town.

Mama's was bustling when Ivey eased into a booth at the diner, prepared for the worst. Em barely glanced at her, busy with the morning rush.

Ophelia Lyndstrom and Kevin Morrison were sitting in a booth on the other side of the restaurant, and as they were leaving, they veered in Ivey's direction.

She braced for impact.

"We want you to know none of us believes your Aunt Lucy had anything to do with that ugly matter," Kevin said as he took out his wallet.

"Not for a minute." Ophelia patted Ivey's hand.

"Thanks. Because she didn't. She's pretty upset about the

whole thing." Over the phone from Italy, Aunt Lucy had some choice words for Ben Cartwright, the kind Ivey would rather not repeat in front of her elders.

"I imagine she is. The poor dear. You think you know someone."

They were being so nice it was a little strange. Where was the outrage? Aunt Lucy did know how to pick them, didn't she? Even Ivey would have to agree with that.

Kevin put his business card down on the table and slid it across to Ivey. "If you wouldn't mind, dear, give my card to your aunt. We need new advisors to the city planning commission, and I always value the opinions of reasonable people."

And Aunt Lucy sounded reasonable?

Ophelia nodded. "We should go. Have a good day, Ivey."

"You'll give her my card?" Kevin coughed.

"Sure." Ivey put it in her purse, wondering what city coffer or new project needed funding now. Everyone in town knew about Lucy's windfall, and had already hit her up countless of times for donations, investments or loans.

Em popped by to take Ivey's order. "What was that about?"

"I don't know, but I think someone needs money. At least they realize Aunt Lucy had nothing to do with her ex-husband's fraud."

"No one thinks your aunt had anything to do with that swindle. It's always the men who cheat. Always the men."

Well there was a story there, but Ivey didn't have time for it this morning. First order of business: get Marissa on board. She'd then start referring midwives to the hospital for work, and everyone would be happy. Possibly not everyone, but perhaps most people. Good enough.

"I was worried about you last night when I saw the

broadcast. Where are you staying now?" Em asked as she poured Ivey some coffee.

"Um, well, I'm staying at Jeff's in the spare bedroom until I find another place."

Em didn't bat an eye. "Isn't he a sweetheart? I'm telling you, Dr. Garner would give the shirt off his back to any one of us."

Of course he would. He's rather fond of taking his shirt off.

She thought about those muscles, and what it might feel like to run her hand down his chest down to his crunch-worthy abs. To feel the strong beat of his heart under her fingers.

"So what are you doing today?" Em's voice jerked Ivey back to reality.

She was sitting alone in the diner, thinking about her ex's abs. Probably a bad sign. "I'm meeting a friend."

On cue, Marissa walked into the diner and waved to Ivey. But she wasn't alone. With her was a beautiful Amazon of an exotic-looking woman at about 36 weeks of gestation, Ivey would say, give or take.

Marissa made the introductions. The woman was Asia Foster, one of Marissa's patients.

"This is my first baby," Asia said. "And I want everything to be right. Perfect. I've timed it down to a science, and I should be having the baby sometime tomorrow. That's actually the anniversary of the first day we met. The labor will be smooth and progress swiftly, and then I'll give birth right on my bed. My husband will hold my hand and recite a poem of his choosing right as our baby is born into the world."

Asia reminded Ivey of Jeff on steroids. The woman liked to plan too, and unfortunately would soon find out that babies did the planning. And didn't tell you about it ahead of time. Not to mention the fact that according to everything

Babs said, they continued to do that for the next few years of their lives.

Ivey and Marissa exchanged a meaningful look, fine-tuned by midwives all around the world. *How precious. First time mothers. Gotta love them.*

"What makes you think you're going to give birth tomorrow?" Ivey asked.

"Months of visualizing techniques. Works every time."

"So the problem is," Marissa said, with a look that implied this would be no problem at all, "I'm going out of town tomorrow to visit my sister in Oregon. I hate the Grape & Wine Festival. All those people worshipping a vine. It's ridiculous. So Asia is a little bit worried."

"A lot worried. You're my midwife. Who knew you'd be taking off when I give birth?"

"This is Asia's first baby, and I've tried to explain babies have their own time table, and being that she's barely now at thirty-eight weeks gestation, it's highly unlikely the baby will come tomorrow. And I'll be back Monday morning. But my idea, Ivey, is that you would cover for me while I'm gone. To ease Asia's mind. Again, I doubt that the baby will come—"

"Oh he's coming," Asia said with a slight whistle.

Because Ivey had never met a mother who could determine her baby's day of birth, she was 99.9% certain that covering for Marissa would mean maybe a phone call from Asia asking why nothing was happening and not much beyond that.

"I'd love to. Don't worry, Asia, if your baby—"

"*When,* you mean."

"Sure. When your baby comes, I'll be there." Ivey leaned over to pat the woman's hand, an empathy trick she'd learned from Babs.

Asia's eyes narrowed. "But you don't look old enough to be a midwife."

"I've already gone over Ivey's qualifications. She studied under a colleague, Babs Holiday. I trust her completely."

Fortunately, it didn't look like either one of the women had seen the news last night or made the connection between Aunt Lucy and Ivey, or maybe they'd have other thoughts.

To put Asia at ease, Ivey went over her experience and qualifications again. All the skills she'd put on the back burner for the past few weeks that she'd been back in town—first taking care of Aunt Lucy and now fighting for a job in a hospital. Fighting to be acknowledged. But it occurred to her that she missed bringing babies into the world. Even though Asia's baby would not be arriving on her watch, she had to get back to the business of birth sooner rather than later. This was probably Marissa's gentle way of reminding Ivey where her priorities should be, and she did have a point.

Asia finally left with Marissa, reassured that her baby wouldn't be brought into the world by an incompetent. Now Ivey could get to the grocery store and take care of someone else's incompetence.

"You're kidding! But it's for the kids! How can you do this to me on such short notice?" Em shouted into the phone. The diner did take-out orders, and Ivey wondered what kind of an order would elicit that kind of reaction. "That's a fine how-de-do. Yeah, yeah. Goodbye."

Ivey picked up her ticket and swung by the register to pay. "What was that about?"

"My niece informs me she can't come down and help me with our booth at the festival like she does every year. Leaves me hanging the day before. How do you like that?"

Ivey would be dropping by the festival, because that's what people in Starlight Hill did. She'd make an appearance, say hello to everyone so they realized she wasn't judging them for loving the vine, and then leave. Maybe she'd rent a movie afterwards or download another book for her Kindle. Great, she was starting to sound like the town spinster.

Em was eyeing Ivey in a way she never had before, sizing her up. "Are you about a size six?"

Ivey cleared her throat. More like a size seven. Her "girls" kept her from the smaller sizes, since they had their own zip code. "Er, about that. Why?"

"I have to ask you for a huge favor. It's for a good cause, and I know you'll be perfect for it."

With that, Ivey braced herself once again.

CHAPTER 10

"She has got to be kidding," Ivey muttered the following day as she inspected the costume she'd promised to wear to the festival.

She'd agreed to help out at Em and Si's booth—some kind of Medieval theme—and that meant wearing a costume. Because she wanted to show how much she appreciated the town's support, and also because it was a bit difficult to say no to Em, Ivey agreed to pitch in. It would mean that she'd meet some people at least, and wasn't that what a woman intent on not being the town's spinster should do every once in a while? Sounded like a good idea at the time.

Big mistake. Unless the intent was to look like a Swiss Miss in a size-too-small top. *That's the last time you lie about being a size six.*

The tight, off-the-shoulder white top and black lace-up waist cincher pressed down on her like a vice, her body ready to bust out at any given moment. The red skirt was short, which would at least be a relief during the scorcher predicted today. The outfit was completed with a red scarf and fishnet stockings which were definitely not going on her legs. A girl had to have some pride.

"You're helping a friend," she reminded herself in the mirror. She tiptoed out of her bedroom. If she timed things right, she could get out of the house before Jeff got a glimpse of her.

No such luck, as she passed Jeff in the kitchen, drinking some of the milk she'd purchased. That same milk nearly came spewing out of his mouth. "Holy Swiss Miss. Wow."

"Stop staring. This can't be a size six, or maybe it shrunk. This doesn't fit," she said as she pulled up on the top, glossing over the fact that she hadn't worn a size six since high school.

"Oh, it fits." He grinned.

Since he wore low slung jeans and a gray baseball team jersey, she got the message that he wasn't on his way to work. "You're not going to the festival, are you?"

"I'm stopping by the hospital first, but I'll be there later." He folded his arms and leaned against the kitchen counter. "The whole town goes to the festival. You ought to remember."

"Right. See you there." She didn't like that gleam in his eyes. It told her maybe there was something else. Something she didn't know. But damned if she was going to indulge him by asking.

Ninety degrees at nine in the morning was never a good omen, but there it loomed displayed on the trip computer of her SUV. *August in California.* Anyone in their right mind would be in their air-conditioned home, or seeking AC elsewhere. The rest of them would be at the festival. Drinking.

Burt the police chief would be out tonight, making sure everyone took advantage of the free rides he provided in the back of his cruiser.

Wine tasting booths from the local vineyards were set up all around the center of town, prepared to sell out of chilled white wine and even some of the red stuff—Cabernet or whatever. There were booths with oil paintings from local artists and handmade leather boots and belts from the Williamson family. Balloons and cotton candy for the kids and lots of beer on tap for the few people who didn't do wine. In the distance, a crew worked to set the stage for the bands that would play tonight. Brooke would be in the crowd somewhere. Ivey hadn't seen much of her lately.

When she reached the diner's booth, Ivey waved her arm from her top to the bottom of the short skirt. Si wouldn't even look at her. "Is this some kind of a joke?"

"You look great." Em was dressed in a matronly Renaissance gown, more of what Ivey had in mind. Em caught her eyeing her gown. "You don't want to be in this. It's too hot."

But then Ivey saw another sign—a sign which caused her to hitch her breath and break out in a sweat that had little to do with the weather. *No.* Ivey picked up the small sign, waving it at Em. "What—–exactly—is *this?*" The sign read *Kisses from Swiss Miss - $1.00. All proceeds go to St. Vincent's Home for Unwed Mothers.*

"Isn't it wonderful? My niece does this every year. It's for a good cause, and with you being a midwife, I knew you'd want to help out," Em said with a straight face.

"This is why you thought I'd be perfect?"

"Consider it a compliment, dear. We always get the prettiest and best endowed girl we can find. Like I said, my niece, Miss California, couldn't come out this year."

Best endowed? "I don't like this at all." She was no beauty queen and her endowments would get far too much sun in this getup. "Can't I help you serve the food?"

"It's a kiss on the cheek, for goodness' sake. I'm not running a brothel," Em said with a laugh.

If that were true, why did Ivey feel dressed to work in one?

Before long, a line formed at their booth, and Ivey reluctantly settled in behind the counter.

Sometimes an entire family came up to order, donating a dollar without collecting a kiss, but every now and again there was the random teenage boy standing in line. Ivey became nervous and self-conscious about her PG-13 rated clothing, and threw occasional pointed looks in Em's direction. The boys were mostly perfect gentlemen as they turned their cheek for a kiss, and only later did she see them point in her direction, making her feel sixteen all over again.

Adding to the feeling of being sixteen was noting Jeff in the line near the end of the day. Before long he'd somehow made his way to the front, skipping ahead of several customers with ease. Most of them seem to know and like him, calling him "Doc" and letting him cut in line.

Jeff ordered Pirate's Grog and a smoked-beef-brisket sandwich and paid Em. Then he handed Ivey a ten-dollar bill.

"That's very generous of you, but you can't have ten kisses," she said, taking the bill from his hand. "I think it's against the rules."

"How about a ten dollar kiss then?" He grinned.

Some of the men behind him whooped and laughed.

"You can't have that either."

"Be reasonable," he said, pointing to his cheek and leaning in closer.

People were beginning to stare at their exchange, including Em and Si. The bigger deal Ivey made out of a simple kiss, the more attention she would call to it. She'd have to play along even if the thought of kissing him made her knees feel like Jell-O on a hot day.

"Fine," she said, leaning forward. "A ten dollar kiss."

Her heart did a flip as she and Jeff drew closer than they'd been in years. She aimed for his cheek, but did not expect him to take her face in his hands as though he would be the one doing the kissing. Too late she saw him headed straight for her lips, but as their noses touched Ivey whispered, "Don't."

Her tone must have been pleading enough, and his eyes gazed into hers with what seemed to be a quiet agreement and his lips turned toward her cheek. Ivey closed her eyes as his prickly chin touch her face, causing more shivers to run down her spine. He kissed her lightly on the cheek as one hand held the back of her head, his fingers threading through her hair. His lips felt hot like a brand, and she prayed the soft moan hadn't really come out of her throat. Time seemed to suspend and Ivey couldn't stop herself from resting her hand on his shoulder. His very smell was too familiar, the memory of him far too intoxicating, until she forced herself to pull away.

"There! A ten-dollar kiss." She turned to find a small crowd staring, including Si, his jaw slack.

Em slammed the Pirate's Grog in front of Jeff, her lips a thin straight line. "No more ten-dollar kisses, Doc. Any more of that and the two of you need to get a room."

As dusk settled over the park and the band began to play, Ivey was issued a reprieve from her duties. After a moment to change into her well-worn jeans and tank top, Ivey headed out to the lawn with her blanket to find a good spot.

Brooke was at the Serrano booth, serving up drinks with the same man who had spirited her away. The boss who had the hots for her.

"About time you dropped by," Brooke called out.

"I've been busy helping at Em's booth."

"So I heard. And saw the outfit." Brooke grinned. "How'd you get roped into that?"

"Don't start with me. I didn't know about the costume until it was too late."

"And knowing you, you weren't going to bail on her at the last minute."

"Well, no."

"I'll be working till we're done here, but we'll catch up later," Brooke said.

But Brooke seemed too caught up with the boss to want to spend any time with Ivey. And if it were really love, Ivey couldn't blame her, except that from where she stood it looked more like lust than anything else. Brooke might well be the only woman who could keep her heart from being involved, but even so Ivey had her doubts.

She found an empty spot to spread her blanket out and wait for the band to play, as all around her couples sat wrapped in each other's arms. Maybe if she sat here for a while, she wouldn't be alone for long. But alone or not, she'd be okay. *Keep telling yourself that.*

* * *

ALL RIGHT, so Jeff may have pushed a bit too far with the ten-dollar kiss. Only Ivey had the ability to turn him into a testosterone-driven horny adolescent. It hadn't even been Ivey's plea that stopped him from kissing her on the lips, but the sudden realization that he was about to set a precedent, and he sure as hell didn't want anyone else paying for a ten dollar kiss.

He stayed in the shadows, searching for Ivey. He spotted her sitting on a blanket, wearing jeans the way only she could wear them and a pink tank top that displayed the great rack that still headlined his fantasies. He wasn't surprised to see she'd become a quick-change artist, but a little bit unnerved by how she still made his heart pound.

Relationships weren't like hitting the pause button and resuming again. Even though it felt that way at times—like no time at all passed. Like the whole separation had been a mistake.

Was Ivey right about the fact that they couldn't do this again? Did Ali make sense when she thought he ought to stay away? No matter what his head said, his heart seemed to have other ideas. He'd never let it lead before, but maybe it was time.

Ivey's long dark hair caught a glint of the moonlight, but there was a slight problem with the picture. Mr. Williamson's boy Jimmy, who had to be all of eighteen-years-old, sat with her on the blanket. Jimmy had hopes of touching heaven too, and Jeff almost felt sorry for him as he prepared to dash those dreams.

"Hey, Jimmy. So, your mom is calling you. Something about watching your sister while they pack up," Jeff lied as he emerged from the shadows. Something told him that Mrs. Williamson wasn't going to object to some help with her youngest, and Jimmy would only look like a good son thanks to him. No harm, no foul.

Jimmy's face fell as he rose from the blanket. *Ah yes, so close and yet so far. Sorry, buddy.*

"See you later, Ivey. Don't forget my band is playing tomorrow night."

"Okay, Jimmy, I'll be sure to clap the loudest."

Jimmy smiled as though he'd won the lottery.

Jeff sat down beside Ivey. "How dare you? He's a child."

"What? I didn't do any—" Ivey protested. "Oh. You're teasing me."

"I'm sorry, but you make it easy sometimes."

"That was a mean thing to do today. Do you know how hard it was for me to stand there looking like the town wench while teenage boys ogled me?" Ivey slapped his shoulder.

"I know how hard it was for me," he said.

"You and your ten-dollar kiss." Her words scolded, but her eyes were smiling.

"You can't blame a guy for trying."

Ivey turned her head toward the music again, as the band broke out into Lionel Ritchie's song *Truly*. Couples began to slow dance to the song. Jeff sucked in a breath through clenched teeth, and his gut pinched with envy. He was so tired of being alone, so weary of the temporary nature of every relationship he'd had since Ivey.

"So what made you go online to find the perfect love match?"

She turned to him, her posture suddenly defensive. "Why would you ask me that now? Don't you believe me?"

"Believe what?"

"That I found someone online."

"Why wouldn't I believe you? My question is why. Isn't that supposed to be the move of the desperate?"

Ivey fingered the threads of fringe on her blanket. "Leave it to you to make fun of people who need a little help in the love department. You probably never had any trouble getting a date."

"I didn't think you would either."

"Shows you how much you know."

"All right, fine. I'm not judging you or anyone else who uses those services. It takes all the fun out of it. Doesn't it?" Sure, he believed in planning, but even he realized you couldn't plan who you fell in love with.

He'd known that the first time he met Ivey, who'd nearly chopped off her finger in a high school Home Ec cooking class. He'd been the one tasked to take her to the office for first aid, which he'd administered himself when the health clerk had been otherwise occupied.

"Don't you know how to hold a knife?" he'd asked, his bedside manner at the time sadly lacking.

"I guess not," she'd answered as she smiled at him through watery eyes. "Thanks for helping me."

He'd looked at her. Really seen her for the first time. He didn't see Beth Lancaster's daughter, the dyslexic girl who'd been placed in an at-risk group early on. He only saw Ivey, and something in his heart had pinched and constricted.

He'd never been the same again.

"As someone who plans, you should try online dating. You can pick the qualities you want in a mate."

He supposed that was a dig, but a person didn't get an MD after their name without some preparation.

"I'll pass. But if I'd been able to pick from a list of qualities, I might have picked someone who could cook." Unless it came out of a can or a box, Ivey would have starved to death.

"Funny."

"Is that what you did? Looked at a list of qualities you wanted and checked them off one by one?"

She sighed. "I don't want to talk about this anymore."

Well if they weren't going to talk, he had some other ideas of how to fill the time. He stood, taking his chances, and held out his hand. "Dance?"

Ivey rose to meet him. "You want to dance? But you don't know how. Have you learned?"

"All right, you got me. Not really, but I want to hold you tight."

"At least you're honest." She didn't resist when he took her in his arms right there on the blanket and pressed her against him. He held his hands near the small of her back, and her arms rose to his neck, as she gazed right into his eyes. He swallowed hard.

He couldn't still love her. Could he? Love didn't stay in a suspended state of animation for years and then suddenly surge to the front. This was lust, pure and simple. He had it bad for Ivey. Always had.

"Hey, do you remember when we used to listen to concerts here?" Ivey smiled up at him.

He did. And if he didn't stop thinking about that, he would soon be too hard to continue this slow dance of torture. "Yeah," he managed to say. *He'd forgotten his brain stopped working when she was this close.*

He ran a hand through her hair, the silkiness making his fingers feel like sandpaper. Ivey gazed up at him, but he couldn't figure out if what he saw in her eyes was desire or plain confusion. Still, he took his opening and bent down and covered her mouth with his. He tried not to groan as her mouth opened in welcome and he deepened the kiss. She tasted like vanilla and memories, the best ones—long summer nights by the river when the choice between her and *Gray's Anatomy* had been a no-brainer. Funny how the pain she had caused him faded into the background now.

He could feel her hands clinging to him like she used to when she'd been filled with need, but her fingers shook as they wrapped around his arms. "You're trembling," he said, stroking the curve of her face.

"I'm sorry," she whispered. "You do that to me."

"Yeah? Totally flattered." It took him a minute to realize the song had ended and the rest of the crowd danced to a different one he didn't even recognize.

Still they stood holding each other like maybe they were trying to make up for lost time. He leaned his forehead against Ivey's and heard her sigh. A warm summer night, the hint of honeysuckle in the air, Ivey in his arms at last. It was too perfect.

Which is why it shouldn't have surprised him when Ali walked up and almost wedged herself between them. "Hi, Ivey. Welcome back."

"Ali," Ivey said, taking a step away from him.

"So this is embarrassing. Looks like I might have interrupted something." Ali glanced from Ivey to him, and pierced him with her Big Sister look.

He and Ivey spoke at once.

"You didn't interrupt anything," Ivey said.

"Yes, you did."

"Mom and Dad are around here somewhere. Have you seen them?" Ali continued, despite his do-you-want-to-die stare. The look had worked when he was fourteen and she had made it her mission to make sure he stayed on the straight and narrow—otherwise known as tattling—but the glare wasn't working for him now. He loved Ali, but he already had a mother.

"Nope, but I'll catch up with them later."

Ali turned to Ivey. "So what's this I saw on the news about your aunt's condo being repossessed? Wow, that's some excitement, huh? We don't get the FBI much in little ole Starlight Hill."

The unspoken message seemed to be: "leave it to you and your aunt to bring the FBI to town." It took great effort to remember that his sister was only looking out for him, and that she didn't want to see him hurt again. Without thinking, he reached for Ivey's hand and squeezed it. "This all has to do with Ben Cartwright, and making restitution to his investors. It has nothing to do with Ivey or her aunt."

Someone or something slammed into his knees, and he looked down to see Becky. Bob followed behind her, holding a sleeping Liam.

"Hey, squirt."

"Uncle Jeff! I saw a clown! He painted my face! And I have a balloon!" Becky babbled. The kid was so filled with excitement he half expected her to levitate.

"She's had too much sugar," Ali said, by way of explanation.

"Becky, this is my friend, Ivey." Jeff introduced two of his favorite girls. Once Ali would have qualified too, except that right now he wanted to kill her.

"Hi! I'm four! How old are you?" Becky asked, reminding him of a spinning top.

"You don't ask grown-ups how old they are," Bob the Saint corrected with a sigh.

But Jeff couldn't help notice that Ivey smiled at Becky like she'd seen the sun set in gold, red, and orange. "That's okay. I'm old, too old to count."

"No, you're not!" Becky laughed, and climbed out of his arms. "My Grandma's old." She started running in the general direction of the street, Bob following quickly behind.

"I better go too," Ali said with a conciliatory look in her eyes. "Nice seeing you."

Jeff turned to Ivey when they'd left. "That's Ali's family. Becky isn't usually wound up like that. She's smart as a whip though."

"And adorable."

"Thanks. I am rather partial to her." Someday if he were lucky enough to have children, he hoped they'd challenge him as much as Becky did. She made him see things in new ways, in different colors and shapes. Ali said kids had a way of doing that.

He took Ivey's hand, and she went willingly with him away from the crowds and closer to the creek that ran in the back of the park. "I'm sorry about Ali. She's worried about me."

"Worried about you?" The tone in Ivey's voice suggested that she couldn't fathom a reason why Ali would worry about big, capable Jeff Garner. "Surely she knows you left me."

He cleared his throat. This was the hard part. Not the way he worked, but maybe it was time to make some changes. He would have to let his heart take the lead, because his brain was currently disengaged. "Yeah, of course she does. But here's the thing. She also knows what I haven't told you yet."

By the creek, a slight breeze kicked up and he instinctively pulled Ivey closer.

"What haven't you told me yet?" He could feel it as her tiny frame tightened in expectation of another blow. Not surprising, since she'd lived her life recovering from a series of small shocks.

He let go of her and dragged a hand through his hair. "This isn't easy to say."

"Say it."

Right. "What you don't know is that after I said I needed a break I regretted it. Instead of calling you, I planned a surprise. You like surprises, I know that. Anyway, I asked for my grandmother's wedding ring, came home right after finals and picked it up. But you weren't home because you went to meet up with the guy you met on a dating service. And that's the truth."

Humiliating though it was, the truth felt liberating. And now he didn't feel like such an asshole. Yeah, maybe he'd made a selfish mistake, but he'd tried to correct it. He expected Ivey to be happy now, to know that he too had regrets. And that the joke had been on him.

But of all the things he expected, not one of them was to watch her burst into tears.

CHAPTER 11

"*B*efore I apologize, I need to know what I did wrong." Jeff pressed his forehead to hers.

The strong beat of his heart pulsed under her fingertips. With a slight push she turned away and faced the creek, trying hard to swallow a sob. "You did nothing wrong."

Every star winked back in the inky black night, but she had no words. No words for the unfairness of it all. For the irony. If she'd only waited one lousy month. She wouldn't have even been showing, so she would have had the pleasure of a proposal knowing it hadn't been born out of necessity. But beyond that, not much else would have been different.

He still might have had to drop out of school. They would have still wound up hating each other. No, she'd done the right thing.

She'd fixed it. Fixed everything. Only problem, she'd never had what she wanted. Maybe now it was finally her time.

Perhaps from this point forward she wouldn't cheat herself

anymore. Stop making excuses and believing she didn't deserve to be happy. Tell the truth and let people deal with it. Take what she wanted, and try like hell to be happy. Life was too short.

And this man happened to be all she'd ever wanted from the moment she'd first laid eyes on him. Granted, most people didn't discover the love of their lives at sixteen, but she wasn't most people.

Neither was he for that matter. He happened to be—everything. And she deserved him.

Jeff came up behind her, his arms encircling her, head bent low to her neck. "Tell me you're okay."

She turned to face him. "I am, but we're going to have to set Ali straight."

"Don't worry about her." His thumb traced the edge of her eye, wiping away a tear.

"I have to worry about her. She's your sister, and she loves you. She's upset with me, and I get it. But she has to know that I'm not letting you go this time."

The furrowed brow eased and his face broke out in a smile. A surge of love kicked her in the gut so hard that it spread down and around to the back of her knees.

"Yeah?"

She rose to the tips of her toes to kiss him square on the lips, where she'd wanted to kiss him for weeks. He deepened the kiss, and she felt warmth as it spread down her legs, and to the soles of her feet. He tasted so good, warm and wet and hard under her touch. She let her hands wander down his back and then up his flat stomach, while his fingers threaded through her hair, holding her firmly in place. As if she would dream of going anywhere.

She pulled back, breathless and hazy but most of all certain. "Let's go."

They didn't bother saying goodbye to anyone as they left

the park, and Jeff tugged on her hand like he thought if he didn't hurry she might change her mind.

Once at the cottage, when the door to the rest of the world closed and they were two lovers alone with their thoughts and their history, Jeff kissed the hollow of her throat and whispered near her ear. "Are you sure?"

She answered by leaping into his arms and wrapping her legs around his waist. Holding the back of his neck she kissed him hard, letting all the hurt, regret, anger, and pain slide right out of her body. "What do you think?"

He carried her to his bed and gently lowered her, his arms cradling her like she was something precious and breakable. She wanted to show him that she wasn't fragile any more. Instead she was strong and capable and ready to risk it all.

Eager, she fumbled to take her jeans off, fighting with a zipper that didn't understand how important this moment was to her. He'd once whispered that nothing turned him on quite as much as her eagerness for him, but he stayed her hand before she removed her black bra and panties.

"Slow down, Little Face." He ran his fingers under the satiny strap, and the warmth of his hand made her shiver.

"I don't know if I can."

"Me either, but I'm going to try," he said as he pulled her bra strap down and his mouth covered her breast.

In the back of her mind there was something she hadn't told him, but for now the uncomfortable truth faded to black because it was so much better to feel, to love, to touch him everywhere. The rest would take care of itself. She had to believe it.

Her eyes were closed, and she hadn't realized it until Jeff spoke. "Look at me."

And she did, taking it all in, the way he moved above her, causing her such pleasure she might jump out of her skin.

"I see you," she said on a sigh.

She saw everything she'd ever known about him and never forgotten. The way he knew how to love her, never judging her, seeing her heart even before she'd ever showed it to him.

As wave after wave of pleasure hit her, there were no words left. Only sensations that carried her away.

* * *

IVEY SIGHED in Jeff's arms and snuggled in closer. This was bliss, lying in his arms. Feeling his heart beat next to hers. She hadn't wanted to admit it, but all that serial dating had amounted to the fact that there had never been anyone else for her except for Jeff Garner.

"I don't want to go anywhere else, ever again. Let's stay right here."

"Deal." Jeff ran his hand along the small of her back, and she settled in to the fact that his hands were not going to stop touching her for the foreseeable future. A little bit like heaven. "Maybe we should sleep for a while. I don't want to tire you out. The first time we were both a bit carried away, and it was too quick for me, but the second time felt more like we were getting reacquainted. And the third time we tried something new."

She felt a blush coming on. "I liked that."

"I could tell." He kissed her forehead. "We may get into the swing of this the fourth time."

"But first I need to rest. For a little while." Ivey laid her head on his chest, listening to his strong and steady heartbeat. She'd missed this—him—so much that fears clouded her vision. She could lose him, because she had once before. He'd told her his secret. Now could she tell him hers? Would he still want her after that?

Yes he would. He wanted to marry you, remember? If he still didn't feel that way, would he have told her at all?

Her cell phone rang and Jeff groaned. She reached for it, but it was closer to him so he grabbed it first.

He playfully held it out of her reach. "Give me. It might be important. Remember I'm covering for Marissa this weekend."

"What will you give me for it?" He had a wicked smile on his face.

"I think you know what I'll give you." Ivey let her hand dive under the covers and he jumped.

"You've got a deal," he said as he handed her the phone.

When Ivey answered she heard a moan on the other end. So either someone was having sex or about to have a baby. "This is Ivey. Hello?"

"It's Asia. Foster. Ow! Oh, mother of God that hurts. Are you going to help me or what?" Asia sounded pushy and in pain.

"Of course I will," Ivey said as she swatted Jeff's hand away from her breast. "What's going on?"

"I'm having a baby, Einstein. Are you sure you're qualified to do this?"

All right, so maybe Asia was a little bitchy as well. "How far apart are the contractions?"

"That's the thing. There's no pattern. Eleven minutes, seven minutes, eight minutes, twelve. What should I do? It's not like it says in the book!"

Ivey jumped out of bed and collected clothes from the floor. How had Asia done this? She was about to have a baby on the day she'd planned. It was one wild coincidence. "It's enough of a pattern. I'll be over in a few minutes. Don't worry. We still have plenty of time."

"You have to go," Jeff said when she hung up.

For the first time since she'd been doing this, she'd rather stay home than go deliver a baby into the world. That might be because Jeff lay on his back, arms splayed behind his neck, only the thinnest of sheets covering him. Especially difficult, because she was well acquainted with what lay under the sheet.

"Lousy timing, but babies have their own schedule."

"So I've heard."

"I'll make this up to you." She leaned down and gave him a long, deep kiss.

He grinned. "You better."

* * *

ONE QUICK SHOWER LATER, which Jeff couldn't talk Ivey into sharing with him, and she was off. Now he stood alone in the kitchen, fully dressed but not happy about it, heating up a can of chicken soup. It took him a few minutes to realize he was whistling. *Whistling.*

A couple of uninterrupted hours with Ivey had done that. At first he hadn't known what to expect, being together after all these years, but it was better than he could have imagined. Better than his oldest fantasies. He hadn't been a monk all these years, but he had cheated himself. There was nothing quite like sex with someone you loved, and he'd done that for the first time in years tonight.

She remembered him. The way he liked to be touched, everything he'd taught her about how to please him. And she'd done that tonight, with the kind of passion he remembered. Ivey wasn't shy or retiring with him, she was eager and took what she wanted. This had to be love, the kind that didn't fade away, and from now on he wasn't going to settle for anything less.

If it meant he had to make more sacrifices, give up more of himself, lose sleep, he'd do it. He didn't know how Ivey felt, but he'd find out soon enough. This time, he wasn't going to let her walk away without an explanation.

There was a short, insistent knock on the door, and Jeff halfway convinced himself that Ivey was back, having forgotten her key. Instead an older woman stood in front of him, dressed in a peasant top, jeans, and Birkenstocks.

"I heard from my friend Marissa that Ivey Lancaster is living here. Is she here now?"

"Sorry no, she's with a patient."

"Don't tell me at the hospital."

"She's covering for a midwife who's out of town. It's going to be a while, I think." He hoped the woman would get the message. She should come back later.

"Fine. I'll wait for her if you don't mind. I'm up from LA, trying to talk her into letting go of this foolishness with the hospital. I heard all about it from Marissa. Ivey and I used to work together."

Jeff moved aside and waved the woman inside. Apparently he would have company for a while. "You must be Babs. She's talked about you."

Babs took a seat on the couch, and for the first time he noticed the overnight bag. Great. Did she think she would stay the night here? He stared at the bag, trying to mentally telegraph that she wasn't going to be able to. On the other hand, Babs could have Scott's room and Ivey could stay with him. Face it, as far as he was concerned, she'd never sleep in Scott's room again.

"Ivey and I go way back. Never would have thought I'd mentor one of my own patients, but Ivey was special."

He froze. "Excuse me?"

"I said she was special."

"You said she was one of your patients. Maybe I heard wrong." Wouldn't she have told him if she'd been pregnant? They'd been discussing labor and delivery for weeks, and she never thought to add her own personal experience? Why hide that from him? Did she think he of all people would judge her? Or — the other thought that immediately ran through his mind was too terrible to be true.

Bab's eyes narrowed. "Wait a minute. What did you say your name was again?"

"I didn't. How long ago was she your patient?"

Now she looked nervous, and Jeff could feel anger roiling around in the pit of his stomach. But it couldn't be true. Ivey wouldn't have done this to him.

"I think you should talk to Ivey," she said with a mortified look that gave him his answer.

But it was much too late for her to stop talking now. He forced himself to speak calmly. "Answer the question. How long ago? A year ago? Five years ago? When?"

Babs sighed and looked directly in his eyes. "I'm not going to say anymore, but you're asking the right questions. Ivey was my patient five years ago."

His baby? How did he miss it? Five years ago, Ivey had been suddenly clingy and tearful. Out of the blue she'd asked him about family housing for married students. He'd only felt the noose tighten around his neck and made up some lame excuse about it being too crowded. Too expensive. Too late to sign up. He'd wanted her to be patient. It was going to be bad enough being married on a resident's salary, but he couldn't stand the thought of having his wife work to put him through school. No, waiting and planning was best.

Obviously he hadn't had all the facts. Ivey had been pregnant with his baby. Didn't think he had a right to know. Phased him out, just like that.

Jeff had never felt hot molten lava course through his veins before, but damn if there wasn't a first time for everything. "I have to go. Stay here as long as you like."

"Wait. Where are you going?" The woman wouldn't stop

talking, but he could barely hear her words, little bites of sound in the distance.

Suddenly the past had ringing clarity to it, even as red seemed to cloud his vision.

His fingers tightened around the steering wheel, and he hit the dashboard with his fist. So many questions to be answered from the one woman who couldn't seem to stop hurting him. This one final dig, taking his child away, was almost more than he could take.

He didn't care that he'd be interrupting, as he drove to the Foster house. He didn't care anymore because he needed answers and he wasn't going to wait another second for them.

CHAPTER 12

*I*t might be a long night with little sleep for any of them, but at the end of it Asia would hold her baby in her arms for the first time. Ivey still wasn't sure how Asia had managed to nail her delivery date so accurately. Call it luck or good timing, but the Fosters seemed to have both in spades.

"You're sixty percent effaced and two centimeters dilated." Ivey took her gloves off.

"Two? Only two? Tell me why I feel like I'm at twenty."

"Honey, it's okay." Asia's husband Derek massaged her back.

"Don't touch me."

Derek looked wounded, and Ivey gave him a little apologetic smile. "Prodromal labor is hard, but you'll get there. You probably have a big baby, and he or she is tiring your poor womb out. But this is going to happen soon. We need to wait the baby out. So far everything looks great."

"You'll stay with us. Right?" Derek asked, the high pitch in his voice and the terror in his eyes giving her a clear idea of his level of apprehension. She'd give him a ten, ninety-nine percent effaced. Poor guy.

"I'm not going anywhere. Why don't you get her some more ice chips?"

Derek, given a green light to do something away from his wife, took off at a near run.

"Remind me why I did this," Asia said. "Why have his baby? He's so damn big, no wonder his baby is big. Why couldn't I have fallen in love with someone smaller? Thinner?"

Glad Derek was out of the room, Ivey wiped Asia's face with a soft, damp towel. "Because you love him?"

"Oh, God help me, I do." Asia sobbed. "I was so mean to him. Derek! Come back here. I didn't mean it. I love you, baby."

Derek didn't waste any time hightailing back into the room with the ice chips, the look of a happy puppy dog in his eyes. "You called me, baby?"

Ivey left the bedroom, giving them a moment. This was the best part of a home birth. *Home.* She'd be in the kitchen if they needed her. In a few minutes, she'd be back to suggest that Asia take a walk and move around some more. Meanwhile, time was their best friend.

But it wouldn't be the same in a hospital setting, even if the women's center had birthing rooms they'd designed to look like bedrooms. It wasn't home, and Ivey could see Marissa's point.

Being an employee of the hospital would mean that Ivey would be used for more than one function and maybe more than one patient at a time. It was in the economy of health care. Time spent waiting for nature to take its course might not fit into the natural ebb and flow of the hospital.

From the kitchen window, Ivey saw the bright headlights of a car pull up the driveway. The Fosters were private people, and they hadn't invited any extended family to the event. They weren't expecting anyone.

Ivey made her way to the front door to discourage any eager friends or relatives from coming any further when she noticed Jeff. One look at him, his purposeful stride towards the house, and she realized something had changed. It was in the set of his jaw and in the way he held himself like a tightly wound cord. In an instant she knew.

She rushed to meet him on the front lawn of the home. They couldn't do this. Not here, not now. She needed a minute, or another month. Another year. She wasn't ready, even after all this time.

"We need to talk," Jeff said.

"Now's not a good time."

"Then make it a good time, because this isn't going to wait."

"It has to wait. I have a patient—"

"What did you do with my child?" He took another step toward Ivey, the heat of his anger nearly emanating off of him in waves.

Oh, not this. She'd wanted to spare him all along. Maybe she'd been selfish, or maybe she'd been selfless. Either way, Jeff was about to hurt in places he didn't even know existed and all because of her.

"Answer me!"

The emotion she heard in his voice mixed in with the anger turned her answer into a strangled sob. "There *is* no child. I had a miscarriage."

He flinched like he'd been slapped, and his body seemed to cave in a little at that answer. "Why?"

She realized that he wasn't asking why she'd lost the baby. It was a bigger why. He wanted to know why she'd never told him.

"You didn't want me anymore. If I told you, I knew you

would have done the right thing. You would have married me, and you didn't want to get married. Not then. I have enough pride to want to be married because someone loves me and not out of obligation."

"So this was all about you? No—you made a decision for both of us. And you didn't have the right to do that."

Those words were like bullets hitting her heart. Yeah, she had no right, but she'd done it anyway. "You wouldn't be a doctor today. You might have had to drop out of school."

"So you did it for me?" The tone in his voice left no doubt that he didn't believe her for a second.

"For you and for me. I was going to tell you someday."

The words sounded so empty. So false. Because they'd been the words and thoughts of a scared and stubborn twenty-year-old who didn't know any better. Who wouldn't listen to what anyone else told her.

"Some. Day."

"If I'd given birth, I would have told you. Eventually. I would have let you be a part of our baby's life."

He slashed a hand through his hair. "Would you? That's really big of you."

He moved another step toward her, closing the distance between them.

"Look, I get that you're mad. But this is not the time or the—"

"Mad? Ivey, what you did went so far over the line that the line is a dot in the distance."

"But—I did it for you. You had our lives planned out, and the baby didn't fit in." Why couldn't he see the noble sacrifice she'd made so that he could finish school without complications? What about that?

"We made love tonight. What if you'd gotten pregnant? Would you tell me this time or would you walk away again?"

"That's not fair. Of course I wouldn't. It's different."

"What's different? I loved you then, and I love you now. I don't care about any of the details. We would have worked it out."

With one swift move his right hand pulled her forehead to his own and held it tightly in place. She felt the strength of his anger, barely restrained and bubbling beneath the surface. But it was the tears forming in his eyes that caused another sob to hitch in her throat.

"I'm sorry."

"You. Had. No. Right."

He released her and stomped back to his car, taking off without another look in her direction. She stayed rooted to the spot on the Foster's lawn, right near the azalea bush. Wondering as she watched Jeff drive off if those were the last words he'd ever say to her.

Turned out that no one thought having their choice taken away was any kind of favor. Jeff included. She ought to know that better than anyone. Wasn't she fighting so that women could have more choices in a hospital setting? And yet she hadn't given Jeff the same respect.

It dawned on her how much she'd hurt him.

"Miss Ivey?" It was Derek, calling out to her from inside the screened front door. "You okay?"

Ivey kept her back to him as she wiped the tears away, and squared her shoulders. "I'm fine."

"I thought I heard shouting."

She turned to see the concerned look of a Daddy-to-be, already in full-fledged protective mode. He'd be a good dad.

Like Jeff would have been.

And suddenly Ivey couldn't breathe. Maybe this was why she hadn't wanted to come home for so long. Why she'd stayed away. She'd already lost enough, hurt enough, and cried enough.

But not with him.

The only person who'd ever said anything that made any sense was Babs, who after the miscarriage had told Ivey that no one but the baby's father would fully understand her grief. But she hadn't shared that with him. She hadn't shared her grief with anyone.

Everything had been all right while she pretended, while she kept the truth locked away safely in her heart.

"Miss Ivey?" Derek stood at the door, and it didn't look like he'd be going back inside anytime soon.

Ivey swallowed back a sob. "It was a big misunderstanding."

The width and span of which might be too great to ever get over.

* * *

JEFF DROVE because he had to keep moving. If he didn't move, he would have to hit something. Hard. He had to get away from Ivey, because he was too angry to talk any more. Too hurt to try to understand. Like a lighthouse to a ship, the hospital beckoned. The best thing to do after a shocking, life-changing event had to be something normal. Routine. That's what he needed right now.

And he still wanted to check on Frank. When he'd dropped by earlier in the day, Frank had been out of his room for more tests. Jeff still wanted to know what he'd missed. In the ER he'd run every test he could think of and come up with nothing. Somehow, though, he'd missed it. Frank had a heart condition.

He took the elevator up to the cardiac wing of the hospital and asked the night shift nurse for Frank's room number. By now he was under the care of a specialist, and maybe Dr. Bryans would have some answers.

Jeff ran into Dr. Bryans in the hallway. "How's Frank Sullivan? I came to check on him."

"He'll be fine. Thanks to all those tests you ran on him, I had a basis of comparison. He's healthy for the most part, but his heart shows some cardiomyopathy, probably from the undiagnosed arrhythmia. Never caught it on the EKG, so it's probably paroxysmal. Something his regular doctor should have caught with a twenty-four hour Holter monitor."

"He didn't seem to have a regular doctor." Something Jeff should have pressed Frank on. Should have demanded to talk to someone at the assisted living center or a relative and make sure they followed up.

"Yeah, that's what he told me." Bryans grabbed the elevator. "Not to worry. He'll be fine."

Jeff wasn't fine though. He'd had Frank in the ER for a few hours at a time, sometimes several times a week, and he'd still missed it. Sometimes if you turned your head for a second you could miss so much.

More and more it appeared emergency medicine wasn't for him. He wanted, needed, to be more involved in the outcome.

Ivey had denied him that, but no one else would ever again. He should have been there for her, in those days when she would have been scared and alone. When he might have made a difference. Or not.

But at least he would have been there for her, for their baby. She hadn't given him that chance, maybe because she didn't trust him enough. Couldn't trust that he'd take care of her, because no else ever had. And she didn't believe he loved her. Not enough.

And whose fault is that, idiot?

Jeff sat on an empty chair beside Frank's bed for several minutes until the man's eyes fluttered open.

"Well, hot damn. My favorite doctor."

"Thought you might want to see what I look like without a stethoscope around my neck."

"No bags under the eyes, either. Doc, have you been relaxing?"

"Something like that." He supposed he'd been happy, for about a nanosecond. And Ivey had something to do with it, like as she had everything to do with his misery now. "I did have a couple days off."

"Just what I ordered." Frank winked.

"You're going to be okay," Jeff reassured him. "Now that we know what's wrong, we can fix it."

"What about you? Can we fix what's wrong with you?"

"I'm fine," Jeff closed his eyes and pinched the bridge of his nose. Or he would be anyway. Someday.

"If you say so, Doc. But if I promise not to come to the ER any more, will you promise you won't always be here? I'd like to think of you, young as you are, enjoying life."

"Why? Work is a good thing." It was all he would have now, and maybe all he'd ever need.

He'd see about switching specialties soon, maybe cardiology or pediatrics. Something in which he could be around for the duration. Witness the outcome. He'd have to start over again but that was okay. Ivey had done it, and so could he.

"Work is great, it's just not enough. No lie, trust me, it'll never be enough."

Jeff didn't believe him. For years now, medicine had been front-and-center in his life and he hadn't questioned it. Not until Ivey had come back to town and sent his heart and hormones into overdrive. "Let's talk about you. Do you have any family? Someone who can be here with you?"

"I have kids, but I hate to bother them."

"How many?"

"Six." Frank grinned. "I was a busy man in my youth, Doc."

"Yes, you were. I'm sure they'd want to know what's going on with you. Did someone call them?"

"I have my oldest son on the contact list. He's flying out from Utah." Frank sighed. "He won't be happy."

"I'm sure he's worried."

"It's not that. He works all the time. Anyway, I can't complain because his salary pays for the prison—I mean the assisted living center. Because you know, I'm too old to remember how to turn off a stove. Might burn the place down." Frank rolled his eyes.

They continued to talk about Frank's family and kids for several minutes. It turned out Frank was a widower, and he still got teary mentioning his wife's name. After about half an hour, Frank's eyes were at half-mast, and Jeff decided he'd tired him out enough.

"Rest. I'm glad you're going to be okay." Jeff patted his arm and rose to leave.

On his way to the parking lot, he saw Lillian leaving. She caught up to Jeff, and they walked out to the lot together.

"Thanks to your and Ivey's recommendation, the board agreed to hire one midwife to start the trial. We'll see how it goes from there. I want to thank you. You had an open mind, and I appreciate that."

"Thank Ivey. She's persuasive when she wants to be." And a good liar too.

"Do you think she's still interested in the position?"

"You should call her."

"I will. I don't want to lose her." Lillian waved as they parted ways.

He hadn't wanted to lose her either, but it seemed inevitable now. He'd lost her a long time ago.

He couldn't go home, so he drove out of town and back again. Then wound up where he should have all along.

Ali opened the front door. "Providence. That's what this is. Pure and simple providence. Bob is working late and Becky won't go to sleep. Here, you take Liam, and I'll go in and hold her down till she falls asleep."

He must have given her a weird look, because she shook her head. "I'm not really going to hold her down."

"I didn't think so, Ali."

He carried Liam to the couch, plopped him down, and sat next to him. Liam was two and didn't like Jeff much. Or at least it always felt that way, because Liam didn't say a peep around Jeff, and word out on the street was that Liam had learned to talk. Jeff and Becky were pals, but for Liam, it seemed like the jury was still out. Jeff couldn't blame the kid since they didn't see each other often enough.

Liam, pacifier firmly stuck in his mouth, scrambled off the couch and handed him items from the coffee table. The remote control, a deck of cards, every single coaster on the table. Was he supposed to hold everything the kid gave him? Jeff set them back on the table, but Liam handed everything back to him. The kid was on some kind of mission to unclutter the coffee table.

Finally he picked up a magazine—*Ladies' Home Journal*—handed it to Jeff and climbed in his lap, where he proceeded to flip each page with the finesse of an orangutan.

"Don't worry, kid. You'll get those fine motor skills."

Liam looked up at him, as if he questioned Jeff's sanity.

When Jeff started reading the Oil of Olay ad out loud to pass the time, Liam actually snuggled up to listen.

"Erases fine lines and wrinkles." He kept reading, and Liam kept getting limper in his arms. So this was the secret. Bore them to sleep.

Kids weren't so difficult. He didn't know what Ali was

always whining about. Liam's soft blonde hair brushed against Jeff's chin and the smell of Johnson's Baby Shampoo brought back a childhood memory.

He wondered if he and Ivey would have had a boy or a girl. Whether it would have hurt any less to know when she'd miscarried, instead of being blindsided now.

"Bless you. He's asleep. How'd you do it?" Ali whispered, lifting Liam out of his arms.

"Oil of Olay."

Ali made a face. "I never understand your jokes."

The story of his life. When Ali came back, she had a glass of wine in each hand.

Now it was his turn to be grateful as she handed him the glass of chilled white wine.

"Chardonnay, Clos La Chance 2011," Ali said, because she fancied herself a wine connoisseur. "It's not bad. To what do I owe this unexpected visit? Did they finally decide to give you a day off?"

"Something like that."

"Well, why don't you look happier? Wait. Let me take a wild guess. Ivey."

"You have no idea." And then, because Ali was his big sister and he didn't currently owe Ivey a lick of loyalty, he told Ali everything.

She didn't speak for a moment. Maybe she was also thinking about the fact that in a different outcome, he'd have a child Becky's age. Then Ali's eyes watered, which made his stomach clench some more. "I'm so sorry. What a lousy way to find out."

"Why didn't she tell me? Maybe you can do me the favor of explaining womankind to me. You are my sister, and I did let you have my ice cream cone that one time you dropped yours because you're such a damn klutz."

Ali rolled her eyes. "I can't explain womankind to you,

because even I don't always understand women. We're all different, and contrary to what you men think, there's no secret handshake. You and I both know that Ivey had a lifetime of keeping secrets, protecting those she loved. It doesn't seem like such a stretch to think she'd try to protect you too. Yeah, it was lousy and it was wrong, but the truth is I kind of understand."

"I can't believe you're defending her."

"I'm not defending her. I hate what she did. But I said I understand why she did it."

"She didn't have to do me any favors. Didn't she think I could handle being a father? Is that how little she thinks of me?" He heard the sound of his own voice, sounding like a stranger's. Angry. Bitter. Hurt.

"Shhhh, you'll wake the kids. You're going to make a great father someday, weird jokes aside. But you weren't ready to be a father back then. Think about it. I actually recall you saying the words 'I'm dying here.' You didn't have time to come home for the weekend, what makes you think you had time to be a father?"

"Ouch." Ali had a way of cutting to the heart of the matter.

"I'm not kidding. This is my life." She waved a hand, spanning the room. "I'm deliriously happy to be having a glass of wine at nine o'clock and some grown-up conversation. Do you know what I found the other day? Do you?"

"I have a feeling I don't."

Ali got closer, ruffling her hair and pointing to her scalp. "There! See that? Can you believe it?"

Ali had always been a bit dramatic. Mom was right about that, come to think of it. "I don't see anything but hair. What am I looking for?"

"My first gray hair! Can't you see it?" Ali continued pointing to her scalp.

"One gray hair? How am I supposed to find it?"

"I'm thirty-two years old and I have my first gray hair. Found it right after Liam was born." She sat back down on the couch, smoothing her short brown hair back into place. "That is what kids will do to you."

"I don't care about gray hair."

"See, you would have as a medical student with a wife and child. You probably would have a full head of gray hair when all was said and done."

He was about to say that it worked for George Clooney, but he was beginning to see Ali's point.

Ali turned to him with that annoying superior-big-sister look she'd spent years refining. "Not to mention you and Ivey would have wound up hating each other."

He scoffed. "Ironic, since we're not together now."

"Yeah, sure. Like I believe that. Do you know how many young marriages end in divorce? What's the divorce rate for doctors?"

"Okay, okay, I get it. I wasn't ready back then, but I'll never believe that I didn't have the right to know. To be involved. It was my baby too."

Ali nodded. "So what are you going to do?"

"I don't know. The problem is I think I still love her."

"Shocking," Ali said. "I called it. Like magnets."

"But I can't trust her." He pulled out his phone. It had been buzzing on and off for the past couple of hours, and he'd been ignoring it on purpose. The hospital would page him, and he wasn't even on call. He had a good feeling who had been calling him, and it didn't surprise him when he finally took a look.

Several missed calls from Ivey. And two text messages: *You don't understand. Please let me explain.*

Maybe it was time to listen.

CHAPTER 13

When Ivey returned the following morning, she hadn't expected to find Babs napping on the couch in the family room. Ivey stifled the groan that formed in her throat. She wouldn't have to ask Jeff how he found out.

Babs sat up, rubbed her eyes and stretched. "What is wrong with you young people? I visit, and that man leaves me here alone. For hours! What if I was a thief or worse, an ax murderer? Where's his sense of safety?"

"What are you doing here?"

"Marissa called me, and I needed to see you in person. This is important." Babs stood and smoothed down her rumpled jeans. "But first, I'm afraid I spoke out of turn earlier."

"I know. And your timing is horrible."

"Well, I'm sorry about that. I didn't tell him much, but he guessed. Anyway, I know about the women's center, and I've come here to give you my opinion in person."

So Marissa had called in reinforcements. But Ivey had

already made up her mind, especially after last night. "I don't need your opinion. I've already made my decision."

"Good. I was worried after Marissa called and told me."

"I'm going to do it." Baby boy Foster had been born early this morning on the same bed where his parents likely conceived him, bathed by the soft light of his mother's reading lamp, while his father wept (he couldn't read the poem after all). Ivey didn't think a hospital could replicate that in a hundred years.

Not without her there to help them.

"Didn't I teach you better than this? Doctors don't understand birth. Even women doctors. I don't know what they do to them in medical school, but you'd think that labor and delivery were something they have to cure."

"Look, I understand. Believe me. Tonight Asia Foster gave birth at home, and it was beautiful. I wish every woman would do that. But the truth is they're not. For whatever reason, they're going to feel safer in a hospital setting. I know it's not the easy thing to do, and I'm sorry if I'm letting you down. Jeff and I turned in our recommendation to the board. And if they'll have me, I'm going to work at the women's center. I want to make sure that every woman can have the childbirth experience they want."

"But the doctors aren't going to let them have that experience!"

"Well that's exactly why they need me there."

"You're one tiny girl, up against territorial doctors who are going to defend their livelihood to the death."

"Let them. I'm fiercer than I look, and you ought to know that."

Babs' gray eyes softened. "I still remember the young girl who came to me pregnant with her first child, wanting to have that perfect birth. You'd read everything you could get your hands on and already knew what you wanted."

"I didn't get very far." Ivey's breath hitched, for one minute drawn back to that time when she thought for a few months that she'd been blessed. Finally, she must have done something right. She'd failed to take care of Mama, because she hadn't been able to stop her from driving off the road. Failed to plan ahead, like so many times before. But this time, she wouldn't fail.

Only she had. Even eating the healthiest diet, taking her vitamins, doing everything she'd been asked to do and then some, she'd lost the best mistake she ever made.

Babs gathered Ivey in her arms. "You never get over losing a baby, honey. I tried to tell you that, even as you wanted to act like delivering someone else's babies would somehow make up for the fact that you never got to have your own precious child."

Is that what she'd done? "I thought it was all in the past as long as I didn't think about it. But when I came back home, when I saw him . . . "

"It all came back, didn't it?"

Not while she could pretend for a while that it had never happened. Jeff didn't know, after all. Except that now he did, and she was somehow reliving the hurt all over again.

The memories—bleeding and in agonizing pain, rushing to the hospital. Babs had met her there and tried to be a friend because the client-midwife relationship was over. Aunt Lucy had come to see Ivey a few days later, insisting that it was all for the best and that someday she could try again. Saying all the wrong things, even with the best of intentions. But the pregnancy hadn't been an inconvenience to her. It had been her baby.

Like so many good things in her life, the joy hadn't lasted. Didn't have staying power. "I wasn't ready to tell him."

"It's good that he knows. You need someone to grieve your loss with you as only he can do."

Like he'd been summoned, Jeff chose that moment to walk through the front door.

Babs stared from him to Ivey, then back again. "I'll leave you two alone."

Ivey didn't even say goodbye, because her eyes were riveted on Jeff, who looked like he wanted to say a million things or maybe nothing at all.

He held the door open for Babs, nodded to her as she left, and shut the door again.

"Where were you?" It was the only thing she could think to ask him. Not "will you ever forgive me," or "can't you at least try and understand?"

"Driving, mostly. I stopped by the hospital, and I stopped by Ali's. And then I kept driving until I thought I could be calm enough to listen to you." He scrubbed a hand across his face, and from the looks of it, he still hadn't yet reached that point.

"You have to understand—"

"I don't have to do anything, Ivey." His jaw quivered almost imperceptibly, but she noticed it.

"Okay, you don't have to. But if you would try to imagine how I felt—"

"What do you think I've been doing for the past few hours? Over and over in my mind I've thought about how scared you must have been. What it must have felt like to lose our baby. All the physical pain you went through. And all I can think is that I should have been there, but because of you I wasn't. You didn't trust me enough. Didn't think I could handle it."

"No, it's not that," she protested. "I didn't want you to feel obligated. I didn't want to ruin your plans for the future."

"Screw planning. Maybe I needed something to show me that the best things in life just happen. You didn't give me a choice. You lied to me. I've never lied to you."

"I know I was wrong. But can't you forgive me?" She moved closer to him, but he was a hard, solid wall of anger.

And he didn't answer for a few lonely seconds. "I don't know."

The answer made the tight fist of fear in her stomach open up and spread to the tips of her toes.

Ivey fingered the soft bristles on his jawline and tucked a lock of his hair that had fallen over his eye. "I love you, and you love me. We can get past this." *Please, God, let us get past this.* She'd never wanted anything more in her life. Another chance. Did anyone really get over their first love? She never had.

His eyes were wet, and she thought maybe she really would die right here and now because she'd done this. She'd caused him this pain.

He took her hand and kissed the back of it. "I don't know. I need some time."

Time. Right. Time away from her. She was familiar with that refrain. "Maybe I should go stay with Brooke."

This was where he would protest, and let her stay here where maybe within the next day or so they'd be back in each other's arms again. But he only gazed at her with red-rimmed eyes and said, "Maybe you should."

* * *

IVEY AND BROOKE hadn't tripped over each other yet, but they had bumped into each other several times over the past week. Hard not to in a nine-hundred-square-foot cottage.

Even so, Brooke wouldn't hear of any other arrangement.

"This is temporary, because you two will be back together in no time," Brooke said as they stood hip to hip in what passed as the kitchen.

"Don't be so sure. You might be stuck with me, and rentals don't come up every day."

"You're telling me. I've wanted to get out of this place for years. I've got enough money saved up and no place to rent. But I've got my eye on Mrs. McCreety's place. She's ninety. How much longer can she last?"

"Brooke!" Was that what it had come to? Wishing people dead?

Brooke only shrugged. "The thing to do is buy land. One of these days I'll get my hands on some of it."

Everybody had to have a dream. Ivey had received part of her dream a few days ago when Lillian phoned with the job offer. She'd start next month, working in the women's center. One of her proudest achievements, and she wasn't sure why it didn't feel like enough.

Now, the tears—she'd shed enough of those. It had been a week of staying in, feeling sorry for herself, and waiting for a phone call. But she was all done with pathetic and ready at the very least to go to lunch and maybe for a little retail therapy.

Brooke drove, since she had a nice BMW company car and Ivey had still to go car shopping. Brooke cruised down Main Street. For a Saturday in the middle of the day, it wasn't all that busy. Then again the grape harvest had come and gone, and summer and tourist season were about to close up shop.

"Where to?" Brooke asked. "Anywhere. It's my treat."

"Anywhere but Mama's Diner." Ivey might run into Jeff there, and she wasn't ready. She'd need to be ready by next month when she started her job at the hospital, but by then, well, she didn't know what she would do, but she'd figure something out.

"Let's try Sweet Southern Buns. It's brand new and I haven't tried it yet."

Ivey didn't notice the ribbon until they were at the front door to the eatery. But right there, poised prominently on the front door—a beautiful and large pink ribbon. Clearly new and fresh, not an old faded one from the past.

"Oh no," Ivey breathed, but Brooke pretty much pushed through the front door.

"Don't worry, I'll find out what this is all about," Brooke said, waving to a petite young redhead.

"Hi, Brooke. I ordered my pink ribbon as soon as I heard. And you must be Ivey. I'm Genevieve, and I own this place. Bought it from Mrs. Lewis." She waved a hand around the small bakery filled with porcelain, teacups, and pictures of Paris on the walls.

"Why do you have a pink ribbon?" Ivey managed to squeak out.

"I heard you two broke up again and the chamber decided to go back to the ribbons. It's the best way of letting everyone know which side we represent."

"Sides? There are no sides," Ivey said as she took a seat at one of the wrought-iron tables.

"It's fun. Don't you love small towns and all their little quirks?"

"No," Brooke answered.

"Remind me again why I decided to go out today." Ivey threw a pointed look at Brooke.

"To show your face. Let everyone know 'Hello world, it's me, Ivey, and I'm not going to go down without a fight.' Something like that, anyway."

"Oh yeah. I forgot." Ivey tried to break out a smile and it took such effort she was sure it died before it even got to her lips. Not happening today.

Brooke noticed. "See that? That's exactly why I'm never falling in love."

"What?"

"That look on your face. Love hurts. And you've let love for that man torture you since you were sixteen years old."

"I should have told him."

"All right, so maybe I was wrong. Next time don't take advice from a woman who's never been in a serious and committed relationship. I can't do much more for you, but I promise you I'll take care of those pink and blue ribbons."

"I don't mind, actually. It's kind of sweet."

"How is it sweet?"

"They do it because they care about us. They're showing their support the only way they know how. And Genevieve is right. It is kind of fun. All the blue and pink ribbons all over town. Like a party."

"That's a new way to look at it. I remember how upset you were when you first heard about it."

But when she'd first come home, she'd tried to move forward and pretend she hadn't lost everything. She'd always felt like the wronged one, but it turned out that hadn't been entirely true.

Seemed also that she was stronger than ribbons.

After lunch, Brooke and Ivey walked past storefronts covered in pink and blue ribbons. For the first time, Ivey noticed many storefronts with both a pink and a blue ribbon and people who were smiling and winking. This, she supposed, passed for entertainment. No harm done.

They heard the loud voice of a woman inside Ed's Hardware store. "Seriously, get a hobby. Get a life. Stop giving these out!"

"Give those back to me. They're for paying customers!" Ed could be heard shouting back.

"Send me the bill." Ivey nearly collided with Ali as she stormed out the front door, carrying a box of blue ribbons. "Sorry about all this. I know how it must seem."

"I don't mind anymore," Ivey explained. But she couldn't stop staring at the box of blue ribbons in Ali's hands.

"We've decided it's quaint," Brooke offered.

Ali smiled. "Is quaint the new word for crazy?"

All three of them had a good laugh, while Ed eyed them suspiciously through the front glass door entrance.

Ali pulled Ivey to the side. "But seriously, please don't give up on him. I happen to know that he loves you."

"I know. And I love him." She would until the day she died, but maybe love wasn't enough when two people had hurt each other so much.

"He's super stubborn when he's hurt. He usually nurses his wounds for a while, like a grumpy bear. And I know work has been strangling him from the inside out for some time. Please be patient."

"All right," Ivey said with a shaky voice.

Ali waved good-bye, throwing the box of ribbons in the trunk of her car and slamming it shut with a loud thump.

"Wow. That was something, huh?" Brooke asked.

Amazing, seeing Ali come to Ivey's defense that way. Ivey would have expected even worse from her, once she'd found out about the big lie. Not this kind of compassion and understanding from the woman who would have done anything to protect Jeff.

Unless she was finally clear on the fact that he didn't need any protecting from Ivey.

CHAPTER 14

"Are you certain?" Dr. Cooper asked.

"I haven't come to the decision lightly. I'm sure." Jeff sat across from the chief of cardiology.

"I know how hard you've worked for the hospital. If I'm being honest, I'd love for you to come on board."

No, it hadn't been part of the plan, but there it was. Emergency medicine wasn't a good fit, and the more Jeff had considered it over the past two weeks, cardiology fit right with where he wanted and needed to be. He didn't want to wind up four years later, unhappy with his career, still questioning whether or not he was doing any good. And was there anything more important to the human condition than the heart?

"And a pediatric cardiologist? Dr. Leonard is doing great work here. He'll be thrilled."

"I guess it's a matter of waiting for an opening now. I've already informed my attending."

"Right. I'll meet with Lillian, and we'll see how fast we can get this done."

Jeff made his way to the lounge and his locker. He wasn't

kidding himself. It might be a while before there was a resident slot in cardiology. But now that he was certain of where he needed to be, he didn't mind waiting.

He still had a lot on his plate for today. Okay maybe he was still a little bit into planning, but who would have thought he'd wind up pursuing a specialty in pediatrics? Still, the more he'd thought about it the better it felt. Seemed right, rang true to him. He'd always liked kids, had once planned to have three of them with Ivey's help. And in some small way, he thought maybe if he could help sick kids, he'd be making up for the fact that he hadn't been there for his own baby.

Yeah, it hadn't been his fault. Not entirely. But maybe if he hadn't been so insistent on planning every aspect of their future life together, Ivey might have felt comfortable coming to him. She might not have thought she'd be ruining everything. Maybe if he hadn't been so wrapped up in medicine, in his career, expecting Ivey to meekly come along as a silent partner, he would have seen the signs.

Some things in life did require planning. Only not when it came to love. He hadn't expected to fall in love in high school. Certainly hadn't thought he'd want to marry his first love. But that's exactly what would happen, if Ivey would still have him. Because he couldn't be without her. Not like he hadn't tried. They both had. Five years and she wasn't out of his system. When she'd waltzed back into town, something in his heart popped open, and it was almost as if his life had been on pause for five years. Then Ivey had hit "play" again and they'd been off to the races.

He was a long way from being able to support a wife in the style he'd planned at one time, and he had a few years ahead of him before he could be in practice. But he'd leave it up to Ivey this time. They didn't have to wait another minute to be married as far as he was concerned. There was an official courthouse in the next town over, and if that didn't work, there was a rumor that Burt the chief of police was secretly an ordained minister.

Now all he needed was the ring.

* * *

A WEEK LATER, Ivey had avoided it long enough, and now it was time to visit Mom's grave. It must have been hard for Mom to live in wine country, trying to pretend that she was like everyone else and could stop at one or two drinks.

Speculating wouldn't do any good now, because Mom hadn't stopped drinking even after child protective services threatened to take Ivey away. She didn't stop drinking for Aunt Lucy, who didn't understand why Beth couldn't go out drinking Friday night with her without winding up under the table.

The cemetery where Mom had been buried was on the outskirts of town, ironically on land rumored to have long ago been occupied by a vineyard that had gone out of business. Ivey hadn't been here since the day of the burial.

Along the way, Ivey stopped at a flower stand and bought a dozen gardenias, Mom's favorite flower. Ivey heard a florist say that gardenias were not a good idea in arrangements— they were fragile and required a precise amount of light and cool nights and the leaves turned brown after being touched, making them almost impossible to work with. But maybe Mom should have what she'd wanted in death, even if she couldn't have it in life.

Ivey bent down and replaced the plastic flowers with the gardenias, even if they wouldn't last long in this environment.

Kind of like Mom.

Ivey didn't know what to say to a gravestone. Mom

wasn't really here, but maybe Ivey could pretend for a minute. Despite the fact that Mom had made life at home a minefield, Ivey didn't blame her anymore. Some people could be as fragile as the gardenias, and couldn't help but make mistakes. Mom had made a lot of them, but so had Ivey.

She was learning to forgive herself.

"Hi, Mom. Sorry it's been so long. I hope you don't mind me asking, but if there's a special place in heaven for babies that were never born would you please find my baby there? Give her a hug from me."

She didn't want to cry, but when a memory of Jeff's warm hand slipping inside hers on the day of Mom's funeral came to mind, tears flooded her view.

She hadn't heard from Jeff in two weeks, and although she tried to tell herself that fourteen days wasn't all that long, every day seemed to be further proof that Jeff couldn't forgive her. Couldn't trust her, and would never get past her betrayal.

But she wasn't going anywhere. Running wouldn't solve anything. If Jeff thought she'd ever give up on him again, he was about to find out different. She'd wait for him, and give him all the time and space he needed. However much time was necessary for him to realize they were meant to be together. She'd be patient this time. Jeff was right in that life sometimes needed a plan.

Or at least a rough draft. Even if she'd always flown by the seat of her pants, like Mom taught her, this time she'd try a plan.

A stop at Mama's Kitchen was precisely what she needed right now to cheer up this melancholy mood, and a double helping of the Knock You Naked Brownies wouldn't hurt. Today of all days she deserved them.

She arrived at Em's in the late afternoon lull before dinner.

"What'll you have, honey? Made some of my pot roast today. Best in a while." Em pulled out her pad.

"I'm having my dessert before dinner today. Life's too short. I want some Knock You Naked Brownies," Ivey said with a sigh.

"Si, are those brownies ready yet?" Em turned to yell.

"No, woman, I said twenty minutes. Hold the phone. There isn't magic in this oven, ya know!" Si shouted back.

"Good Lord that man will be the death of me yet. I told him to put those in two hours ago, as I live and breathe. I'm sorry, dear. Anything else you want right now?"

"No thanks, Em. I think I'm going home."

Maybe it was a sign from the universe that one more helping of those brownies would turn Ivey into double her size overnight.

She walked out the door to an unsettling sight. In plain view outside the diner sat Jeff's car, with a huge pink ribbon draped over the hood. The ribbon was large enough to cover the windshield, and it draped down the sides of the front windows.

She didn't think he'd be too thrilled with the idea, even if, like her, he'd grown used to the ribbons. This one was a bit over the top, and Ivey wondered who the joker could be. She turned in circles and didn't see anyone nearby. Maybe she could take it off herself and he wouldn't be the wiser.

Carefully she began to pull off the ribbon.

"Hey, what are you doing?"

Ivey startled and turned to see Jeff standing in the shadows, leaning against the wall of the building.

"I didn't see you there. I'm only trying to help. Somebody's idea of a joke."

He moved towards her. "Don't take it off."

"Why not?" Her foolish heart beat triple time against her rib cage as he drew closer.

Please calm down. Don't get your hopes up.

"I kind of like it, seeing as I put it there."

"You did?" Ivey's heart did a weird flip when he reached her side.

"What can I say? I wanted to get in on the fun. I hate to tell you this, Little Face, but you're becoming a little predictable."

"Me? What do you mean?"

"Every afternoon around four you're at the diner." He put one hand on top of the hood, effectively blocking her in on one side.

She felt a little bit pinned in, but in a good way. Had he been watching her?

"Where did you get a ribbon this large?"

"Special order two days ago. Did you know you can find anything online?"

"Yes, I do."

But probably not love. At least not the kind that made you ache.

He grinned. "All right, so I'm still a planner. I can't help that. It's part of who I am, like taking care of people is part of who you are. I wanted a big enough ribbon so that the whole town could see how crazy I am about you."

Now her heart had entered the Kentucky Derby since he was so close, and she couldn't speak because there was a good possibility she'd been struck mute. Good thing he wasn't touching her, because if he did there was a good chance her knees might give out on her for good.

"I'm sorry," he said, and she thought she might have heard wrong.

"*You're* sorry?" she finally managed.

"I'm sorry if I ever made you feel like anything was more

important than you are." Both of his strong hands framed her face.

Ivey swallowed. She'd heard wrong, somehow, otherwise how could he say exactly what she needed to hear?

The his finger traced the curve of her lips. "I love you, Ivey. I want to spend the rest of my life proving that you come first with me."

She was dreaming again. This couldn't be real, because it was too good. Too perfect. When Ivey noticed Em and Si walk outside the diner, and then Ivey noticed Ophelia and Genevieve, as well as many other patrons and customers, she had to admit this was no dream. It was her reality, and far better than fiction.

"What's all this?"

Ivey glanced in the direction of their audience, who had formed a semi-circle around them.

Jeff reached inside the front pocket of his slacks. "I thought I could use a little support."

He got down on his knees in front of the mini-crowd. She almost gasped because those were a new-looking pair of slacks, and he was kneeling in a parking lot. Had he thought this all the way through, or was he trying unpredictability on for size?

"Marry me, Ivey. Say my timing is right this time. I'm not going to lose another chance with you." He had a beautiful antique-looking ring in his hand.

Ivey's heart broke open, and a zillion tiny butterflies made their way up her stomach and out her throat.

"Yes! Of course, yes!"

Was that loud enough? God, she hoped so. She hoped people in the next town heard her loud and clear. Her finger shook as Jeff placed the ring on it.

She tugged Jeff up off his knees and threw her arms around his neck. He pulled her up onto her toes and kissed her square on the lips, deepening the kiss like there was no one else in the lot. No one else in the world. People were clapping, possibly, the sound fading in the background.

Sophia appeared suddenly right behind Jeff, trying to aim her phone over his head.

"I can't reach, can you get out of my way?"

"No," Jeff said, kissing Ivey again.

"Well damn, how can I get a selfie with both of you in it?" Sophia complained. "My followers are going to want to see this."

Ivey became vaguely aware of someone, possibly Em, dragging Sophia away, muttering a few expletives. It didn't matter, because she wasn't aware of anything other than the pounding of Jeff's heart beat under the pads of her fingers.

"Let's celebrate, everyone. Knock You Naked brownies on the house!" Em cried out, and Si groaned.

"Should we go inside?" Ivey asked Jeff.

"No. I'm going to knock you naked," Jeff said, smiling against her mouth.

All things considered, that was a much better offer. She did love brownies but not enough to turn Jeff down.

"See you later, Em! Thanks anyway," Ivey called out.

Jeff was still holding onto her like he thought if he let go she might disappear. But she wasn't going anywhere.

Ever again.

"One more thing. I decided to change specialties, so you're going to be the wife of a resident for a while. I don't know exactly what lies ahead, but I hope you'll be there with me."

"It sounds like an adventure."

They drove home in Jeff's car, but first they took the ribbon off.

ABOUT THE AUTHOR

Heatherly Bell loves coffee, craves cupcakes, and occasionally wears real pants.

She lives in Northern California with her family and loves to hear from readers.

Contact her at Heatherly@HeatherlyBell.com.